PAR

OF ROOKS

Haunting Brontë Country

Karen Perkins

First published in Great Britain 2017 by LionheART
Publishing House

This book is copyright under the Berne Convention
No reproduction without permission
All rights reserved.

Copyright © Karen Perkins 2017-2021
ISBN: 978-1-910115-77-0

The right of Karen Perkins to be identified as the
author of this work has been asserted by her in
accordance with sections 77 and 78 of the Copyright,
Designs and Patents Act 1988.

LionheART Publishing House
Harrogate

lionheartpublishinghouse@gmail.com

This book is a work of fiction.
Names, characters and incidents are either a product
of the author's imagination or are used fictitiously.

For Louise Burke and Louise Turner

True Friends.

Author's Note

To reflect both setting and characters as accurately as possible, a flavour of the Yorkshire dialect is used in the dialogue and some narrative, such as the use of were in place of was, and tha (thou) and thee in place of you.

For those not familiar with the accent, there is a short glossary at the back of the book with some of the more – interesting – linguistic attributes of Yorkshire, although all meanings should be clear from the text.

"You are my Demon.
This is my Exorcism."

– Verity Earnshaw

One for sorrow,
Two for mirth.
Three for a funeral,
Four for birth.
Five for Heaven,
Six for Hell,
Seven for the Devil, his own self.

– Old English nursery rhyme

PARLIAMENT OF ROOKS

Haunting Brontë Country

Prologue

Haworth, March 1838

Martha hitched up the bundle strapped to her front. Satisfied Baby John was secure, she grasped the handle and turned it to haul the full bucket up the well shaft.

John barely mewled in protest at the violent, rhythmic action, already used to the routine, and Martha pushed thoughts of the future out of her mind. Her firstborn was sickly, and she was surprised he had survived his first two months. He was unlikely to live much longer.

She stopped to rest, her body not yet recovered from the rigours of the birthing, then bent her back to her task once more. She had too much to do to indulge in a lengthy respite.

Once she had the water and had scrubbed their rooms clear of coal dust and soot, she'd be up to the weaver's gallery to start on the day's pieces.

She stopped again, took a couple of deep breaths, then coughed as fetid air filled her struggling lungs. Bracing herself, she continued her quest for water, cursing the dry February that had caused the well to run so low.

At last she could see the bucket, water slopping with each jerk of the rope. Reaching over, she grasped the handle and filled her ewers.

Adjusting Baby John once more, she bent, lifted, and embarked on the trudge homeward.

'Blasted slaughterman!' she cried, just catching herself as she slipped on the blood pouring down the alley past the King's Arms and on to Main Street. She'd forgotten it was market day tomorrow. The slaughterhouse was busy today.

Another deep breath, another cough, and Martha trudged on, the bottom of her skirts soaked in blood.

She heard the snort of the horses and the trundle of cart wheels on packed but sticky earth just in time, and was already jumping out of the way before the drayman's warning shout reached her.

'Damn and blast thee!' she screeched as she landed in the midden anext the King's Arms, which stank of rotten meat and offal from the slaughterhouse next door.

She clambered back to her feet, checked Baby John was unharmed, then noticed her empty ewers lying in the muck beside her.

Covered in blood and filth she ran after the dray, cursing at the top of her voice, then stopped. That wasn't the drayman sat atop his cart of barrels. It was a trap carrying a passenger.

She watched the carriage come to a halt by the church steps, and a jealous rage surged in the pit of her stomach as the passenger alighted.

Emily Brontë had returned to Haworth.

Part One

December 2016

"I wish I were a girl again,
half-savage and hardy, and free."

Wuthering Heights
Emily Brontë, 1847
Haworth, West Yorkshire

I.

'There she is, about bloody time! I have better things to do than hang about here,' the van driver said, just loudly enough for me to hear.

At the same time, he returned the rude gesture of the Range Rover driver who had squeezed past the van on the narrow, cobbled lane.

Out of breath from my steep climb up Main Street, I forced a weak smile and jangled my new keys at the man and his mate.

'At least there's not much to shift,' I heard one of them say as I unlocked the front door. I wondered if I'd been meant to hear this comment too, but decided I didn't care. No, I didn't have much to shift – just clothes, books, a laptop and a few personal things I could not bear to leave behind in the ruins of my marriage.

I had taken only the furniture and furnishings I'd had when I met Antony; none of the joint purchases. I'd left our CD and vinyl collection alone – the CDs were already in my iTunes library and I had nothing to play the vinyl on anyway – and had even left all the kitchen paraphernalia. Everything held memories; memories I knew I had to leave behind else turn mad.

The only thing I had brought out of the divorce was money – enough to buy the old restaurant, turn it into a guesthouse, and start again. That was all I wanted.

'Them bloody roads ain't fit for vehicles,' the driver's mate said. 'Some bugger's knocked the wing mirror off!'

I landed back in reality with a bump – the actuality of my dream move was car horns, angry men and chaos. Not quite what I'd hoped for from this quaint West Yorkshire village clinging on to a steep hillside in Brontë Country.

I tuned the noise out again and smiled. *Brontë Country.* Charlotte, Emily and Anne had lived a minute's walk away from where I now stood and lived. I could *see* the parsonage from the top windows of my new home. I'd been a fan of their books since discovering them at school, and had dreamt of living here one day.

'That'll be going on the bill,' the driver said, stomping through the entrance, arms full of suitcases.

'I told you to park in the museum car park,' I said.

'I'm not paying four quid to park the van and carry stuff further than I need to.'

'Seems cheap now, though, doesn't it?' I smiled at him with no sincerity. He'd done nothing but complain since he'd arrived to collect my belongings. He hated the roads, hated his satnav, hated the hills, hated the cobbles, hated his job, life and pretty much everything else. I was beyond irritated, but I would not let him spoil this for me.

'I want everything upstairs in one of the guest rooms. Through that door, up the first set of stairs, then left through the arch. I'll take it from there.'

'Are you sure you don't want us to sort it into the right rooms for you?' the driver's mate asked.

'No – I have a load of work to do first.'

'Ain't that the truth,' the driver said, looking around at the empty, damp and dingy foyer. 'Not exactly welcoming, is it?'

I stifled a retort and forced myself to smile again. 'It will be by the time I open,' I said. 'Is there much more to come in?'

'Give us a chance, love, this is only the first load.'

I nodded, my point made, and went outside, unwilling to spend any more time in the man's company. A few seconds later, I was in the heart of the village.

Whatever the removal men's faults, I had to admit they had a point. These roads had not been built for cars; their narrow blind bends and cobbles were far more suited to slower horse and cart.

I looked up, startled at the clop of a horse's hoofs, and waved at the rider – a young girl in a hi-vis vest. For a moment I'd half-expected to see a nineteenth-century carrier's cart loaded with barrels or coal sacks.

Having left Leeds that morning – for good – I felt like I'd stepped back in time, such was the contrast.

Instead of a bustling, modern city centre, Haworth Main Street plunged in its full cobbled glory to the Worth Valley below. The moors rose opposite in magnificent frosted green and winter shades of brown – heather, grasses, bracken and gorse – with snow heaped against the dividing dry stone walls.

Slate roofs slanted, soot-stained and age-darkened millstone grit walls leaned, and cobbles rose to trip the unwary or infirm. Even the accoutrements of modern living – benches, telephone poles, red telephone box (yes, Haworth still had one), lamp posts and the rest – tipped, dipped and sloped, all having to accommodate at least one unexpected angle, rejecting all human effort to tame this wild land.

Yet people were still here. They carved out a living; they enjoyed a holiday; they walked, shopped, explored.

It was an uneasy balance, made even more precarious by the flocking tourists anxious to follow in the footsteps of their literary heroines and characters. But something told me Yorkshire was not yet done; the power of the earth was too strong here, too prevalent. Nature would yet prevail over this insidious human invasion.

3

'Hello? Where the hell has she got to?'

I sighed at the driver's distant, grating voice and turned back, unable now to summon even a ghost of a smile for him as I approached.

'All done, you just need to sign the worksheet, then we'll be on our way.'

'Right then,' I said, took his pen, and hesitated. Much as I wanted this annoying man out of my dream home as soon as possible, I could not bring myself to sign without checking everything first.

I led the way back into what would soon be my guesthouse, ignoring the heaving sigh of irritation behind me, and examined the piles of boxes, suitcases, and scraps of furniture, mentally checking everything off.

'And the van is definitely empty, is it?' I asked when I re-emerged into daylight, my head swimming.

The driver glared at me, but his mate grinned, slid open the side door and I inspected the interior. If anything had been left behind, it wasn't in there.

I signed the paperwork and the driver snatched it out of my hands, clambered behind the wheel, and slammed the door.

'Good luck in your new home,' the mate said, touched his cap with a grin, then sighed before joining his colleague. I had never been so glad to see anyone drive away in my life.

I walked back into the building and looked around me. The proud smile drained from my face as the enormity of what I had taken on hit me. I had left everything I knew behind me, and my future was blind.

2.

A shriek outside made me jump, then I relaxed and smiled at the sound of high heels and laughter accompanied by the rumble of trolley bag wheels on cobbles. Lara and Jayne.

Opening the door, I stared pointedly at Lara's feet as she tottered down the steep, icy ginnel, clutching an enormous bouquet of flowers. Jayne was pulling two cases and wincing at the ferocity of her friend's taloned grip on her arm.

'I told you to wear flats,' I said. 'You'll break your leg in those things here.'

'I don't do flats, darling,' Lara said, unconcerned. She let go of Jayne to swathe me in a floral-scented hug. 'Welcome to your new life, Verity.' She handed over the flowers. 'It's very . . . you.' She beamed, clearly pleased with her non-committal phrasing.

I turned to hug Jayne and was almost knocked off my feet by an excited Irish terrier the colour of sandstone who'd been chased from the car park by Lara's ten-year-old daughter, Hannah.

'You need to keep hold of his lead,' Jayne admonished, bending to pick up the leather leash. 'He has no car sense whatsoever.'

'Sorry, Aunt Jayne, he's just so strong and excited.' Hannah took back possession of Grasper and tried to pull him away from me and all the interesting smells around the front door. He only acquiesced when I ceased petting him and finally embraced his mistress.

5

Accepting a bottle bag with a very promising gold-foil-covered offering inside, I led the way. 'Welcome to The Rookery,' I said.

'So where exactly are we sleeping?' Jayne asked, perched on her case and clutching a mug of champagne. She peered around the foyer. 'Are the guest rooms at least serviceable?'

'No, not yet,' I said. 'I've a camp bed set up in the best one for myself. I thought you three would put your sleeping bags out here – you did bring sleeping bags, didn't you?' I eyed their cases.

Jayne spluttered champagne, Hannah clapped in delight at the prospect of camping, and Lara grinned.

'Nearly had me going there, Verity,' she said. 'Now put Jayne out of her misery and tell her where we're really staying.'

I smiled. 'Sorry, ladies, I couldn't resist. No, I'm not inflicting this place on you – not until it's furnished anyway. I've booked you into the Old White Lion; it's literally thirty seconds down the street. I'll take you over in a bit so you can check in, then I thought we'd have dinner there.'

'Cowbag,' Jayne said, and Hannah giggled. 'How long will it take to get this place ready for guests?'

'I have three months. I'll make the website live and sign up to all the booking sites as soon as the wiring is done and I have broadband. With any luck, I'll be taking bookings from the first of March for Easter onwards.'

Lara looked around the foyer and Jayne laughed. 'I hope you have reliable tradesmen – that doesn't leave you much time if anybody lets you down.'

'They've all been highly recommended and they start on Monday. I've been speaking to the foreman, Vikram, quite a bit on the phone and so far I'm impressed.'

'Oh yes, Vikram is it? What does he look like?' Lara said, eyebrows raised.

'They're starting the week before Christmas, are you serious?' Jayne said.

I chose to answer Jayne. 'Yes, the joiners are in first to wall off part of the back there – they'll make another guest room, then the remainder of the space will be a kitchen for the guest breakfasts, plus an office. The electricians and plumbers will do their thing too then start on the existing bedrooms upstairs, and the joiners will move up to partition off the en-suites when they've finished down here. I don't have to have every guest room ready for Easter, but I do need the downstairs area, as many guest rooms as possible, and my own living quarters to be ready on time.'

'Then what, you'll have work carrying on while guests are here?'

'If need be, although only after breakfast hours for as little disturbance as possible.'

'But it'll all come to a grinding halt before they even get started,' Jayne predicted.

'Only for a few days over Christmas,' I said.

'Do you really think it'll be ready in time?' Lara asked.

I looked around me, unwilling to admit my fears.

'You don't, do you?' Jayne was far too good at reading people.

'Yes, it'll be ready. Okay, okay.' I raised my hands to hold off more naysaying. 'I admit when the movers left and I was here on my own for the first time, I had a moment of doubt, but I can do this, I know I can.'

'Of course you can, Verity,' Lara said, putting down her champagne mug.

I really must get some proper glasses, I thought as she tottered across the flagged floor and embraced me.

'Don't listen to old Grumpy Drawers over there, and don't be too hard on yourself. You've gone through hell with the divorce and everything. This is your new start. It sounds like you have everything organised and you'll be on site to keep an eye on things – and we'll help as much as we can. I know the village seems isolated, but it's really not that far away – it only took us half an hour to get here, we'll be here all the time!'

'Don't forget she needs the rooms for guests.' Jayne joined the huddle. 'She has a business to run, you know. Sorry, Verity, I didn't mean to come across as negative.' I felt her lift her head to glare at Lara. 'I was just trying to make sure you're on top of everything and have a good plan.'

'Always bloody planning,' Lara said.

'And just as well, too – my planning has got you out of more than one scrape, remember?'

'Enough!' I laughed. Jayne and Lara were so different on the surface, one a building society manager: practical and stern; the other a complementary therapist and single mum, and one of the strongest women I'd ever met. But both of them had big hearts and matching values, and despite the outward bickering, all three of us had been best friends for years.

'What's wrong with Grasper?' Hannah's voice penetrated our hugfest.

Jayne swung around in concern, then smiled at her pet's antics. 'He's just bored, probably needs a walk and some attention.'

'Hmm,' Lara said, digging in her bag for her phone. She ignored Jayne's scoffing and filmed the Irish terrier as he jumped and twirled about, tongue lolling in delight.

'Have a look at this,' she said, playing the video back.

Jayne and I peered over her shoulders.

'There – did you see it? And there – another one.'

'Let me see, let me see,' Hannah begged.

'Just a moment, Hans.' She ran the video again. They were still there: two circles of light dive-bombing and circling the dog.

'Those are orbs, Verity. Spirits. You've bought a haunted house.'

3.

'Oh good thinking, Verity,' Jayne said, sitting down on the padded bench next to me and pouring a glass from the bottle of Prosecco on the table in the bar of the Old White Lion Hotel.

'Well, it's a celebration,' I said. 'It's not every day you finalise a divorce, complete on a haunted guesthouse, and move to a village where you don't know anybody.'

'Cheers to that,' Jayne said with a smile at my attempt at a joke, and we clinked glasses.

'What are we toasting?' Lara asked as she sat down.

'Verity leaving her cheating husband, upping sticks and moving to the middle of nowhere,' Jayne said.

'Don't forget the bit about the ghosts,' I added.

'Pour me a large one,' Lara said. 'I'll drink to that!'

'Pour your own, you lazy cow,' Jayne said. Lara stuck her tongue out at her and did just that.

'Can I have a glass, Mummy?' Hannah asked, and Jayne spluttered over her next sip.

'No, you can't have wine, Hans. Water, squash or apple juice.'

'Coke!'

'Not at teatime, you won't sleep. Water, squash or apple juice.'

'Aww, please, we're celebrating, Auntie Verity said so. Please?'

'Water, squash or apple juice.'

Hannah sat back, arms folded in a sulk.

'Let me know when you've decided,' Lara said, then turned back to us. 'So how does it feel, Verity?'

'What? My cheating husband or the haunted guesthouse?'

'Cheating *ex*-husband,' Jayne said.

'True.' I raised my glass in a toast once more and took a long gulp, blinking back unexpected tears. I'd thought I'd already shed all those.

'Did he ever give you an explanation?' Lara asked.

I shook my head, thinking back to the day I'd found Antony's emails and messages not to another woman, but to many, going back years. 'He didn't seem to think he'd done anything wrong – once the initial shock of being found out had worn off, anyway. Apparently virtual cheating doesn't count. Despite the intimate pictures, the webcam sessions, the fact that he proposed to at least one of them, and declared his undying love to a few more. He just can't understand why I'm so hurt or feel so betrayed.'

'Idiot,' Jayne said.

'Bastard,' Lara countered.

'Mummy!' Hannah admonished.

'Sorry, Hans, quite right.'

'Well, at least the judge understood,' Jayne said.

I said nothing, and sipped my wine. Finding out what Antony had been doing for so long had turned my world upside down. We'd been together for years, I'd thought we would always be together. It had turned out that I didn't know him at all.

'Have you decided yet?' Lara asked Hannah, and I gave her a grateful glance for changing the subject.

'Juice.'

'Juice what?'

'Juice, please.'

'Okay. I'll get us another bottle as well, ladies. Might as well make a night of it.'

11

'You're a bad influence, Lara,' Jayne scolded.

'Rubbish, you were both thinking it.'

I looked at Jayne and laughed. Lara's observation was spot on.

'This is supposed to be a working trip, not a girls' weekend,' Jayne complained.

'The work starts tomorrow,' Lara said. 'Tonight is the celebration. Relax and enjoy yourself, Jayne.'

'I hope Grasper's okay over there. Those light things were freaky.'

'He'll be fine,' Lara said. 'Dogs aren't allowed in here, there's no way he can sleep in the car, and the orbs were friendly, they were playing with him.'

'Let me see it again,' I said, and Lara dug out her phone.

We watched as Grasper jumped at a ball of light, then spun in a full circle as it teased him before shooting off. I could almost see the indecision on the terrier's face – torn between chasing the one and playing with the other. The second orb hovered around his head then shot to his tail, where it followed the wildly wagging appendage as best it could – not an easy task as Grasper was also circling madly, trying to catch it. I realised I could see the orbs more clearly each time I watched the video.

Then the first rejoined the fun and Grasper was truly lost. Snapping at one then the other, he settled for watching them, tongue hanging out in a sappy grin. He only joined in their whirling dance when one approached him.

A moment later, they were gone, and Grasper settled down on the floor, exhausted but happy, looking up at Jayne with his usual level of adoration.

'Whoever they are, they're friendly,' Lara said. 'Grasper would react very differently if they were dark forces.'

'*Dark forces*? What nonsense!' Jayne said in

12

exasperation. 'They're flies or something, that's all. Not spirits or ghosts, and certainly not demons!'

'They're not flies, Jayne. Look at them, they're circular balls of light. Have you never watched *Most Haunted* or *Ghost Adventures*? They're orbs – spirits.'

'You're freaking me out,' I said before Jayne and Lara descended into a bickering spat. 'I'm going to be on my own there most of the time – at least until I open. I don't want ghosts around.'

'Ghosts? Oh, you must be the lady who bought Weavers.'

We looked up at the waitress – blonde, pretty and young; it seemed very strange hearing her talking about ghosts.

'Yes. I'm Verity Earnshaw,' I said. 'I'm turning it into a guesthouse, and should be opening in April.'

'Earnshaw? Well, you'll fit right in round here then.' The girl laughed. 'I'm Tess, welcome to Haworth.'

'You know about the ghosts?' Lara asked.

'Village is full of them, but I only know about one at Weavers, the Grey Lady. She's not seen very often, but the sightings are consistent – she's a bit of a celebrity round here. People reckon she's Emily Brontë.'

'Are you seriously trying to tell us that Verity's guesthouse is haunted by a Brontë sister?' Jayne asked.

'No one knows for sure, but she only appears around December 19th, the date of Emily's death.'

'Next week,' Lara said, glancing at me.

'Yeah, she's said to climb up a flight of stairs that are no longer there – the wall that adjoins the row of weaver's cottages. But she's always smiling and has never done any harm,' Tess added, no doubt in reaction to me. I felt cold and horrified, and presumably had gone pale.

'Don't worry,' Jayne tried to reassure me. 'It's fanciful tales, that's all.'

'Oh no, that's where you're wrong. There's plenty of

ghosts round here,' Tess said. 'Nothing fanciful about them – you should go on the ghost tour, find out all sorts of tales you will.'

'Verity, relax,' Lara said. 'It's Emily Brontë – how wonderful is that? That's why she played with Grasper, she loved animals and even had a dog herself called the same, that's where Jayne got Grasper's name from.'

Jayne nodded in agreement.

'And I told you,' Lara continued, 'those orbs are friendly. You've nothing to worry about.'

'Orbs?' the girl asked. 'What orbs? What did you see?'

Lara showed her the video, which she watched in silence.

'Well, I've never seen owt like that before,' Tess said. 'Will you show me mam? She's behind the bar – if there are any stories, she'll know.'

She didn't wait for an answer but shouted across the bar, her Yorkshire accent broadening further.

'Ey up,' her mam said after viewing the clip. 'Now there's a thing.' She turned and went back to the bar, and the three of us looked at each other in confusion.

'Don't worry. She takes a while to warm up to strangers. If she knew anything, she'd have said. But she'll find out, you can be sure of that. Are you ready to order?'

Subdued, we ordered food and wine – and an apple juice for Hannah. When we were alone again, Lara reached over and grasped my forearm.

'Don't worry, Verity. You'll have Grasper with you tonight, and I'll cleanse the whole building for you in the morning. You'll be fine.'

I shuddered. Spirits were unknown and unknowable, and I hated the idea of strangers in my new home. Then I grinned at the absurdity of that thought. In a few months, I'd be running a guesthouse – constantly inviting strangers into my home. I raised my glass and took a long gulp, realising I was committed. The Rookery was my home and would soon be my livelihood. I had nothing else. I was stuck here, ghosts or no ghosts.

4.

The camp bed creaked as I turned over, and I startled awake, the image of a man clear in my mind. Dark-haired with black eyes and sun-baked skin. I shivered, rolled over again, and went back to sleep.

He beckoned to me and I joined him, walking across the car park behind my guesthouse, wincing as my bare feet found stones and the debris of tourists.

Towards the parsonage then down Church Lane to the graveyard, I followed the enigmatic figure in shirt and breeks – barefoot like myself.

I chided myself at every step, yet could not halt my feet. He pulled at me, beseeched me, drew me in, yet never touched me.

Past the early graves, the slabs of stone flat against the earth and butted up to each other so closely, Nature had no chance to exert a living presence. Some altar graves, then the newer tall, carved monoliths standing sentinel and guarding the valley below.

I hesitated, shivering again as the man I followed disappeared into fog. What was I thinking?

I took a couple of hesitant steps backwards, but was too late; the fog was quick, falling down the hillside, enveloping me until I could see naught but grey and white swirls of cloud.

Then light, and I moved towards it, the misty tendrils releasing me, and I saw him again.

Standing with the sun behind him, shining on him, he

spread his arms wide as if to show me something. I looked past him and gasped at the majesty of the moors: grim, yes, but also beautiful in their barrenness.

But no, not barren. Buzzards, hawks, even red kites circled above. I spotted a kestrel, hovering in place despite the wind, then diving down on to its prey.

I looked closely at the ground, a mixture of heather and tough, tussocky grass, and spotted rabbits playing, then scattering as a young fox cub bounded into their midst – too young and unskilled to do anything but scare them away. That would soon change.

The man pointed, and I twirled to see a herd of deer run past on the hillside below me. I grinned in utter delight, clasping my hands together, and watched the hardy beasts until the last flash of white from their hindquarters disappeared. I turned back to the man.

He beckoned again and I stepped forward, but he turned and walked away. I followed, hardly thinking about what I was doing, back into the swirling, enveloping fog, then jerked to a standstill as it cleared and I found myself perched on a rocky ledge at the edge of a precipice, the man's hand on my arm to steady me.

I opened my mouth to berate him, to tell him to be more careful, but he gestured to the valley below, and my complaints died in my throat.

The moors stretched out in all directions, a seemingly endless and full palette of browns and greens, yellows and oranges, maroons and purples, all swirled together as if by the hand of a great master in a grand passion of artistic creativity.

I pulled my gaze down and looked over the valley, only now seeing the towering, elongated chimney stacks belching black smoke to mingle with the clean moorland mist.

All that burning coal to produce the steam needed to run enough jennies, mules and looms to clothe gentlemen and ladies alike in the finest worsted wools.

I counted what now looked like vents from Hell as I pictured the children crawling about under that relentless machinery, literally risking life and limb with every crash and rattle of iron, every yard of yarn. A dozen, no, more – eighteen – factories of slavery and torture littered the valley, and I realised they must provide work for the occupants of near every house I could see.

The small slate roofs jumbled together in clusters, mimicking the outcroppings of ancient rock that interrupted the swathes of colour on the moorland above.

How many people lived and worked in those tiny cottages? Streets swimming with filth, children close to starvation, disease rampant.

I shook the dreary thoughts away; the vista was so beautiful, why did I feel so forlorn?

I gasped as the man pulled me, and mist eddied around us once again until we were on the edge of the moors and I recognised the parsonage by the church – although something was wrong. The parsonage was missing a gable; the museum buildings at the back, as well as the car park, were not there. Neither were there any trees in the churchyard, and all the memorial stones were flat. Everything seemed very . . . bleak.

Six children walked up the lane and I smiled, charmed by their fussy Victorian clothing, the smallest girls looking the cutest of all in bonnets, clogs and aprons over full skirts.

I looked more carefully and realised they were all close in age; no more than a year or two between each, and they were not all girls – a boy walked in the middle, herding and shepherding his charges along. Well, trying to; his sisters did not appear to appreciate his efforts.

It struck me who they were, and I turned to my companion to confirm my suspicion of the identity of the family, but he was entranced by the large black rook perched on his wrist.

It took flight, was buffeted by the wind, but soon righted itself and swooped low to the gaggle of children.

One of the smaller girls – Emily, I decided; there was only one younger who would be Anne – raised her face to the bird in delight and stretched out her arm.

The rook alighted on its new perch, shuffled and flapped its wings, then settled.

The children stepped back from Emily in amazement, either scared of frightening the creature away or of its sharp, curved beak, but Emily took the visit in her stride. She lifted her arm close to her face to whisper a few words to the bird, then looked up at us and waved with her free hand.

The man waved back, and a smile – the first expression I had seen from him – broke across his harsh features, softening them, animating them, and my heart thumped hard at the sight of the crinkles around his eyes, the love and sheer delight reflected in his pupils, and the shape his mouth formed.

I gasped at the crushing pain in my chest and clawed my way to a sitting position, blinking in utter confusion at my surroundings. Then I realised I'd been dreaming.

The sense of crushing disappointment was accompanied by a strange smell – one I could not place, but knew belonged to the moors – and I felt in the bed next to me for Antony.

Reality coalesced as I touched no husband nor soft, luxurious bedding; merely a sleeping bag and the frame of a camp bed. A moment of sadness, then I remembered the man from my dream and identified the still-lingering smell as wild garlic.

Heathcliff, I thought, smiling. *I just met Heathcliff.*

I hugged myself, and realised a wide smile – a smile to match his – stretched across my face, despite the absurdity. I was in Brontë Country after all; I'm sure many people dreamed of their own version of Heathcliff when they visited this village.

Feeling lighter and more positive than I had for many years, I disentangled myself from my sleeping bag, eager to get on with the day.

5.

'Coo-ee, Verity, are you here?'

I made my way downstairs to greet my friends. 'Goodness, you're early, couldn't you sleep?'

Jayne gave me a funny look. 'Verity, it's nine thirty, we were expecting you for breakfast an hour ago, are you okay?'

'What? Nine thirty?' I fished my phone out of my pocket to check and saw I'd missed three calls from them.

'Goodness, I'm sorry, I completely lost track of time and I didn't hear your calls.'

'Are you sure you're all right?' Lara asked. 'You look a bit flushed.'

'I'm fine.' I blushed a deeper red – I'd been fantasising about Dream-Heathcliff. 'I slept really well, got up early and took Grasper out, then started cleaning. I only meant to do half an hour, then meet you for breakfast. I guess I got carried away.'

'Well, find somewhere to sit,' Lara said. 'We brought breakfast to you – a bacon butty and coffee, hope that's okay.'

'Perfect,' I said, realising I'd built up quite an appetite. I had no furniture yet, so used the windowsill as a table.

'Verity,' Jayne said slowly, 'aren't the workmen coming in on Monday?'

I nodded, my mouth full of bacon and soft, white, fluffy bap.

'Then why are you cleaning now? There doesn't seem to be much point.'

21

'I was working in my quarters, trying to make them a bit more habitable – I'm not having any major work done up there and it would be good to set up a sleeping area and be able to use the kitchen and bathroom. The basic fittings are still here from the previous owners, and they'll do until I can afford to upgrade.'

'Oh, we'll give you a hand – we'll soon have it right when the three of us get going on it.'

'Thank you.' I looked around, startled, just noticing the quiet. 'Where's Grasper gone?'

'Hannah's taken him out again,' Jayne said. 'How was he last night? No more weird stuff?'

'He was fine, Jayne, no trouble at all, and nothing weird, don't worry.'

'And what about you, how did you get on?' Lara asked.

'I went straight to sleep, I was shattered,' I said. 'No ghosts, no ghouls, orbs, nothing.'

'Did you dream?'

'I did actually – very vividly,' I said, then stopped. I didn't want to share the dream man with them.

I changed the subject to forestall what looked like the makings of another question I didn't want to answer. 'Weren't you going to do a cleansing or something, Lara?'

'Yes, it's always a good idea to cleanse a new home anyway to clear it of old energies, and I brought some sage with me so I could do the guesthouse for you. We'll get started when you've finished your breakfast.'

'What does it entail, exactly?' I asked.

'Sage is cleaning and protective. I'll light the smudge stick—'

'The *what*?'

'Smudge stick, Jayne. Don't look so sceptical, it's been used for centuries.'

Jayne grimaced but stayed silent.

'Anyway,' Lara continued, 'I'll use the smoke to clear out the old energies of the people who used to live and work here, and invite in all things positive for Verity. You'll be surprised at the difference it will make to the feel of the place.'

'And will it get rid of those things, those orbs, from last night?'

'I don't know to be honest, Verity. We can only try it and see.'

'I've been thinking about that. There's all sorts of things those could have been. Insects or moths, for example,' Jayne suggested once more.

Lara pulled her phone out and played the video again. 'Do you see any wings, Jayne? And anyway, it's December, not exactly bug season.'

'Dust, then.'

'When have you ever known dust to move like that? Plus we'd have been able to see it when we were watching Grasper without the phone. And before you say it, they weren't lens flare, else Grasper wouldn't be reacting to them, they weren't torchlight or headlights, nor were they dandelion clocks or any other kind of seed in December. And we're inside, so they're not raindrops.'

'It does smell a bit damp in here though, it could be moisture.'

'When have you ever known water droplets to form and move like that? They're orbs, Jayne, accept it. What else can they be?'

Jayne said nothing.

'All right, I'm done, let's get started with this smudge-sticking or whatever it's called,' I said to break the charged silence.

Lara smiled. 'Smudging,' she said. 'Come on then, we'll start upstairs and work our way down.'

***

'Just what *exactly* is this supposed to achieve?' Jayne asked, disapproval distorting both her face and her words.

Lara ignored her and continued dancing around the room, waving the smoking, tightly bundled baton of sage into every nook and cranny. She finished her circuit of the window frame, then of the rest of the room before standing in front of us.

'As I said before, I'm clearing out any and all energies that no longer belong here,' she said, staring into Jayne's eyes. 'I'm getting rid of any and all negativity so that Verity's positivity, hopes and plans for her new life can flourish. Your attitude is not helping the process, Jayne.'

Jayne scowled and I hurried to speak before she could pour more scepticism on to Lara. 'It can't hurt, Jayne, and it might help – I like the idea.'

'It smells like dope,' Jayne said.

'It's not cannabis, it's pure sage – grown in my own garden,' Lara said, her irritation barely concealed. 'Just keep an open mind, Jayne, that's all I'm asking. Now, you're in the way.'

We moved from the door to let Lara finish, then she stepped into the corridor and moved on to the other rooms. Jayne and I followed behind, staying out of her way.

'This will be my quarters,' I said, taking the conversation away from Lara, herbs and energies. 'Kitchen and lounge up here, bedroom and bathroom below.'

'Isn't that upside down?'

'What does that matter? This house is four nineteenth-century cottages converted into one property – you've seen the maze of rooms and staircases. I can get four double and one single guest room – all with en-suites – from it without having to knock through any stone walls, apart

24

from doorways, and this is the space that's left.' I spread my arms, indicating the doors around us.

'I'd rather have a larger lounge than bedroom, and a bigger kitchen than bathroom, wouldn't you?'

'Fair enough.' Jayne went back into the room behind us – the lounge – and looked out of the window. Finally, she smiled. 'It's one hell of a view, Verity. You can see right up on to the moors. Oh, what's that?'

I joined her and looked down at the line of smoke. 'Steam train. It runs from Keighley to Oxenhope. They used one of the stations to film *The Railway Children*.'

'Oh wow, can we go on it?'

I laughed at her transformation from stern disapproval to almost childlike delight. 'Absolutely.' I turned to look back into the room. 'I'm going to paint everything white.'

Jayne nodded. 'A blank canvas,' she said.

'Exactly! I don't know what my future will hold – other than this place, of course – or who I'm going to, or even want to be. I like the idea of clean, fresh walls. A new start in every way.'

'What about the guest rooms?'

'I'm taking my inspiration from the Brontës,' I said.

'What? Wild moors and crumbling ruins? Mad wives in the attic, that kind of thing?'

I laughed. 'No, from their home, the parsonage. It's all very tasteful and understated. The wallpapers are floral, but two-tone and are as masculine as they are feminine – delicate patterns intertwining. Classy.'

'And the furniture?'

My face darkened. 'Well, all dark wood, nineteenth century of course, but I don't want it to overpower the space. I'll have to go to Ikea.'

'What? You can't be serious!' Jayne scolded, loudly enough to bring Lara running.

'What's going on now?'

25

'Verity has this wonderful plan for beautiful wallpaper in the guest rooms, then wants flat-pack furniture!'

'I can't afford solid wood,' I said. 'I can only do what I can to furnish five bedrooms.'

'Nonsense,' Lara and Jayne said together, then looked at each other and giggled, best of friends once more.

'What's your budget for each room?' Jayne asked.

I shrugged.

'Well, that's the first thing to do. We'll sit down this afternoon and go over the figures, work out what you can afford to spend.'

'Then we'll go round the second-hand shops and auction houses,' Lara said. 'I bet we'll find some nice stuff in Ilkley and Skipton, and even Harrogate isn't that far away. We can sand it down and varnish or paint, the rooms will look stunning.'

'And everything you do have to buy new: beds, mattresses and the like, well, its sale season in a couple of weeks, the perfect time to buy.'

All of a sudden, I felt like bursting into tears. I couldn't afford to do everything at once, and had made the decision to focus on the basics – plumbing, electrics, structural alterations – then gradually upgrade the furniture in the rooms as and when I could. It hadn't occurred to me to buy used pieces and renovate them. 'That could work,' I mumbled, and grinned at my friends.

'It would add character too,' Jayne said.

'Thank you, I don't know what I'd do without you two.'

'Well, you'll never have to find out,' Lara said.

'Probably starve,' Jayne said, and we both looked at her in confusion.

'You have no food, no microwave and no kettle. As soon as Lara's finished her smoking—'

'Smudging.'

'Whatever. And when Hannah's back with Grasper, we're off to Asda. We'll get these rooms liveable this weekend and move your camp bed in, but there's no way you can put us to work without regular cups of coffee!'

6.

'Fish and chips times four,' Jayne said, puffing as she came through the door and put the bag on my new kitchen table. 'Bloody hell, Verity, you'll soon get fit living here – there are hills everywhere. And then this place, I've never been somewhere where I've actually had to *look* for the next staircase! I nearly got lost on the way up.'

'It's a great place for hide and seek,' Hannah piped up. 'I could hide for *hours*! You'd never find me, I'd win easily!'

I laughed as I found the salt, vinegar and ketchup in the array of Asda bags lined up along the wall ready to be unpacked into the newly cleaned kitchen cupboards. We'd eat out of the boxes for tonight. 'Yes, you probably could, Hannah. Once all the alterations and decorating are done, it will look very different though, and should be easier to navigate.'

'I bet your guests will still get a bit lost though,' Lara said.

'You'll need lots of signs guiding people to their rooms,' Jayne said, ever practical.

I brought the condiments to my new camping table, and Lara carried wine and glasses.

'We did a good job today, thank you, ladies,' I said, looking around the upstairs of my flat. We'd scrubbed, washed and swept, and I had a living space with basic cooking facilities. 'I'd never have got this done without you, not before Monday.'

'I know it's rudimentary,' Jayne said, glancing at my

'furniture': camping table, four foldaway chairs and a camp bed doubling as a sofa in the large, open-plan kitchen and sitting room. 'At least you have somewhere to escape to while all the work is going on.'

'We can decorate next weekend,' Lara said. 'It won't take long to slap some paint on the walls and then you'll be ready for proper furniture as soon as the New Year sales start.'

'Are you both coming for Christmas? Have you decided?'

'Definitely,' Lara said. 'Jayne talked to the receptionist at the Old White Lion about Christmas lunch and rooms, and we're all booked in, so we can help out here over the holidays. It's our Christmas present to you.'

'I don't know what to say,' I said, feeling emotional as I hugged them both. 'I can't believe you're giving up your Christmases.'

'We're not,' Jayne said. 'We're spending Christmas with friends. Now come on and eat, the food's getting cold.'

Lara and I laughed, and Hannah sidled up to her mother. 'We're not giving up Christmas, are we?'

'Oh, no, Hans,' Lara said with a laugh. 'Don't worry, it's just an expression. We're going to come here for Christmas.'

'We'll still have turkey?'

'We certainly will – at the hotel where we're staying now.'

'So you won't be cooking?'

We all laughed at the hopeful expression on Hannah's face. Lara was an enthusiastic cook, but rarely followed a recipe or the recommended cooking times. She usually got away with it, somehow, but there had been one disastrous Christmas lunch two or three years ago which had come with an extra gift of food poisoning for all who'd tasted her undercooked turkey.

'No, I won't be cooking,' Lara said with good grace, 'and Grasper will be here to play with.'

'Yay!' the girl said, clapping her hands and hugging the dog.

'Right, wash those hands again, young lady, then come and eat.'

Jayne poured the wine. 'To your new home,' she toasted.

We all clinked glasses and I looked around. Yes, this could be a home – my home. I started to relax. I could be happy here, couldn't I? Okay, at the moment it reflected my life: bare, empty, and in need of decoration and filling, but that wouldn't last.

I looked at Lara and Jayne, and raised my glass again. 'To best friends and an empty guesthouse,' I said with a wry smile.

'From small beginnings are grand dreams realised,' Lara said.

'I'll drink to that,' Jayne said.

'So what's the plan for tomorrow?' Lara asked, closing the lid of the cardboard fish-and-chip box.

'Day off, it is Sunday, after all,' I said. 'I thought we could do the touristy things, explore Main Street, visit the Brontë Museum, ride the steam train, maybe even go for a hike over the moors.'

'What, with Lara in high heels?' Jayne laughed. 'You know its stilettos or bare feet – nothing in between.'

'Too right,' Lara said, lifting one of her legs and wiggling her toes. 'A girl has to have standards.'

Jayne snorted, but said nothing.

'I don't want to go to a museum,' Hannah said from the camp bed where she was cuddling – and surreptitiously feeding – Grasper.

'Someone needs to look after Grasper anyway,' Jayne

said. 'Unless we lock him in which doesn't seem fair when there's so much countryside about.'

'I can take him for a walk!' Hannah said.

'Is it safe?' I asked.

'Grasper will look after her – she's part of his pack,' Jayne said.

'Okay, as long as you don't go far and you have your phone switched on – but only while we're in the museum, all right, Hans? And you go no further than I say.'

'Okay, Mum,' Hannah sang, then she turned to Grasper. 'We're going to— oh!'

'What is it, Hans?' Lara turned to her daughter. 'Oh my God. Verity, Jayne, look!'

Grasper leaped from the camp bed, high enough to clear Hannah's seated form, although she had ducked out of his way, then circled a couple of times and jumped back on to the bed, ran over Hannah's lap, then tumbled back on to the floor.

'What the hell was that?' I cried.

'I saw it too,' Lara said, fumbling in her large handbag. 'Damn it, where's my phone? We need to video this.'

'I'm on it,' Jayne said, iPhone in position and already recording her pet's antics. 'I want to make sure it wasn't a glitch or a special app on yours, anyway.'

'An app?' Lara was insulted at the suggestion, but was distracted by Hannah's giggle as she dived away from . . . nothing. Although I did think I saw a flicker of light near her head as she ducked.

I glanced at Lara and knew she had seen it too. 'Wasn't that sage-smudging stuff supposed to get rid of those orbs, or whatever they are?'

'It would have if they were negative energies. If they're still here, they must be of the light – good.'

'Then why have you gone white?'

'It just dive-bombed my daughter and I don't know who or what it is!' She rushed to Hannah's side, although Hannah didn't need comforting; she was still giggling.

'Oh settle down, Lara,' Jayne said. 'You're over-reacting.'

'Am I? Don't you want to know what Grasper's playing with? If anybody is interacting with my daughter, I want to know who they are and what they intend.'

Jayne did not answer.

'I need to know. We have to hold a séance.'

I looked at Jayne and shrugged. I didn't expect it to help in any practical way, but if it put Lara's mind at rest then I was happy to do it.

'You can't be serious, Lara!' Jayne was not so easily persuaded.

Lara raised her eyebrows at her friend. 'Why not?'

'You can't mess with things like that, you're likely to make things worse, not improve them.'

'I'll be careful. Anyway, do you have any better ideas?'

Jayne shook her head, then looked at me. 'Verity?'

I glanced at Grasper, who was still dancing with things we could not see. I spread my arms and held my hands high, palms up. 'I don't think we have much choice.'

Jayne nodded, although she did not look happy about it. The three of us might bicker like siblings most of the time, but when we needed each other, we were there, no matter what that entailed.

'I'll go put Hannah to bed and see if that Tess girl will keep an ear out for her, then I'll be back.'

7.

Lara, Jayne and I sat at the camping table, which we'd covered with a new white cloth. Under Lara's direction, we spread our hands out and connected our little fingers to make a circle.

Lara took a deep breath before intoning, 'Is anybody there?'

I glanced at Jayne, then averted my gaze. Both of us felt it was ridiculous and clichéd.

Lara filled her lungs again, but didn't comment, yet I felt chastened, and knew Jayne felt the same way. I glanced up at Lara and smiled to encourage her to continue.

'We only want to talk to you, we will not harm you. Will you talk to us?'

Silence.

'Please talk to us or give us some kind of sign that you're here. Can you knock on the wall or tap on the floor?'

Silence.

'Knock once for no, twice for yes.'

Nothing.

'Please,' I said before Lara could continue. 'We'd really like to talk to you, don't you want to talk to us?'

Grasper barked when two sounds echoed through the near-empty room. He jumped off the camp bed and ran in circles around the table.

Jayne broke the circle to reassure her pet, as simultaneously I snatched my hands away, shocked that we'd elicited a response.

Grasper calmed, but refused to budge from Jayne's side.

'Are you okay if we try again?' Lara asked her.

Jayne glanced at me then said, 'Maybe we should leave this.'

'No,' Lara said. 'I need to know who this is and what they want with us.'

'Are you sure?' I asked, glancing at Grasper. Although quiet now, he was still alert, his eyes wide.

Lara nodded and I pursed my lips to indicate my own agreement.

We placed our hands back on the table.

I shivered and blew out. My breath condensed and the mist of it dissipated within the circle. Lara and Jayne simultaneously blew a long breath and the same happened.

'It's so cold,' Jayne said.

'It's an old house,' I said. 'The heating isn't working yet.' I wasn't sure if I was defending my new home or trying to deny the sudden drop in temperature.

We gasped when two knocks reverberated around the room.

'Lara,' Jayne warned, 'don't push it.'

I realised our hands had split again and wordlessly splayed my fingers on the tabletop. I was not in the mood for banter now.

Lara took a moment to gather her thoughts, then asked, 'Did you live here?'

One knock.

'No. Did you work here?'

Two knocks. Yes.

'Are you the Grey Lady?'

Nothing.

'Are you a woman?'

Silence.

'Are you a man?'

Two knocks.

I gasped and pulled my hands away.

'Oh calm down, Verity, that's hardly conclusive,' Jayne said.

I couldn't speak; an image of the man in my dream last night filled my head. I knew it was him; just *knew* it. The thought crossed my mind that this was the time to tell my friends about my dream, and how much it was affecting my thoughts, but I stayed silent. I wanted to keep him for myself; I was not yet ready to share him.

'Jayne's right,' Lara said. 'We need to be careful not to get carried away.'

Jayne raised her eyebrows at her and Lara smiled, then became serious once again.

'Spirits can lie, just as people can. We need to keep in mind the Law of Three. Ask the same question in three different ways and only trust the answers if they concur.'

'That makes sense,' Jayne said, albeit reluctantly. 'And those answers didn't meet that criteria.'

'No,' said Lara.

'But the temperature,' I said slowly, ready now to face the truth of it. 'I could see your breath – I know it's winter, but it isn't that cold in here, despite what I said about the heating not working. Anyway, we've had the new portable heater going.'

'I didn't say nobody was here,' Lara said. 'I just said we shouldn't blindly trust what they're saying.'

I shivered when I noticed she was picking the nail varnish off her nails, something she only did when very stressed or nervous. Grasper barked and chased his tail for a couple of circuits.

'I think we're done,' Jayne said. 'Grasper needs his night walk, we're all spooked, and to be honest, I'm ready for my bed.'

Lara looked as if she would protest, then said, 'Yes, time to call it a night.' She stood. 'Sorry, Verity, I feel I've given you more questions than answers.'

I hugged her. 'Well, I'll be here for quite a while – plenty of time to find those answers.'

'Goodnight, Verity, hope you sleep well.'

I jumped. For all the world, it had felt like somebody had blown a breath on the nape of my neck. I put my hand there but felt nothing.

'What's wrong, Verity?'

'Nothing. Goodnight, sleep tight.'

8.

I put the rubbish out before the whole Rookery took on the smell of fish and chips, then climbed back upstairs to my bathroom, below my kitchen. It didn't feel quite *right* down there, as if I hadn't moved in on that floor yet, and I was glad to get back upstairs and climb into my sleeping bag and camp bed, despite the dog hairs Grasper had so kindly left both on and somehow inside the sleeping bag.

As I thought this, he made a chuffing sound and I stroked his head; he'd stretched out alongside the camp bed, putting himself between me and the rest of the room.

I wondered briefly if Jayne would mind leaving him here when she went home. Somehow he just fitted in here at The Rookery, and I felt safer for his presence. I knew there was no way she'd go without him though.

Antony rolled away from me and I reached out to him, imploring him to stay in bed just a little while longer, even though I knew he was on the breakfast shift.

I let him go, reluctantly, and he walked naked to the bathroom to shower.

I stretched out in the bed, luxuriating in Egyptian cotton sheets, wondering if he'd have time to bring me a coffee before he had to leave for the hotel and its hungry guests.

A flashing light caught my eye and I realised Antony had left his phone on silent. I rolled over, grabbed it and dropped it in shock as my eyes focused on an intimate picture of a stranger that had just been sent to my husband via WhatsApp.

I scrolled through, and saw picture after picture, some of her, some of him.

The images sliced though my brain, preventing coherent thought, and dropping a depth charge straight into my heart.

I knew I could not hide from the truth any longer; no matter what I wanted the truth to be, it was time to face the reality of my life and my marriage.

I scrolled to the main menu, and saw a list of names I didn't know. Gina, Isa, Patsy, Sindi. I tapped on one and dropped the phone when I read the words written there amidst naked pictures of *another* woman. *I love you so much, I can't wait to marry you.*

'What?' I whispered, amazed at how calm I was as I struggled to grasp what was happening. I guessed I was in shock; my voice hadn't caught up with the emotions racing through my body. Whoever these women were, I wanted to leap through the phone, shove my arm down their throats, rip out their hearts and drive a stiletto heel through them. Then spit on them, chuck them on a fire, and feed them to the pigs. Then do something else that I wasn't yet capable of thinking of at that moment.

I dropped the phone, then belatedly realised I hadn't cleared the screen and could still see the evidence of Antony's betrayal, but I could not – would not – bend to his mistress, no, mistresses. Had he really proposed to someone? How many women was he swapping intimate pictures with? When and how had he met her – them? He was a chef in a five-star hotel and when he wasn't working, he was with me. And even when he *was* working, I was at the reception desk; most of the time, anyway.

When had he found the time and opportunity for one affair, never mind multiple betrayals? It certainly wasn't at work. Yes, okay, hotels were notoriously incestuous, but I had my ear very definitely plugged into the gossip grapevine. He was not doing the dirty at work, I was sure of that. Anyway, everybody there knew we were husband and wife.

Antony walked back into the bedroom, mostly dry and still naked after his shower. I glared at him, stared at his groin. I'd trusted him. Had he really stuck that elsewhere? Did I need to get tested? I looked away in disgust.

My practical side crumbled, the emotion overtook me, and I scowled at him, pouring my hatred through my eyes until I found my voice.

'Babes, what's wrong?' Antony rushed over, full of concern, and took me in his arms.

'Get off me!' I screamed. 'Don't touch me! You bastard, you cheating scum bastard!' Too late, I thought about playing it cool, then dismissed my own recrimination. There was no way I could handle this coolly – my heart had just broken. If I didn't take my anger out on him, I would take it out on myself.

'What? What the hell's wrong with you?'

In silence, I pointed at the phone on the floor, still displaying his proposal to another woman.

'Babes, babes, I'm so sorry. I can explain. I love you, I do, honestly. I've never even met her—' he picked up and brandished the phone at me '—not in person, just playing online.'

His words stabbed me and I lost the tenuous control I had over my temper. I grabbed his phone, opened the window and got ready to throw it on to the patio below.

I was too slow. He caught me; grabbed hold of my arm – hard enough to make me scream in pain – but I did not care. I flicked the phone up, caught it with my left hand and launched it through the window. Not as hard as I'd have managed to do with my right arm, but it was still somewhat satisfying.

39

Antony ran to retrieve it.

I followed as far as the top of the stairs and thought I should have gone after him and locked him out as soon as he went into the garden, but I didn't think of it in time. Instead I stood there, numb, unable to comprehend what had happened.

We'd been married for thirteen years, and we'd never tired of each other. Our sex life was still healthy; we had no shortage of conversation or laughter. I'd thought we were happy; solid; soul mates. What a fool I was.

He came back inside and climbed the stairs. Stood in front of me.

'She's nothing, it was just a game,' he said. 'It's you I love, we can fix this.'

I stared at him. *Is he for real?*

My fists clenched at my sides and it took every ounce of willpower I possessed not to raise them. I wanted – so desperately – to lift them; to launch them at him; to push him; to thrust him back down those stairs; to kill him.

I forced them to stay by my sides. I stared at my husband and his face changed. He wasn't Antony any more, his features morphed to those of the man in my dream the previous night, and I relaxed. Heathcliff. Heathcliff was here.

He held out his hand and took mine, then led me back to the bedroom, I climbed into the bed and he sat on the mattress next to me and stroked my hair; calming me, soothing me, sending me deep into sleep.

Except I wasn't falling into sleep, I was falling out of it.

awareness coalesced. I wasn't snuggled in Egyptian cotton on a soft mattress; once again I was in a sleeping bag, on a flimsy canvas camp bed.

I tried to roll over, but couldn't. My mind was awake, I knew where I was, what had happened, the challenges that lay ahead; but I couldn't move. I couldn't even twitch.

But I wasn't scared; I just watched myself sleeping in that bed.

His hand stroked my hair. I knew I should be terrified, but I also knew I was asleep so I was not frightened; I was just aware, observing, fascinated.

I grew more cognisant; realised my mind was awake even if my body was not. I enjoyed the feeling of relaxation and peace that I had rarely known before.

I grunted as my body tilted, but I did not have the capacity to fend off whoever was there.

My awareness grew and I understood the camp bed was sloped and skewed as if someone were sitting on one side of it. But there was no one there. I could no longer see my dream man.

The bed lifted and I felt a hand in my hair again, smoothing it.

My heart pounded, jerking me awake, and I stared wildly around the room.

No one was visible. But I *knew* somebody was there. I stretched my hand down to find solace in the fur of Grasper's head. He didn't need any more encouragement and jumped up to join me on the bed.

I realised he was just as confused as I was.

9.

'Blimey, that lad in the old Hovis ad had some legs, didn't he? He almost *ran* up a hill just like this,' Jayne said, stopping for breath yet again.

I didn't need any persuasion to rest with her. 'It gives new meaning to the words "high street", that's for sure. I feel more like Ronnie Barker than the Hovis lad – do you remember that TV sketch?'

'Hill? More like mountain,' Lara complained from behind us before Jayne could answer. 'And these bloody cobbles will be the death of me.'

'Well, they might be the death of one of your ankles,' Jayne said. 'Why on earth wouldn't you just borrow a pair of Verity's trainers?'

'Heels, darling, heels,' Lara said. 'When they make a pair of trainers with heels, then I'll try them. Until then, not a chance.'

She caught us up, bags flung over each shoulder – she'd stopped at almost every shop on Main Street as an excuse to have a rest from the climb – and I took pity on her. 'We're nearly there, Lara. The pub at the top is just there – see?'

'Pub?' Lara said, hope in her voice. 'Pub? Why didn't you say so? Come on, Hans, help me up this last bit – it must be lunchtime and it's definitely wine time.'

Recovered, refreshed and replete, we left the Black Bull and made our way up the lane, past the church, and towards the parsonage for a gentler afternoon exploring the home of the Brontë sisters.

'Oh wow, look at that graveyard,' Lara said. 'That is seriously spooky.'

'It's definitely atmospheric,' Jayne agreed. 'Shall we have a look around?'

Lara was already halfway down the path, Hannah and Grasper in her wake, and Jayne grinned at our friend's enthusiasm for a cemetery.

'Are you all right, Verity? You're very quiet today.'

I squished my lips together in a pathetic attempt at a reassuring smile, then gave up. 'Bad dreams,' I said.

'Antony?'

I nodded. 'That morning I found his phone and found out about those women. I know it was months ago, but it still hurts.'

'Of course it does.' Jayne put her arm around me and squeezed. 'It devastated you – Lara and I have been really worried. But it's a good sign you're dreaming about it, it means you're processing it, starting to deal with it, deep down.'

'You sound like Lara.' I attempted a laugh and faltered.

'Well, I spend enough time with her.' Jayne's smile was genuine. 'But seriously, Verity, dreams are how we deal with what life throws at us. You've not stopped since it happened; the divorce has only just been finalised, and you completed on the guesthouse two days ago. The past *is* now the past, and you've embarked on a different future; it's no wonder you're dreaming about him – you're getting him out of your system.'

'I hope so.' I shuddered. I hadn't told anybody just how close I'd come to pushing Antony down the stairs. Did the fact I dreamt about that moment mean I still wanted to kill him?

'What? There's something else,' Jayne said, as astute as ever.

I decided on the lesser of two evils. 'Well, it was weird – I relived the phone call, the arguments, the emotion, everything—' I broke off before I said too much. 'But right in the middle of it, Antony changed.'

'What do you mean, changed?' Jayne sounded guarded.

'He became . . . well . . . someone else.'

'Did he *look* like Antony?'

'No – nothing like.'

'Well that's a relief! I thought for a moment you'd changed the way you think about him, but it sounds like you might be getting ready to meet someone else.'

'Don't be ridiculous, Jayne. No one's ever getting the opportunity to hurt me like that again.'

'I know, honey,' she said. 'But don't tell Lara or she'll be signing you up to all the dating sites.'

This time my laugh was genuine. 'Not a bloody chance,' I said. 'Don't you dare say anything to her!'

'Anything about what?' Lara said. 'What's up with you two? Come on and have a look at this place, it's amazing.'

We followed her into the graveyard, and I understood why she was so enthralled. Six-foot-by-three-foot stone slabs lay so close together not a blade of grass could grow between them. Just like my dream. If not for the names etched on them, it would look like a patio.

'There must be ten names on that one,' Lara said, pointing. 'How deep would the grave need to be for ten coffins?'

I shook my head, unwilling even to think about it.

'Oh God, they're so young!' Jayne said. 'Look – aged two, four, six, twenty six. I haven't seen any age above thirty yet.'

'Not a great place to live in Victorian times,' I remarked,

then jumped as a flock of birds took off as one from the nearby trees.

'A parliament of rooks,' Lara said. 'How fitting.'

'What are you talking about?'

'That's what a flock of rooks is called, a parliament. They were believed to be the souls of the dead. It's quite profound to see them in a graveyard.'

We walked on in silence, all of us a little overawed by our surroundings.

'Is that the parsonage?' Jayne asked, pointing between the trees.

'Yes,' I said. After my dream it looked strange with the extension, although the addition now looked as aged as the rest of the building.

'What a place to grow up, looking at this through your windows every day,' Lara said. 'Those poor children.'

'I don't think there were trees then, either,' I said, then shrugged at Jayne's enquiring glance. 'I did a bit of reading up on the village and its famous residents before I moved in.'

'Glad to hear it. At least this bit has more character than the patio down there.'

The graves here were still flat, but some were raised – either a couple of inches or a foot – resembling altars of death. I wondered what it would have been like as a child, growing up with intimate knowledge of a working graveyard like this, surrounded by death every day.

'Apparently at the time of the Brontës, life expectancy was about twenty two,' I said, falling into the defence mechanism of tour guide to avoid the emotion of it. 'Patrick Brontë performed about three hundred baptisms a year, and then did the funerals for most of them, often only a few years later.'

Jayne shivered and hugged herself. 'Goodness, and think

how many babies would have died even before baptism. It doesn't bear thinking about.'

'It wasn't a healthy time to be alive, that's for sure,' Lara said, staring at a stone filled with names. 'Where's Hannah?'

I started at the panic in her voice, then spotted her. 'Over there, look, by the upright stones.'

Lara hurried off and I glanced at Jayne, both of us fully understanding of Lara's sudden protective instincts. It was humbling to see so many children's deaths recorded in stone.

'Mummy, Mummy, stop it, I'm playing with Grasper.' Hannah squirmed out of her mother's arms and chased after the Irish terrier.

'Grasper!' Jayne called, and I glanced up at the sharpness in her voice. She was more spooked than I'd realised. 'Here boy!' The terrier ran to his mistress and she took hold of his lead then passed it to the child. 'Keep hold of him, Hans. He shouldn't be running around the graves, it's disrespectful.'

'Yes, Aunt Jayne,' she said solemnly and clenched the leather leash with both fists.

I looked up at the hillside, dotted with six-foot-high carved monoliths to celebrate and mourn the dead. 'They look like sentinels,' I said. 'Guarding the village below from the moors above.' I realised I was lapsing into my first dream and quietened.

Lara and Jayne said nothing, and we stood in silence for a while, contemplating the rows of individually engraved millstone grit.

'I don't know which is sadder,' Lara eventually said. 'The stones with a long list of names, or the ones that are only half full.'

I followed her gaze and spotted the stone that was

affecting her. Two names at the top, then four feet of blank.

'Their family didn't survive,' I said. 'They died before they could have children.'

'Can we get out of here?' Lara said. 'I've had enough.' She shuddered. 'There's something about this place, something not right.'

As one we turned and left the dead to re-join the living.

10.

I climbed into my camp bed utterly exhausted. I couldn't remember the last time I'd seen Lara so spooked. She wouldn't leave Hannah alone, even for a second, and had said she could not 'cope with the museum and more death'.

Instead, we'd come back to The Rookery, Hannah had become fractious and emotional from the unaccustomed fussing from her mother, and they'd left just after an early tea.

I missed them already. I knew I had a busy week ahead, but it seemed to stretch out emptily until Friday evening when they would return.

The phone buzzed and I jumped, then scrabbled for it, a sinking feeling in the pit of my stomach as I wondered what had happened.

With relief I registered that the caller was not Lara or Jayne as I swiped the answer icon. I instantly regretted it when Antony said, 'Verity? Hello?'

'Hello Antony,' I said, resigned to the conversation, but determined to keep control of my temper and emotions. 'How are you?'

'Not good, Verity, not good.'

My heart sank. It was one of *those* calls: self-pitying and maudlin drunk. 'What's happened?'

'Nothing, I'm just really low. I miss you, I've messed everything up.'

'Yes, you have.'

Antony huffed in frustration. He wasn't sorry, he just wanted absolution. And probably the divorce settlement back. 'I know, I know, things were just so hard – we hardly saw each other, always on different shifts, and we weren't getting pregnant.'

I gritted my teeth. I would not cry. I would not.

'I was lonely, Verity, so lonely.'

'We worked at the same hotel, Antony, we lived in the same house. If you had put the effort into us instead of that slapper—' I broke off and squeezed my eyes shut in frustration. The last thing I wanted was to argue with my ex-husband. Even by being on the phone he was tainting my new home; my new life.

He said nothing for a while, then changed tack.

'You can't put it all on me, you know. You could have made more effort.'

I said nothing, wondering if I should hang up or if that would make things worse.

'You were so cold, and always complaining, it's no wonder I looked for comfort elsewhere.'

'What? You can't put this on me! *You* were the one cheating!'

'We were arguing all the time.'

'Probably because you were chasing other women!'

'Verity—'

'No! No, I've had enough. Please, it's over, it's done. We're divorced, we're separated. You go marry your slapper, and I'll get on with *my* life. Goodbye, Antony.' I finally hung up.

Within seconds, the phone buzzed again. I ignored it.

And again.

I switched it off, lay back down, and stared at the ceiling somewhere above me in the dark.

Tears rolled down the sides of my face and pooled in my

ears. I stifled a sob, furious with myself for allowing him to upset me again. I'd cried a river since that day. It was time to move on, to get over it, over *him*.

But how *did* you get over a broken heart? How did you put the pieces back together again? How did you ever let anybody in again?

I sobbed once more as a lonely, empty future stretched out before me. *Would* there ever be anybody to share it with me?

A face swam in front of my vision. Dark, handsome, piercing eyes, infectious smile. He held out a hand to me. I took it, and sank, swirling into a dark mist, letting go, drifting away from the bleak reality of my life.

II.

I woke with the image of those same eyes staring into mine, and lay frozen for a moment, my heart beating hard. My chest seemed to be the only part of me able to move as my breathing matched my heart in its intensity, clouding the air above me with evidence of life. For a moment I had been so disorientated I'd been unsure if I were alive or dead.

I caught my breath. What was that noise? And again! *Footsteps*? I listened until I had to release air and take in fresh – the action violent enough to shake me out of my torpor. I laughed at myself – in silence and without mirth – of course it hadn't been footsteps; just an old house on a winter's day, and the remnants of a nightmare.

I remembered Antony's call last night. That would have been enough to spark all sorts of weird and frightening mirages in my sleeping brain.

Shaking it off, I forced myself out of my warm bed into the cold morning air – the sooner the heating system was sorted properly, the better.

Shuffling to the shower – thank goodness for fluffy slippers and fleecy onesies! – I remembered the eyes I'd woken to. They hadn't been Antony's blue irises; they had been dark, brooding, intense.

'Oh for God's sake, Verity, it was a bloody dream, stop spooking yourself!'

I laughed at the sound of my own voice in the emptiness and switched on the shower. Time to be thinking about the day ahead, not the night behind. I undressed and stepped under the thankfully warm spray, then lifted my face to the waterfall.

The builders would be here before too long, ready to start work on making the place mine.

I soaped myself, thinking about my plans, my dream of how the next part of my life would be.

The Rookery would have five bedrooms, and I was determined to make it spectacular, going that extra mile to make people feel welcome and valued. After living and working in the centre of Leeds for so long, I wanted to embrace country living: fresh air, a real community, and a slower, more enjoyable pace of life.

I loved the Brontës' books, and couldn't be closer to the parsonage – one of the reasons I'd chosen this property – and I wanted to reflect the history of this place in my design and management decisions.

The house was attached to a row of weaver's cottages, so I'd use plenty of local textiles, and it stood to reason that Emily Brontë, and then Charlotte would have been regular visitors to the people who lived and worked here. In the 1840s, Emily had returned to live with her father and Branwell, and carried out the duties of curate's wife – even though she was daughter. Then Charlotte when she returned to Haworth after a small taste of fame and the city life in London to care for her father, then as Arthur Bell Nicholls' wife until her own premature death in childbirth in 1855.

I sighed at the tragedy of so many talented and driven siblings dying so young. Poor Patrick; first burying his wife, then seeing all six of his children in their graves. Maria, his firstborn, at age eleven through to Charlotte, the most famous of his brood, at thirty eight.

The pain and unfairness of it had me close to tears and I

lifted my face to the spray of water and leaned back into the comforting hand around my waist. It had been a long time since Antony had joined me in the shower.

Then I remembered and spun around, my grasping hand on the tiles only just saving me from a nasty fall.

I yanked the shower curtain back and used it to cover myself in one movement, then peered into the small bathroom as I fumbled around for the shampoo bottle. Not much of a weapon, but all I had to hand.

I listened hard to silence as the steam cleared, then stared at empty tiles, mirror and closed door.

There was no one there.

12.

Chaos had never felt so safe. Noise, people, dust, destruction, rubbish. If I couldn't have Jayne and Lara, Keighley Building Services would do until the girls could get back to Haworth.

I handed out mugs of strong, sweet tea and looked at what had been accomplished so far. The build team – Omar and Woody – had ripped out a couple of internal walls in the lobby, covering everything with rubble and curses.

They had not yet managed to find a single level surface – on any plane – and had launched into a constant bicker with each other and the project manager, Vikram, about how to go about turning the drawn plans into reality.

Sarah, or Sparkly as she seemed to be quite happy to be called, was the only female electrician within twenty miles and very proud of it. She was not taking the state of The Rookery's wires very well; mainly because she was struggling to even find them, and she took every frustration out on poor Snoopy, her apprentice, real name Charlie Brown.

Thick, stone walls were introducing themselves at most inopportune moments, and two hours in, nobody understood the original construction or subsequent alterations of the building.

'Look at this,' Omar said, gesturing at the architectural plans I'd had drawn up at great expense. I hung back, not wanting to get embroiled in yet another row.

54

Vikram leaned in closer, a look of resignation on his face. He was a funny bloke; big features in a rugged face, and I suspected he'd get better looking as he got older and grew into his looks. But he definitely looked interesting. Tall and surprisingly strong – he'd heaved some pretty heavy loads out to the skip along with Omar and Woody – I was not quite sure where his lanky frame was hiding the muscle. I wondered what he looked like when he smiled – if he ever did. I'd seen no hint of one so far, not even in greeting.

'Architect has us moving this wall 'ere, but its bloody stone. Then there's this en-suite upstairs – I've got no idea how the plumbers are going to pipe it in.'

'And the wiring will have to be completely redone,' Sparkly put in. 'And I can't go off these plans, I'll have to go through the whole place and find out for mesen which walls are stone and which I can work with.'

This was beginning to sound expensive. I couldn't just leave them to it. 'But why are there so many issues? Surely the architects sorted all that out when they surveyed the place.'

'It doesn't look like they did survey it,' Vikram said. 'It looks like they've just gone off the plans that have been lodged with the Land Registry and not checked to see if they're correct. And with a building this old . . .' He shrugged.

'So what was the point of me paying them all that money?'

Vikram shrugged again. 'First off, you'll have needed them for planning permission for the alterations, and to be honest, having architects come out to the property to survey it really would have cost a fortune.'

'And we'd still probably have had to chuck it all out when the real work started,' Omar interrupted.

55

'Don't worry, love, we'll work out how to sort it, you don't have to bother yourself,' said Vikram.

'My name's Verity, and this is my home, business and livelihood. I will very definitely bother myself with it.'

'All I meant was, we'll work out how to sort it,' said Vikram. 'Verity. We've all grown up and spent our working lives in buildings like this. If we can't understand the place and make it work, no one can.'

I nodded, mollified. 'That's good to hear.' Then, keen to ease the tension, I said, 'So what do you think we should do about that wall?' I pointed at Omar's most urgent problem: the stone wall that bisected my proposed reception area.

'Give us a minute, love. Verity,' Vikram corrected, glancing up at me.

I gave him a small smile and he held my gaze a moment, then returned his attention back to the plans and room.

'Well, we can't knock it down,' he said at last. 'It's original and solid – it's been there over a hundred and fifty years, and ain't shifting without some serious resistance.'

'So we need to work around it,' Omar said.

'How about instead of having your reception area against that front wall, you move it there.' Vikram pointed to the left of the back wall. 'Then that wall can stay and we can widen the doorway into an arch,' more pointing, 'and you've still got room for seating and stuff there and there. Would that work?' He looked to Omar and Sparkly first for approval before turning back to me.

I walked to the doorway in the problem wall and looked into the space that would have to house my guests' breakfast room. 'It's a bit tight. I need five tables with chairs as well as a buffet table, and I don't want everyone on top of each other.' I looked at the far wall. 'It might work if that's moved back.'

Vikram sighed, strode to the latest offending wall, knocked on it a couple of times then opened the door to examine the other side. 'It's timber and plasterboard,' he said. 'It can be done, but it'll mean a smaller kitchen.'

'I realise that. But I'll only be cooking breakfasts, not three-course dinners as the restaurant did.'

'Don't forget we'll be putting a bedroom in over there.' Vikram pointed again.

'I haven't forgotten.' I took a deep breath and did my best to speak builder. 'If this wall was moved back two feet, and with the new room and en-suite at that end, what would the dimensions of the new kitchen be?'

'Omar?' Vikram barked, clearly not amused to be challenged.

'Well, if we put the new wall in here,' Omar laid a batten on the floor, 'and the wall for the new bedroom will come to— Hang on a minute.' He nipped back into the lobby, presumably to check the plans, then reappeared and paced, thinking hard. 'Here.' He placed another batten, then turned and spread his arms. 'This will be your kitchen.'

I looked at the large space, then up at Vikram. 'Perfect. We'll do that, then. Can I leave it with you? I have a few errands to run.'

Vikram nodded – still no smile – but Woody grinned at me as I escaped.

It would take more than two months to be ready for guests, and I was ready to pull my hair out after two hours. I couldn't do this alone.

I fished my mobile out of my bag and dialled. 'Jayne? Tell me again why this was a good idea . . .'

13.

'Oh you've got to be kidding me,' I muttered as I drove down West Lane. Builder's vans and skips had taken over and there was nowhere to park. *Not the best way to introduce myself to the neighbours.*

I drove on, crawling down the almost vertical Main Street, managing not to hit any of the winter tourists – even though a fair few of them didn't realise it was a functioning road with actual traffic – and made my way back round to the top of the village. I'd have to park in the museum car park and unload the car later.

I glanced over at the rear gable of The Rookery and walked in the other direction. I simply could not face Vikram and his army yet. Maybe later – when they knocked off for the day. His comment about not bothering myself tickled at my memory, but I shoved it away.

I continued walking. Past the parsonage and into the graveyard. It seemed quiet, peaceful. The odd tourist was wandering around, but the bustle of village life was absent. Best of all: no builders.

I sat and sighed, feeling my shoulders physically drop as I relaxed. Then I jumped as my phone beeped.

Embarrassed, I fumbled it out of my bag, pulled off my glove, and checked the text. Antony. *I'm sorry about last night. I didn't want to argue. I miss you. Call me xx*

I stared at it then switched the phone off. Why couldn't he leave me alone? Did he not realise how deeply he'd hurt me? How much I was still hurting? Every reminder of him and his betrayal just made it worse. I shoved away the memories of that night and what might have been, took a deep breath, and looked around me; searching for the calm that had descended on me when I first sat down; furious with myself that despite it all, I missed him too.

The clop of horses' hoofs broke into my reverie and I smiled – that was such a sound of the past. I realised I couldn't hear any cars or any other noise denoting the twenty-first century, just the buzz of insects, the horses, and a cock crowing. Even the distant voices could have come from the age of the Brontës.

I sniffed. No exhaust; no ozone; just damp fresh earth with a hint of something familiar. A distinctive smell I recognised. I'd smelled it the first morning I'd woken in my new home: wild garlic. *In December?* I dismissed the discrepancy as the bare trees above rattled their smaller branches in response to a gust of wind, and a rabbit shot across the path in front of me as if being chased by a ferret.

The great slabs of stone themselves stayed stoic, whether laid on the ground or standing upright in rows. Each was a different shape, a different design, and heavily carved, but all were of a similar imposing size. Indifferent custodians of the dead.

I shivered when I remembered 44,000 people were believed to have been buried in this vastly inadequate patch of earth; far too many of them children. I counted the names on the nearest upright stone. Twelve. Twelve people in one grave. I shuddered, remembering Lara's question about how deep these graves must be. Had they dug it deeper every time there was a death in the family? How often in the past had this cemetery been scattered with rotting coffins as more room was cut out of the earth below?

Was my dream man one of them? Were his bones commemorated by one of these stones? Had those forceful eyes rotted away into the earth beneath my feet?

I caught a movement between the stones – a flash of white. Him? I stared. There it was again, but too far away to make sense of it. Then again, in the other direction.

I shook my head. This was getting ridiculous; at best I was descending into a world of fantasy and ghosts, at worst I was losing my mind.

Startled, I looked up as the rooks took wing as one, lifting from the skeletal treetops in reaction to some unseen threat.

I shivered as I realised they had done so silently – with no cawing of warning or intention – before settling once more in their roosts. Somehow it felt a portent.

I shook myself, ashamed of being so melodramatic, and I glanced around at the stone sculptures surrounding me. *Well, no wonder my imagination is running away with me in here.*

I stood and belatedly realised my bench was in fact an altar grave. I silently apologised to the occupants and peered at the worn letters.

After a few moments, I picked out *cliff* and my heart leaped. *Heathcliff, really?* I sank to my knees and activated the flashlight app on my phone, then shone it from the side to pick out the rest of the letters in the winter's afternoon gloom.

Not Heathcliff, Sutcliffe.

I hung my head and snorted with laughter at myself, then got back to my feet and went home.

I shouldered open my front door, cursing at the shopping bag straps digging into my arms and shoulders, then swore more violently as Woody barged into me and sent me flying.

He didn't stop to apologise, never mind help me up or pick up the food and wallpaper samples now scattered over the dusty, rubble-strewn floor.

'What the hell?' I shouted at Vikram as he rushed in to see what all the noise was about. 'Your bloke just shoved me over! What's going on?'

'I'm sorry, love, I don't know what's got into him. One minute he was measuring up, the next he bolted.'

I rubbed my elbow, then pushed up my sleeve to try and examine it, but couldn't see.

Vikram took hold of my arm. 'That'll bruise, you should get some ice on it.'

I snatched my arm back. 'One of your staff assaults me, and that's all you have to say?'

Vikram stared at me. 'Don't worry, love, I'm sure it was an accident, but I will deal with him, don't doubt that. Are you hurt anywhere else?'

'No, no, I don't think so.' I was mortified to hear my voice shake, and stepped forward, but winced and rubbed my hip. 'Spoke too soon.' I tried to smile. It was a poor attempt.

'Get yourself upstairs and pour yourself a nip of summat. I'll bring this lot up.'

'What's happened? Is everything all right?' Sparkly appeared at the door to the stairs.

'Where's Woody buggered off to? What's going on?' Omar said, pushing past her.

'I dunno, he just bolted, knocked Verity over.'

'What? Are you okay?' Sparkly asked.

'What's he done that for?' Omar said. 'What's got into the lad?'

'I'm fine, just a bit shaken,' I answered Sparkly.

'Dunno,' Vikram repeated to Omar. 'He never said a word, just ran. But he was as white as a sheet.'

'I'll go after him, find out what's up.'

Vikram nodded and bent to gather up my shopping as Sparkly led the way upstairs, asking new questions with every step.

That nip of something Vikram had mentioned was getting more and more tempting, and I found myself praying the bottles had survived the tumble.

14.

I stared at the ceiling, alternately willing sleep to come, then doing my utmost to stay awake when I felt my eyelids falter. I desperately wanted my dream man to visit again, but at the same time he scared me. When my lids finally closed I remembered the caress in the shower this morning and snapped awake.

If I wasn't already going mad, it wouldn't take much longer at this rate.

I drifted awake, becoming aware that I must have succumbed, but with no idea how long ago. The mixture of relief and disappointment I felt at not having dreamt dissipated in a flash. Was that a footstep? And another?

I tried to move, but once again was paralysed, helpless to do anything but listen and wait.

There was no doubt now: footsteps climbed the stairs, growing louder and resonating deeper the closer they came.

They were in my apartment now, approaching the room where I slept. I cast my mind back, wondering if I'd closed my bedroom door – I didn't think I had.

A floorboard creaked – that was in my room!

I could not open my eyes, never mind move my limbs, and now my breath faltered too. I focused on expanding my chest then pushing the air back out, trying to dismiss the creaking footsteps as imagination.

My breath caught and I forgot to expel it. My mattress had dipped as if someone had sat on the edge of my bed.

My chest strained, but I still did not breathe, then I felt fingers brush my cheek and I let out the stale air with a yell and sat up.

I scrambled to switch on the bedside light and stared around the room – eyes wide and breath now panting in and out of my abused lungs. No one. The room was empty.

I bolted out of bed, showered with no further incident, dressed and was downstairs fifteen minutes later. I'd get breakfast from the closest café.

When I got back to The Rookery, Vikram and the build team were waiting for me. The expected complaints didn't come as I let them in, instead Vikram introduced the new face amongst them.

'This is Gary, he'll be working with Omar to replace Woody.'

'Morning, Gary, pleased to meet you.' I held up my hands full of coffee and bacon butty to indicate I couldn't shake, but he wasn't bothered.

'Hiya, mush. That smells good.'

Mush?

Sparkly saw my expression and laughed. 'And you thought "love" was bad! Best just to ignore them – I've been trying to train them for years, I'd have better luck with pit bulls.'

I smiled, still too shaken by this morning's rude awakening to get upset about the pet name.

'Pit bulls are very intelligent,' I said with a smile and Sparkly gave a very loud, very throaty laugh that had the men grinning along.

'So what happened to Woody?' I asked.

'He saw the Grey Lady,' Sparkly said. 'Freaked him out – he doesn't believe in ghosts.'

'Sparkly!' Vikram admonished. 'I thought we'd agreed—'

Sparkly flapped her hand at him. 'She'll find out eventually, and it's not as if she's evil or anything. Woody's just a wimp. Verity, are you okay?' Her tone changed. 'You've gone as white as Woody did.'

'Just get to work, all of you,' Vikram barked. He dragged a sawhorse closer. 'Here, sit on this.'

I nodded at him gratefully and perched on the paint-splattered trestle.

'You've seen something too, haven't you?'

I shook my head. 'No,' I said, ignoring Grasper's antics with the orbs, then to moderate the lie, added, 'but I've felt things, and had dreams. What did Woody see?'

'The Grey Lady – he's not the only one, plenty have seen her over the years, here and in the row of cottages next door. She's said to be Emily Brontë.'

'Yes, the waitress in the White Lion said something about that.' *But if The Rookery is haunted by Emily Brontë, Who's the man with the dark eyes?* I thought but did not say.

'Oh Tess, yeah, she loves all the ghost stories, does amateur ghost hunts and puts stuff on YouTube. There's not much evidence it *is* Emily, to be honest, just that she's only seen at this time of year, and she wears the right era clothing – big bonnet with a bow, full gown, that kind of thing.'

'Why grey? That was a mourning colour wasn't it?'

'I don't know about that.' Vikram screwed his mouth up. 'People say there's a grey haze around her, which is where the name comes from.'

I sipped my coffee, my bacon butty forgotten. 'So what did Woody see? What actually happened?'

'Right over there.' Vikram pointed to the wall separating The Rookery from the cottage next door. 'She walked up the wall in a diagonal, as if there were stairs there, then disappeared through the wall.'

'That's all?'

'It was enough for him.'

Despite myself, I laughed.

'It sounds like you've had more scares than funny feelings and dreams,' Vikram said.

I smiled up at him, touched by his concern, but reluctant to tell him too much. I didn't want him to talk about me in the same dismissive way he'd spoken about Woody's reaction to the Grey Lady.

'Just intense dreams and a few touches. A man though, definitely not Emily Brontë.' I laughed. 'Probably just my imagination – new start, new home, and in a place with so much history.'

'Not heard of anything like that here,' Vikram said. 'Right, better get on.'

So much for not being dismissed.

15.

I had to admit, despite the problems, Vikram and his team had made good progress. The new floor plan downstairs was coming on – the walls that we'd finally decided would come down were down, although there was still a lot of tidying up to be done. The new dividing walls should be in place by the end of the week, then Omar and Gary would start on the bedrooms after Christmas, although finding workable room for all the en-suites was going to be a challenge.

Sparkly was happier with the wiring. She'd found most of the existing network and had enthusiastically ripped out every wire. Which meant I was reliant on candles, torches and woolly jumpers until she could get lights and sockets working in my apartment again.

My candles flickered and I switched on the torch and looked around. I really had not thought this through. Instead of a romantic adventure, this was far too spooky. I liked a good ghost story – but not when there was the possibility I was featuring in it.

I unscrewed my bottle of wine and poured my first glass. I didn't normally drink alone on a Tuesday evening, but I told myself the circumstances were exceptional. It would keep me warm and was quite possibly the only way I would sleep tonight. If I drank enough, I might not even dream.

I'd called Lara and Jayne earlier to give them the news that the place was definitely haunted, and wished I'd made

Jayne my second call for her calming, logical reassurance. Instead, I'd been left with Lara's excited squealing and talk of Ouija boards and more séances. Just what I didn't need.

I took a big gulp of wine and called Jayne back.

She answered my call, laughing. 'You called Lara didn't you?'

'Yes.'

'How badly has she freaked you out?'

'Well, I'm sitting in a hundred-and-fifty-year-old haunted house. I have no electricity. I'm drinking wine by candlelight, one of the builders was so scared he ran, even though it might cost him his job, and the man in my dreams keeps touching me. I'd say I'm about nine out of ten on the freaked-out scale.'

'What? The man in your dreams, plural? And he's touched you? You didn't tell me that before.'

I winced and took another gulp of wine. 'Sorry, I didn't mean to tell you now – it's probably just imagination. It's always when I've just woken up and my subconscious is probably dealing with all the Antony stuff.'

'So is the man in your dreams Antony?'

'Well, no.'

'What does he look like?'

'Dark, handsome – very handsome!' I giggled and had another drink. 'And his eyes – the complete opposite to Antony's – they're dark too, I feel like they're looking straight through me, into the core of me. I know I'm only dreaming him, but it's like he's staring into depths of me I don't even know are there.'

Jayne was silent a moment. 'You know who you've just described, don't you?'

'Who?' Although I knew what she was going to say.

'Heathcliff.'

'Great, I'm being haunted by a fictional character!' I laughed and sipped again.

Jayne was the first to stop laughing.

'What?' I said into the silence on the line.

'I just had a thought. He'll have been inspired by *somebody*, the Brontës did draw on the people in Haworth for their characters – more than a few of their neighbours were upset when they realised who authored those novels.'

'So who inspired Heathcliff?'

'Exactly.'

I drained the bottle into my glass, a little embarrassed at how quickly I'd emptied it, and made Jayne promise not to tell Lara about the dreams. I ended the call but dropped the glass before I'd brought it halfway to my lips.

There was a figure, glowing grey, almost brighter than the candles. A woman, and slim. She wore a large bonnet, and a dress tight about the upper torso then flaring out in a full, bell-shaped skirt.

She carried a basket over one arm – I could see it was full, but not what the contents were – and as I watched, she calmly disappeared into the wall.

I stared open-mouthed. *Have I just seen Emily Brontë? Or have I just had too much to drink?*

This was too much. Feeling completely sober despite the wine, I grabbed my handbag and coat and left. Hopefully the Old White Lion Hotel had an empty guest room as well as a warm, comfortable bar with real, *live* people.

16.

The boy bolted and was on the moors before the mill bell had stopped ringing to announce the end of the children's long working day. There was still a glimmer of the late spring daylight left, but the shadows were fast encroaching on the bleak landscape.

He lost his battle with the tears he'd been fighting all day and ducked down behind an outcrop of millstone grit to give in to them in privacy.

He gasped for air between sobs and fell into a violent coughing fit as fresh moors' air hit his wool-fibre-lined lungs. Only one day at the mill and his chest hurt. The fibres had prickled the back of his throat all day, and nobody had paid any attention to his complaints.

Mind you, nobody could hear him over the relentless cacophony of the spinning jennies and mules.

It had been worse than thunder, and there had been no let-up; not from the mill bell at five that morning until the children's bell at six that evening. Even the worst thunder didn't send merciless steel backwards and forwards, threatening to crush unwary hands, feet, or heads.

Fresh tears flooded down his cheeks as the seven-year-old realised he would have to do the same tomorrow, and the day after that, and the day after that, for the rest of his life; however short that may be.

'Why are you crying?'

The boy startled and rubbed his face at the thin but strident voice, then peered at the girl in confusion, unable to decipher her words through the ringing in his ears. She repeated her question and Harry studied her lips to understand what she was saying, then recognised her as water cleared from his eyes.

Emily, one of the parson's daughters. He cringed; to show such weakness in front of a girl!

'I'm not, I just have soot in my eye. I started working on mill floor today.'

'Is that why you're covered in black dust?' Emily asked. 'You'll get the moors dirty.'

He looked down at himself. She spoke true; he was covered in sooty wool fibres. He shrugged. 'Maybe Mr Baalzephon will clean mill up.'

She hooted with laughter. 'Old Man Rook? He'll do nowt of the sort!'

The children laughed, united against the owner of Rooks Mill.

'What's thee doing here?' the boy asked, remembering Emily was a couple of years younger than he. 'Where's thy brother or sisters?'

'Oh they're in the parlour,' Emily said, dismissive. 'I crept out, I wanted to see if the lapwings had hatched.'

'Lapwings?'

'Aye, there's a nest over yonder with eggs. Listen, the mama and papa are calling! Do you want to see?'

'All right then, happen I do.'

'But you'll have to be quiet or you'll scare them away. Why are you shouting, anyway?'

The boy stared at Emily. 'I'm not shouting.'

'Yes you are, you're really loud.'

He thought for a moment. 'Is tha sure lapwings are calling? I can't hear them.'

'Yes!' Emily stamped her foot. 'Listen! There, did you just hear her peewit?'

The boy cocked his head but still heard nothing. 'I think mill's made me deaf already,' he said, then looked at Emily in alarm. 'Has mill taken lapwing's call away from me forever?'

Emily stared up at him. 'They're this way,' she said in lieu of answering his question, and ran up the hill.

The boy followed Emily through the bracken and grass of the lower moor, then through the heather until the little girl turned with her finger to her lips.

She pointed ahead and the boy squinted. There she was! Difficult to see unless you knew she was there, her brown plumage camouflaged her well against the heather stalks, her crest imitating the new growth above that sheltered her and her eggs from the overhead threats of owl, buzzard and kestrel.

'How does tha know there are eggs? It's late in season to be laying,' the boy whispered.

'Shh,' Emily hissed, but too late, the lapwing hen took wing.

'There, see?' Emily said. 'You'd better not have scared her away for good or the chicks won't hatch. I wish I'd never shown you. Come on, come away.'

The boy followed his young guide back down the hill.

I woke with tears flooding down my face. I could *feel* the despair of the boy and somehow understood exactly what it was like for the child to crawl underneath the working spinning mule, brushing down its moving parts, as well as the floor, as it operated; the metal frame clanging into its final position, then making its return journey; back and forth three times a minute, every minute, of every working hour. And there were an awful lot of working hours. No wonder employment of children in the mills had been termed The Yorkshire Slavery.

As I grew more aware, I shrank against the wall before

remembering where I was. The Old White Lion. I clearly didn't need to be at The Rookery for Heathcliff, or whatever his real name was, to visit. He could find me anywhere.

17.

Sitting in comfort, having breakfast served to me and my coffee cup refilled regularly was exactly what I needed and went a long way to bolstering my spirits.

I didn't want to leave the comfort of the White Lion and return to my building site, but it had to be done, and eventually I settled up and walked home.

The build team had beaten me again and were sitting in their vans outside, waiting.

'Morning,' I said as they exited their vehicles and trooped into The Rookery. I received a few grunts in return and a reluctant 'how do' from Vikram.

My good feeling from breakfast disappeared and I wondered what was going on now.

'None of 'em slept well.' Vikram had recognised the look on my face. 'They all had nightmares, but none of 'em will talk about it.'

'So it's catching.'

'What?'

'Nothing. How about you, did you sleep okay?'

He shrugged. 'Well enough. What happened here?'

I followed his gaze and saw the shards of broken wine glass. I'd forgotten about that – they still lay where they'd shattered before I'd fled last night. 'Woody's Grey Lady paid another visit.'

'You saw her?'

I glanced away from him, then back. 'I-I think so. But I was spooked after the Woody thing, and had no lights but candlelight. Now it's daylight, I-I'm not so sure.'

'What did you see?'

'Well, what you said. A woman glowing grey with a big bonnet, a gown with a large skirt, and carrying a basket.'

Vikram said nothing.

'What?'

'I don't remember telling you about the basket.'

'What?'

'I didn't tell you about the basket. Everybody sees it – sometimes that's all people see – but I realised when I got home I hadn't told you about it.'

'Oh.'

Vikram made his habitual shrug. 'It seems your imagination isn't quite so rampant after all.'

I sighed. 'Thanks for that. I feel much better.'

Vikram's answering smile was gone before it was complete as a crash echoed from upstairs and Sparkly's voice carried through the building.

'You daft bugger! I told you to hold on to them wire strippers! Where the hell are they?'

'Sorry, sorry, I don't know where they've got to. I just had them!' Snoopy said. 'Sorry, Sparkly.'

'And why the hell does everyone have to call me Sparkly? My name's Sarah, and I never wear bloody sparkles!'

'You're a female sparky, lass, so you're Sparkly. Get used to it,' Omar butted in.

'I'd better go calm things down before Gary calls her "mush" and she really loses it,' Vikram said, finally smiling and hurrying through the broken glass still on the floor, towards the stairs.

'What on earth is going on here?'

I twirled at the sound of her voice. 'Jayne! What are you doing here? I wasn't expecting you until tomorrow.'

'It sounded like you needed a friend, so I pulled a sickie. Lara can't make it today because of Hannah's school, but she sends her best and wishes she was with us.'

I embraced her and hung on tight. 'Thank you,' I whispered. 'It's so good to see you.'

She hugged me back a moment, then pulled away. 'Right, well, we'd better get that glass cleaned up and then you can fill me in properly on what's been happening.'

'Okay, but not here. Let's take Grasper for a walk – I need to get out of this place.'

By the time we had completed a very slow stroll to the bottom of Haworth Main Street, it was almost lunchtime.

'Let's try Haworth Old Hall,' I said. 'I haven't eaten there yet.'

'Lead the way, Verity. I hope that place isn't haunted!'

I slowed my step. 'In a place this old, with this much history, *everywhere* is probably haunted,' I said, aware my chest was tightening again.

Drinks and menus in situ on the table, Jayne sat and stared at me.

'What?' I asked.

'I think you're worrying too much.'

'Okay,' I drawled, hoping she was right but knowing deep down in the pit of my stomach that she wasn't.

'Antony's put you through hell in the past year, it's no wonder you're having weird and vivid dreams, especially about a man, and especially about a man who's the opposite in looks to Antony.'

'But what about the touches? The footsteps and sitting on the bed?'

'You said yourself, you were either still half-asleep or had only just woken up. You were probably still dreaming.'

I thought back to the caress in the shower. That had not been a dream, I was sure of it. I'd been fully awake for that one. Although, if I was honest, I *had* been daydreaming about Antony, hadn't I? Maybe Jayne had a good point.

'What about the Grey Lady – seeing her last night?'

'Power of suggestion. You're already on edge with the dreams and sleeping alone in a strange house – and a very old one at that. That builder bloke had already freaked out about the Grey Lady – more suggestion, judging by the legend that's passed about. And you'd been drinking by candlelight. It wasn't real, just a shadow.'

'But I knew about the basket.'

'Lucky guess.'

I pursed my lips. 'Maybe.'

I'd run out of arguments, and I really, *really* wanted her to be right.

18.

''Scuse me, love.'

I stepped aside for a strange man carrying plastic piping and watched him climb The Rookery stairs. The plumbers had arrived.

'Does that mean central heating?' Jayne asked.

'I think it might,' I replied, and knocked three times on the closest door frame.

'Wonderful.'

'I doubt it will be operational by tonight.' I laughed at the crestfallen expression on her face. 'We'll still be camping upstairs around the fan heater, I'm afraid.'

Jayne shrugged. 'Why is it so quiet?'

I stopped and listened, confused, then realised what Jayne meant. Whilst there was plenty of banging and clattering – plus the constant rumble of the generator – there were very few voices, and none of the banter I'd become used to.

'I'm not sure I want to know,' I said, glancing at the wall where I'd seen the apparition the night before. 'Come on, let's go up, out of their way.'

'Why can't you leave the generator running for us?' I asked Vikram. 'There's plenty of cable to run lights and heater.'

'Sorry, love. Health and safety. Can't run it when there's no staff on the premises – insurers won't let us.'

'But . . .'

He shrugged. 'Nowt I can do about it, love, sorry.'

'It's okay, Verity, the lamps have plenty of batteries and I'm sure we can work out how to get the camping stove running,' Jayne said.

'They'll have rooms at the White Lion or Black Bull,' Vikram said.

'No, they're booked up for Christmas,' I said. 'I was lucky to get a room last night, but it was the last one.'

Vikram nodded. 'I'll stop in later, if you want – make sure you're okay.'

'We'll be fine,' I said. 'But thank you.'

'Sparkly's not far off getting the wiring sorted,' Vikram said. 'If she doesn't finish it tomorrow, she won't be going home Friday till you have lights and heat for Christmas.'

'Thanks, Vikram.'

'No problem, goodnight.'

'Did you see the way he looked at you when he was talking about staff being on the premises?' Jayne asked once the door had closed behind him. 'He was after an invite to stay!'

'Don't be daft.'

'I'm serious – he's definitely interested.'

I shook my head. Vikram had warmed up since Monday, but he was very definitely not interested in me. 'Shall we go see if the fish and chip shop is open?' I asked to change the subject. 'Then we don't have to bother with that camping stove.'

Jayne wasn't fooled, but let it slide. We wrapped up and stepped out into the freezing December evening.

'It looks so eerie,' Jayne said. 'The way the streetlights look like old gas lamps, and the haze around them; all the stone and cobbles, it really wouldn't have looked much different a century ago.'

'Longer,' I said. 'I think the gas came in the 1860s, so

79

that's a hundred and fifty years at least.' I shivered as we walked. 'You can almost feel the history embracing us.'

'You're not kidding,' Jayne said. 'If not for the odd parked car, I honestly wouldn't be sure *when* we are.'

'We should walk back through the graveyard,' I suggested. 'If you think this is atmospheric, try that place at night!'

'You'll not get me in there after dark! It was spooky enough in full daylight.'

I smiled. I wasn't sure 'spooky' was the right word – it was something more than that; something *heavier.*

'Thank goodness, they're frying,' Jayne interrupted my reverie. 'What are you having?'

Half an hour later, with hot food before us, glasses of wine poured, Jayne's lamps brightening my apartment, and wrapped up in sweaters and blankets, I felt at ease. I wasn't concerned about Haworth's ghosts, not in Jayne's company. I smiled at the thought that she'd shooed them away.

'What?'

'Nothing. I was just thinking how glad I am you're here.'

She grinned. 'What else are friends for but to freeze to death with you in a haunted house four days before Christmas, eating fish and chips and swilling wine?'

I laughed. 'I do appreciate it, Jayne, honestly. More than I can say.'

'I know, love.'

'Oh don't you bloody start calling me love, too!'

'That's better! I was surprised to hear you take it from Vikram.'

I ignored her raised eyebrows. 'I've given up. Anyway, one of the builders calls everyone "mush", so being called love doesn't seem so bad now. I've decided to ignore it.'

'Oh my God, it would drive me crackers!'

'How are Jenny and Michael?' I asked when the laughter had died down.

Jayne's smile relaxed and she sipped her wine. 'They're fine – great. Jenny's well on with her final year assignments, and Michael seems to be settling down at the ad firm okay.'

'Will you be seeing them over Christmas?'

'No. It's their father's turn for Christmas this year, I'll catch up with them in the New Year.'

I nodded, careful not to comment. Jayne had been divorced fifteen years and still hated her ex with a passion.

'Next year, there'll be rooms here for them too,' I said and leaned over to squeeze Jayne's hand.

She shook me off and took another bite of battered fish, making me wait until she'd finished her mouthful before replying. I refilled her glass while I waited.

'That would be lovely – I just hope they won't be too busy in their new lives. They're literally only going for the meal this year, apparently John's furious.'

She smiled and gulped her wine. I followed suit and refilled again.

'But I guess that's what happens.' Jayne visibly pulled herself together – sitting more upright and squaring her shoulders. 'They grow up, don't they, boy?' She ruffled Grasper's fur and fed him some fish.

The subject of children was still too raw for me too. 'I wonder if he'll come tonight.'

'Who, Vikram?'

'No!' I slapped her arm with the back of my hand. 'Behave. I meant the dream man.'

'Ah, Heathcliff.'

'I wish you wouldn't call him that.'

Jayne smiled. 'Well, I hope he isn't Heathcliff,' she said, standing up and clearing away the empty plates. 'You've had enough of dysfunctional men. Ow!'

I leapt to my feet at the exclamation, Grasper's frantic barking, and crash of dropped plates. 'What happened? Are you all right?'

'Someone pushed me!'

'What? Who? There's no one here!'

We looked at each other.

'Are you sure?' I asked. 'It was definitely a push?'

'Yes! Two hands on my back. I was lucky I didn't fall.'

'The floor's pretty uneven, are you sure you didn't just trip?'

Jayne stared at me, worried, then shrugged. 'Maybe. I must have done. It's just this place, it's got me spooked.'

We both jumped at a bang from the window.

'Just a bird,' she said.

I gave a shaky laugh. 'Now you know how I feel.'

We both looked at Grasper who was still very vocal and seemed to be doing a little dance; leaping and twisting, his eyes following something neither Jayne nor I could see.

'Is there more wine?' Jayne asked.

'Plenty.'

19.

'What have you found, Emily?' Branwell called from further down the hill. 'Don't go too far away, you know Papa said I'm in charge and I'm staying over here with Anne.'

Emily gave no sign of hearing her brother, and crouched motionless in the heather over the treasure she'd found.

'Can you hear them?' she asked.

'Only a little bit. How did tha know I were here?' Harry asked.

Emily looked at his wooden-soled clogs, and he understood.

'I ran away from mill again,' he confided.

Emily made no reply. Harry watched her, intrigued as she studied the lapwing nest of chicks. She didn't speak to him very much, but he didn't take offence. She didn't speak to anybody very much, except her brother and sisters, and then only when she had a mind to.

He liked her silence; his world was normally filled with noise: the spinning machines at the mill, and the constant clack of the handlooms in the weaver's gallery which took up the entire top floor of the row of cottages where he and his family had their home. The clop of horses, rumble of wagon wheels and shouts of draymen on the street. And of course the little ones' cries and Ma's sobs at the house.

He lived with his eight brothers and sisters – seven now. The baby had died before earning a name, and someone was always sickly. It was Mary and Robert at the moment, keeping everyone's nerves on edge with their constant coughing and crying. As if on cue, Harry himself coughed, feeling the tickle of the fluff from the spinning room within his throat.

'Hush.' Emily rounded on him, her little face fierce. 'You'll scare them!'

'Sorry,' Harry whispered. 'Can I see?'

Emily regarded him with large, round eyes, considering whether he was worthy of the sight, then nodded and moved aside.

Harry took her place then gasped as the dull, grey drizzle that had offered no respite for over a week turned to a sudden, drenching downpour.

The sky turned so black it almost seemed night, high on the moor above Haworth, despite it yet being early afternoon.

Harry regained his composure and bearings in the violently changed conditions, then lost them again as he saw Emily Brontë twirling in the heavy rain, arms outstretched and face turned to the sky.

'Emily, Emily, come on, we have to find shelter or we'll catch our deaths,' Branwell called, to no avail.

Branwell's small face, turned up towards them, was serious and worried, but he had Anne to take care of, and the seven-year-old took his duty very seriously. Besides, he knew just how stubborn Emily could be.

'*Emily!*' Harry saw him scream. Saw because nothing could be heard over the enormous, thunderous roar that exploded around them.

Lightning flickered, followed by a lesser thunder.

Something wasn't right.

Harry looked uphill and his mouth dropped open in shock. It was moving. The hillside was moving.

Peat, heather and rock slid towards them.

'Emily!' Harry shouted, and ran to grab her. She had seen the danger, but instead of running for safety, she was trying to gather the lapwing nest with its brood of chicks into her hands.

Harry pulled at her, but she resisted, and he had no choice but to pick up the child – thankfully small and thin for even her young age – and run, stumbling out of the path of the relentless, tumbling moorslide.

The four children, Emily still clutching the lapwing chicks, hurried along a path that would take them out of danger, and also bring them back together; Branwell dragging a screaming five-year-old Anne alongside him, and Harry still carrying Emily.

He put her down, his arms shaking, and she barely looked at him, her attention still wholly occupied by the birds. Did she not understand the danger she had been in herself?

'Emily.' Branwell sank to his knees when he reached his sister, and he and Anne clung to her. 'Is all well?'

'I think so,' Emily said, holding out the nest. 'I don't know how their parents will find them, though, they had better come home with us.'

Branwell and Harry looked at the way home. It was a river of gloopy, rocky mud.

'How will we get home?' Anne asked, her voice small and terrified.

Branwell didn't answer, but looked at Harry.

'We'll have to go round,' Harry said.

'No,' Branwell said. 'We'd have to go right round by Top Withens. That's too far, especially in the rain and with Anne. Ponden Hall is much closer. We'll go there and the Heatons can get a message to Papa. He shall come to fetch us.'

***

'Whoever heard of an earthquake in Haworth?' the parson said when he arrived, having ascertained those of his children not yet in the custody of a school were all present and unharmed.

He stared at the lapwing nest, still protected in Emily's hands, then glared at Harry.

'Mam says it were the bog that burst,' Robert Heaton said.

'Nonsense, did you not hear it? It was an earthquake,' the parson dismissed him and his mother. 'Now, who is this?'

Harry stayed silent, scared of the stern cleric who thundered from the pulpit every Sunday. A tall figure, dressed in black with high, white collar, Harry had always been in awe of him.

'Harry Sutcliffe,' Emily said. 'He works at the mill but keeps running away.'

'Does he now? You know you'll be beaten for that, boy?'

Harry nodded. 'Yes, sir.'

'He saved Emily, Papa,' Branwell said, unhappy at being left out of the conversation. 'I was with Anne, looking after her like you told me to, Papa, and Emily was up the hill with her lapwings. I told her to come, but she didn't, Papa. And then Harry came, just before the big roar, and Emily was dancing in the rain and she wouldn't come and she saved the lapwings and Harry picked her up and ran away from the bogslide.' Branwell stopped, out of breath.

His father regarded him in silence a moment, no doubt making sense of his son's rushed monologue.

'I see. Well, young Harry, it appears I and my family owe you a great debt.'

Harry looked up at him in hope. Mrs Heaton had fed them all pork and apple with hot posset when they'd arrived, soaked to the skin and shivering. Dare he ask for more food to take home for his family?

'You work at the mill, boy?'

'Yes sir.'

'Which one?'

'Rooks, sir.'

'And you do not like the work?'

'No sir.'

'But is it not good to have work so your family have food and shelter and cloth on their backs?'

'Yes sir.'

'Then why do you run away?'

'It is so loud, sir. I can't hear the lapwings call, and I cough all the time, and my brothers and sisters cough all the time, and I keep getting hurt.' He held out an arm showing thick red weals on the pale skin. 'And—'

'Enough.' Patrick Brontë held up a hand. 'I have heard enough.' He glanced at Emily.

'Do you miss the lapwings' call, Harry?'

'Yes sir.'

'Well, I cannot find you work with birds,' the parson said, and Mrs Heaton tittered. 'But the mason is looking for an apprentice. There is just too much work for him these days . . .' He lapsed into a thoughtful silence, then blinked. 'It is hard work, but skilled work and would give you a trade. Would you like that, boy?'

'Yes sir, thank you, sir.'

'Very well, report to the mason's workshop behind the parsonage first thing tomorrow morning. I shall inform your father and Mr Rook.'

'Yes sir, thank you, sir,' Harry said again, so overjoyed at not having to return to the mill, he had not yet considered that he would be carving memorials for the remainder of his life.

'What about me, Papa?' Branwell asked, a little sulkily. 'I looked after Anne and saved her. I dragged her away out of the danger, didn't I, Anne? Didn't I?'

Anne nodded. She had not spoken since reaching safety.

'I should expect nothing less from you, Branwell. It is your duty to care for your sisters.'

At Branwell's crestfallen face, his papa ruffled his hair. 'Now, let's get you all home, Tabby and Aunt Branwell are very worried about you all and are making an extra special supper for us all tonight: liver and onions. And you have earned a double helping, Branwell. What do you think of that?'

'That will do very well, Papa, thank you,' Branwell said and beamed at his father. It was his favourite.

20.

'Morning, Vikram, what's the plan for today?'

'Morning, love.'

Jayne smirked at my continued non-complaint about the generic pet name. I ignored her.

'Plumbers want to finish getting the pipe laid for the central heating so they can crack on with the pipework for the en-suites after Christmas. And Sparkly's putting the final touches to the wiring – with any luck, you'll have light and sockets by the end of the day. But it might be best to stay out of her way. Things can get a bit . . . fraught when she flicks a switch and things don't happen quite as they're supposed to.'

'I know the feeling,' Jayne muttered, and I grinned.

'I think we can all relate. Well, what do you think about visiting the museum, Jayne? I don't think Lara's too bothered about it, so it would be a good opportunity.'

'I don't mind where we go as long as we get out of here for a while.'

I glanced at her, realising she was more affected by last night than I'd appreciated.

'More ghosts?'

'Something like that.' I smiled at Vikram, took Jayne's arm and led her out of The Rookery, then stopped at Vikram's touch on my back.

'Verity?'

'Wait for me outside,' I said to Jayne, then turned to Vikram, surprised at the way my heart had speeded up at the sound of my name in his voice.

'Is everything all right?'

I shrugged. 'A bit stressful, to be honest, but that's to be expected.' I gestured at the chaos in the room.

'Are you sure that's all?'

'Yes. I'm fine, honest.'

He had no choice but to believe me, although we both knew I was lying, but I smiled, turned and left; at least for the day.

We entered the front garden of the parsonage and I almost felt Jayne's shudder.

'Jayne . . .' I started, but she shook her head, clearly not yet ready to talk about what had happened.

'I didn't realise the extent to which death surrounded the Brontë sisters,' she said after a while. 'They lived surrounded by gravestones.' She indicated the churchyard bordering two sides of the garden.

'I know, it must have been a very strange way to grow up, although of course the graveyard would have been much smaller then.'

We both looked up as the resident parliament of rooks took wing and wheeled about the memorials before settling to roost once more. Jayne shuddered again and I looped my arm through hers.

'Even though the front looks down over the older part and the church, the standing stones are newer, so it wouldn't have been so obvious they lived surrounded by graves. And there would have only been a few to the side as well. It wouldn't have been quite as grim then as it appears now.'

'Yes, but still – young kids growing up here?'

I shrugged. 'They were different times. Death was very much a part of life and childhood then, no matter where you lived. And look at the house they enjoyed – other kids their age were sleeping nine to a room, and a small room at that.' I gestured to the handsome, millstone grit building as we turned.

Framed by the moors behind, it was true that the nine windows on the front aspect regarded the church and its yard, but each was made up of smaller panes, and lined with the darker stone that picked out the corners of the building. A white portico framing the front door was in vast contrast to The Rookery – once four cottages, each housing large families.

'Come on, let's go in,' I urged. 'Enough doom and gloom. Whatever you think about its situation, wonderful books were inspired and penned here.'

'I'm starting to see why they're so bleak.'

'Come on, Jayne, this isn't like you. And I know you love *Wuthering Heights* and *Jane Eyre.*'

Jayne sighed. 'I know, you're right, sorry, I'm just a bit out of sorts this morning.'

I opened my mouth to speak as we climbed the steps to the front door, but she rushed on to stop me. 'Not yet, I don't want to talk about it yet, Verity.'

I nodded, handed in our tickets, then led the way into the Brontës' dining room and became lost in the world of Charlotte, Emily and Anne, and the tragic tale of their family and lives.

'Even the pub backs on to the graveyard,' Jayne said as we settled into our seats at the Black Bull.

'Worse than that,' I said. 'We're downhill, bordering it, and one of the village's main wells was in the backyard here.'

'You are kidding me!'

'Nope. The water from the moors filtered through the cemetery then ran into the village's drinking water.'

Jayne stared at me in horror.

'No wonder the churchyard is so full,' I said. 'Now, what would you like to drink?'

Jayne pulled a face at me. 'Something fermented, and preferably shipped in.'

'Sauvignon blanc?'

'That will do nicely.'

I fetched two glasses and a bottle, which Jayne frowned at.

'I know its lunchtime, but it's nearly Christmas.' I smiled.

Jayne paused and said, 'It's strange to think those wonderful books were all plotted and written in that dining room. I could almost see Charlotte, Emily and Anne walking around the table in a frenzy of creativity, skirts swishing.'

'They didn't have much room, did they?'

'I guess they didn't need it,' Jayne said. 'They needed each other more.'

'Yes, it was interesting to see all that stuff about Angria and Gondal, the fantasy lands they created together as children.'

'I know, and those tiny books!'

'No wonder there's so much fascination about the sisters and their lives,' I said. 'The whole family certainly did things their own way.'

'You can say that again. Can you imagine waking up to your father discharging a pistol out the window every morning?'

'Not really.' I laughed. 'That's one hell of an alarm call!'

'It must have been awful to live every day – and night – in fear, and if the father felt it, the children must have too.'

'Yes, I guess the threat posed by Luddites and campaigners against the working conditions in the mills was a lot deeper than I thought.'

We both sipped our wine, then I tried to lighten the mood. 'What did you think about the décor? I want to decorate the rooms at The Rookery in the same style, although keep each different and original.'

'That sounds like a great idea, and very appropriate given the building's age and location.'

'Yes. I also thought about naming the rooms rather than numbering them, just because everything's on different levels and numbers wouldn't flow – they could cause more confusion than assistance. What do you think about Charlotte's Room, Emily's Room etcetera?'

'A bit clichéd isn't it?' Jayne asked. 'Might be a bit over the top.'

I shrugged. 'Maybe. I'll give it some more thought.'

'Are you ready to order?'

'Oh, sorry,' I said to the waitress. 'Too busy chatting, can we have a couple of minutes?'

'Of course.'

We sat in silence to study the menu, ordered our food, then I topped up our glasses and looked at Jayne, my eyebrows raised in silent question.

21.

'It was a definite push, Verity.' Jayne took another gulp of wine. 'I felt hands, and they had force. How can that be?'

'I don't know, Jayne. Maybe Lara can shed some light on it when she gets here tomorrow.'

'Has anything like that happened to you?'

I shook my head. 'Just the dreams, which are getting more vivid, and seeing the Grey Lady.'

'But you've been touched?'

I said nothing.

'Verity?'

I took a deep breath, then a sip of my own wine, then nodded. 'A couple of days ago. In the shower.'

'In the *shower*?'

'Yes, but it wasn't trying to hurt me, it was more of a caress.'

'So, let me get this straight.' Jayne pressed together her index fingers to emphasize her first point. 'The Grey Lady, supposedly Emily Brontë, has only been seen occasionally over the years, yet has appeared twice in the last two days to two different people.'

She moved to her second finger. 'You're dreaming about the same man every night, and occasionally the Brontës as children as well.'

I nodded.

'Three. You're getting caresses while wide awake and I was pushed by invisible hands. So what does that tell us? Verity—?'

I'd stopped listening, jumped up, knocking the table, and rushed out of the pub. I stood staring down Main Street when Jayne caught up with me.

'Verity? What is it? You're white as a sheet.'

'I thought I saw ...'

'Hey!' The waitress had dashed after us, holding two plates of food. 'You haven't paid!'

'Sorry,' Jayne said. 'My friend was taken ill. It's okay, we're not doing a runner, we'll be right there.'

The girl looked at us dubiously, then behind us at our table and realised our coats were still there. She went back inside, carrying our lunch.

'Verity?' Jayne said. 'What happened?'

'I just ... I thought I saw ...' I stopped, not quite sure now what I'd seen. 'Sorry, Jayne, I thought I saw the man I've been dreaming about, but he was gone by the time I got outside.'

'You saw his ghost?'

'No, I don't think so. He was wearing jeans and a parka, no Victorian costume.' I shivered. 'Come on, let's go back in.'

'Okay, but I want to know every detail about the dreams. Something is going on here and it's escalating. I have a bad feeling. Oh, and there's no way we're sleeping there tonight. If the White Lion's still booked up, we'll find rooms elsewhere.'

'*Everywhere's* bloody haunted around here. You'll not get away from Haworth's ghosts that easily.' I managed a laugh and followed Jayne back into the Black Bull, though I had lost my appetite.

I regarded the age-blackened wood panelling which had been hacked into to accommodate modern plug sockets, and the uneven stone flags that had been shined by centuries of shuffling feet and which were now breaking away to reveal more stone beneath. The building was a complex jigsaw of colour, texture, age and use, and I wondered just how many ghosts were resident here, too.

The waitress gave us a funny look as she checked on us and watched Jayne pick up her phone despite our half-full plates. 'There *was* a bog burst,' she said. 'On Crow Hill in 1824. And Patrick Brontë *did* think it was an earthquake.' She looked up at me. 'If that's true, the rest is likely to be as well, but I don't see how we can check it.'

'What about the name? Harry Sutcliffe.'

'Nothing comes up online, but it's a common enough name. We could have a look at gravestones, see if we can find him.'

I shuddered, remembering the altar grave I had sat on in error. The name on that had been Sutcliffe. 'But even if Harry is real and I am dreaming real events, that doesn't explain the caress in the shower or the push last night.'

'No,' Jayne mused. 'Oh God, I wish Lara were here, this is more up her street than mine.'

'I know, but it's good to talk about it now. You know what she's like, she'll get all excited and carried away and I could really do with getting my head round it all first.'

'I don't think there's much chance of that,' Jayne said. 'By the sounds of it, the story your dream man is telling you has only just started.'

'You think he's telling me a story?'

'Isn't he?'

I shrugged.

'Well, whether he is or isn't, maybe you should keep a dream diary. It might help us put the pieces together and understand what's happening.'

'That's a good idea,' I said. 'We'll stop off at the Tourist Information shop on the way back to The Rookery and I'll pick up a notebook.'

'Verity?'

I looked up to see Vikram. 'What is it? Is anything wrong?'

'No, not wrong, but Sparkly's panicking a bit over the security cameras. She needs you to confirm exactly where you want them.'

'Cameras?' Jayne asked.

'Yes, I'll be running the place on my own so I'll need to be able to see the public areas and front door from the kitchen and my apartment. There's the security aspect too.'

Jayne nodded, and I scrunched up my napkin.

'Oh, finish your meal first, love. Sparkly will wait – as long as she knows you'll be back after dinner.'

I nodded and smiled at him and he took his leave.

'If your dream man is jealous of *me*, that guy had better watch out,' Jayne said.

'Oh Jayne, stop it.'

'You like him, I can see it in your face.'

'It doesn't matter. I'm not ready, not after Antony, it's still all too raw.' I sipped my wine and shared out the remainder of the bottle. 'Drink up, it could be a trying afternoon.'

'Things have been trying enough already,' Jayne said, picking up her glass. 'I'm not sure I can cope with more just yet.'

22.

'Coffee, please,' Jayne said. 'Plenty of it and keep it coming.'

The waitress – Tess – smiled. 'No problem, I'll bring the pot. And for you?' she asked me.

'I'll share her coffee,' I said.

Tess glanced at Jayne. 'I'll make it a large pot.' She visibly relaxed as Jayne smiled.

'Are you always this grumpy in the morning?'

'Only until my third cup of coffee. Ah, at last.'

I glanced up at Tess with an apologetic smile. She really could not have been any quicker. I dreaded to think how Jayne had behaved earlier when she'd taken Grasper out while I was still getting ready.

Jayne poured, sipped hers – black and scalding – and sighed, her shoulders discernibly lowering to a more natural posture.

'All right now?'

'Much better. I'm so glad there was a cancellation and my room was available a day early.'

'And that it's a twin,' I added.

'Definitely. You know we can share for the rest of my visit, too.'

'What, and face a coffee-less Jayne every morning? I'd rather deal with the ghosts over the road!'

Jayne scowled at me, then laughed. 'Well, it's up to you – the offer's there.'

'Thank you. I do mean that, Jayne. But The Rookery is my home, I need to claim it.'

Jayne nodded. 'That makes sense. But wasn't it a relief not to dream? I'm also worried about that push – if whatever it is, is getting violent, you might not be safe.'

'He's not been violent to me – quite the opposite – and there's never been any hint of threat from the Grey Lady either.'

Jayne pursed her lips. I didn't want to tell her my nightly visitor could find me here.

'Anyway, this place is haunted too, you know.'

'What?'

'Yes, a balloonist who died in the '20s, Lily Cove. She fell to her death on the moors and apparently still haunts her old room at the White Lion.'

'Which room?' Jayne had gone very still.

'Seven, I think.'

She relaxed again. She was in Room Six. 'Is there anywhere *not* haunted in Haworth?'

'I doubt it. There's a lot of history here, and much death over the centuries, a fair bit of it . . . unpleasant.'

'What do you mean?'

'Well, Lily for one. Then there's a witch's house up the road connected to Pendle. And don't forget all the mills, the accidents and lung diseases there, plus horrendous living conditions: overcrowding, bad water, shared privies, TB, cholera and all sorts of other diseases.'

Jayne shuddered. 'But it's such a pretty, picturesque village.'

'Well yes, it is now. Wasn't so great living here in the 1800s.'

'So what do you think about that Sparkly woman yesterday?'

I raised my eyebrows at Jayne's abrupt change of subject, then shrugged.

'She's normally lovely, I don't know why she's been in

99

such a bad mood the last couple of days. I guess she's just under pressure with such an old and complicated building to rewire.'

'Strange her tools keep going missing, though. You don't think your ghosts are stepping up their game?'

Ah, so it hadn't really been a change of subject after all. 'I doubt it, it'll be the lads winding her up – they seem to really like her, but are constantly on her back.'

'Or hope to be.' Jayne sniggered and I laughed with her.

'Probably, yes.'

'Come on, let's order some food.'

'It was strange Vikram turning up like that last night,' Jayne mused, as she refilled her cup.

I shrugged. 'It's a small village – no real surprise we bumped into him in one of the main pubs.'

'I suppose,' Jayne said, smiled at me, then focused on the rest of her breakfast.

'Lara's just texted,' Jayne said as we approached the door to The Rookery. 'She'll be here after lunch.'

'Great,' I said, then looked up as a flock of birds cawed above us. 'I wonder what she'll make of everything that's been happening.'

Jayne groaned. 'I don't even want to think about it. She'll be in seventh heaven and having us do all sorts of weird and wonderful stuff. We'll be like *Ghost Adventures* or *Most Haunted*!'

'We might get some answers,' I said as I pushed open the door to my guesthouse and stopped dead.

Sparkly was in full flow, ranting about missing tools and cable, the lads shuffling awkwardly, trying to defend themselves, but only succeeding in angering Sparkly further. Even Vikram looked lost for what to do.

'What's going on?' I asked, and was ignored.

Jayne slammed the door and I asked again, this time at the top of my voice, and hush descended over the rabble of squabbling tradesmen and -woman.

Sparkly took a deep breath, faced me, and opened her mouth, no doubt to begin her tirade afresh, but Vikram stepped in front of her.

'The cameras have disappeared,' he explained. 'Expensive ones.'

Sparkly shouted over him, 'And I know you guys have done it for a joke, but it's gone too far. I need to get them all up today. I've got everything else finished. There's only the cameras left to fit, then I'll be done – I want to finish today. Just tell me where they are, you buggers!'

Vikram held up a placating hand. 'I'm not denying we don't wind you up for a laugh – but none of us want to hold the job up. The sooner we get done, the sooner we get off for the Christmas break. Nobody's taken the blasted cameras. They must be here somewhere.'

'I've looked top to bottom, and in every damned cranny in the place!' Sparkly stamped her foot and Vikram's face reddened.

'I suggest you look again, start at the top.'

She opened her mouth to argue, then shut it again. Vikram had turned away from me so I couldn't see his new expression. Judging by Sparkly's about turn, followed by the rest of the gang, it was probably just as well.

He turned back to me. 'Sorry about that. Things are just a bit fraught for her around Christmas – family stuff, you know.'

I nodded, I was feeling a bit fraught myself to be facing my first Christmas as a divorcée – but at least I had good friends around me.

'How is everything else coming on?' I asked.

'Pretty good, actually,' Vikram said. 'We're a little

behind, but not much. Sparkly's got all the sockets and lights working, and the plumbers are well on with the new pipes for the en-suites. I was hoping to have all that done before Christmas, but we're not quite there I'm afraid. Nothing to worry about though,' he added hastily. 'It's to be expected in an old building. We'll have you ready to open on time. It's just these blasted cameras . . .' he tailed off.

'I'll help you look,' I said. 'Sorry, not much fun for you.' I glanced at Jayne.

'Don't worry, I need to take Grasper for a long walk, get rid of most of his energy before Lara and Hannah arrive.'

I nodded. 'That sounds like a good idea – he'll likely tear the place up again if you don't. Joke,' I added, seeing the look on Vikram's face. 'He'll be fine.'

'He'd have to face that lot if he isn't,' Vikram said, jerking his thumb at the stairs, still flooded by the sound of animosity.

I grimaced.

'He'll behave,' Jayne said. 'Verity's just having you on.'

'I'd like to get some mince pies and mulled wine in as well, just as a thank you for everyone working so close to Christmas.'

'They'd like that, although would probably prefer cans of Stella and Black Sheep to mulled wine,' Vikram said. 'Have a word with them at the Black Bull, they'll sort you out. Assuming we find those damned cameras, we'll be done by two.'

'Great, I'll sort it for then. Would you split this between everyone too?' I passed him an envelope.

He laughed. 'They'll appreciate that even more! Thank you.'

'One way to make sure they'll come back in the new year,' Jayne said.

'Oh, go and walk your dog. And have another coffee.' I smiled to take the sting out of my words, realising the atmosphere of the constant arguing was getting to me. 'Sorry,' I added. 'I'm feeling a bit on edge with all this going on.'

Jayne nodded and gave me a hug, then called to Grasper who, we just noticed, was once more doing his crazy dance – presumably chasing more invisible balls of light.

23.

'Everyone seems much happier,' I remarked to Vikram, watching the build team tuck in. The Black Bull had been more than happy to cater the beer and wine, and one of the local cafés had done us proud with sandwiches and nibbles. Everything looked . . . festive, despite The Rookery being more building site than guesthouse.

'Yes the cameras turned up, and we all pitched in. Sparkly's relaxed, and that makes all the difference.' He swigged from his can and I wasn't quite sure how light-hearted his comment truly was. I decided to ignore it and mentally apologised to Sparkly for my lack of female solidarity.

'Where were they in the end?'

'Well, that's the strange thing,' Vikram said. 'They were on the top stairs – that's what all the shouting was about earlier. One camera on each tread. Cables neatly coiled, all very carefully. Sparkly went ape.'

'So had one of the guys done it to wind her up?'

'I don't see how. She'd searched the place top to bottom, there's nowhere they could have hidden them – then they were set out in plain view. No one's been on their own, and everybody swears it wasn't them. I believe them.'

'Sounds like your ghost is playing tricks.'

I swung round at the familiar voice. 'Lara! How wonderful to see you!' We hugged, then I released her to hug Hannah while Jayne embraced Lara.

'How long have you been standing there?'

'Long enough to hear you've been having fun and games without me, and apparently not long enough for anyone to offer me a drink.'

'Oh sorry! Mulled wine?' I turned to pour her a glass without waiting for her nod. 'What's up with you anyway? It's not like you to wait until you're asked – you certainly know you don't need to stand on ceremony here.'

Lara shrugged. 'You have company, I was trying to make a good impression.'

'That ship sailed with your ghost comment,' Jayne said, laughing. 'Seriously though, it's good to see you.'

Lara raised her eyebrows. 'Why do I get the feeling I don't know even half of what's been going on?'

Jayne and I shrugged in unison, and Lara narrowed her eyes but checked her curiosity for the time being and turned to her daughter who was tapping her arm, trying to get her attention.

'Can I take Grasper for a walk, Mummy? Can I? Can I?'

'You'd best ask Aunt Jayne.'

'Can I, Aunt Jayne, can I take him walkies? Pleeeaasse.'

'Well, now you've said the magic word—'

'What, walkies?' I said, laughing as I indicated Grasper's excited and downright manic circling.

Jayne smiled. 'Of course you can. Just watch out for that Main Street – I took him down there earlier and it was lovely. The only problem was getting back up it!'

The adults laughed, but Hannah looked confused. 'Why? It's just a hill.'

The laughter died and Jayne held out the Irish terrier's lead with a resigned smile. 'Now I feel old,' she said. 'From the mouths of babes . . .'

'I'm not a babe, I'm ten!' Hannah said, full of indignation. She clipped on Grasper's lead and marched out of The Rookery, head held unnaturally high.

'You've got a right one there,' Vikram said.

'Oh, Lara's more than a match for her,' Jayne said. 'She keeps us all on our toes, though – doesn't let us get away with anything!'

We all sipped our drinks, then Lara said, 'Oh, I meant to tell you, Verity – you need to get some netting or spikes on the window ledges and gutters. You know, the ones town centres use to keep the pigeons from roosting and messing up the front of the buildings.'

Vikram scowled. 'We don't really have much problem with pigeons here – the buzzards tend to scare them off.'

'Well, whatever they are, there's loads of birds perching outside. I dread to think what your window cleaning bill will be if you don't sort it out.'

Jayne and I looked at each other in confusion. 'I haven't noticed anything,' I said.

'No, nor me,' Vikram added. 'Let me go and have a look.'

'Good idea,' Jayne said, and we moved to the door.

'Mistletoe!' someone shouted from behind us – Omar or Gary, I'm not sure, and the build team filled the place with laughter as Vikram and Jayne looked up to see the offending greenery with white berries hanging over the doorway.

'Bad luck not to give her a kiss, boss,' Gary – definitely Gary this time – called.

'They won't stop,' Vikram said to Jayne and she gave a slight nod to permit his peck on her cheek, then glanced at me in a mixture of apology and embarrassment.

I smiled and we trooped outside – in single file.

'Worse than Spin the Bloody Bottle,' Lara muttered.

Outside we looked up and I gasped. Every window ledge, door lintel, the edge of the roof – every available roost – was occupied. I had a brief flashback to Daphne du Maurier's *The Birds*, then shook myself. They weren't doing anything, they weren't threatening, and they weren't attacking.

All the same, the sight of so many rooks, wing to wing, was unnerving.

'I've never seen owt like it,' Vikram said.

'What made you call this place, The Rookery, Verity?' Lara asked. 'Where did the name come from?'

I shrugged. 'I don't know really, I was playing around with more Brontë-like names, Wildfell, Thrushcross, that kind of thing, then The Rookery popped into my head and just kind of stuck.'

We stayed staring at the façade of the building for a minute or two more, then the build team emerged – in single file again to avoid the mistletoe – to say their thanks and goodbyes.

'I'll leave you to it as well, ladies. Happy Christmas,' Vikram said.

Lara, Jayne and I returned the greeting then went back inside and I topped up our glasses.

'I think you two had better tell me exactly what's been going on,' said Lara.

24.

'There's something you're not telling me,' Lara said, looking at Jayne after I'd told her about my dreams, the touch in the shower, and the sightings of the Grey Lady. 'Jayne, you're too quiet, and too accepting of everything. Why haven't you made any jokes or suggested rational explanations?'

Jayne shrugged, clearly uncomfortable, but said nothing.

'Something happened to you too, didn't it?'

'I don't know. Maybe. It was probably nothing.'

'Jayne?'

She sighed. 'Verity, you tell her.'

I wasn't sure if she was scared, in denial, or just reluctant to admit what had happened after years of poking fun at Lara for believing just this kind of thing. Whatever was going on with her, I did not want to make things harder, and told Lara about the push.

'Do you feel safe here?'

I was surprised at Lara's response, but nodded. I did feel safe. I was curious and confused, but I didn't feel threatened.

'No.' Jayne's reply was unequivocal. 'And I worry about Verity staying here. I think she should sell up.'

'What?'

'Something's going on, Verity – something strange, something powerful, and even if you feel safe, I don't. I could have been badly hurt. The builders don't like it here either – one's run off already and the others all keep falling out. It's all centred around this place and you.

You've only been here a couple of weeks and it's escalating. I think you should go.'

'Verity?'

I was flabbergasted and needed Lara's prompt to gather my thoughts. 'I can't go. Look at the place, I could never resell with it like this, and I've invested everything into it. Anyway, I don't want to move.' I sat back and folded my arms.

'To be honest, it sounds like it may already be too late,' Lara said.

'What do you mean? How can it be too late?' Jayne asked.

'There are different types of hauntings,' Lara began. 'Take the Grey Lady – from the sound of it, she's a residual impression of something that happened a hundred and fifty years ago. It may be something that happened often and regularly, or maybe something else happened around the woman – whether she's Emily Brontë or not – that has kept her stuck in that action. It's almost recorded into the fabric of the building – a bit like the way sound used to be recorded on to iron oxide in the days of cassette tapes. There's no interaction, no consciousness there, just a repetitive image.'

'Okay,' Jayne said, drawing the syllables out. 'I guess that makes sense.'

To her credit, Lara didn't bat an eyelid at this apparent acceptance of her theory. 'But the man – the man's different. He's communicating – at first just with Verity and through her dreams, but he's getting stronger. The dreams are becoming more focused, he's touched not only Verity, but you too, Jayne, and I think he's connected to Verity rather than the building. He's sentient, and if Verity leaves, I think there's a good chance he'd go with her.'

'But he didn't last night,' Jayne objected. 'Verity didn't

dream about him last night when we stayed at the White Lion.'

'He may have overexerted himself, weakened himself. Plus you were both relaxed, focused on each other, and I'm guessing had quite a bit to drink.'

'Well . . .'

'That's a yes then. Even if you did dream about him, Verity, your sleep could have been so deep that you just can't remember it.'

'Oh. Yeah, I guess.' I wasn't sure if the prospect of having to drink to silence him was more unsettling than the idea that if I did drink, I would miss him.

'Talking of drink, I need a refill,' Jayne said, rose and fetched a bottle of merlot. On her way back to our makeshift seats of sawhorses and trestles that Vikram and the team had left us, she stopped, visibly shook herself, then rushed over.

'You're freaking me out,' she complained.

'What happened?'

'I just came over all cold.'

Lara stood and moved around the same area that had frozen Jayne. 'A cold spot. He's here.'

'Well, tell him to go!'

Lara slowly shook her head at Jayne as she returned to her seat. 'No. He's here for a reason. We need to find out what that is, then maybe we can help him and he'll leave us alone.'

'What if what he wants is Verity?'

We looked at each other – Lara and I now sharing Jayne's fear.

'Then we protect her,' Lara said at last.

Neither Jayne nor I asked her how. We were both too scared that she may not have an answer.

'So what do we do?' I asked after more silence.

'We find out all we can about this place and the people

who lived here,' Lara said. 'We do our research – books, the museum, and is there a ghost walk or anything? This is a tourist village, there must be a ghost walk.'

'Yes, there is,' I said. 'But I don't think they're running at the moment, we may have to wait until the New Year.'

'Well, I'll get stuck into the books and Google,' Jayne said. 'You two can do the ghost walk, then all of us can go to the museum again – I'll find out when it's open over Christmas and the New Year, and if we can access their library.'

'Oh ghost walk, ghost walk! Can I go on the ghost walk, pleeaasse?'

'Hans, are you sure?' Lara turned to greet her daughter as Grasper hurled himself at Jayne. 'It might be scary.'

'I'm not scared of stupid ghosts. Anyway, Grasper will look after us.'

'Well, okay, if you're sure, but tell me if you get too scared and Auntie Verity will bring you back here, okay? I need to stay to the end of it, I don't want to miss any of the stories.'

'I won't get scared, Mummy, promise. Can we go tonight, can we? Can we?'

'No, not tonight, Hans, we'll have to find out when the next one is. Anyway we're all a bit tired, we'll just have a nice evening together and an early night.'

'Okay, Mum.' Hannah looked crestfallen. 'Do you promise we will do it, though?'

'I promise.'

'Hans,' Jayne said, 'did you see the birds when you came in, are they still there?'

'What birds?'

Jayne breathed a visible sigh of relief.

'Mum, what's Grasper doing?'

We turned and looked. Hackles up, growling – something I couldn't remember hearing him do before –

Grasper had placed himself between us and the cold spot Jayne and Lara had found earlier. He did not like whatever it was he could see.

25.

Harry stood back watching Uriah Barraclough – the master stonemason and the man he was now apprenticed to – and John Brown, the sexton, push the tiny coffin into its final resting place within the Brontë family vault underneath the church.

Opened just four years ago for Maria, the parson's wife, ten-year-old Elizabeth had now joined her mother and elder sister,

Her father, Patrick, remained stoic and calm, but Harry had already seen enough pain etched into too many faces not to recognise the same in his.

And no wonder. When his wife died he had been left with six children to care for. Now, consumption had taken the two eldest within little more than a month. What would become of those surviving: Charlotte, Branwell, Emily and Anne?

Harry risked a small smile at Emily, but she turned her head. He kicked himself. It was hardly the place for a smile.

He concentrated on watching Mr Barraclough and Mr Brown carefully secure Elizabeth's carved memorial in place next to those of her sisters, then they stood back and the Reverend Brontë cleared his throat to speak.

I woke with a sob. *Those poor girls. That poor family.*

I rose, went to the loo, washed my face, and took a long drink of water. Maybe Jayne had been right and I should have joined them at the White Lion after all.

No. I shook my head to emphasise the thought. This was my new home, my new business, my new life. I could not run away from a few dreams. I pushed thoughts of caresses, pushes, orbs, cold spots and Grasper's odd behaviour out of my mind and went back to bed, accidentally on purpose leaving the bathroom light on and pretending not to notice.

Harry found Emily in one of her favourite places; the little waterfall only half a mile up the moors, over the clapper bridge. She was sitting on a rock and staring at the summer trickle of water, her new puppy, Grasper, at her feet. Harry suspected she would find a wild winter torrent more to her taste today.

'How do,' he said, and she grunted.

'It's hard,' Harry tried again, 'when a sister dies. I remember when our Rebekah went last year, it were like a light had gone out of the world.'

'Two,' Emily said.

'Beg pardon?'

'Two sisters. *Two* sisters died. *Two* sisters in their coffins. *Two* sisters in the vault. Two, two, two, *two!*'

She jumped to her feet and ran through the heather – her sure feet jumping from tussock to tussock as she somehow kept her skirts away from the grasping branches of the tough, hardy plants.

The inevitable happened and she fell.

'Emily!' Harry cried. He had been following as quickly as he could, but heather was not easy to run through – poor little Grasper had to bound in a series of jumps to make any headway.

Harry reached down to help his friend up, and she kicked and scratched. 'Don't touch me, don't touch me, get away!'

He sat next to her and stared, waiting for her to calm down.

'I still miss Rebekah,' he said. 'And Charlie, and John.'

'Who's John?'

'The babby. Died before he got a name really, but I think of him as John. Don't know why.'

Emily sat up. 'I remember Rebekah. She cried when Black Tom caught a chaffinch.' Black Tom was Emily's cat. Even by age seven she'd collected a menagerie of stray and injured animals, not all of them four-legged. 'I liked her.'

Harry nodded. 'The consumption took her too.'

Emily pulled Grasper on to her lap and tugged on his ears in affection. 'It was that school. That school killed them. I'm not going back, neither's Charlotte. They can't make us.'

Neither spoke, knowing full well that Emily and Charlotte had no choice in the matter.

'I want to be here,' Emily said. 'Nowhere else. I just want to be here. In Haworth, on the moors. Here.'

Harry shuffled sideways and put his arm around her. 'I want thee to stay here too,' he said. Emily relaxed into his embrace and sobbed her grief for her beloved sisters.

Harry was just glad she couldn't see the tears on his own face.

26.

'Morning, ladies. Happy Christmas Eve,' I said as I opened the door to my friends. We all looked up, startled at the thrash of wings, and a dark cloud lifted to the sky.

Hannah ducked as the rooks rose overhead and all three dashed into safety as Grasper raced around in circles, barking at the birds.

'I think you're right about that pigeon netting, Lara,' I said.

'You might need spikes to deter that lot,' Jayne said.

'I'll get Vikram on to it as soon as they're back at work,' I promised.

'Ugh,' Hannah said. 'One's messed on me!'

We laughed then immediately sobered as the child neared tears.

'Don't worry, Hans, it's supposed to be good luck,' Lara said. 'Take your jacket off and we'll give it a good wash.'

'Yes, the new washing machine is working,' I said. 'Come on up and I'll put the kettle on.'

'Oh goody, I'm ready for a coffee,' Jayne said, and Lara and I laughed.

'When are you not?' I spluttered.

'You know, when we came down this morning, the breakfast staff had a pot ready brewed and waiting for her.'

'Well-trained,' Jayne said.

'Terrified of you more like – you've only been here a couple of days and you have your name on a coffee pot!'

We laughed again – even Hannah – the tension broken.

'They had a cup-to-go ready for me when I took Grasper out first thing,' Jayne admitted, 'with two extra shots.'

'Do you bleed red or coffee brown?' Lara asked sweetly.

'Definitely red,' Jayne answered, 'but the nurses swore they could smell coffee brewing last time I donated blood!'

Laughing, we reached my rooms and I filled the kettle.

'Guess which room Lara and Hannah have,' Jayne said after she'd taken a scalding sip.

'No,' I said. 'You're not in Room Seven?'

'Yep,' Lara said, hugging Hannah to her. 'Aunt Jayne told us all about the stories at breakfast.' She glared at Jayne. 'But it's a lovely room, isn't it, Hans?'

Hannah nodded but said nothing.

'Come on, give me that jacket – I'll rinse it off and get it in the wash,' I said. 'You can borrow one of mine if you want to take Grasper out later, okay, Hans?'

Lara handed me the jacket as Hannah nodded and slid to the floor to play with Grasper, looking a bit more cheerful.

'What the hell is that noise?' Jayne asked, lifting the sash window and leaning out. 'Oh, Christ!'

'What is it?' I joined her at the window, closed my eyes and sighed.

Antony's car was blocking the narrow lane, and neither he nor the man trying to drive in the opposite direction were giving way.

'That's all I bloody need,' I muttered.

'Do you want us to go and give you some privacy?' Lara asked.

'No – thanks, Lara, but no. You are invited, he is not; you are the ones I want to spend my Christmas with, not him. He is not chasing you out of my home, no way.'

She nodded, but cast Hannah a worried glance.

I looked out of the window again. The men had sorted

out who owned which bit of the road, Antony had parked up, and was hammering at the door.

'I'd best go and see what he wants,' I said, 'before he upsets the rest of the neighbours.'

'Happy Christmas!' Antony beamed and held out a box.

I looked at him, stared at the box – unwrapped – for a moment, then lifted my eyes back to his. 'What are you doing here?'

'I just wanted to wish you well,' he said. 'It is the season of goodwill after all.'

I arched my eyebrows at that.

'It's a Christmas tree.'

'What?'

He waggled the box. 'Just a small one. I didn't think you'd have had time for decorations or anything and thought it might brighten the place up for you. First Christmas . . .' He faltered and reddened.

'First Christmas alone, you mean?'

He cast his eyes down briefly then gave me a small smile. 'For both of us. I just hoped, well . . .'

'Yes?'

'Well, that we could start afresh, you know, put the divorce behind us and move forward.'

I stared at him. 'You want us to move forward? What – get back together?'

'No.' He squeezed his eyes shut a moment then said softly, 'No, I don't mean that, I know we're over. But we shared a lot of years together, a lot of laughs, and yes a lot of tears, but we had some good times. I just don't want us to be strangers.'

I nodded in understanding, but wasn't ready to respond to that. 'You'd better come in.'

He looked around the lobby, horrified at the mess and all the work that still needed to be done.

'I've only been in a couple of weeks,' I said, angry with myself for feeling defensive. 'The build team have worked like Trojans to create this chaos.'

He disguised his mocking smile with a sage nod. 'When do you open?'

'Easter, all being well. There'll be a lounge and breakfast room down here, plus a bedroom through there, and a kitchen of course.' I led the way to the stairs, pointing out the rooms as I went.

'Will it be ready in time?'

'Early days yet, but I don't see why not.' I tapped the wooden bannister three times for luck, then started to climb, before stooping to pick up an iPad from the next tread. I looked at it in confusion for a moment, I was sure it hadn't been there on the way down. 'The electricians are more or less done, and the plumbing and partition walls for the en-suites started. As long as everyone comes back to work after Christmas and don't let the ghosts scare them off, I'll be fine.'

'Ghosts? You're kidding, aren't you?'

I shook my head, annoyed at myself for opening up to him, even a little.

He seemed happy to drop the spectral subject though, and opened one of the doors I'd indicated as we passed. 'Good-sized room this.' He crossed to the window and peered out. 'Oh, is that the parsonage?'

'Yes, great view, isn't it?'

'One of the best.' He walked towards me and I backed out of the doorway and continued up the next flight of stairs to my private quarters, Antony following close behind, still carrying the box.

'And these are my rooms,' I said, stopping in and turning just in time to catch his look of dismay as he spotted Lara and Jayne.

27.

'Oh, hello,' he said to the cold glares he was greeted with, then glanced at me. 'Not a Christmas alone after all then.'

'No, I'm not alone,' I replied. 'You can put the tree down over there.'

'Tree? Is it a Christmas tree, Uncle Tony?' Hannah asked, and I winced at the 'uncle'.

'It is, do you want to help me put it up?'

'We can do that later,' Lara said.

'Of course. I can't stay long anyway, I'm on a split shift, and the restaurant's full tonight.'

'Would you like a coffee?' I asked, depositing the iPad on the table.

He glanced at Lara and Jayne, then shrugged. 'Sure, why not?'

I glared at Jayne to warn her not to answer that question, and went to fill the kettle.

'You could have told me *they* were here,' Antony hissed in my ear and I jumped. I hadn't heard him follow me.

'Why? Our lives are separate now, Antony. I don't need to run things past you or check with you before I make a decision or plan, *or* invite my friends to stay.'

'I know, but you could have warned me downstairs, I wouldn't have come up.'

'Why, too ashamed to face us?' Jayne approached us.

Antony said nothing.

'Hannah and I are going to take Grasper for his walk,' Lara said, and I smiled at her in apology, recognising her desire to get Hannah away from the souring atmosphere and threatening argument.

'Check in my wardrobe for a jacket for her,' I said. 'My fleece should be in there.'

'Thanks, Auntie Verity. Bye, Uncle Tony.'

'Bye Hannah, happy Christmas.'

She ran over and gave Antony a quick hug before Lara could stop her, then turned her attention to the increasingly agitated Irish terrier. 'Come on, Grasper, walkies!'

Hannah and the dog pounded down the stairs as Lara collected my fleece, looked at Antony but said nothing, then followed her daughter.

Silence filled The Rookery, and we sipped coffee.

'You're right, Jayne,' Antony said at last. 'I am ashamed, I deeply regret the way I hurt Verity.'

Jayne snorted. 'Only because you were caught. How could you do it? Lie and cheat all that time?'

A red flush of anger crept up Antony's neck and jaw. 'I don't have to justify myself to you. I've already been through this with Verity. We're divorced, I've paid for my mistakes, just leave it.'

'Just leave it? Are you kidding? Lara and I were the ones who picked up the pieces while you indulged in your fantasy life.'

'I'm not doing this with you, Jayne. It's between me and Verity.'

'No, it isn't. You mess with her, you mess with me.'

'Jayne, please, it's all over and done with. Leave it,' I said.

'No, I will not leave it!' She slammed her mug down and looked at me, 'Don't you remember what it was like, Verity? You were a wreck.'

'Jayne, please,' I said, glancing at Antony in embarrassment. I did not want him to hear this.

The twitch of his mouth sent a chill down my back. Was he amused? Pleased? *Proud*? My eyes narrowed and I clenched my jaw in an effort to refuse my emotions.

'And what the hell were you thinking, turning up here, at Verity's new home, new *life*, and on Christmas Eve? Haven't you done enough? Can't you just stick to your cheap tarts and leave Verity alone to get on with her life?'

'We broke up.'

'I bloody know you broke up! She found you out and kicked you out for God's sake, that's hardly news.'

'You broke up? With *her*?' I interrupted Jayne. If anyone was going to argue with my ex-husband, it should be me, not her, however passionately, and I was letting the side down.

Antony nodded and a feeling of vindictive smug satisfaction spread through me – echoed on Jayne's face with the ugliest smile I had ever seen her pull.

'So did she check your phone too?'

Antony paled but said nothing.

'And so you've come crawling back to Verity,' Jayne sneered. 'I wouldn't expect anything better from you. Did you think she'd warm your bed for you while you trawled the Net for your next bint?'

'I thought nothing of the sort,' Antony retorted. 'I just came to wish her a happy Christmas.'

'I am here you know,' I said, my emotions finally under control.

'Well, you're too late,' Jayne said in triumph as if neither of us had spoken. 'She's already moved on.'

'What?' Antony and I said together.

'Am I interrupting?'

I whirled round to see Vikram standing in the doorway.

'I – er – I've misplaced my tablet,' he said into the sudden silence. 'I need it to work out the wages. I must have left it here somewhere.'

'Hi, Vikram, sorry,' I managed to say, quite calmly. 'This is Antony, my ex-husband. Um, yes, I found it on the stairs, I meant to ring you.' I crossed over to the table to pass it to him.

'On the stairs? What was it doing there?'

I shrugged.

'Anyway, thanks. I'll leave you to it.' He glanced at Jayne and Antony, recoiled from the animosity of Antony's stare, then glared back until Antony dropped his eyes. 'Well, thanks again.' He waved the iPad at me. 'Have a good Christmas, and I'll see you next week.' He rushed out, his footsteps beating a rapid tattoo on the stairs.

Antony rounded on me. 'Is that him? Are you seeing him?'

I shook my head.

'It's only a matter of time,' Jayne crowed. 'She's a catch is our Verity, and now with her own business too, she's causing quite a stir in the village.'

I shot her a warning glance, but she was far too interested in winding Antony up and doing her best to hurt him.

'She's not the meek little wifey you thought she was, not any more, not now she's free of you. She can do anything she wants, with whomever she wants – she doesn't need you!'

'Jayne, please, enough.'

She ignored me, her full attention on Antony. She'd been waiting a long time for a chance to tell him what she thought of him.

A slow grin spread across his face and my heart sank. I knew that look.

'Antony, I think you should go.'

He ignored me too.

'Meek little wifey, is that what you think? Maybe you don't know our Verity as well as you think you do, there's

123

nothing meek and mild about her, not when she gets going – a right little hellcat she is.'

Jayne sneered.

'You haven't told her, have you?' He turned to me. 'And I thought you told your girls everything. Not so honest when it comes to your own shortcomings, are you, Verity?'

'Antony, please don't.'

He turned back to Jayne. 'What has she told you about the day we broke up?'

I jumped as my coffee cup fell off the table, but Antony and Jayne didn't notice.

'I know she found your catfishing harem on your phone,' Jayne shouted. 'I know the messages went back months – years – with different women. How many *were* there? You're a fantasist, you've got a serious problem!'

'Just words,' Antony said. 'A bit of fun online, none of it meant anything.'

'It did to Verity! How do you think that felt, her reading your declarations of undying love, never mind the webcam footage and phone sex?'

'I've got a fair idea,' Antony said. 'She made it pretty clear at the time.'

I jumped at another crash, this time from the kitchen area, but was more fearful of what Antony was about to say. I grabbed his arm, but he shook me off. There was no stopping this.

'I should bloody well hope she did,' Jayne shouted. 'I'd have killed you if it had been me!'

'She tried to!'

'Antony!' I shouted.

Antony opened his mouth to say more, but was startled by a loud bang from the kitchen.

'What the hell was that?' Jayne said.

This time I ignored her. I glared at Antony in silence.

'Verity?' Jayne said. 'What's going on? What did you do?'

I sighed. 'Nothing. I was just so angry and hurt and humiliated. He wouldn't get away from me; he kept trying to hug me, talk to me, *lie* to me. And I wanted, wanted to—'

Tears were running down my face now and I was dimly aware of noise but I was lost in the memory of that moment.

I screamed as Antony launched himself at me and we crashed to the floor. Winded, I struggled feebly, then with more strength.

'Stay down!' He rolled on top of me, his weight pinning me, and I screamed and struggled harder.

Jayne's screams matched mine and I grew aware of the other noises: the banging of cupboard doors; smashes and crashes as plates, glasses and mugs hit the walls above our heads, showering us with shards as sharp as knives; the whistle of the kettle, suddenly come to the boil; the gush of water as the taps spouted torrents of water.

I squirmed my head free just in time to see a bottle of wine on the worktop explode, coating the walls behind with streaks of red. Hysterically, I thought of the TV show, *Dexter*, and wondered how he would analyse the splatter. Then it stopped.

The door opened.

'What have you done to them?' Lara launched herself at Antony, kicking him off me. 'Are you all right?'

'Nothing, I didn't bloody do anything!' Antony pushed himself off me, clambered to his feet, and backed towards the door, his face white with shock. 'What the *hell* is going on here?'

He turned and ran.

Lara offered me a hand up off the floor and all three of us looked around the mess of the room.

'I guess your ghosts like Antony even less than they like me,' Jayne said.

'At least they have good taste,' Lara said, breaking the tension. All three of us gave a high-pitched giggle, then sobered at the desperate sound of it.

'Well,' Jayne said. 'I think it's time for a drink.'

'White Lion,' Lara said, and hustled Hannah down the stairs, Grasper leading the way.

Jayne and I hastily gathered up our coats and handbags, then I dashed downstairs to collect a change of clothes and my toiletries bag. Nothing would induce me to sleep in The Rookery tonight.

Part Two

28th December 2016 - January 2017

"Be with me always – take any form – drive me mad! Only do not leave me in this abyss, where I cannot find you! Oh, God! It is unutterable! I cannot live without my life! I cannot live without my soul!"

Wuthering Heights
Emily Brontë, 1847
Haworth, West Yorkshire

I.

The twelve-year-old girl trudged towards the parsonage, exhausted and chilled after a day in the fresh winter air, yet reluctant to descend from the moors.

'Emily!'

She stopped at the shout and turned towards the stonemason's workshop.

'Tha just walked past without passing the time of day,' Harry complained.

'Good afternoon, Harry.'

'That's better, see, no harm in passing a friendly greeting is there?'

Emily smiled at him and Harry beamed in response to the rare show of affection. Emily didn't make friends easily – not of the two-legged variety anyway. He glanced at the strange collection of animals that seemed to be forever in attendance on Emily Brontë, and smiled when he noticed the new additions of a goose and a pheasant amongst the usual cats and dogs.

He was proud of the fact he was likely Emily's only friend outside her family. He knew no other who was as self-sufficient and happy in her own company as Emily – even her siblings were social extroverts in comparison – and he was honoured that she viewed him as friend – even if the other lads in the village teased him over her, calling her savage. And when her temper was roused, she could indeed be savage; but they had never seen her charm a hurt lapwing on to her hand to be carried home and nursed back to health. They had never seen her free a coney from a snare and care for it until it could return to its warren.

Although it never had gone back to its own kind, he mused, as he watched it awkwardly hop up to join the rest of Emily's coterie. The fur never had grown back on that hind leg and, although slower than the rest of its kind, the little bobtail was never too far away from its saviour.

'Tha'd live up there if tha could, wouldn't thee, lass?' Harry said, nodding at Haworth Moor rising behind Emily.

She turned and looked at the landscape. Most would consider it grim and barren at this time of year. Not Emily; she saw naught but life up there and loved it all, even the wind, no matter how hard it bit.

'I'd love to,' she replied, her voice childlike in the simplicity of her answer. 'Away from the cesspit of human habitation.' She wrinkled her nose at the stench of the privies and midden heaps of Haworth – a smell diluted by the position of the parsonage and mason's workshop beyond the church and away from Main Street, but still powerful enough.

'It would be much better to live with the coneys and the foxes, the buzzards and the owls. They drink the purest water and eat the freshest meat.'

'Apart from the foxes that scavenge from the midden heaps,' Harry said with a grin.

Emily shrugged. 'Only in the winter, when there's less food about. Then they're back on the moor, the air fresh, and the footing sound.'

Harry grimaced, knowing what Emily was referring to. The recent rains had sent a river of waste from the privies and middens at the top end of Main Street down to the bottom. The steep hill had been lethal, even more so than normal; and people, horses and carts had slithered down it with a filthy, stinking regularity over the past few days.

He shuddered. 'The sooner they lay them cobbles they keep talking about, the better.'

Emily didn't appear to have heard him. 'I love the . . . space . . . up there. No one else to annoy you, just fauna and flora.'

Harry scowled at her fancy words mixed in with her Yorkshire dialect, itself not as strong as most in the village. That more than anything highlighted the differences between them, and at times he struggled to understand her meaning.

He glanced at the parsonage then thought of his family's cottage. Nine of them in two rooms; and that was only because four of his siblings were already in their graves.

'Been up to Top Withens today,' Emily continued, having mistaken Harry's silence for interest. 'Love it up there.'

'Aye, tha can see for miles and there's no folk to spoil the view,' Harry said.

'Yes,' Emily exclaimed. 'That's it exactly!'

'Mebbe one day we'll live up there, together.' Harry was aware of his fierce blush, wondering if he'd gone too far, but Emily didn't seem to have understood his meaning. Either that or she had far more tact than people credited her with.

'I'd love to live up there,' she said. 'But Papa would never allow it. What time will Mr Barraclough release you?' She looked at Harry, irritated, and he knew he'd taken too long to respond to her change of subject. He popped his head inside, and received a nod from his master.

'Whenever tha wishes. What service can I do thee for?' He smiled and winked, but again Emily failed to react.

'Come to the parsonage for tea. In about an hour. Papa was complaining this morning that he doesn't see enough of you.'

'Have another sandwich.' Charlotte proffered the plate.

The eldest at fourteen, Harry knew, yet she was so diminutive, even her youngest sister Anne more than matched her for height.

But whatever her stature, she was the perfect hostess, with impeccable manners, even if she did have a strange manner of peering at her guests through lenses the size of ha'pennies.

Must be all that reading she does, Harry thought, *that makes her squint so. Bad for thy health, all them books.*

'I've just finished *Don Juan*,' Branwell announced. 'I found it to be an absolutely fascinating, if a little shocking, study of today's society. Have you ever read Lord Byron, Harry?'

Harry refused to let his true reaction to this pretentiousness show on his face. He couldn't abide Branwell, who lorded it over boys of his own age, especially those of the village. He idolised his father's sexton, John Brown, and tried to pretend he was of the same age and life experience, despite the thirteen-year gap. Little did Branwell know, instead of appearing learned and a man of the world, he was viewed as a pompous ass by everyone in Haworth under the age of sixteen – unless their surname was Brontë.

'No, I have not, Branwell,' Harry replied, mocking the other boy's upper-crust way of speech. 'My reading tends to be limited to the memorial stones Mr Barraclough carves.'

Charlotte reclaimed the conversation with a small rebuke to her brother as she defended their guest. 'Don't be silly, Branwell, Harry doesn't have time for such pursuits as poetry, he must feed his family, especially with young Mabel so poorly. How does she fare, Harry?'

'Ailing at the minute, Miss Charlotte, but still breathing so there's hope.'

'Well, you must take the rest of these sandwiches home

with you. Some apples too, we have a good stock, they'll do her the power of good.'

'Thank you, Miss Charlotte.'

'Ha!' Branwell interrupted, determined to regain the upper hand from his elder sister, and waved a newspaper over the children. 'Look at this! Mr Rook will have a fit when he sees it.'

'Sees what, Branwell?' Charlotte asked. 'Which publication is that?'

'*The Leeds Mercury*.' Branwell cracked the paper open in emulation of his father.

'That scoundrel, Richard Oastler, is at it again, he's blatantly calling for millworkers to strike!'

'No scoundrel, Branwell,' Emily said. 'He speaks for many, and there is truth in what he preaches, even Papa says so.'

Branwell scowled. 'He should not talk against the mills. Without them Haworth would starve.'

Emily snatched the newsprint from her brother. 'You know as well as I the perils of working in the mills. Even now Harry's sister is in her bed, barely able to breathe for the fluff in her lungs, and only ten years old, the same age as our Anne!'

'Emily,' Charlotte cautioned with a concerned glance at Harry. His face was white, but he showed no other sign of emotion.

Emily ignored her sister. 'Richard Oastler speaks for all the mill children who have no voice. Their parents too.' She jumped to her feet in her passion, her features pinched as she struggled to express the outrage flooding through her. She pointed at the newspaper, then her brother, and stamped her foot.

'The Yorkshire Slavery he calls it, and slavery it is. Nippers crawling under those awful machines, and girls not much older running those huge spinning frames.'

'Have a care, child. I will tolerate no Luddite tendencies under this roof.'

Emily jumped, paled, and sat down all in one motion at the sound of her father's rebuke.

'I am sorry, Papa. I am not speaking against the machines, only the lot of their operators.'

'Those operators are lucky to have the work,' a new voice said. 'Without it, their families would starve. Is that not so, Mr Sutcliffe?'

'Yes, Mr Rook,' Harry said.

Baalzephon Rook, as owner of Rook Mills the employer of the majority of Harry's extensive family, nodded and put a hand on the shoulder of his son, Zemeraim.

'What say you, Miss Brontë?' he said, glancing at Emily. 'Should I allow those families to starve?'

Emily met his gaze, lifted her chin, and opened her mouth.

'Come now, Baalzephon. You shall get no sense from a child,' Patrick Brontë said with a cautionary glance at his most wayward of daughters, who blessedly kept her silence.

'They show rather too much interest in a world they neither understand nor have no business therein,' Rook Senior pronounced.

'Nonsense, Baalzephon. 'Tis good for the new generations to learn about their world, surely?'

'They do not seem to be learning, but passing judgements beyond their capabilities.'

Patrick shot another warning glance at Emily, then replied, 'Merely a step on the road to enlightenment, my friend, 'tis all.'

'And I'm surprised at you, Harry Sutcliffe, keeping such company.'

Patrick narrowed his eyes, unsure whether Harry or his own offspring were being insulted, but before he could enquire, Baalzephon and Zemeraim had taken their leave and departed.

Emily looked at Branwell, whose face resembled a thunderous sky at the perceived slight, and giggled.

Patrick sighed in exasperation.

'I think I should also take my leave,' Harry said, flustered. *Why could folk not just say what they mean?*

'I shall see you out, Master Sutcliffe,' Patrick said, and Harry fled.

'Not so fast, boy.'

Harry froze on the stoop.

'She's not for you.'

He did not turn.

'I encouraged your friendship, I know. My Emily does not make friends with ease, not the human kind. You have been good for her. You have saved her life at least once. But she will never be your wife. My largesse shall not extend to that. Set your sights on another.'

Harry walked away. He did not look back. He would not allow Patrick Brontë to see the angry flush his words had ignited on his cheeks.

He passed through the gate from the parsonage garden to the churchyard, past the grave of his sisters, past the church, towards home on Weaver's Row.

Patrick watched him go, wondering if he had done the right thing. Harry was the only person outside the family and household who understood Emily, who accepted her as she was, who loved the birds and animals as she did.

But he was a stonemason's apprentice, and a weaver's son. Emily was a parson's daughter.

With a heavy sigh, he swung shut the front door and turned to see Emily staring at him.

One of the few things in the world that could make the Reverend Patrick Brontë flinch, was his daughter Emily's fiercest stare. He not only flinched, but stumbled backwards against the closed door.

2.

'Are you sure you should move back in there?' Lara asked.

'Yes, I can't afford to stay at the White Lion indefinitely when my own place is just across the street. It was lovely over Christmas, but I need to face whatever is going on at The Rookery. Anyway, Vikram and the gang are back today, I can't put it off forever, and nothing has happened since Antony's visit.'

'And you've had no more dreams?' Lara asked.

'No,' I lied, and Lara narrowed her eyes, but with a glance at her daughter, she stayed silent. 'And even if I had, the dreams aren't the problem.'

'No, just your friends and your ex-husband,' Lara pointed out.

'Well, I don't think Antony will pay another visit.'

Lara laughed. 'You can say that again – I've never seen anybody run so fast. Or look so pale.'

'Like he'd seen a ghost,' Hannah repeated the joke we'd been telling all over Christmas. 'Like Scrooge.'

'Just like Scrooge,' Lara agreed, and Hannah buried her nose back in her book. I was struck anew by the way Hannah seemed to cope so well with such strange and frightening events. Yes, she was terrified when these things happened, but within a day she'd accepted it as normal. I envied her.

'Anyway, I have to check out today, the room isn't free again until after New Year. Apparently there's a big do on in the village and they're booked up already.'

'I just wish Jayne had been able to stay longer,' Lara said, and I looked at her in surprise.

She shrugged. 'We may not agree on everything, but we do agree on looking out for you.'

I nodded and Hannah looked up from her book again and said, 'And Grasper could have looked after you too, Auntie Verity.'

'He certainly could, Hannah. What are you reading?'

Hannah showed me the book – a history of Haworth. 'It has all the ghosts in it,' she explained.

'Hannah woke up on the floor this morning,' Lara said. 'Seemingly, it's because of the ghost of the balloonist.'

'Yes, Lily Cove,' Hannah explained. 'She parachuted out of her hot-air balloon, but the parachute didn't open and she just fell.'

'And you're not scared?'

'No. I was at first, but she just wants to tell people what happened to her and it's difficult because she doesn't have a voice or a body any more. That's what Mum says. Maybe that's what your ghosts are doing, Auntie Verity, trying to tell you what happened to them.'

'You could be right, Hans,' Lara said. 'Have you finished your breakfast?'

Hannah nodded, put a large black feather into her book to mark her page, then closed the book.

'Where did you get that?' Lara asked with a shiver.

'Outside Auntie Verity's house. There are lots on the ground from those big black birds.'

Lara and I exchanged a glance, then I threw my napkin on to the table. 'Right, come on. I need to get my stuff and settle my bill, then once I've spoken to Vikram and the build team, the rest of the day is ours.'

***

'What's that lot for?' I pointed at the bag of crystals, amulets and other odds and sods Lara had bought from the new-age shop on Main Street.

'If you're moving back into that place, you'll do so with some protection,' Lara said.

'Stones, herbs and symbols?' I scoffed.

'I'm willing to try anything,' Lara said. 'And don't mock this stuff, used properly it can be very powerful.'

'But you've already cleansed The Rookery. That didn't do much good.'

'How do you know? You've no idea if things would be even worse without that cleansing.'

I stayed silent, but knew my apprehension was clear in the set of my face and shoulders.

'We'll cleanse again tonight after the builders have gone, then every evening – and you need to carry on doing it after Hannah and I go home.' She stopped in exasperation at the look on my face.

'Look at it this way, Verity, it can't hurt and you'll keep me off your back.'

I relaxed. 'You're right, Lara, sorry.' I gave her a quick hug. 'I guess I'm a bit freaked out by it all. When the stuff in the kitchen started smashing, well . . .'

Lara glanced at Hannah, who was peering into shop windows and not paying us any attention.

'It must have been terrifying,' she said. 'But no one was hurt – and they could have been had the spirits wanted to. They're clearly capable of it.'

'They?'

Lara shrugged. 'Well, yes, there were two orbs, remember?'

'My dream man and the Grey Lady,' I said.

'I don't think so – I don't think the Grey Lady has anything to do with this. But whoever they are, we need to make sure you're safe.'

'I don't think they want to hurt me,' I said. 'If anything, I think Hannah's right, he – they – want to tell me something.'

'Maybe, but to be honest, they're going to a lot of trouble and energy to merely tell you a story. No, there's something more going on here, and I'm not sure we want to find out what.'

'I doubt they'll give us the choice, they've been pretty insistent so far.'

'That's what's worrying me so much,' Lara said. 'How much further will they go to make you understand?'

I hesitated, then said, 'Okay, I'll do whatever you want: spells, potions, rituals, the works. Even dance naked in the graveyard under the full moon if that'll make you happy!'

Lara laughed with me. 'We don't need to go that far, Verity, not unless you really want to.'

'I'd rather not – even if it appeases the ghosts, which is unlikely, I can't see my new neighbours taking kindly to that spectacle!'

'Why are you laughing, Mum?' Hannah had grown bored of window shopping and re-joined us.

'Oh, just picturing Auntie Verity dancing around the gravestones with no clothes on.'

Hannah looked thoughtful for a moment. 'Why would you picture that, Mum?'

I joined in Lara's laughter. 'Yes, why would you picture that, Lara?'

'I wish I never had,' she spluttered. 'Shall we get on with the shopping instead? Didn't you want to have a look at the art gallery?'

Still laughing, I linked arms with Lara, Hannah taking her other side, and we made our clumsy way over the cobbles.

3.

'Auntie Verity!' Hannah bumped into my back and I managed to put one foot in front of the other to make slow progress into the art gallery. The man behind the counter stared at me as intently as I stared at him, but neither of us spoke.

'Hi,' Lara said with a concerned look at me. 'We're interested in local landscapes . . .' she tailed off, glancing between me and the man, then plonked her handbag on to the countertop with an audible thump and broke the spell.

The man diverted his attention to her and finally smiled. 'Over here.' He moved towards the far wall of the shop. 'They're my speciality – if there's a local landmark you're thinking of in particular and it isn't here, just let me know and I'll paint it for you.' He shot another glance at me, his colour high.

'Oh, you're the artist too?' Lara asked.

'Aye, William Sutcliffe. At your service.' He gave an awkward bow, the blush in his cheeks undiminished.

'How wonderful,' Lara said.

I still could not form words of my own and thanked my lucky stars that we'd done this today and Lara was here to speak for me.

'Do you paint people too?' Hannah asked.

'Aye, sometimes, if someone takes my fancy.'

I met his eyes again then looked away just in time to catch Lara's smirk.

'Have you ever had your portrait painted, lass?'

'No, only photographs,' Hannah said, deadly serious. 'I'd love a painted portrait, though. Mummy, can I have one?'

'I think that might be a bit too expensive for your pocket money, Hans,' Lara said, with a smile.

'Ah well, you'll just have to save up, lass. I'll do you a good deal.' He winked with a smile.

'Or I could get a job, just like Aunt Jayne.'

'Maybe in a few years. Come and have a look at these,' Lara said. 'Which do you think would look nice in Auntie Verity's hotel?'

'The spooky ones,' Hannah answered promptly. 'So the ghosts feel at home.'

I laughed – finally finding my voice. 'They already seem to feel quite at home, Hannah, don't you think?'

Hannah shrugged as the man – William – said, 'Ghosts? You've bought in Haworth then, there's barely a house without a ghost story on this hill.' He smiled at me as I gave another nervous laugh.

'Yes, we're getting that impression.' I stuck my hand out. 'Verity Earnshaw,' I said as we shook. 'I've bought The Rookery – the place on West Lane with the skip outside,' I added as I remembered that nobody but myself, Jayne, Lara and the build team knew the building by that name at the moment.

'Ah, the old weaver's cottages. Aye, I know the place. Have you seen the Grey Lady yet?'

'Auntie Verity has, and one of the builders did. He ran away scared, didn't he, Mummy? I'm not scared though, not any more, not of her or the man. Or the ghost in our room at the hotel. I'm not, am I, Mummy?'

William looked rather taken aback by this, but rallied valiantly. 'It sounds like you're a very brave girl – that's a lot of ghosts not to be scared of.'

'It is, isn't it, Mummy? A lot of ghosts. They don't scare me though.'

'Okay, Hannah, how about we look at these pictures?' Lara tried again to distract her daughter.

Hannah's babbling had at least given me time to recover my wits, and I turned my attention back to William. 'I'm looking for a couple of dozen landscapes,' I started.

'Prints or originals?'

'Prints – preferably related to the Brontës and the village.'

William nodded and I realised he'd hear this criteria from most of his customers.

'They're to go in the guest rooms as well as the public areas,' I continued, 'and be available for sale to guests, so I was hoping we could make a sale or return arrangement.'

'Sale or return,' he repeated. 'And when would you return them if they didn't sell?'

I stayed quiet, unprepared for this question, but he took pity on me and broke the silence.

'I can't do that I'm afraid,' he said. 'If I did I'd have prints hanging in every guesthouse and hotel in the dale, but I'd have no money coming in. This is how I make my living, I do need to sell my work.'

He sighed and rubbed his hand over the dark stubble on his chin. I wondered if the growth was from overnight or if he had indeed shaved that morning, then caught myself and brought my mind back to the business at hand.

'As you'd like a bulk order, I can offer you a 25 per cent discount on the lot, or you can buy half at full price, and I'll let you have the rest on sale or return – but only for six months. If you don't sell any, I'll take them back, or you'd need to buy them.'

'At 25 per cent off?'

He shook his head. 'One or the other, I'm afraid. It's up to you and how many you think you can realistically sell.'

I stayed silent, thinking.

'And if she buys them at the discount, then sells, what would you offer at that point?' Lara asked.

William smiled, but didn't take his eyes off me. 'If you're making sales, then we can definitely renegotiate.'

He stared at me a moment longer, his colour rising once more. 'When do you open?'

'Easter,' I said.

'So you wouldn't need them straight away,' he mused, then met Hannah's eyes – big, grey and round, staring back at him, full of hope – and his face softened, then hardened once more as he returned his attention to me.

'Earnshaw did you say your name was?'

'Yes, my father grew up in Keighley, but his ancestors came from this area. He always joked one of his relations inspired Emily Brontë's Cathy.'

'But you're Verity.'

'My middle name's Catherine.' I blushed; I hated admitting that.

William nodded. 'Well, you're a local then.' He smiled. 'Tell you what, if you let me hang the pictures and have my card in the frame, I'll let you have them for three months after opening, on spec. Then you decide which deal you want. Can't say fairer than that.'

Hannah clapped her hands, but was silenced by her mother's hand over her mouth.

I considered for a moment, then held my hand out. 'Deal,' I said. 'Nice doing business with you.'

He took my hand and I jolted at the sensation of the touch of our palms. By the look in his eyes, he had felt it too.

We let go at Lara's cough and I wondered just how long we'd been standing in the gallery holding hands. I was surprised to hear myself say, 'When would you like to pop in to have a look around The Rookery? We'll be in tomorrow.'

'Tomorrow it is then, as soon as I've shut up shop.'

'See you then.' I hesitated, unwilling to leave, but eventually followed Lara and Hannah back out on to Main Street.

Hannah ran on ahead up the steep hill and Lara linked her arm with mine as we followed far more slowly.

'What was all that about? Why were you acting so weird in there?'

'That,' I said, 'was the man I've been dreaming about.'

4.

'I clear this space of all negative energy and call in angelic light and love to fill this place,' Lara intoned yet again, then held the smouldering bundle of sage under the tap before putting it into a bowl.

'When it's dry you can relight it and do the same again,' she said.

'Uh huh,' I replied, my arms folded and my nose wrinkled in scepticism.

Lara glanced at me, frustrated. 'I thought you were going to try this, Verity.'

'We are trying it.'

'No, you're watching me try it – again. This is your home, you need to embrace it or the intentions have no power.'

'It'll only work if I believe in it, you mean?'

Lara sighed. 'Essentially, yes.' She held up a hand to forestall my mocking harrumph. 'It's all about intention. If you believe and mean the words, that gives them the power to manifest – become true.' She paused and looked at me in exasperation.

'Have you ever lost something?'

'Of course I have.' I laughed.

'And what do you say to yourself while you're looking for it? Say for example, you can't find the TV remote, what's running through your head while you're searching?'

'Um, where's the bloody remote? I can't find it anywhere. Something like that.'

'And do you find it?'

'Eventually.'

'But not while you're telling yourself you can't find it, right?'

I thought for a moment and relaxed a bit. 'Well, usually I've given up, gone to get a cup of coffee or glass of wine, come back into the lounge and then I find it.'

'Probably somewhere you've already looked, right?'

'Well, yes, usually. That could just be age though.' I laughed.

Lara smiled. 'Or it could be that you didn't see it because you were telling yourself that you couldn't find it, and you believed that.'

I shrugged. She was starting to make sense.

'Next time you lose something, instead of telling yourself you can't find it, tell yourself it will be in the next place you look.'

'If I tell myself that often enough, it *will* eventually be in the next place I look.'

'But I bet you find it long before you give up, get a drink, then find it somewhere you've already searched.'

I said nothing. I'd have to try it first.

'It's the same thing here – the cleansing we're doing with the sage and candle is about setting your intention. In the same way as telling yourself you will find what is lost, you are telling yourself and anything listening that you want only peace here.'

'Okay, I guess that makes sense,' I admitted, 'but do I really have to wave burning herbs around? I can't imagine my guests enjoying the smell, it stinks like a doss house!'

'Yes, unfortunate that burning herbs all smell the same – including cannabis, as Jayne so kindly pointed out before Christmas.' Lara smiled. 'No, just do the sage when the place is empty and you're cleaning and airing the rooms anyway. The rest of the time use a candle.'

'How do I do that?'

'I'll show you, we'll do it now.' Lara dug into her shopping bag and pulled out a small votive candle in a glass holder. She lit it and handed it to me.

'I want you to move it in continuous clockwise circles,' she said. 'Get into every corner of every room, and spend a bit of extra time in the well-used places like I did with the sage: over your bed, the dining table, sofa, that kind of thing. And keep repeating the intention.

I nodded and started. 'I cleanse this place of all negative energy— I feel like a right wally,' I interrupted myself, self-conscious again.

'No one's laughing at you, Verity, and being a right wally may not be the best intention to set, no matter how apt it is at the moment.'

I narrowed my eyes at her and she laughed.

'Keep going. I did it and I'm none the worse for wear.' She smiled to reassure me. 'It doesn't feel so weird after you've done it a few times. Trust me.'

I held her gaze for a moment, then nodded. I did trust her, and I had no better ideas.

I raised the candle again and made my way through the rooms, circling and chanting – with the odd prompt from Lara.

'I cleanse this place of all negative energy and call in angelic light and love to fill this space.'

We moved through the building, pausing in my bedroom to check on Hannah – fast asleep on my bed, exhausted from her insistence on running up Main Street ahead of us, then returning to chivvy us along up the steep slope.

'Downstairs too?'

'Every single room on every single floor,' Lara said. 'And every single day, too.'

'What?'

'You need to keep doing it until you fully believe in what you're saying, until the intention of light and love is as much a part of you as the blood that runs through your veins. Then you'll be safe.'

'How long will that take?'

No answer.

'Still feel like a wally?'

'No-no, I don't. I feel weird, peaceful somehow.'

Lara nodded, smiling.

'Probably all the candle and sage smoke gone to my head!' I joked.

Lara's smile grew wider, her eyes crinkling in honest pleasure. She said nothing, though, just poured us both a glass of wine. 'I think we've earned this,' she said. 'Cheers.'

We clinked glasses and drank.

'What?' I said, defensive again at the look in her eyes over the rim of her glass.

'What do you think about a tarot reading?'

'I don't know, Lara, that makes me uncomfortable.'

'You're spending too much time with Jayne,' she said. 'There's nothing to worry about, nothing sinister about the cards, they're just a tool to allow us to understand what our subconscious and intuition already know.'

'Oh what the hell,' I said. 'In for a penny, in for a pound. Just don't go telling me when I'll die or anything like that.'

'The cards don't predict death,' Lara said, 'only the most likely outcomes of current situations.'

'I thought there was a death card.'

'There is – but it means change, a letting go of a way of life, not the end of a life.'

I nodded. To be fair, I was intrigued by the tarot. Lara had never been wrong in the past when she'd persuaded me to sit for a reading. Something about them just unnerved me though, and I'd never embraced the cards.

'Best to do it quickly before we have more wine,' Lara said, and I laughed as she took another gulp, then I gulped myself, took the bottle and followed her to the table.

As she unwrapped her cards from the silk purple scarf in which she kept them, I topped up our glasses.

'Dutch courage.' I shrugged at her frown and took a sip.

She said nothing, but shuffled the cards, her eyes closed and face blank in concentration.

I sipped again as I waited, then took the cards when Lara proffered them, and shuffled them myself as she instructed.

Handing them back, she laid them out, face down in three columns of three cards each, then looked at me. 'Ready?'

I gulped my wine, noticing that Lara had drunk no more, then took another drink and set my empty glass down. 'Ready.'

Lara turned over the top row of cards.

'This represents your past,' she said, 'and there are no surprises here – always a good thing at this stage.' She smiled up at me and I refilled my glass.

'Seven of Cups. That's delusion, believing somebody who's been lying to you.'

'Antony,' I confirmed, sipping again.

Lara nodded. 'Then the Three of Swords. Discord – that's the divorce card – and the third one is the Tower. Your old life falling down.'

'Sounds about right,' I said, lifting the glass to my lips again. I quirked an eyebrow at my friend. 'Are you sure this is a good idea? I think we'll need more wine if it carries on like this.'

Lara reached over and laid her hand over mine. 'This is a reflection of the past, Verity. It's nothing you don't already know, and actually the Tower is a good card to end on.'

I stared at the picture on the card. A bolt of lightning striking a tall, lone stone keep, fire spewing from the upper floors, stonework tumbling.

'It means the slate's wiped clean and you can rebuild, with stronger foundations. It means a new life is beginning.'

I grinned, looking around me and opening my arms wide to indicate The Rookery. 'Very apt.'

Lara smiled and bent her head back to the spread of cards. 'The next row is your present. The Fool, the Chariot and the Eight of Wands.'

'The Fool, that sounds about right.'

Lara ignored me. 'The Fool means you're at the beginning of a new journey, and judging by the Chariot that follows it, it'll be quite a ride!' She looked up and took a sip of her wine. 'You'll need willpower and hard work, but you have both of those in you in spades. And you'll persevere.' She spread her own arms out, repeating my earlier gesture. 'I think this place will be a success.'

'I'll drink to that.' I giggled, growing tipsy now.

'Then this one.' Lara tapped the Eight of Wands. 'These are the arrows of love.'

'The arrows of love? Christ, I don't need any of that, thank you very much. Antony has very definitely rid me of any appetite for love!'

'Really? Watching you in that art gallery today, I could have sworn I saw you salivating.'

I blushed, but I wasn't ready to talk about that – I needed far more wine before I could even start to get my head round meeting that man. 'And what about the next cards, the future?'

Lara unsuccessfully tried to hide a smug smile, then grew serious again. 'The Moon, the Hanged Man, and the Lovers,' she said as she turned the cards over.

I stayed silent, my heart doing funny things at the appearance of the last two cards.

'The moon is about your dreams,' Lara said, eyebrows raised.

'You're joking!'

She shook her head. 'Pay attention to them, truths are contained within your dreams, truths you need to know and understand.'

I sipped my wine, feeling unaccountably sober again. 'And the Hanged Man?' I almost whispered the words.

'Does *not* mean death,' Lara reassured, her hand once again atop mine. 'It can mean sacrifice, or can be about perspective. Coming after the Moon card, I think it's telling you to look at things in a different way. See how the man is hanging upside down from his foot? He's telling you to be open-minded, don't jump to conclusions, and look at things from every angle before acting.'

I nodded then giggled again. 'You don't have to tell me what the Lovers means!'

Lara tilted her head to her right shoulder. 'Not quite what you're thinking – it indicates choices to be made, although probably to do with a lover. It can often mean the start of a significant relationship.'

I giggled again, my earlier protestations forgotten.

'Verity.' Lara grabbed my hand again and I winced at the strength of her grip. 'Make the right choice – be very careful.'

I wrenched my hand away. 'Lara, what the hell?'

She blinked a few times and looked confused, then gasped.

Two balls of light hovered over the spread of cards on the table, then slowly moved around each other and rose to the ceiling, where they circled around the room.

I jumped to my feet, Lara a split second behind me,

when I spotted the hazy figure of the Grey Lady standing in the kitchen area, her back to us.

Lara and I grabbed each other and stood frozen, fingers intertwined, and stared as the figure turned to look at us.

She was petite, barely taller than Hannah, and very slender. Her hair – it was impossible to see the colour of it but it seemed dark – was bound up under a bonnet, but careless curls, not quite ringlets, escaped its confines and framed her bony, pinched face.

Her gown was modest; the lace trimming the neck of it brushed the base of her skull, the sleeves puffed from the shoulders, and the waist was impossibly nipped in.

Corset, I thought. *She's wearing a corset.*

The skirt bloomed large from the hips and brushed the floor – no, extended *through* the floor.

I raised my eyes again to her face, and gasped. She was staring at me with such a look of pity and – sorrow – yes, that was it, sorrow, I felt tears prickle my eyes.

She turned her face forward again and moved, very slowly, until the kitchen units, then the wall swallowed her up.

She was gone.

Lara dragged her hand out of mine and fell back into her chair – hard enough to hurt. She stretched out a shaky hand, took hold of her glass, and after a couple of attempts, drained it in one.

I retook my own seat and stared at her.

'Bloody hell, Verity,' she said. 'Tha-that was a ghost. That was a real ghost.' She took a deep breath. 'I've never actually *seen* a ghost before!'

5.

The Reverend Patrick Brontë regarded the couple standing before him, and a rare smile flitted across his face as his eyes met the groom's. *The lad's left it long enough,* Haworth's parson thought, *but it's good to see him wed at last.*

'Harry Sutcliffe, wilt thou have this woman to be thy wedded wife, to live together after God's ordinance in the holy estate of Matrimony? Wilt thou love her, comfort her, honour, and keep her, in sickness and in health; and, forsaking all other, keep thee only unto her, so long as ye both shall live?'

'I will.'

'Martha Earnshaw, wilt thou have this man to be thy wedded husband, to live together after God's ordinance in the holy estate of Matrimony? Wilt thou obey him, and serve him, love, honour, and keep him, in sickness and in health; and, forsaking all other, keep thee only unto him, so long as ye both shall live?'

'Aye, I will.'

Emily watched from the back of the church with her siblings. Charlotte and Branwell were in charge of taking the collection, and it was Emily and Anne's duty to distribute then re-collect the prayer books and hymnals before and after every service; whatever the service may be: wedding, funeral, christening or Holy Communion. It was a nice change to attend a wedding, the most common service by far was the funeral.

Emily was glad to see Harry wed before she left for her teaching post at Law Hill. She knew he'd been holding out to wed her, but had finally given up hope. *A pity*, she mused, *if I am to have a husband, Harry may have been a tolerable one. But better to have a teaching life, than be a stonemason's wife, that's what Papa says. Maybe I'll find a husband on the moors one day.*

Emily's attention was brought back to the church as the congregation stood to sing. It was her favourite hymn, *All Creatures of our God and King*, and she joined in with gusto until Charlotte elbowed her in the side, and she lowered her voice to a more melodious tone.

Martha looks lovely, Emily thought when the hymn was over. *Not like her usual slovenly self at all.* The bride wore a new cotton gown, especially made for the occasion. It would have taken the Earnshaws a couple of years to save up for the material, but was worth it. A lovely earthy pattern of dark red stripes on a gold background, it would likely be Martha's best dress for the rest of her life, worn for every special occasion.

I hope they've been able to leave plenty of spare material at the seams, Emily thought. *If Martha's anything like her mam, she'll be needing to let it out plenty afore too long.*

Emily breathed deeply as the distinctive, fresh smell of wild garlic wafted over her. *Garlic for courage and health*, she thought and squinted at Martha's bridal bouquet to see which other flowers and foliage she'd chosen; what her hopes for the future were.

Gorse: endearing affection. Emily scowled, that wasn't Martha at all. Maybe Harry had given her that. White heather for dreams to come true, honeysuckle for the bond of love, and of course pussy willow for motherhood. Hence all the garlic. Babies rarely saw their first birthday, and nearly half of those that did would not see their seventh.

Papa's certain it's the wells. If water stinks that much outside, what does it do to us inside?

Emily smiled at Harry as the couple passed, genuinely happy for her friend, then recoiled at the strength of Martha's glare.

The two had never got on, not even as girls, but Emily hadn't paid too much attention. She didn't care what the village girls thought of her.

They had never hated each other though, but that's what Emily saw in Martha's face as she walked out of the church, her new husband on her arm: a deep, malevolent hatred. And something else too. Triumph?

Verity jerked awake, her fists clenched, heart racing. But not for love, her heart was racing in anger.

Her breathing calmed as she grew aware of her surroundings and century. The dream had seemed so *real*, and that was William who'd been getting married – for all he was called Harry in her dreams.

Verity's gut twisted at the thought. *Jealousy? Am I seriously jealous from dreaming about a man I don't know getting married over a hundred years ago?*

She threw the covers aside and jumped out of bed. *This is getting ridiculous.* Even more ridiculous when she caught herself hoping that Harry would visit her in the shower again.

6.

'It's not good enough, Gary,' Vikram said into the phone. 'You and Omar swore to me you'd be fit for work this week.'

He listened a moment, then, 'Food poisoning, my arse. Alcohol poisoning more like. Just get here when you can – I don't care how much your head hurts.'

He hung up with a curse, then winced and apologised for his language when he saw Hannah.

'Problem?' I inquired.

'The labourers have hangovers,' he said. 'It'll slow us down some.' He indicated the two men standing behind him with cups of tea. 'Both Pramod and Darren are qualified plumbers, and now they'll have to work together on one en-suite rather than getting on with two.'

I shot an enquiring glance at Lara, then said, 'Can we help? If it's labourers you need, we're more than happy to help out – we can fetch and carry with the best of them.'

Lara laughed. 'Yes, we'd been planning to visit the museum but it's closed until after New Year. We have the day free if you can use us.' She stared in all innocence at Vikram as he blushed.

'Well . . . if you're sure . . .' He hesitated and looked to his colleagues, then shrugged. 'If you two can help Pramod, I'll help Darren. We'll be laying pipe for the bathroom suites, and connecting everything up.'

'Like the pipes game on your phone, Mum,' Hannah butted in.

'Well, summat like that,' Vikram said. 'It shouldn't be all day, with any luck, those two layabouts will drag themselves here at some point. They'll need to earn some dosh for their next pub crawl! You'll need safety gear though: hard hat, hi-vis vest and steel toecaps.' He paused and stroked his chin.

'Steel toecaps? Do those come with heels?'

Vikram stared at Lara, for a moment lost for words, then he seemed to decide she was joking. 'I should have enough gear in the van, but I don't think I'll have anything to fit you, lass.'

Hannah looked crestfallen.

'Not to worry, Hans. It'll be all dirty and dusty,' Lara said. 'You wouldn't like it. Why don't you go up to Auntie Verity's rooms and do some colouring?'

'I want to read,' she replied, lips pouting in a sulk.

'Okay, I'll pop over to the hotel and get a book. Which one do you want?'

'*Gangsta Granny.*'

I raised my eyebrows at the title, then followed Vikram to the van as Lara and Hannah crossed the road to the White Lion.

'I was sorry to intrude on Christmas Eve,' Vikram said.

I shook my head. 'Don't worry about it, you weren't the one intruding.'

'The ex?'

I nodded.

'Are you okay?'

I gave a smile that I knew barely touched my cheeks. 'Yeah, I'm fine. He won't be back in a hurry.'

'Is that a good thing?'

'Definitely.' This time my smile was genuine.

He nodded and clambered into the back of his van, emerging with an armful of safety gear. 'Boots'll be a bit on the big side, you'll have to stuff socks in them or summat.'

'No problem, it's not as if we'll be walking far. Oh, you've got three hats, Hannah will be chuffed!'

'Aye, three vests .an'all. It'll be too long for her, but at least she won't feel left out.'

'That's very thoughtful of you.'

'Aye, well, I've three nippers of my own, I know how they get.'

'Oh, I didn't realise you had children.' I mentally kicked myself; his private life was none of my business.

'Yeah. Don't see enough of them, though.'

We were interrupted by the return of Lara and Hannah, who immediately cheered up with the presentation of a hard hat and a fluorescent yellow vest, then we turned to go back inside.

'Bloody hell,' Vikram said. 'Sorry,' he added with a glance at Lara. 'Again.'

'She's heard worse,' Lara said. 'What's wrong?'

He pointed. 'The rooks again. I've not known them roost on the buildings before – they tend to stick to the graveyard, away from folk. Well, living folk, anyroad,' he amended.

'Yes, I was meaning to mention that to you. Can you put up netting or spikes, something to keep them away? As soon as possible.'

'Aye, no problem. It'll have to be in the New Year though, when I've got a full team back.'

'That should be okay – as long as it's before guests start arriving.'

He nodded. 'You know, it's said they're lost souls.'

'Yeah, I'd heard something about that.'

'Aye, unable to find their way to peace, that's why they congregate in graveyards.'

I shivered and noticed Hannah step closer to her mother, pressing against Lara's side. Vikram must have seen too.

'Load of superstitious nonsense,' he said, his tone brighter. 'Shouldn't have brought it up. Right, are you ladies ready to go to work?'

'I am absolutely exhausted,' Lara said, collapsing on to one of the camping chairs.

'Hey, watch it, you're filthy.'

'I'll clean it later.'

I took pity on her. 'Tell you what, grab a quick shower and change, and I'll treat you and Hannah to lunch as a thank you for this morning.'

'Done,' Lara said. She held her hands out. 'Drag me off this chair and I'll do that.'

I laughed, grabbed her hands and hauled her to her feet. 'You've only done two hours' work, and most of that was sitting and holding pipes in place!'

'Harder than it looks,' Lara said. 'Right, Hans, are you coming with me or staying here with Auntie Verity?'

Hannah cast a disdainful look over her mother's dust-laden and generally grimy appearance and stuck her nose back into her book. 'I'll wait here.'

Lara and I grinned at each other, then went our separate ways in search of cleanliness.

'Meet you in the Black Bull?'

'Half an hour.'

As it transpired, Hannah and I passed the Old White Lion just as Lara emerged.

'You look like a new woman,' I said.

'Good job too. You don't scrub up too badly yourself.'

Giggling at Hannah's eye roll, we linked arms and followed Hannah to the Black Bull and lunch.

I stopped dead as soon as I stepped through the interior door.

'Is that . . .?'

'Yes.'

'It's the painting man,' Hannah exclaimed and ran over to him. 'Hello, have you painted my picture yet?'

William Sutcliffe glanced down at her, stared a moment, then raised his eyes to mine. He lifted his hand to his flat cap and tweaked it, then regarded Hannah once more, tilting his head first one way then the other.

'Not yet, lassie, but one day. Setting has to be right, though.'

'Mummy, Mummy, he's going to paint me!'

'That's lovely, Hans.' She raised her eyebrow at William, and he shrugged.

'She's persuasive, that one.'

Lara relaxed. 'Yes, she certainly can be.'

He turned his attention to me. 'Ms Earnshaw.' He touched his cap again.

'Mr Sutcliffe.'

'I'll be seeing you later as agreed?'

I nodded, then followed Lara and Hannah to a table.

'Seeing him later?' Lara asked.

'He wants to come and see The Rookery,' I reminded her. 'To get an idea of where his pictures will hang.'

'It seems a bit early for that.' Lara pursed her lips, but amusement shone in her eyes.

I shrugged.

'Lara,' I said, 'can I ask you a serious question?'

'Of course, what is it?'

'How can he be a ghost if he's flesh and blood?'

'Why, Verity,' Lara laughed, 'he can't be. You must have seen him on one of your trips here before you moved in, he's made an impression on your subconscious and that's why he's popping up in your dreams.'

'No. No, that's not it, it's more than that. Besides, if I'd seen him, I'd have remembered.' I blushed at the lifting of Lara's eyebrows, then recovered myself.

'There are at least three ghosts, right? The Grey Lady and the two orbs.'

Lara nodded.

'Because of the dreams and what else has happened – Jayne being pushed, Christmas Eve when Antony was here, last night . . .' I tailed off then gathered my thoughts, grateful that Lara had the patience to wait for me. 'Well, how can he be a ghost if he's standing right there?'

'He can't.'

'So what is he?'

'I have absolutely no idea,' Lara said, and reached over to grasp my hand. 'I'm sorry, but I don't. We don't even know that the man you've been dreaming of is one of the orbs. At least we know the Grey Lady and the orbs don't mean you harm.'

'How do we know that?'

'They still appeared after we'd cleansed and protected The Rookery. They're not evil or demonic.'

I stared at her in shock.

'Don't look so worried, Verity. Those orbs were white light, and the sense around the Grey Lady was one of peace. They're beings of light.'

'But what do they want?'

Lara opened her mouth then shut it again. She had no answer.

I looked up in time to see William tip his cap to me again and leave the pub.

7.

William Sutcliffe eyed me from head to toe, then frowned at the birds overhead and pushed past me into The Rookery.

'I'm going to dinner with Lara and Hannah when we've finished here,' I said, then mentally berated myself. Why on earth was I explaining my outfit to this man? Although, I had to admit, I hadn't chosen my V-neck dress for Lara . . .

'Uh huh,' he said, scanning me once more, then he lifted his eyes to take in the building site that was still my foyer. 'Still got a bit of work to be getting on with.'

'Yes,' I said. 'They're getting the en-suites sorted at the moment, then the plasterers and decorators can take over.'

'It'll take time for the plaster to dry.'

'Yes, I know that,' I said through gritted teeth. 'It's all in hand, the schedule's been devised for an Easter opening.'

He nodded. 'Are you going to give me the tour then?'

I bit my lip, wondering if he was being deliberately rude or if this was his habitual manner. I decided to give him the benefit of the doubt. For now.

'These will be the public rooms,' I began. 'Lounge area there, reception desk, then breakfast room through there.'

'And will you have pictures on all the walls?'

'All but that one and the corner.' I pointed. 'Those will be covered with book shelves.'

'I see.' He looked at me expectantly.

He was older than the man in my dreams, I suddenly realised, his skin more weathered and tanned. The eyes and the shock of curly dark hair were the same, though – apart from the threads of grey at his temples.

He still hadn't shaved, and the stubble was nearly long enough to be called a beard. I wondered if my dream man had the same need to shave so often, then realised I was staring.

I tried to hide my blush by rushing towards the stairway. His smirk told me he had noticed my colour.

'There will be one bedroom through here.' I placed my hand on the wall. 'They'll knock through and partition it off from the existing kitchen, but it's a bit of a mess at the moment.'

'Double or single?'

'Double with wetroom, and accessible for a wheelchair.'

He nodded, then pushed past me to the stairs.

'What will be down here?' he asked, indicating the first corridor.

'Housekeeping cupboards, then a single room at the end. Branwell's Room.'

He cocked an eyebrow in question.

'I'm calling each room by the name of a Brontë sibling. Charlotte's will be the room downstairs, Emily's and Anne's will be doubles on the next landing, then Elizabeth and Maria's at the top.'

'I thought you said five bedrooms.'

'Yes, Elizabeth and Maria's will be a twin.'

He said nothing, but opened the door to Branwell's Room and crossed to the window.

We were at the front of the building, away from the parsonage, and looking out over the rolling, green hills of the Worth Valley.

'You'll be able to see at least six mills from here when it's light,' William said. 'An image of the mill race and waterwheel would look well there, then a study of the mill floor on that wall.'

'I was thinking more of Brontë landscapes.'

'You can't have the Brontës without the mills,' he said. 'The mills were a major part of life here when they lived. The whole village depended on them. It would add a bit more interest too, rather than the same old images you see everywhere. England's dark satanic mills,' he quoted. 'William Blake, *Jerusalem*.'

'Well, I suppose so – you're the expert.'

He nodded, pointed to the door, then brushed at his face, cursing cobwebs. He pushed up his sleeves: he meant business now, and I led the way to the next rooms, listening to his suggestions, not only on subject matter and placement, but lighting too.

My initial shock at meeting him yesterday had morphed into a combination of suspicion, trepidation and . . . fascination. Yes, that was the word; he fascinated me. Why was I dreaming about him? Or a version of him, anyway.

'You know the place is haunted, don't you?' he said.

'What? Well, yes, I do as a matter of fact.' I laughed.

He held out his arm for me to inspect before I could elaborate.

Cautiously, I stepped closer and gasped when I saw every hair on his arm was standing on end. I stretched out a finger to stroke the strands and was rooted to the spot by a rush of electricity.

More energy lifted my chin – his finger, I dimly realised – and our eyes met.

'That's not static,' he said, his voice hoarse and gruff.

'No,' I said – or tried to; my own voice was misbehaving and it came out as a whisper. 'I don't think it is.'

His head lowered and my breathing accelerated. Very slowly, his lips inched closer, until his breathing was mine and mine his.

My phone rang, startling us both, and I pulled away and fumbled it out of my pocket; partly with relief that the spell, whatever it had been, was broken, and partly with exasperation at the loss.

Crestfallen, I hung up.

'Not going to dinner then?'

'No. It was Lara, Hannah's poorly – only the sniffles and a headache, but she's running a temperature and Lara's put her to bed.'

'Guess you're on your own then.'

I frowned at him, my patience running out and my mind whirling with confusion. Then my heart lurched as a smile transformed his gruff, whiskery, taciturn features.

'Sorry, that was rude. What I mean to say is, I'm dining alone as well, will you join me? Only at the Black Bull like,' he added, 'but they do a mean curry.'

I heard myself agree before I was aware I'd decided. I didn't feel as if I had any choice; not one inch of me wanted to depart from his company.

8.

The noise was tremendous, a surreal cacophony that shut out the world and exhausted the senses. Five floors of wheels, gear levers, travellers, carriages, and row upon row upon row of spinning bobbins created a rhythm more urgent and regular than her own heartbeat.

It took over everything; every movement was made to the percussion of the spinning frames. Those working the cap frames walked to a different beat to those at the ring spinners, who were out of step with the mule spinners, their wooden clogs – no hobnails allowed in here for fear of sparks – reinforcing the beat of the iron machines they tended.

The only thing out of rhythm was the staccato coughing of the women and children in attendance on these marvellous monsters of modern ingenuity. Throats dried within seconds of walking on to the spinning floor, and lungs breathed in the fine wool fibres flying off the machines like spider silk.

Even kerchiefs tied around mouths and noses couldn't keep the stuff out, and most didn't bother. For some, it filled their bellies, driving away the hunger pains, despite providing no sustenance.

Martha doubled over with the violence of her coughing fit. She had been drifting, standing with her mouth hanging open like an old clodhopper. Sarah grabbed hold of her and yanked, then pointed to forestall Martha's swinging hand; a verbal protest had no power in this place.

Instead, Martha mouthed, 'thank you', knowing Sarah would understand. Even the five-year-olds here could read lips.

The carriage of the spinning mule thumped into position at the end of its traverse, gears changed, and it trundled back to reunite with the rack of bobbins. Had Sarah not acted as she had, Martha would have gone with it, screaming at the top of her lungs and unheard.

Pull yourself together, lass, she scolded herself. *No point worrying unduly. What shall be, shall be.* She took a deep breath and immediately regretted it as another coughing fit racked her body. She clutched a protective hand to her belly, just in case, and her mind wandered back to her growing concern.

With her mam so poorly, and Harry's passed, there was no one at home to look after a bairn; all her sisters and Harry's were on this mill floor. She'd have to stop working and stay at home and they'd never manage without her few shillings a week.

Harry seemed not to be bothered, but Martha couldn't believe Mr Barraclough would up his wages by that much, even if he *was* a married man now. She'd have to see about doing some weaving, Old Dan Walker was struggling to grasp the shuttles now his fingers were so crooked. Maybe she could do the weaving and him take a cut for the use of his loom? The money wouldn't be as regular, but better than nowt.

Dan worked in the weaver's gallery over the row of cottages she lived in with Harry and his family. She could easily keep the bairn in a basket by her stool. No one would hear it cry over the noise of the looms, and the rhythmic whooshing of the shuttles soothed bairns. It would be perfect.

'What's going on?' Sarah's voice penetrated the ringing

in Martha's ears, and she startled back into the present. The machines weren't moving.

She'd never known the machines to still in the middle of a shift.

Martha met Sarah's eyes, wide with fright. Martha knew her own betrayed a similar emotion.

Bartholomew Grange, the overlooker, stood by the door, silent and unmoving. More confused now than scared, the women and children gathered together to hear the news. Whatever had happened was serious to bring the mill to a halt.

Baalzephon Rook, his son Zemeraim, and even the youngest, Jehdeiah – rarely seen on the mill floor – entered amidst the sound of shuffling feet and constant coughing. Now the overpowering noise had stopped, Martha noticed the smell for the first time: lanolin and grease; a sickly combination.

Suddenly she missed the unholy racket that had been the overwhelming signature of her days for as long as she could remember.

'Silence,' Grange roared, slapping his dreaded alley-strap, the one he liked to call 'The Dasher', against the door frame. It made a different sound against wood than skin, Martha mused. Even she could hear that.

The mass of shuffling wooden-soled clogs against wooden floorboards stilled, but not even the threat of the overlooker's leather paddle could silence the coughing.

The Rooks, at least, understood that and ignored it, despite Grange's scowl.

Baalzephon Rook stepped forward and cleared his throat against the fine wool fibres still dancing in the air. 'The king is dead,' he announced. 'His niece, Victoria, has taken the throne.' He just managed to utter the final word before a coughing fit overtook him.

'Long live the queen,' Zemeraim finished his father's speech.

Martha and the other spinners, piecers and mule rats stared at him in silence. A girl of eighteen their queen? No king? How could a young lass be their queen?

9.

'She's recovered quickly.' I indicated Hannah, who was chasing rabbits across the heather, squealing in delight as their white tails flashed.

'Resilience of youth,' Lara said.

I narrowed my eyes at her. 'Was she even ill or was it just an excuse so you could play Cupid?'

'Verity! How could you suggest such a thing? You really think I'd lie about my child being ill?'

I said nothing, but stared pointedly at Hannah, who was standing, hands on hips, searching for her next four-legged victim in her game of hoppity tag.

Lara sighed. 'It turns out I may have been a little over-cautious,' she allowed. 'But you can't be too careful – especially with kids. You just don't know what will be a temporary sniffle and what will knock them on their backs for a fortnight.'

'Well, thank goodness she's okay,' I said, and Lara grinned at me.

'So, are you going to tell me? What happened last night?'

I shot another glance at Hannah to make sure she was out of earshot, then returned Lara's grin.

'It was . . . interesting.'

'Interesting? In a Chinese curse kind of way or an, I met the man of my dreams kind of way?'

I laughed. 'I'm not sure – could be either, or both, I suppose.'

Lara grimaced, then brightened again. 'Come on, stop stalling, spill.'

'Well, after you interrupted our first kiss—'

'What? How did *I* interrupt anything?'

'When you rang to cancel dinner.'

'But that was early on! Are you telling me you were already snogging?'

'No. Well, not quite, but I think he was about to kiss me.'

'Fast mover,' Lara remarked. 'Or was something else going on?'

I quirked one corner of my mouth. 'Something else. All the hair on his arm was standing on end, and it was like we were being pulled together; caught in an energy tow or something.'

'An energy tow?'

'Yes, electricity was literally shooting through me and I couldn't step away from him. Even if I'd wanted to.'

'The arrows of love,' Lara whispered. 'So then what happened?'

'You rang and broke the spell.' I laughed. 'Then we finished the tour and talked about the pictures – he has some really good ideas, you know.'

'Yeah, yeah, get on with the juicy bits.'

I gave a snort of laughter, then pulled my expression into one of seriousness. 'And then we went out for dinner.'

'Thank God for that,' Lara said. 'Things aren't as serious as I thought. There's life in you yet!'

I gave her a playful shove, then grinned at her.

'And it looks like you lived very well,' she said.

I nodded. 'We just couldn't stop talking. Once the shock of seeing him wore off, it was like we'd known each other for years. Although I can't remember what we were talking about now!'

'Hmm. Both of you *did* look shocked when we walked into that gallery.'

'Yes, but it's weird, he's not quite the guy I've been dreaming about. He's older for a start.'

Lara shrugged. 'That doesn't mean very much, it could still be the same man.'

'No, there's something in his face – the jawline. It's subtle, but it's not the same.'

'Did you dream about him last night?'

'No, not really. He took me to the mill and left me there. It was frustrating actually – I couldn't get a proper look at him.'

'Mum, Auntie Verity, the waterfall's just up here.' Hannah grabbed the hands of both Lara and myself, and tugged us up the path to the Brontë Falls. I glanced to the side where the path fell away into a steep valley, and felt a touch of vertigo, but Hannah pulling my hand kept me steady and we allowed her to drag us along.

Sunshine had greeted us this morning and we'd come up Penistone Hill to make the most of a perfect winter's day. Blue skies contrasted with the grim brown moor, and pockets of frost lingered in the hollows. The wind was biting, but luckily not too strong, and was no match for the layers of cotton, fleece and Gore-Tex we all wore. Although Lara and Hannah – and no doubt myself – sported red noses; their eyes were bright and skin glowed with health and fresh air.

I reflected that this was the very land that the Brontës had loved so much and thought I could understand how it inspired such wild and dramatic novels in the young girls.

From where we stood, the moors stretched for miles over rolling hills, bare but for the hardy heather and the odd weather-battered tree or farm standing sentinel and providing the only shelter for the creatures that made their home here. I spotted a couple of farmhouses – in ruins now – and I wondered which one was Top Withens – the farm Emily had supposedly used for Wuthering Heights. Probably neither – that one would be further 'oop dale', I thought, coining the Yorkshire expression as I stared at the horizon: a dark, unbroken, unwavering line of hills against the blue.

'Just how much further is it, Hans?' Lara asked.

'Not far, just up past this big stone. Look, there they are!'

I stared at the small stream tumbling over little rocks and shrugged at Lara as she mouthed, *waterfall*?

The falls we had trekked to see were little more than a stream cascading through a cleft in the moor. Pretty and quite dramatic after the recent snows, the waterfall was not as large as I'd expected.

Lara perched herself on a nearby rock.

'Your throne, madam?' I asked.

'Just keeping an eye on things,' she said, watching her daughter, and swinging her feet to tap against the stone.

'Have you forgiven me yet for making you wear walking boots?'

Lara lifted her legs to regard her feet and frowned. 'I suppose I'd better get used to clodhoppers now you've moved to the country.'

I laughed then sobered as I thought about one of my early dreams – the bog burst – and remembered it had probably happened near here. I decided not to remind Lara about it.

'You didn't tell me how the evening ended,' Lara said. 'Did you . . .?' She left the question hanging.

I kept her in suspense a moment then shook my head. 'It was a close run thing, though.' I laughed, remembering my parting from William. We had stood, still talking, outside the Black Bull for an hour, neither of us wanting to separate, neither quite daring to take the next step so soon.

I was sure the bereft expression of regret on his face as I finally broke away from his arms, had been echoed on my own face.

'When are you seeing him again? Tonight?'

I shook my head, although the temptation had been almost unbearable. 'Tonight is for my girls.' I smiled. 'Jayne's back this evening, and I thought we could all try out the ghost tour.'

'And tomorrow?'

'Well, he did let slip he'd be in the Black Bull, but we really should make the most of New Year's Eve, don't you think? There's a torch-lit procession planned – all in Victorian fancy dress, it should be very atmospheric, and a bit different.'

Lara grinned. 'A torch-lit walk to the Black Bull it is then. I'm looking forward to it.'

'Hmm.'

'What's wrong?'

'Everything's just so . . . odd. And sudden. I don't know what to make of it all. The dreams, the orbs and birds at the house, the *ghost*. And now him. One minute I'm overjoyed, the next I'm terrified.'

'To be fair, that's normal for anybody falling for someone new.'

'Who said anything about falling for him?'

By way of reply, Lara arched her eyebrows.

'Well, okay, maybe I did give that impression, a bit,' I admitted.

'*Aren't* you falling for him?'

I looked at her, helpless, unable to deny it yet afraid to confirm it.

She jumped down from her stone throne and hugged me. 'It'll be okay, Verity. Just take your time, don't do anything before you're ready, be careful of your heart, but above all, enjoy it! The last year has been hell, you deserve a bit of fun, you deserve smiles and laughter; you deserve to love and be loved.'

'But what about all the weird stuff?'

'Well, if he's connected to the man you've been dreaming about, which he must be, somehow, then he's likely to be connected to the answers too. But I think you need to decide now – do you want to understand what it's all about?'

'Yes,' I said. 'If I don't, it'll drive me mad, and someone's likely to get hurt too.'

'Then we spend New Year's Eve, or at least part of it, at the Black Bull,' Lara said. 'And we travel this road wherever it takes us.'

'Jayne may not like that idea – what if it makes everything worse?'

Lara met my eyes, then said, 'That's a risk we have to take, Verity.'

'A risk *I* have to take, you mean.'

'No, I meant what I said. Jayne and I are in this with you, wherever it takes us.'

10.

'Aunt Jayne,' Hannah cried, waving madly before dashing to hug Jayne.

I smiled as Jayne's face lit up in an expression of pleasure I'd seen nobody but Hannah evince in her since her own son and daughter had left home. Hannah had been the one who had convinced her to join us this evening.

Escaping Hannah's clutches, Jayne greeted Lara and me, waiting patiently on the church steps.

'Auntie Verity's got a boyfriend,' Hannah announced before we'd barely had chance to say hello. 'He's going to paint my picture. And Mum wore walking boots without heels. All day!'

'Are you serious? I've been gone less than a week!'

'We've got a lot to tell you,' Lara said, then approached the gentleman dressed in top hat and tails to collect a couple of lanterns he was handing out.

Jayne squeezed my arm and looked at me. 'Verity?'

'Not now,' I said, nodding at the top-hatted man. 'The tour's about to start, we don't have time – I'll fill you in later. I could do with your advice.'

'Okay,' Jayne drawled. 'Are you all right?'

'I'm not sure, to be honest.'

'Ladies and gentlemen, boys and girls,' Top Hat said, forestalling all conversation for the moment. 'The ghosts of Haworth welcome you and invite you into their world.'

'Had enough of that already,' I hissed to Lara.

The man glared at me, then bade the small group across Main Street to Gauger's Croft.

I leaned against the stone wall of the narrow, covered passageway and relaxed as I listened to the man weave his story of inns and slums, horses and carriageways, ladies in full skirts dropping small curtseys in response to the lifted top hats of gentlemen's greetings.

I peered out at Main Street; it seemed to have grown darker, much darker, and I blinked when I realised the modern-day streetlamps – fashioned to resemble olde worlde gaslights – had disappeared. In their stead were the broad, dancing naked flames of pitch torches.

I gasped and clamped my hand over my mouth as I emerged on to Main Street to investigate further. The place stank. The underlying smell of burning pitch and coal fires added a singed accent to the overpowering stench of raw sewage and rot.

I lifted my foot to investigate what I had stood in, and realised the entire street was filth. The cobbles were gone and muck flowed down the steep hill.

I jumped backwards to avoid the two gentlemen about to walk into me, and shouted after them, but they did not acknowledge my presence.

Turning to Lara, my mouth dropped open. She was gone, as were Jayne, Hannah and the rest of the ghost tour group. They hadn't passed me, so they must have moved deeper into Gauger's Croft. I hurried after them and was again halted by the overpowering stench of sewage.

Houses were crammed together so tightly the air could barely circulate around them, and I did not want to think about the constituents of the stinking piles the dim torchlight revealed.

Midden heaps, I thought. *Those are midden heaps.*

Fear solidified into a twisted ball in my stomach and I

stepped back into the passageway then whirled around at the crack of a whip and a shout behind me.

A horse loomed above me, whinnying crazedly, and I screamed as the cart it pulled bore down on me.

White faces stared at me, and Jayne and Lara both put hands on my arms.

'Verity? Are you okay?'

'What happened?'

I gaped at the strange faces watching me with a mixture of curiosity and contempt, and apologised. 'It's nothing, I just got a bit carried away.'

The tour guide moved the group on, past the Black Bull, the King's Arms and the White Lion, but I barely listened, still spooked by the experience I'd had in Gauger's Croft.

It had seemed so real; the smell, or the memory of it, still stung my nose, and I had honestly believed I was about to be trampled.

Hannah's squeal brought me back to the tour, and I saw we were outside The Rookery. I was one of the stops on the ghost tour.

Flanked by Lara and Jayne, I listened in fascination as Top Hat described numerous sightings of the Grey Lady, painting a picture of exactly what I had seen, although there was no mention of orbs of light, or people being pushed.

'Auntie Verity's seen her, twice,' Hannah informed the tour guide. 'That's her house and she keeps seeing the ghost. Mum's seen her too, but I haven't, not yet. I've only fallen on the floor in that other place, the White Lion, that's the only ghost I've seen,' she continued, oblivious of Top Hat's irritation at this interruption to his narrative.

His eyes narrowed as he shifted his gaze to me and I nodded, then shrugged in apology. His expression grew thoughtful and he moved us on, introducing the 'witch's house' at the end of West Lane.

'I don't like it here, Mummy,' Hannah said. 'I feel funny, I want to go.'

'Shush, we'll be moving on in a minute,' Lara said. 'I want to hear the story about the witch.'

'But I don't like it,' Hannah cried. 'I *really* don't like it.'

'I'll take her back to the White Lion,' Jayne said, taking Hannah's hand. 'We'll have hot chocolate by the fire and wait for you there.'

'Okay, Aunt Jayne, let's go.' Hannah almost dragged Jayne away, casting an accusing glance back at her mother, and Lara met my eyes.

I couldn't decipher the expression in them, and wondered if she was feeling the same sensation I was: my chest tightening so much I was having to make a conscious effort to deflate and inflate my lungs for air.

Top Hat raised his voice as he came to the climax of his story – either that or he was just sick of the interruptions caused by me and my friends. I heard the words 'hanging from the rafters' and reached my limit. I glanced at Lara, who nodded, and we placed our lanterns on the low wall bordering the path, walked away from the tour, and hurried after Jayne and Hannah.

'Whatever that is in there, Pendle witch or not, it does not come from the light,' Lara said. 'That's a dark energy, thank God Jayne took Hannah away so quickly. I should never have brought her on this tour.'

I said nothing. I'd had enough of ghosts; I wanted hot chocolate by the fire with my friends.

II.

Martha glanced into the churchyard as she passed, able to see the site of the Sutcliffe grave where they had lain Baby John to rest before he had seen his first year out. She sighed at the memory of him, then turned her attention back to the living and stooped to pick up Edna – her little legs not quite up to the full walk to Harry's workshop. Mr Barraclough was handing more and more of the work to Harry these days, and he was fast gaining a reputation as a master stonemason in his own right.

Not surprising, all the work he does in that churchyard, Martha thought. Memorial stones had grown more intricate in latter years, the more successful families opting for altar stones rather than the more usual flat slabs laid directly on the ground, and were happy to pay for elaborate carvings to commemorate the passing of their loved ones.

Martha stopped in her tracks at the sound of voices rather than the regular percussion of hammer and chisel. *That's a woman's voice.*

She hefted Edna in her arms, and strode to confront her husband – the pail of bread and cheese she was bringing him for his dinner swinging, despite the coughing the exertion brought on.

Her expression hardened when she recognised the interloper's voice. Emily Brontë.

'It's a travesty,' she was saying, 'throwing Richard Oastler into The Fleet.'

'Aye,' Harry replied. 'It's nowt to do with debts, neither, that's just trumped up. It's to stop him acting against the mills.'

'They just don't know what to do with him – a Tory organising strikes!'

'That Thomas Thornhill has much to answer for – it's his doing, mark my words. Oh hello, love. Has tha brought me lunch?' Harry noticed Martha in the doorway.

'What's going on?' She put Edna down, who waddled over to her papa.

'They've arrested Richard Oastler, you know, The Factory King. Him who's against young 'uns working in the mills so much,' Harry explained.

'The Yorkshire Slavery he calls it,' Emily said. 'Have you read about him?'

'She don't read much,' Harry said. 'Worked in the mill since she were not much older than our Edna here. Never got to go to school.'

Emily nodded but said nothing more.

Martha added embarrassment to the cauldron of emotions boiling within her. She glared at Emily. 'Had to work for food,' she said, her voice strident. 'All of us did, couldn't swan off to no fancy school.'

Harry shot her a look of rebuke. Emily's two eldest sisters had died as a result of their time at Cowan Bridge School, something Martha knew well.

He noticed Emily's expression darken, and hurried to forestall Emily's words; trying to protect his wife from the wrath of his friend.

'Mr Oastler is for the Ten-Hour Movement,' he said, his voice unnaturally loud. 'No more getting out of bed at four and working till nightfall. And no young 'uns to be working in mill afore their tenth year.'

'But how will families manage?' Martha protested. How will they feed little 'uns without that wage?'

181

'Mills will have to pay a better living to them that do work,' Emily said.

'I can't see Rooks or any of t'other mill owners agreeing to that,' Harry said. 'Law or no law. They've paid no mind to the Factory Act, and that's been in place seven year now.'

'Aye, but there was no way of proving a child's age,' Emily argued. 'Nearly every child in the mills is "small for his age" or undernourished. Now the queen is forcing every birth to be registered, they'll not be able to get away with it no more, they'll have to prove their age with a certificate.'

'Aye, that's true enough, lass. Though for folks like my Martha here, there's not a lot of point to a certificate they can't read.'

Martha thumped Harry's lunch pail down and glared at him.

He cast his eyes down in apology, but Emily didn't seem to notice Martha's pique.

'But the authorities can read it. People like my papa write them out, and the mill owners will be kept in check. Things will come good.'

'I hope so, lass, I really do,' Harry said, then switched his attention to a safer subject by picking up his daughter to swing her round in a circle, confident Edna's giggles would soften Martha's mood.

He risked a glance at his wife, and grinned when he saw his ploy had worked.

I woke with a smile at the delightful sound of Edna's simple joy. Then realised where I was, alone in my new bed in The Rookery. My hand drifted to my stomach, a belly that had never expanded with new life, and I felt a sense of profound loss. Surprised and feeling a little shaken, I got out of bed to start the new day.

12.

'Wow, just look at that!' Lara exclaimed as Haworth Old Hall came into sight. Morris dancers were in full swing, their shin bells marking the steps of their dance as they wielded their sticks in minutely choreographed strikes.

Flames glanced off top hats and canes, breeks and clogs, bustles and bonnets, and I staggered as the tarry smell of the burning pitch hit my nostrils. For a moment I was back in Gauger's Croft, the horse and cart bearing down on me.

A tug on my arm brought me back to the here and now. 'What's that, Auntie Verity? Is that woman holding a dog? Why isn't it moving?'

I chuckled. 'No, it's a muff, Hans. It keeps the lady's hands warm.

Hannah looked thoughtful. 'Why doesn't she just wear gloves?'

'Back in Victorian times, ladies didn't wear big, thick gloves, only thin, dressy ones.'

'But it's like her hands are tied in front of her.'

'Not really, she can get her hands out easily.'

'Oh.'

'Welcome.' It was the man who had led the ghost tour. 'No scares tonight, hopefully,' he said as he recognised us. 'Just a walk back in time before we see the New Year in.' He held his flaming torch aloft. 'Lanterns are over there, and there's plenty of mulled wine left. Please help yourself, and we'll be setting off soon.'

'Can't we have a torch?' Hannah asked.

'No, 'fraid not. Only the organisers have those – health and safety.'

Ten minutes later, the procession of tourists and locals, all dressed in a sometimes curious mix of nineteenth-century fashion, began the climb up Main Street, the flickering torchlight reflecting off dark windows and wet slate lending an eerie atmosphere to the walk, despite the mulled wine and music, as Top Hat weaved his tales of the history of each building we passed.

The pace was slow, and slowed further the higher the cobbled street rose. The distant sound of a brass band urged us on, our feet trying to march in step to the deep beat of the tuba, although with little success, until we neared the church.

Rebuilt in 1879, the base of the tower and the crypt below were the only parts of this building that the Brontës would have known. The sandstone almost glowed in the light of half a dozen torches, and the Haworth Band was arranged on the steps and into the square at the top of Main Street with a full complement of tuba, trombones, and trumpets.

We paused to listen. There was something almost magical about the music in this atmosphere of biting cold, pitch torches, and centuries-old buildings. I could almost imagine the Brontës enjoying a similar spectacle, and wondered if they had even listened to the same tunes.

'Well, I've worked up a thirst now,' Jayne said, hitching up her skirts yet again after catching the heel of her ankle boots in her extravagant petticoats. I smiled, she'd been very quiet since Jenny had called to say she and her brother Michael had decided to go to Edinburgh's Hogmanay celebrations for New Year, and would call in to see her on their way back south.

'What those women went through,' Lara said, pulling at

her stays. 'Corsets *hurt* – and that's without the tonne of cotton silk and lace we're hauling about. Everything digs in and pinches, and *squeezes*. Who thought it would be a good idea to climb *that* hill in this lot?' She flared her skirts in a sulk.

'We'll be at the pub soon, then you can loosen up. Your corsets, I mean,' I added at Lara's glare and Jayne's laugh.

Lara gave a pretend swipe at my head with her palm, then giggled. 'I can't wait to get back into jeans. Even bras don't seem so bad anymore.'

'So,' Jayne said. 'Black Bull, King's Arms or White Lion?'

'Verity'll want the Black Bull,' Lara said.

'*William* will be there,' Hannah said, drawing the name out, then her face grew serious. 'Should I call him Uncle William?'

'No!' I said, too loudly, then, 'Sorry, Hans, I didn't mean to startle you. Just William is fine, he isn't your uncle.'

'But you're not really my aunt, and I still call you Auntie Verity.'

'That's because your mum and I have been such good friends for so long, we're sisters in all but blood. We've only just met William.'

'Oh.'

'So,' Jayne said, 'Black Bull, then?'

They moved in that direction, but I hung back.

'What's wrong?'

'Let's make tonight about us,' I said. 'No men, no ghosts, no dreams, no complications, just us. It's New Year's Eve – I want to celebrate with you, not William, or Harry, or whoever he is.'

Lara and Jayne walked back and linked arms with me.

'Verity, are you crying?'

I wiped awkwardly at my face, almost dislodging Lara's arm, surprised to find it wet.

'I-I—' My breath hitched in a sob.

'Verity, it's okay,' Lara soothed.

'I'm sorry.' I got a tenuous grip on myself. 'I don't know what just happened.'

'Don't worry about it, and there's nothing to apologise for,' Jayne said as Lara rubbed my back. 'You've had a lot going on. Getting divorced and moving house are two of the most stressful things you can do. Add to that starting your own business, the renovations, and the hauntings, I'm surprised you're not having a breakdown!'

'Oh, a breakdown sounds good,' I said, forcing a laugh. 'Can I go somewhere quiet and have a rest?'

Lara laughed. 'That's what a guesthouse is supposed to be about – quiet and rest!'

My chuckle was genuine this time. 'I suppose you have a point, but that tends to be the guests, not the proprietor.'

'You can always come and stay with us – anytime things get too much,' Lara said, and Jayne agreed.

'Vikram seems very capable, I'm sure he'd cope if you spent a few days with one of us,' she said.

'Thank you.' I gave them both a squeeze. 'Even the thought of it makes me feel better. Look, no tears!' I raised my face up and showed them first one cheek then the other. 'But I am ready for a large glass of something.'

Arm in arm, we crossed the road and made our way to the White Lion, only now realising Top Hat was standing nearby, awaiting the return of his lanterns.

13.

'Ah, that's better, loose corsets and wine,' Lara said, sinking down on to her seat, her skirts narrowly avoiding knocking drinks off three tables as she did so.

'Saucy,' I said. 'Careful, you'll give people the wrong impression.' I smiled at the family on the next table.

'Or the right one,' Jayne said, deadpan.

'I'll drink to that,' Lara said, unfazed, and lifted her glass. Giggling, Jayne and I joined in.

'Better?' Lara asked me.

I nodded. 'Things just got a bit much,' I said. 'Plus it's New Year's Eve, and that always gets me – especially this year with the divorce and everything.'

'Yes, it's definitely been a year of big changes,' Jayne said. 'But you're moving forward positively. New home, new business, new man . . .' She raised her eyebrows and smirked.

'Ghosts, spooks and nightmares.' I aped her expression.

'We'll fix all that,' Lara said. 'It's only frightening at the moment because we don't understand what's going on. But don't forget, the cleansing and protection I did doesn't work.'

'You say that as if it's a good thing,' Jayne said, eyebrows raised.

'It is,' Lara insisted. 'It means the spirits, whatever or whoever they are, mean no harm.'

'Is that why one tried to push me down the stairs?' Jayne shot back. 'Or destroyed Verity's kitchen and sent Antony running.'

'Maybe that was the point – getting rid of Antony,' Lara said. 'Protecting Verity.'

'And me? Does Verity need protecting from me, too?'

'Of course not. What was going on when it happened though?'

Jayne paused, then a strange look crept across her face. I remembered at the same time.

'We were talking about my dream man. Don't you remember, Jayne? You were wondering if he was Heathcliff, and warned me off dysfunctional men.'

'That's interesting,' Lara said.

'Enough,' I said, forestalling Jayne's reply. 'Sorry, but can we just have a break from it all tonight, please?'

Lara nodded as Hannah climbed on to her lap. She stroked her daughter's hair as Hannah's thumb found its way into its owner's mouth. 'Are you sure you don't want to go to bed, Hans?'

She shook her head.

'She's determined to stay up till midnight,' Lara said with a smile. 'First time ever.'

'Sunday tomorrow,' Jayne said. 'We can all have a lie in and a quiet day.'

'Actually, I wondered if it would be a good idea to go to church tomorrow.'

'Church?' I repeated.

Lara shrugged. 'Can't do any harm, and a bit of prayer may help.'

'I'm willing to try anything at the moment,' I said.

'Talking of willing,' Jayne said, indicating the door behind me. 'I didn't know they were friends.'

I turned to see William and Vikram standing at the door looking awkwardly around the room.

'I almost didn't recognise him,' Lara whispered, and I pulled my eyes away from William's to consider Vikram. He looked more the artist than William did, and without a trace of builder. His chunky black collared sweater hugged his body and suited him almost as much as his black flat cap and dark-rimmed glasses. I smiled; Lara and Jayne would be fighting over him before the year was out.

My eyes slid back to William. He hadn't made as much effort as Vikram, but was simply dressed in a white, open-necked shirt and jeans. The ensemble set off his dark eyes perfectly, and his freshly shaved jaw took years off him.

Thank goodness he hasn't got dressed up, I thought, shifting uncomfortably in my Victorian-style gown, *I'd have thought him to be Harry.*

Vikram led the way to our table, but before the greetings were completed, William escaped to the bar and I stared after him, my heart beating hard, then glanced at Vikram in consternation.

Vikram shrugged and looked embarrassed. 'I hope you don't mind.'

'Of course not, it's good to see a friendly face,' Jayne said. 'Why don't you sit down, join us?'

We shuffled round and Vikram squeezed in on the bench next to Jayne.

'Happy New Year,' I said to him, draining my glass. 'I'm surprised to see you here, I just expected tourists – I thought you'd be going up to town.'

'No, it gets too much – full of teenagers falling over,' he said. 'I'd rather just go down the pub with my mates.'

'I didn't realise you and William knew each other.'

He gave me a funny look. 'Known him since I were a lad. I didn't know *you* knew him.'

I opened my mouth then closed it again. Why had I said that? Vikram was right, *I* was the incomer here. *I* was the one who didn't know anybody in Haworth, who had no ties here.

William plonked a couple of pints of bitter on the table, then left again, all without saying a word.

I glanced at Jayne and Lara, who asked Vikram, 'Is he always so friendly?'

Vikram smiled and sipped his beer. 'He's Yorkshire. Tends to keep himself to himself, but he'll speak when he has summat to say. Then you won't shut him up.' He replaced his pint glass on the table and looked thoughtful. 'He has been a bit out of sorts, though, lately. He was gutted when you didn't show up at the Bull, Verity.' He winked then jumped as a bottle of Sauvignon blanc was slammed on to the table.

William glared at his mate, then turned to me and said, 'Tess behind the bar says this is the one you're all drinking.'

'Th-thanks, yes,' I stammered, and shifted on my seat to make more room.

Jayne coughed and I realised she hadn't met him yet.

'This is Jayne,' I said with a hand flourish. 'And this is William.' I flourished my other hand.

'He's the painting man,' Hannah said, proving she was still determined to stay awake. 'Auntie Verity's boyfriend.'

William spluttered into his beer and I shut my eyes for a moment then busied myself pouring wine, unsure what to do or say, and unable to look at him.

Lara came to my rescue. 'I think it's a bit soon to be saying that, Hans.'

I gulped my wine, still not daring to look at William, yet very aware of him squashed up beside me.

'Yes, the rule is three dates,' William told Hannah, his voice serious, and Jayne nudged my leg on my other side. 'You're not boyfriend and girlfriend before three dates.'

'And by then you'll know whether or not you want to be,' Vikram added, laughing, then leaned towards Jayne and muttered something I couldn't hear.

'Oh, I see,' Hannah said and paused. 'Is this a date?'

'This is just friends meeting up to celebrate a new year,' Lara said.

'So what would make it a date then?'

'I'll tell you later,' Lara said, 'in private.'

'Ah, kissing,' Hannah said, stuck her thumb back in her mouth and wriggled on Lara's lap until she was comfortable again.

'How did you enjoy the procession?' Vikram asked, covering Lara's shocked silence, Jayne's poorly stifled giggles, and the matching blush on William's face and my own. 'Looks like you went to a lot of trouble.'

'You didn't fancy the Bull then?' William spoke softly in my ear as the others discussed the merits of various items of Victorian dress.

'I'm sorry, it was rude of me to stand you up.'

'So why did you?'

I sipped my wine, then looked up at him. 'Everything's just been so full on lately, then with all the brass band stuff, the Bull was heaving, I just felt overwhelmed. I guess I needed a quiet evening with the girls. I'm sorry, it was a last minute decision.'

'You don't need to apologise,' he said. 'Are you okay with us being here? Do you want us to go?'

'No,' I said, a little louder than I'd intended. 'No, it's good to see you, I'm enjoying this.'

'Not too full on?' he teased.

I said nothing, my mind whirling.

'I know what you mean, though,' he added. 'Something's going on here – it has me a bit, well, freaked too.'

'Freaked?' I raised an eyebrow then put my hand on his knee before I realised I'd done so. I moved to hold my wine with both hands. 'Sorry. Yes, freaked is a good word.'

He leaned towards me at the same time as I turned to him.

'Ow,' he said, holding his nose as I rubbed my temple.

'The fireworks are starting!' Hannah shouted,

scrambling off her mother's knee, and I looked round in surprise to see the bar was almost empty.

'Blimey, is that the time?' Jayne said, echoing my own thoughts and we grabbed drinks and shawls, then hurried outside.

Fully aware of William standing next to me, I did my best to ignore him. I couldn't decide whether I wanted to engage him in intelligent conversation, or tell him to leave me alone, so instead I oohed and ahhed with everyone else at the white, green and red flowers depicted in the skies above Haworth Moor.

'Ten, nine, eight, seven . . .'

My breath froze as I realised what the chant meant. What it was leading up to. It had been so long since I'd enjoyed a New Year's Eve celebration as a single woman, I'd forgotten about the pressure.

My heart beat faster and I could feel the warmth spread over my chest and head.

'Four, three . . .'

'Verity?'

'Umm?' It was all I could manage, and I risked a glance upwards, just as an almighty barrage of rockets, Roman candles and mines put everything that had gone before to shame.

His lips were on mine before I registered he'd leant in, and the scratch of his new stubble tickled my jaw.

That's really going to irritate my skin, I thought, before sensation took over doubt, fear and sense.

I kissed him back, my tongue meeting his, teasing, playing, exploring. My lips allowed him to lead the dance and my misgivings melted away – at least for the moment.

We parted with a gasp, both of us short of breath, and my flush deepened at the stares of Jayne, Lara, Hannah and Vikram.

14.

'Let us confess our sins in penitence and faith,' the vicar of St Michael and All Angels intoned.

'Verity!' Lara nudged me and passed me a packet of tissues.

I gave her a puzzled glance.

'Your nose,' she hissed.

'Live in love and peace with all.'

I put my fingers to my face. They came away bloody. I fumbled a tissue out and held it to my nose – just in time as blood gushed from me.

'Head back,' Jayne whispered, then smiled reassuringly at the woman in the pew in front of us who'd turned to see what was going on. I kept my head bowed, not wanting to swallow the blood.

'Lord, have mercy.'

Lord have mercy, indeed, I thought, echoing the vicar's words. *Why now?* I had suffered from regular nosebleeds in the early days of my breakup with Antony, but I hadn't had one for months now. Until today.

'Keep it back,' Jayne insisted, passing me a fresh tissue.

I glared at her, but this was not the time to debate the correct head position during nosebleeds.

The congregation stood to sing a hymn, and I risked moving the tissue away. A mistake.

'I need to go,' I said as best I could.

'You take her, Lara,' Jayne said.

'You're not coming?'

'No, I'd like to stay. Unless you need me, Verity?'

'No.' It came out more like 'doe'. 'I'll be okay. You stay too, Lara.'

'I'm coming,' Lara said in a tone of voice I knew not to argue with. 'But we'd better hurry.'

Jayne slipped out of the pew to let us out and I hurried out the door, closely followed by Lara and Hannah, grateful we'd chosen a pew at the back.

'Why was that lady staring at us?' Hannah asked. 'Couldn't she see Auntie Verity had a nose bleed?'

'Probably thinks I did something to deserve it or there's something wrong with me,' I said dryly, 'and shouldn't set foot in a church.'

'Stop that right now, Verity,' Lara said. 'It's a nosebleed, nothing more, nothing less.'

I handed her the packet of tissues to extract another for me, then placed the fresh tissue to my nose.

'I think it's getting better, Auntie Verity.'

'Yes, it's definitely slowing,' Lara added. 'Come on, let's get you home and cleaned up.'

'Jayne's taking her time,' Lara said as she handed me a mug of coffee and took away the now-melted bag of peas to replace them in the freezer.

'Umm,' I said. 'She's up to something.'

Lara shrugged, sat beside me, and sipped her coffee. 'How are you feeling?'

I brushed my fingertip under my nose, and gave it a quick check. Clean. 'It's stopped.' I touched the tip of my nose and winced. 'All a bit sore, though.'

'You've got a red nose, like a clown, Auntie Verity,' Hannah informed me.

Lara laughed, which somewhat negated the impact of her, 'Don't be rude, Hans.'

She recovered herself and touched my arm. 'It's just the frozen peas, Verity.'

I smiled. I knew well what I must look like, and doubted Hannah was far wrong. I pulled a face at her, immediately regretting the nose scrunch, but the laughter was worth it.

'I think I'll just go and change,' I said, tugging my top to show off the blood drips, but was stopped by Grasper's frenzied barking.

'Aunt Jayne's back,' Hannah announced from the window. 'She's got the vicar with her, he's still wearing his dress.'

'Cassock,' Lara corrected as she joined her daughter at the window and peered below. 'Looks like you were right – she *is* up to something.'

'Well, that was a waste of time,' Lara said as we found a free table.

'Couldn't hurt to try,' Jayne said. 'Do you both want wine, shall I get a bottle?'

'Coke, please, Aunt Jayne.'

'Apple juice or water for you, miss,' Lara corrected.

'Apple juice.' Hannah pouted then added, 'Please,' at her mother's raised eyebrow.

We sorted menus while Jayne went to the bar.

'It was a good idea, Jayne,' I said when she returned. 'Thanks. Though I'm surprised you persuaded the vicar to come straight over after the service.'

'He said it's not the first time someone's had a spontaneous nosebleed in his church,' Jayne said. 'And if you were that stressed, the least he could do was come round as soon as the congregation had left.'

'He probably wanted a look-see at what you're doing to the place,' Lara said. 'You know what these villages are like, everyone wants to know everybody else's business.'

'Probably,' I said with a laugh. 'Either that or he was looking for the Grey Lady.'

'Behave,' Jayne said. 'It was good of him to give up his time to bless the house – it's his busy day, you know.'

We all laughed then, the tension broken. Truth be told, I had found the blessing comforting – and very similar to Lara's cleansings. I couldn't quite understand why she was being so sarcastic and resistant. I shrugged; maybe she just wanted to be the one to solve the issue.

'What's up?' Jayne asked.

'Nothing, just trying to make sense of the last few days,' I said.

'Are the dreams back?' Lara asked.

'No.' I blushed. 'I couldn't sleep last night – not a wink.'

'Ah, thinking about William,' Jayne teased.

My blush deepened.

'You're one to talk, Jayne, did you dream about Vikram, or did he keep you up all night too?'

'What?' I stared at Jayne, whose blush was in competition with mine. She was the scarlet of a hunting jacket.

'Yes, Vikram and our Jayne at midnight,' Lara said. 'Giving you and William a run for your money – I had to cover Hannah's eyes.'

'No, I saw them.'

'Oh, thank goodness,' Jayne said as Tess approached with our wine. 'I need a bloody drink.'

'Roast beef and Yorkshire puddings all round, please,' Lara said to Tess. Then, to us, 'What?'

'We might have wanted something else!'

'Tough – it's a Yorkshire roast for you while you both fill me in on your men. And be aware of young ears!'

15.

Deep breath. You can do this, I thought, then reached out and pushed my way through the inner door to the Black Bull.

I paused, self-conscious, my eyes scanning the interior, trying to check each nook and cranny without appearing too obvious.

Then I saw him. Hand raised. Smiling. At the bar. Waiting for me. William Sutcliffe.

The worry that he wouldn't be here, and the fear that he would be, coalesced, but now the churning in my stomach was infused with warmth. He was here, and I was here. Everything else – caution, memories, Antony, my dreams – hadn't been powerful enough to keep me away. Whatever the evening would bring, I was here; he was here.

I realised I was still standing near the entrance, blushed, smiled, and walked towards him.

'Hi, I was worried you were going to stand me up again.'

My heart leapt into my mouth, and I realised I'd made a mistake. 'You weren't expecting me to turn up? You didn't mean it?'

'Oh,' he held the flat of his hand out to me, 'no, that's not what I meant. I was just trying to make a joke.'

'Oh,' I said, 'I see.' I was lost. Was this a date or wasn't it?

'Shall we start again?' He grinned, and my heart leapt again, this time more pleasantly, at the lopsided smile and resultant dimple in his right cheek. I nodded.

'Hello Verity, it's good to see you.' The dimple deepened. 'Would you like a drink?'

'Yes please, a large one.' I found myself wishing for dimples in my own cheeks to match his.

'That bad is it?'

'Getting better.'

Deeper still. A pause, then a quirk of his eyebrow.

'What's wrong?'

'*What* would you like to drink?'

'Oh, yes. Umm, dry white wine please.'

He ordered it, plus another pint of Black Sheep for himself. 'Haven't done this for a while.'

'No, I'm a bit out of practice.'

'I meant me.'

'Oh.'

'Shall we sit down?'

'I think we'd better.'

We found a seat in the corner by one of the lopsided leaded windows, and looked at each other in silence for a few moments.

'Shall we start again?'

'Okay.'

We laughed then, the awkwardness dissipating in the absurdity of the situation. A couple of nights ago, we'd been in each other's arms at the birth of a new year, a couple of nights before that we'd hardly been able to stem the words; now we seemed incapable of conversation.

'It's good to see you,' William said.

'You too. Cheers.' I held my glass up to clink, then we drank, our eyes locked on each other.

I realised he was younger than I'd originally thought – probably mid-thirties rather than early forties. His face was tanned, but what I'd taken for wrinkles, I now saw were pale lines – crease lines, I realised. He must spend a lot of time outdoors, squinting into the sun.

'You've shaved,' I said, out loud, then gasped and clamped my hand over my mouth.

'Well, I am on a date,' he said dryly, his eyebrows raised. 'Though it's a damn strange one so far.'

'Sorry, I'm out of practice,' I reaffirmed.

'Good.'

I took another drink, cursing myself for injecting discomfort back into the evening.

'It looks good.'

'What does?'

For answer, I stroked my chin, though in truth it wasn't a good look on him, the skin of his jaw was two shades paler than the rest of his face.

'Thanks.'

'Have you ever grown a beard?'

He shrugged. 'Once or twice, but it comes in grey and is a bugger to trim. Easier to shave it off.'

I nodded and sipped my drink again. *Why on earth am I quizzing him about his shaving habits? How would I like it if he asked me about mine?*

'Should get rid of these really, too,' he continued, running his fingers through his sideburns. I realised he was just as nervous as I was, and glad to have something – anything – to talk about. 'Rebekah won't let me though, insists they make me look distinguished.' He wobbled his head in mockery with the last word.

'Rebekah?'

'My sister.'

Relieved, I said, 'She's right, they suit you – give you a certain . . . gravitas.'

'Gravitas?'

I shrugged. 'When the word fits.'

'I'll tell Rebekah that next time she comes to cut my hair.' The dimple reappeared.

'Is she a hairdresser?'

'No, a historian.'

I laughed. 'And the sideburns now make perfect sense!'

We clinked glasses again.

'So how is The Rookery coming on?'

'On schedule so far – thanks to Vikram,' I replied and surreptitiously tapped the wooden table three times. I noticed William watch my fingers, but he didn't remark on the habit. He definitely had better manners than I did.

'Aye, he's a good man is our Vikram. He's very taken with your mate, you know.'

'Jayne? Yes, I heard they got close on New Year's Eve.'

Silence fell again as our eyes met, both embarrassed as we remembered how we'd 'got close' at the same time, and I wondered if he felt the same tingle of excitement I did.

'So, Sutcliffe,' I said, 'no relation to Peter?'

He groaned. 'Why do women always ask me that? No, I'm no relation to the Yorkshire Ripper. Another wine?' He got up without waiting for a response and went to the bar.

When he returned, I thanked him for the drink and apologised.

'No, it's fine, it's a fair question. The man terrorised the area – I can remember my sister being banned from going out alone, most lasses were – thank God he's rotting in Broadmoor or wherever they moved him to. I just hate that we share a surname, does me no good on dates.'

I smiled at the sight of his dimple.

'Tell me about your family,' he said. 'Why did you choose Haworth?'

'Well, I got divorced about a year ago – the details have only just been finalised.'

'So you're starting over?'

'Exactly.'

'Why here?'

'My dad was from Keighley, we used to come here at weekends when I was a child – this place holds my happiest memories – in fact, my dad's family may have originated here, they definitely worked in the local mills.'

'Have you never looked into it, ancestry.com and all that?'

'Have you tried sticking "Earnshaw" and "Yorkshire" into any search engine? There are millions of hits thanks to *Wuthering Heights*.'

'Yes, I can see that would be a problem.' He smiled. 'Maybe Emily based Catherine on one of your ancestors.'

'God, I hope not!'

16.

'Your turn,' I said when I rejoined him, fresh drinks in hand. 'Have you always lived in Haworth?'

'Born and bred,' he said, his pride evident in the smug cast of his smile – no dimple. 'Apart from three years at art school. This is my home – I hated being away, and I can't imagine living anywhere else. We can trace the family back here over three hundred years. I love the moors, the people, the way of life here, both past and present. I just have to paint it, all of it.'

'Wow, so you're not an adventurous breed then?'

I cringed, wondering if I'd been inappropriate again, but he continued without a flinch.

'My grandda and his before him, and his before him, were stonemasons – carved most of the stones in the churchyard they did, and built most of the houses of their time.'

I felt cold and faint headed, but if I'd paled as well, he didn't notice.

'The business struggled when they stopped burying people in the churchyard.'

'Why did they stop?'

'Overcrowding, and the stones were laid flat, so the gases and rot from decomposition were trapped in the ground. Some of those graves are twelve corpses deep, and there's no spaces between them. Supposed to stop in the 1850s they were, after the Babbage Report pretty much condemned the village. But nobody took much notice –

folk want to be with their folk, it takes a lot to come between family in these parts.'

I nodded. 'Who was Babbage?'

'An inspector in the 1850s from the General Board of Health – Patrick Brontë had him come out, actually, the sisters' father. Anyways, the living conditions here were atrocious: life expectancy early-twenties; at least one funeral every day; over two thousand people sharing four wells and twenty five privies. Not good.' He shuddered, and I joined him.

'One of the wells was out back here by the graveyard, and another next to the morgue, where the Tourist Information is now. Can you imagine? Even the cows wouldn't drink from it, folk had no chance. Anyroad, things started improving after he came, and eventually they stopped digging graves.'

'Not before time, by the sounds of it.'

'But it meant no one needed new headstones. I think it was a blessing really when the museum people bought the parsonage – they knocked down the old mason's workshop to make room for the car park.'

'That must have been difficult for your family,' I said. 'The stonemason's workshop would have been a big part of Haworth's history, especially with it having been so close to the parsonage.'

'Aye, just not the sort of history that brings in the tourists,' William said with a smile – dimple evident this time – and took a long drink.

'Anyway, they didn't do too badly from the sale of the land, enough to set the family up in other businesses. My father had the shop on Main Street – shoemakers it was in his day, then when he retired, I took it over and reopened as an art gallery.'

'What did he think to that?'

'Not a lot,' William admitted, 'but he's starting to come round now.'

'How long have you been open?'

'About ten years.'

I laughed. 'And he's just starting to come round to the idea?'

William shrugged. 'Yorkshire folk don't like change. Things are best done the way they've always been done.'

I raised my eyebrows and pouted. I had plenty of memories of my dad saying exactly the same thing.

'I didn't have it as bad as Rebekah, though. You should have heard my dad when she told him she was going to university to read history. Well, most of the village did hear him!' He laughed, but with no mirth, and took another drink.

'Still complains to this day, though we're both making good livings. Not sure he means it now, though, just does it to keep up his curmudgeonly reputation.'

I giggled. 'He sounds like quite a character.'

'Oh aye, that he is, right enough. Just beware when you meet him, he'll have all sorts to say about you opening yet another guesthouse.'

'When I meet him?'

'Aye, well.' He coloured. 'Bound to before long, living here.'

The bell behind the bar rang, and William jerked his head round to stare at the barman.

'Bloody hell, last orders already? Can't be.'

I checked the time on my watch. 'Eleven,' I said. 'Funny, living in Leeds, I haven't heard a last orders' bell in years. Everywhere just stays open.'

'Aye, well, you're in the country now. Things are done the way they always were,' William said. 'And we forgot to eat! Everywhere will be closed now too, dammit.'

'Not to worry, let's get a last round in, then we can go

back to mine – I should be able to rustle up an omelette or something.'

'You sure?'

'Yes, but I'm only offering food, mind, it *is* only a second date.'

We smiled at each other, eyes locked together, then William pulled away at the shout of 'Last orders, please!' from the bar.

'Blimey, what's going on?' William ducked as a couple of birds swooped at us.

'Oh yes, they seem to like roosting here – it turns out calling it The Rookery is very apt!'

William looked up at the gable and windows of The Rookery. 'They never used to roost here before.'

'Really? They've been bothering me since I moved in. I'm sure there are more of them every day.' I gave a nervous laugh and found the keyhole with my still unfamiliar key.

'I've only ever known them roost in the churchyard,' William said. 'My sister used to tell me they were the souls of all the babies buried there. Scared the life out of me, she did – I couldn't go near the place for years.'

'She sounds lovely!' I laughed.

'Aye, but she's also a big sister – had to have her fun with me.'

I switched the lights on and led the way to the stairs. 'The only working kitchen at the moment is the one upstairs, I'm afraid.'

'Vikram's still got a lot to do, hasn't he?'

'Yes, but there's time. They're doing well, actually, on schedule so far, despite the holiday season.'

'That doesn't sound like him – mind you, I guess he's only just started.' William laughed, then realised what he'd said when I turned to him.

'What do you mean? Should I be worried?'

'No, no, not at all. Sorry, me and my big mouth. He's one of the good ones is Vikram, we were at school together. When he does a job, he does it proper – even if it takes him a bit longer. He'll see you right, don't worry about it.'

I nodded, mollified, and led the way up the narrow staircases.

'So why didn't you come to the Black Bull on Saturday – the real reason?'

I didn't turn. I couldn't look at him. 'I-I'm sorry. I shouldn't have stood you up like that. I've taken so much on with The Rookery, and especially after all the stuff with the divorce, it just seemed too much. And Hannah was with us, too, of course.' I paused. 'I'm glad you and Vikram came to the White Lion, though.'

'Yes, me too. I wasn't sure if you'd turn up tonight.'

I giggled. 'I couldn't do that to you again. Anyway, I enjoyed New Year's Eve.' Now I did turn, smiled, and led the way to my apartment.

I opened the fridge. 'Wine or lager?'

'No bitter?'

'None I'm afraid.'

'Guess I'll have to make do with lager then.'

I glanced at him, ready to apologise, but relaxed when I saw his dimple, and passed him a bottle of Becks. I poured myself a glass of wine, then regarded the fridge once more.

'Well, it looks like cheese omelette – that do you?'

'Cheese? At this time of night? You'll give us nightmares.'

'To be honest, it doesn't seem to take cheese to have strange dreams at the moment, I've been having them since I moved in.' I glanced at him, then away again as I put eggs and cheese on the worktop.

'Strange dreams?'

'Hmm.'

'Verity?'

I turned and looked at him properly.

'I've been having strange dreams too,' he said.

'Really? I bet mine are stranger!'

He grinned. 'I've been dreaming about you.'

'What?'

'I've been dreaming about you, for a couple of weeks now. Then you walked into my gallery and I felt pretty much how you look right now. Come and sit down.'

He took my arm and led me to the sofa. A loud crash made me scream and my glass fell, smashing and drenching the floor with Pinot Grigio. 'What the hell was that?'

William left me at the sofa and rushed to the window. 'One of the birds,' he said. 'Must have been mesmerised by the light. I'm afraid it's cracked the window. More work for Vikram.'

'Is it dead?'

'Unlikely. It landed on the tiles, probably just stunned. Best thing is to leave it to sort itself out if it can.'

'And if not?'

He shrugged. 'Nowt we can do. Why did you look so shocked when I told you I'd been dreaming about you? It sounds like a corny pick-up line, I expected you to laugh.'

'Get me a new glass of wine, and I'll tell you.'

17.

'Tha romantic devil!' Martha exclaimed as Harry presented her with a bouquet.

'Well, three years to the day since we were wed,' he said. 'Look, I got gorse, garlic, pussy willow.'

'And the honeysuckle too – the same as my bridal flowers!' Martha held the blooms to her nose and breathed the scent in. She could just make out the delicate scent of the honeysuckle under the more powerful wild garlic.

'Lizzie's happy to have Edna, one more don't make no difference to her now.'

'What, all day?' Harry's sole surviving sister was not normally so free with offers of help.

'Aye, well, special occasion, ain't it?'

'Tha's paid her, ain't thee, Harry?'

He shrugged. 'Special occasion,' he repeated. 'And we're doing all right. I've plenty of work on, and there'll be no let up, not with the smallpox rife. We can afford it, love. Relax and stop worrying, at least for today.'

Martha did as she was bid and leaned her head on her husband's shoulder for a moment. 'So what does tha have in mind?'

'Get out of this village, for one. I've bread and cheese,' he kicked the pail by his feet, 'and a couple of bottles of porter—'

'Tha *is* splashing out!'

Harry raised his eyebrows at her and she stilled her protest.

'I thought we could go up to Harden Woods, it'll be pretty there, the bluebells might be out, too.'

'That sounds lovely.' Martha smiled at her husband and kissed him full on the lips.

'Hang about, woman. We're in public! Plenty of time for all that later.' He grinned and smacked Martha's rump, enjoying the sound of her resultant squeal. He hadn't heard that mock-protest in a very long time.

Harry dropped the pail of food and beer, grabbed Martha – to another squeal – and spun her around in much the same way he did with Edna, then kissed her. Not like the way he did Edna.

He pulled Martha to him as she responded, their bodies reacting to each other in the way they used to. It had been some months since they had shared more than a discreet fumble in a room full of sleeping bodies, and both wanted to take their fill of each other.

Martha pulled back and smiled at Harry, brushing away the hair that flopped over his eyes, then stroked his whiskers.

'Tha's looking very distinguished these days,' she said.

'Well, I'm a master mason now. Folk expect a bit of distinguishment.'

Martha giggled. 'Is that even a word?'

'Don't know, I'll have to ask Emily.' He could have bitten his tongue. Of all the stupid things to do – mention Emily Brontë to his wife.

He didn't understand Martha's antipathy towards her, apart from the usual wary regard most of the village folk had for Emily. But with Martha it was something different, something more.

'She'll likely not know either,' he added in an attempt to undo the harm. He kissed his wife again, melting her heart towards him once more, and grabbed her rump to pull her close.

He was rewarded with another squeal and he hooked her legs, bent her body, and landed her on the ground with a thump. He got slightly more than a squeal for that, but there was no real sting in her slap.

He straddled her and gazed down at his wife of three years. *Why can she not accept that I love her and no other?*

Along with the grief of losing their firstborn, John, that was his only sorrow, knowing that she had no real faith in him. God knew, he had done nothing to deserve her distrust; had always been true to her, unlike many of his peers. But nothing would persuade her of his fidelity and loyalty.

He pushed the thoughts away and smiled down at Martha. Today may well help in that regard.

'You're as pretty as a picture,' he said, and meant it. Her flaxen curls framed her face, and she was surrounded by the greenest grass which brought out the little flecks of green in her otherwise blue eyes, a similar hue to the bluebells which nodded their trumpet heads in the April breeze.

The smile he was granted warmed his heart and he bent his lips to worship it.

I woke, blinked and groaned. I tried to move my arm to grasp my aching head, but it was trapped. I shifted and tried to roll, then realised my body was not the restraint.

Wide awake now, I scrambled to a sitting position, throwing away William's embrace and startling him to wakefulness.

'What the hell?'

I stared at him, stricken, then relaxed in the warmth of

his smile and the slow realisation that he was still dressed. I glanced down. So was I.

Thank God.

William wiped his face with his hands, then seemed to be brushing something away. He looked at his hands, bemused, then turned his gaze back to me and shrugged. 'Felt like cobwebs, but there's nothing there, must be the remnants of a dream.'

'Cobwebs?'

He smiled and showed his hands. 'No. Nothing there. Good morning.'

I relaxed a little more. 'Morning.' I smiled, shy. I had not woken up with a man since Antony. It had been a long time since I had been so intimate, even if we were still fully clothed.

Slowly, the events of the evening before materialised in my memory. The rook striking the window and cracking it, the draught, the cold. Me freaking out, knowing those birds were just outside that broken pane of glass.

We'd made omelettes so quickly we could qualify for the Saturday morning omelette challenge, scarfed them down, then brought the rest of the alcohol into the bedroom, closing the door on the cracked window.

Then we'd talked.

And talked, and talked.

I'd fallen asleep in William's arms and, thinking back now, hadn't felt so safe for a very long time.

Then I'd panicked when I'd woken in those same arms.

Ashamed, I cuddled up to him. 'I had the strangest dream.' I blushed, remembering the bluebell wood.

He gave a humourless laugh. 'I'm not surprised, with everything that's been going on, I had a weird one too. Very interesting it was.' Our eyes met, and I saw he was as embarrassed as I was.

As one, we reached for each other and kissed. Lips soft against mine, tongue gently exploring, his breath feathering my cheek. My heart thumped then settled into a faster rhythm and I could feel his matching mine.

My hands moved down his arms as his crept down my back and cupped my waist as I reached his hips.

Then we broke apart – together – and rested our heads on each other's shoulders, panting hard.

Again as one, we sat up straight and found each other's eyes.

'I can't quite believe I'm saying this—'

'But I need to wait,' I interrupted.

William nodded. 'This is something – I mean *really* something. I don't want to rush it or get it wrong. I want to do things right.'

'Me too,' I whispered. 'These old-fashioned values are quite romantic, really,' I said with a smile, brushing my thumb over his lips.

'Hmm. Not quite sure when I adopted them, though.' He laughed.

'Nor me.' I lowered my face with a smile and glanced up at him through my lashes. 'Coffee?'

18.

I opened my front door the following Friday evening, and flung it wide to usher in Lara and Jayne. I cast a suspicious glance upwards, but the rooks were no threat.

Today, at least.

We hugged, then I stood back and saw a glance pass between Lara and Jayne.

'What?'

'It's just good to see you,' Lara said.

'We haven't heard much from you the past week,' Jayne said with a sidelong glance at Lara. 'We've been worried.'

'Worried?' I scoffed. 'I'm fine, better than fine, I'm in love!'

'Already?' Jayne asked.

I glared at her.

'A week ago you were avoiding William,' Lara pointed out. 'Now he seems to have taken you over. We're concerned, that's all.'

'Yes, you've been through a lot lately, we just want to be sure that life is being kind to you now – for as long as possible.' Jayne smiled.

I hesitated before answering, then relaxed. 'It is, it *is* being kind. William is amazing. I'm so sorry I've been quiet all week, truly I am.' I smiled and held my arms out to embrace my friends once more. The hug was slightly awkward, but none of us remarked on it.

'It's like we've been in our own fantasy land,' I continued, leading the way upstairs.

Lara and Jayne didn't answer.

'Our own little Gondal, that's what we say.' I giggled as I turned to them. 'After the world Emily Brontë created with Anne.'

Jayne gave a small smile, and I faced forwards again and began the climb up the next staircase in silence, wondering what they were both thinking. I couldn't remember the last time I'd felt so awkward around my friends.

I opened the door to my apartment and ushered them in, then stared at the empty staircase behind them. 'Where's Grasper?'

Jayne's jaw tightened and I was embarrassed that I had only just noticed his absence.

'I left him at home with a neighbour. Didn't want him distracting us tonight.'

'And Hannah's with her dad,' Lara said, clearly hurt that I'd missed Jayne's dog before her daughter. 'After virtually ignoring her over Christmas and New Year, he thinks a weekend at Center Parcs will make up for it.'

'Selfish bastard,' I said. 'Glass of wine, ladies?'

I watched as Jayne and Lara shared another glance, then they acquiesced.

'What the hell is that?' Lara exclaimed, staring at the window.

'Oh, CDs,' I said. 'William strung them up for me to scare away the birds until Vikram can put something more permanent in place. They're actually not too bad now, can be a bit unnerving in the morning when they first catch the sun, though.'

'What happened?' Jayne asked, noticing the three small panes covered by cardboard and brown tape. 'Why are so many windows breaking?'

'It's the birds, isn't it?' Lara said, her voice soft. 'They're attacking.'

214

'They're not *attacking*,' I said. 'They're just . . . congregating. And the lights are confusing them, that's all.'

'Is that what William says?' Lara asked.

I shot her a sharp look, hearing the scorn in her voice.

'What does Vikram say?' Jayne interceded, breaking the tension.

'The same,' I said. 'Here.' I passed glasses of wine round, then sipped my own, staring at my friends over the rim of the glass.

Lara and Jayne

'The bar's still open,' Jayne said as she and Lara entered the White Lion.

'Thank God for that. You collect the keys, I'll order us a bottle.'

A couple of minutes later, Jayne joined Lara at the table in front of the fire, which was still blazing, and handed her the key to Room Seven.

'I'd have thought you'd had enough of that room,' Jayne said. 'Isn't that the haunted one?'

'It's not the ghosts in this place that worry me,' Lara said as Tess deposited a bottle of Sauvignon blanc and two large glasses on the table. She looked up to thank the girl, and smiled. 'Don't worry, no strange happenings here.'

'Yet,' Tess said, turned and walked away.

Lara looked stunned, then burst out laughing at Jayne's equally shocked expression. She shrugged. 'Must be a true Yorkshire lass – they're not given to hysterics in these parts.'

Jayne relaxed and joined in her laughter. 'That's probably just as well.' She picked up the wine and poured two generous glasses.

Lara said nothing, but took her first sip before Jayne had even replaced the bottle on the table.

Jayne followed suit, the mood now sombre. She shivered despite the heat of the fire. 'You noticed it too.'

Lara nodded. 'When *did* you last hear from her?'

'I spoke to her yesterday, but only because I rang her – she didn't even text back from my calls earlier in the week.'

'Same here. It's not like her.'

'I thought meeting a man would be good for her,' Jayne said, 'but it's like she's forgotten us. She's just not *Verity* anymore.'

'I know. It's natural to be wrapped up in each other in the beginning, but Verity . . . Normally, the slightest thing happens and she's straight on the phone to tell us about it.'

'Every detail.' Jayne smiled. 'But this time, nothing. It's almost like when Antony was at his most controlling, and she withdrew into herself, do you remember?'

Lara nodded and took another sip of wine.

'What do you think he's doing to her?' Jayne almost whispered the words.

'I don't know. Have you spoken to Vikram much?'

Jayne coloured and glanced down at her hands. 'Just a few texts.'

'Has he said anything about William?'

'We haven't been texting about William.' Her blush deepened.

'I hear you.' Lara smiled. 'I'm glad it's going well.'

'Early days,' Jayne said. 'Hopefully I'll see him tomorrow, but back to Verity. What do you think William's doing?'

Lara didn't speak at first, but sipped her wine again. 'I'm not sure it's him.'

'What do you mean?'

'Whatever's going on, I don't think it's a destructive relationship.'

It was Jayne's turn to silently sip her wine.

'But whatever *is* happening, I think he's as much a part of it as she is.'

'What do you mean? I thought it was the building that's haunted, not Verity.'

'Oh it is – the Grey Lady is definitely connected to the building. But the other, whatever *the other* is, I think that has to do with Verity. And William.'

'But how? I don't understand.'

'There's the million-dollar question. I don't know either, but whatever it is, I don't like it.'

'If we don't know what the problem actually is, how do we solve it?'

Lara smiled at the typical Jayne question.

'Well, to quote someone I know,' she smiled at her friend, 'our first task is to quantify the problem.'

Jayne grinned. 'You're never going to let me forget that, are you?'

'Nope.' Lara swigged her wine, her eyes dancing at the memory. Jayne had been on a problem-solving course at work the previous year and had taken it very much to heart.

'So how do we quantify this?'

'Well . . . I do have an idea,' Lara said.

'Yes?'

'You're not going to like it.'

19.

'Blimey, I didn't realise it was fancy dress,' Vikram said when William and I opened the door of The Rookery.

'It isn't,' William said.

'Really? Never seen you in that getup before, mate,' Vikram replied, unperturbed and indicating William's black slacks, white shirt and embroidered waistcoat. 'Apart from the Victorian dress-up days the village makes us do every year, that is,' he added.

'It's a dinner party.' William shrugged. 'This is the smartest gear I have.'

'Fair enough. Good to see you, mate.'

Finally Vikram and William shook hands, and Vikram led the way into The Rookery.

Glancing skyward and looking relieved to get under cover, Lara and Jayne followed.

'You look nice, Verity,' Jayne said with a glance at Lara.

'Thought I'd get into the spirit of things.' I'd also adopted the Victorian theme with a high-necked, lace-trimmed white blouse and long black skirt. 'Come on through, it's good to see you both.'

I took my friends' coats, draped them over a dustsheet-covered sawhorse and gestured them through to the first of the staircases and upward.

'Wow,' Lara said. 'This looks great, Verity.'

'Thanks, William and I have spent all day getting it ready.'

Jayne and Lara shared another glance, and I

remembered the way they'd looked at me when I'd told them to relax and go to the museum or something, and that I'd see them tonight.

'Don't forget my team,' Vikram said, sounding wounded. 'We've worked ruddy hard to get your new kitchen installed and ready for tonight.'

'Aye, you have that, mate,' William said. 'It's appreciated, and why you've been invited to the inaugural dinner party.'

Vikram took the beer his childhood friend proffered, but didn't say anything.

Lara and Jayne exchanged yet another look, and I sighed inwardly. *What's their problem?*

I relieved them of the bottles of wine they'd brought, checked the labels and deposited them in the fridge, before removing one already chilled. I opened it and poured three glasses.

William opened his can of bitter and raised it in a toast.

'To Verity and The Rookery.'

I smiled at William as the others repeated the toast and drank.

'How's that meat coming on, love?'

'Oh.' I'd forgotten about it. I set down my glass and rushed to my new oven – this was its first use and I really had no idea how efficient it was.

I basted beef and turned potatoes and veg in the roasting pan, then replaced it in the oven, along with an empty Yorkshire pudding tin.

Then back to the fridge and out with a plate of smoked salmon on Ritz crackers with lemon wedges.

I realised the room was silent and caught yet another look between Jayne and Lara.

'What?'

'Nothing.'

'There's definitely something.'

'Well, I was just reminded of when you were with Antony,' Lara said. 'You hated the focus on the food rather than the people in the room.'

'And tonight you seem to be embracing it,' Jayne added, with a glance at William, who was focused on me, helping me with the meal.

Don't they realise how much work we've put into this for them? I swallowed my ire, and said, 'Sorry, the whole day's been a mad panic.'

'You've definitely been busy this week, Vikram,' Jayne said, lightening the mood. 'You've done a great job in here.'

'Thanks,' he said, visibly relaxing. 'The guts of the job are mostly done, now it's everything else.' He laughed. 'We're going from the top down now, getting Verity's accommodation sorted, then each guest room, then the ground floor. Should be a decent place when it's all finished.'

'Oh!' Jayne exclaimed, spinning around on one foot as Lara grabbed her arm – to steady herself as well as her friend.

'It's the CDs we strung up to deter those damned birds,' Vikram said, having rushed to the window to determine the source of the clatter that had startled everyone, then swiping at his face. 'The string's failed.'

'Failed or pecked through?' Lara whispered to Jayne.

Vikram recoiled as a bird landed on the windowsill, opened its beak, and – it seemed – tried to bite the glass with a clack audible in the room.

'Like *that's* not going to get annoying,' Jayne said as the feathered beast did it again, her nervous laugh betraying the confidence of her words.

'The pigeon spikes are due Tuesday,' Vikram said.

'Will pigeon spikes be enough?' Lara asked. 'Those rooks are twice the size.'

Vikram laughed. 'Not quite that big, but the principle's the same. They'll stop roosting here once we've got them all in place.'

He jumped as another beak clawed one of the nine small glass panes that made up each window. 'Can't come soon enough.' His following laugh did nothing to ease the nerves of the others.

'Maybe curtains should go to the top of your shopping list, Verity,' Jayne suggested.

I pouted. 'We're on the third floor, and uphill of the other houses on the other side of the street. I have no intention of blocking any of my view – not considering what I've gone through to get it.'

Jayne's mouth opened, then shut without making a sound.

'These look lovely, Verity,' Lara said to break the tension. She helped herself to one of the smoked-salmon canapés. 'You're really treating us.'

'Then it's sirloin of beef from the local butcher,' William said with pride. 'I could even tell you the colouring of the cow it came from.'

Vikram grinned. 'Old Ed Stockdale,' he said, wiping his face. 'He loves telling people that – picks his beasts out personally he does.'

Lara and Jayne stayed silent, seeming almost grateful for the thump from the window from yet another bird. It meant they didn't have to reply.

'Time to get the Yorkshires in,' I said. 'William, would you help me?'

Vikram squeezed on to the sofa next to Jayne, forcing her and Lara to shift up, then he rubbed his face again.

'Why do you keep doing that?' Lara asked.

'What?'

'Wiping your face. I've seen you do it a few times tonight, but can't remember seeing you do it before when we've met.'

'Oh.' Vikram looked surprised, then regarded his hand before lifting it to his cheek once more. 'It's weird, I keep feeling like I've walked into a cobweb.'

'Really?' Lara glanced at Jayne, who looked confused.

Another rook trying to bite its way through the glass distracted them and conversation stopped for a while.

I gave Lara a quick smile as I caught her eye and poured batter into the piping hot Yorkshire pudding tin, whilst William basted the meat again, then glanced at Jayne who was smiling shyly at Vikram.

Lara sighed, rose, walked to the fridge, extracted a bottle and took it back to the sofa.

'Thanks, Lara,' Jayne said as she topped up the glasses.

Lara's answering smile was small. She looked like she'd made her mind up about something. Something unpleasant.

'I hope you're all hungry,' I said as William and I rejoined our friends in the lounge area. 'Dinner will be ready in twenty minutes.'

20.

'That was absolutely delicious, Verity,' Lara said, pushing her cleared cheesecake plate away. 'You must have been flat out all day.'

'Pretty much,' I said, pleased that the atmosphere seemed to have lightened from earlier. I rested my hand on William's arm, 'But I had a lot of help and I really wanted to treat you after the way you've both helped and supported me through the move and everything.'

'Any time, Verity,' Jayne said.

'We're always here for you, you know that,' Lara added.

Vikram thrust his chair away from the table, startling the others, and swiped his hand over his face.

'Seriously, mate, what's wrong with you?' William demanded.

'It's this place, Will. Something keeps touching my face. It's freaking me out.'

Jayne and Lara exchanged one of their silent glances that expressed so much.

'You okay, Vikram?' Jayne asked.

'Yeah, yeah, it's gone,' he said and pulled his chair back to the table.

'Has anything else been happening, Verity?' Lara asked.

I shrugged, but could not stay my glance towards the window and the bird that was still snapping at the glass. I leaned into William as he grasped my hand. I didn't need to say anything for my friends to understand.

'We need to find out what's going on here,' Lara said.

'You've been saying that since I moved in. So far, nothing's worked.'

'Cleansing and blessing the house hasn't worked,' Lara qualified. 'I think it's time we tried something else and found out exactly what or who we're dealing with and what they want.'

'And how do you propose to do that?' Vikram asked, his scepticism clear in his voice, yet belied as he wiped at his face once again.

'We ask them,' Lara said. 'We hold another séance. Properly this time, and we don't stop until we get answers.'

'What, table tipping and ectoplasm out of your nostrils, all that nonsense?' William asked.

Lara laughed. 'Not quite, but whatever is here does seem to be trying to interact with us – or Verity at least.'

'And William,' I said. 'He's been dreaming too, like me.'

'Of the same man?'

'No, of a woman who looks like me.'

'Okay.' Lara drew the word out as she absorbed this. 'So it does seem there are two of them and they're trying to get through to the two of you.'

'Let's see if we can help them,' Jayne said.

'You're on board with this?' I asked her in surprise.

'Yep. She's quantified the problem and accepts this as the most effective solution,' Lara answered for our friend.

We laughed while both men scowled, not understanding the joke.

'Let's give it a go,' William said, to Vikram's obvious surprise. 'What, mate? Something's going on—' He broke off at another interruption from the window and an opaque crack snaked across another small pane of glass.

He looked back at his friend. 'This ain't normal, and I can't think of anything else to do.'

Vikram didn't remove his stare from the destructive

avian, which seemed to gaze back at him – the light from the streetlamps reflecting in its one visible eye. He nodded.

Jayne and William helped me clear the table, and Lara flung her scarf over the standard lamp.

'What?' she asked in response to Vikram's raised eyebrow. 'It adds to the atmosphere.'

He didn't reply.

Lara pulled three pillar candles from her large handbag and set them on the table.

'You came prepared,' Vikram said.

'Always,' Jayne answered for Lara, and gave Vikram's arm a friendly squeeze. 'You haven't done anything like this before, have you?'

He shook his head. 'Shouldn't mess with things you don't understand.'

'Don't worry, Lara knows what she's doing.'

'I hope so,' he said, then flicked off the overhead light at Lara's instruction.

The room seemed to glow; the pink of Lara's floral scarf complementing the candlelight, and all five of us jumped as a rook pecked again at the cracked pane.

Vikram twisted suddenly.

'What's wrong?'

'I thought I saw something.'

Silence for a moment – even from the birds.

'I think we should get started,' Lara said.

We took our seats and joined hands.

Lara took a deep breath.

'Is anybody there?'

Nothing happened.

'Please come forward, we would like to help you.'

I gasped as the candle flames flickered.

'If you would like to talk to us, please knock or rap the table.'

The candles flickered again.

'It's just the draught from the window,' Vikram said as a second bird cracked another of the small panes.

'One tap for no, two for yes.'

'You'll have no sound windows left at this rate,' Vikram said as a third pane split. 'Mind you, you could probably claim on the insurance if the birds are doing it.'

'Shh,' Jayne said and squeezed his hand.

'One tap for yes, two for no,' Lara repeated. 'Please talk to us.'

Another pane broke.

'It's the birds,' Jayne blurted out. 'They're tapping – answering.'

I screamed as glass showered to the floor, and hung on to William's hand as the others jumped to their feet. The table juddered and thumped against my new rug, and all three candles extinguished as one.

More smashing from the windows and the room was suddenly full of beating wings and outstretched talons.

I heard Jayne shriek as she dived under the table and Lara jumped out of the way as Vikram swung his chair at the invading birds.

'Out, out, out!' he shouted, and I screamed as a bird pecked at my hand.

William threw himself at me, and I fell from the chair to the floor, William's bulk landing on top of me. I welcomed the dark as it rushed to embrace me. I did not want to be inside The Rookery a moment longer.

Part Three

1830-1848

"Terror made me cruel"

Wuthering Heights
Emily Brontë, 1847
Haworth, West Yorkshire

I.

Martha used the foot-treadle to shift the warps then sent the shuttle flying through the resultant gap between the two rows of woollen yarn. Weft picked, she beat the new pick up against the fell of the woven piece, ensuring the new weft was snug against the one before, then worked the treadle and flicked the shuttle back with the next pick. Then repeated. Endlessly.

She had been at this near a year now, and could match most of the men for speed, now that she'd built up the strength needed for beating-up. Though she was still waiting for the day when Old Man Barraclough dropped his chisels for good and Harry could take over the mason's shop.

She wouldn't need to work at all then. She could stay at home, or swan about on the moors like that Brontë lass. She avoided even thinking her name these days, and was furious that Harry still gave her the time of day.

'Her father's the parson,' he'd say. 'They're important in the village. And if I'm to take over from Mr Barraclough one day, I need to keep in with 'em. Most of our trade's memorials. Tha kens that, Martha. Where would we be without the church?'

Martha had no answer.

A cough interrupted her thoughts and she brought her attention back to the piece she was weaving, checked the let off and take up to ensure everything was regular, then glanced down at Edna who was in her basket, playing with her poppet and a couple of bobbins. Happy enough.

She was finding her feet now and Martha did her best to tire the child out throughout the morning, so that when she took over the loom from Old Dan after dinner, Edna would stay in the basket where she put her. The rhythm of the looms seemed to calm the child, but then she'd heard it all her life.

Martha smiled at her daughter, then checked her piece and picked the shuttle. This was the only machine Edna would know, Martha was determined to it. No mill for Edna Sutcliffe, not if she could help it. As a daughter of the master stonemason, she'd be in line for a decent husband who'd keep her in a fine house.

She coughed, adjusted the take up a little on the loom and worked the treadle. *That's better.*

Aye, mebbe it is worth putting up with the Brontë girl if it means Edna and whoever comes next have a decent chance at life.

She caressed her belly, certain more life was growing there, then returned her hand to the loom.

She thought back to that wonderful day in the bluebell woods, certain that was when the child had started. Aye, she was a lucky one to have snared Harry Sutcliffe, though it had taken long enough to get him to the altar. Sarah was green with envy when she told her.

Martha smiled again then glanced down to check on Edna. The basket was empty.

Sighing, Martha scanned the floor of the weaving gallery for her independence-seeking offspring, then a shout alerted her. 'Ower 'ere!'

'Thanks, Alf,' she called and halted the loom to retrieve Edna. Crawling around the way she did, she could easily get trapped under a working foot treadle.

Standing, Martha stretched, then put her hand to her mouth as a more violent cough shook her. She looked around in alarm at the gallery of weavers mesmerised by the rhythm of their looms, recognising a smell that every textile worker dreaded.

Smoke.

'Edna! Edna! Where is she?'

A couple of weavers looked up at her, recognising the note of alarm in her voice.

'Smoke!' she cried. 'There's a fire! Where's my baby?'

2.

'Fire!'

Harry heard the shout, dropped his chisel and mallet – mindless of the memorial stone for Richard Smith's second wife – and dashed outside.

'That's Weaver's Row,' he shouted. 'Martha! Edna!' He ran downhill to his family.

Men flocked to West Lane: slaughtermen, innkeepers, cloggers, druggist; every trader on Main Street. No one from the mills though, they were too far away. It would be up to the village tradesmen to save the cottages; home to near a dozen families, including the Sutcliffes.

'The gallery, is the gallery afire?' Harry cried as he pushed his way through the throng of men.

'Nay, 'tis woolcombing shed. Gallery's safe for now.'

'Where are the weavers?'

No one answered him, and Harry could do naught about Martha as a full bucket was pressed into his hands. A line of men already stretched from the well to the wooden woolcombing shed attached to Weaver's Row, and Harry was one of the closest.

He threw the water at the flames that were singeing the whiskers on his jaw. He didn't notice.

Despite his panic, he knew he had to fight the fire, however much he wanted to find his wife and daughter. Controlling the flames would give them the best chance of getting out.

'There's good men up in that gallery,' Harry muttered to

the next man in line as he swapped his empty bucket for a full one. 'They'll get 'em out.'

The man, Edward Stutterghyll, the proprietor of Haworth's largest ironmongery, nodded, and shouted, 'Happen it'll be all right.' He couldn't have heard Harry's mutter, but didn't need to, to understand the mason's distress.

Everyone in the village knew of Martha's deal with Old Dan Walker, and whilst few approved, no one could argue it didn't make sense for them to share the loom, it was too much for either Dan or Martha to work at for a full day. Besides, fool be the man who denied Martha Sutcliffe anything she'd set her mind on. Including her husband.

Harry swapped another empty pail for a full one, stepped forward and launched the water. They were making progress.

He cursed Martha for insisting on weaving here. Aye, he knew they couldn't yet manage on his wage alone, not with a growing family, but still. Barraclough was getting on now; Harry couldn't see him yet and wondered if he'd managed to shuffle down Church Lane to help out.

He'd have to ask for a raise. He did most of the work now anyway, forty years of working the chisel had left the old man's scarred hands with a never-ending tremble, and he stuck to facing the stones, while issuing a stream of advice to his protégé.

Harry threw another bucket load. *Blasted woolcombers*! This shed, shack really, had been a fire waiting to happen for years. The combers stoked their charcoal fires till they could have forged new combs, never mind heating their existing ones so they slid easier through the greasy wool fibres, pulling at noils and neps to leave the long fibres needed for spinning into worsted yarn.

'Leave shed, leave shed,' Stutterghyll's shout penetrated Harry's thoughts. 'It's gone. Save cottages!'

Harry redirected the path of the water he was throwing on to the stone wall of the first weaver's cottage.

Not afore time, he thought, as steam rose from the stone of his neighbour's home, before being overcome by smoke.

He took a few steps to his right, to better direct the flow of water, and flung his next bucketful.

He noticed more folk had joined the firefighting effort, including Barraclough, and more and more buckets and ewers were being emptied on the cottages. There was barely anything left of the woolcombing shed now, and the steps leading down the stone wall from the gallery were open to the sky for the first time in years.

'Harry, Harry!'

He turned and stared at Edward Stutterghyll. The ironmonger jerked his head, indicating Martha, standing and staring at her workplace, Edna on her hip. Safe and well the pair of them.

'Praise the Lord.' Harry raised his eyes skyward, thrust his bucket at Edward, and rushed to take his wife and child in his arms. Whatever else had been lost this day, he still had them.

3.

'After three,' John Brown said. 'One, two, three, heave!'

Harry and the sexton bent their backs to the altar gravestone. It shifted three inches.

'And again. One, two, three, heave!'

Six feet long and three wide, the heavy memorial shifted another few inches, and the two men strained their backs to lift it enough so that they could slide it on to the neighbouring slab.

'Thanks for giving me a hand, Harry,' John panted while they took a breather.

'It's nay bother, glad to help,' Harry replied. 'It's that busy with the smallpox, I may as well just set up shop int' churchyard, especially now Barraclough's succumbed an'all.'

'Aye, there's half a dozen graves left open after funerals with so many ill. Can't be shifting these things backwards and forwards every time the pox takes another, not when there's whole families taken out at times.'

'I reckon some of graves'll need to be dug deeper,' Harry said. 'And I'm running out of space to add names on the older ones.' He indicated the older, lower part of the churchyard, abutting the Black Bull.

'How do, Miss Emily,' the sexton called. 'Watch tha footing there, there's open graves by the path.'

'Will do, Mr Brown, thank you. Morning, Harry.'

Harry returned Emily's greeting and watched her pick her way down the path from the parsonage, the graves so close, her skirts brushed the flat stones clear of dead leaves and twigs. The cleanest graves in the churchyard were those swept clean by Brontë skirts.

'She's a rum 'un, that lass,' John said. 'Can't get two words out of her normally, in a world of her own she is, but her and her sisters have been out every day taking food and water to the worst-hit families.'

'Aye, I just hope they don't catch it themselves.'

'Aye, our Tabitha has them burning their gloves at end of day, and she's constantly washing gowns. The Reverend's torn; it's their duty to call on the sick, but he don't want to lose any more daughters. He ain't even complaining about buying so many gloves, though they're making do with shoddy.'

'They won't be bothered about that, not them lasses,' Harry said, nodding after Emily. 'They've got more important things going on in their heads.'

'What, poems and them tiny magazines they make? Have you seen 'em then?'

Harry nodded. He still didn't quite know what to make of Emily and her siblings' fascination with Branwell's toy soldiers, or why they wasted their time making inch-long 'magazines' for the toys to 'read'.

'So have you moved into Barraclough's cottage?' the sexton said as he indicated they should resume lifting.

'Aye. Martha's burnt every scrap of fabric and scrubbed every surface, but at last she's happy and Edna's allowed out of her basket.' Harry laughed. He hadn't wanted to move in quite so soon after Mr Barraclough's passing, he thought it unseemly, but Martha had waved aside his objections.

'And how's new bairn coming on?' John asked, puffing after another heave.

Harry frowned. 'Martha's not carrying this one so well,'

he confided. 'I don't mind telling thee I'm concerned about her, but Martha won't ruddy listen.'

John grimaced and shook his head. He'd had his run-ins with Martha Sutcliffe over the years, he knew exactly how forthright she could be. 'Here she is now,' he warned, spotting the newly large figure making her way into the churchyard.

'Lord above, what now?' Harry muttered. 'Let's take five, John.' He turned to meet his wife.

'I've just seen that Emily Brontë,' she said before he had chance to greet her. 'Rushing off with her baskets, doing God's work, that ruddy dog at her heels.'

Martha hated Emily's new pet, an enormous mastiff called Keeper. And to be fair, he was a beast; Emily was the only one able to control him.

'Well she's Reverend's daughter,' Harry said, trying to mollify her. 'She has pastoral duties.' He winked at Edna, who had just peeked out at him from behind her mother's skirts. She hid again as soon as she'd seen her father take notice of her.

'Pastoral duties?' Martha screeched and Harry winced as he realised his mistake. 'Tha's been talking to her again, ain't thee? Using her fancy words!'

'Martha, calm down. It's unavoidable, she's been helping people sort funerals and what wording they want on stones.'

'Hmph.'

'Martha, love. I keep telling thee, tha's nowt to worry about.' He winked as Edna peeped out a second time. She ducked behind Martha again with a giggle.

'That had better be true, Harry Sutcliffe. God help thee if it ain't.'

'Martha!' Harry was shocked she'd cursed him out in this of all places, and in front of the sexton too.

'Aye, well,' she said, embarrassed, but too proud to take it back. 'Anyroad, I'm off to see Sarah Butterworth.'

'Nay! I've told thee afore, Martha. Tha's not to visit any house where there's smallpox.'

'I'll be all reet, Harry.'

'Nay, tha won't. I won't have thee risking thyself nor our child.' Harry stroked her belly and she softened.

'Tha does love me, don't thee?'

'Aye, 'course I do, tha daft .apeth.'

Harry ran his hand around her waist, and squeezed. Her answering squeal told him he'd won this one, at least. 'Now get thee back home and get the weight off thy feet. I'll be late with all this work on, but I'll be home as soon as I can.'

'Aye, all reet then. I'll make sure there's some supper left for thee. Come on, Edna, say ta ta to thy papa.'

The little girl peeped again from her mother's skirts, face beaming. Harry picked her up, swung her round, carefully, then sent her on her way with her mother, both his girls receiving a pat on the rump in farewell.

Harry watched them go, concerned. Martha was hiding it from him, but he knew her too well, and the child she was carrying was paining her; far more than Edna, or Baby John before her. He swallowed his grief for his firstborn, buried just two rows over, and was overwhelmed with concern for his wife and next-born.

Would she tell me if owt serious were wrong? he thought, *Or just refuse to believe it were happening?*

238

4.

Martha clung to Harry's arm as they negotiated the treacherous lane. Half-frozen slush and leather soles, her first pair of proper shoes rather than her usual wooden-soled clogs, did not mix well and she'd nearly been over three times already, even on this short walk homeward from the church.

Harry's hobnailed boots, which she was now glad he'd insisted on wearing to early morning Christmas Mass, were far better suited, and he was as steady on his feet as a newly shod horse.

They still had to hurry though, slush or no slush. It was their first Christmas in the big house. *Well, it's small next to the parsonage*, Martha thought. *But bigger than any I ever had any reet to expect.* She blessed Mr Barraclough yet again for making Harry his heir, then her thoughts returned to the day ahead. Most of her family and Harry's were coming to be fed and were expecting a Christmas feast.

She shuddered at the thought of all the coins and notes she'd handed over to the butcher in exchange for ham and beef. Not to mention the raisins and brandy for the Christmas pudding. But Harry had insisted on 'doing things proper'.

Haworth's winter had been terrible, upwards of four hundred folk dead of the smallpox on top of the usual winter maladies, and there wasn't a family in the Worth Valley who hadn't lost someone. A couple of families, the

Hardys and the Slaters, had been wiped out; there was simply no one left to continue the name.

Those that had survived were in a right state: one minute grieving, then euphoric for those left alive, then remembering once more. Harry was determined that today, at least, the Sutcliffes and the Earnshaws would be celebrating. And he could afford to with all the work he had on.

He was looking at taking on another apprentice too. Martha's nephew, Charlie, couldn't keep up, and Harry's own nephew, Georgie, was coming up to an age where he could be of use.

I could do with an apprentice int' house, she mused. *Or an housekeeper*. She smiled up at her husband; she was still working on that one, but was confident she'd get a kitchen maid at least. Especially once the new babby was here.

She put a hand to her belly and winced.

'Aw reet, love?'

'Aye, I'm fine. Just a twinge, probably just the cold air.'

'Aye, well. Happen tha's got too much on today.'

Martha said naught.

'That's why our Mary'll be joining us a bit later.'

Mary was his elder sister's girl. Nice enough, but a tad slovenly, Martha judged.

'What's tha saying?'

'She'll be giving thee an hand. And living in an'all; she can have the small room next to the kitchen.'

'Tha means—'

'Aye. Merry Christmas, love. We have an housekeeper.'

'Oh Harry!' Martha swung into his arms, nearly knocking them both off her feet in her joy. She'd soon cure Mary of her sloth.

***

Martha looked around her dining table and could have cried. This was the first time both families had come together since her wedding three and a half years before.

Despite the latest additions, Edna amongst them, they were less than half in number. She and Harry had grieved each and every death, but the sum total of their losses hit her.

She looked across at Harry and knew he felt the same, as did everyone around the table; those of an age to understand, anyway.

Both her and Harry's parents had gone now, as had near half a dozen of their own generation, plus twice more little ones. All in three years.

It felt too much to bear at times, and now she did not feel like celebrating this Christmas after all.

Harry brought out the crowning glory of their feast, a huge joint of roasted beef, to a round of diminished yet still heartfelt applause. He picked up the carving set, then put them down again. He looked around the table, tears in his eyes, and Martha knew without doubt that he felt the same way as she.

'It's aw reet, love,' she said, placing a hand on his forearm in a rare public gesture of affection. 'We all know, we all understand, and we all miss 'em.'

'Hear, hear,' Thomas, Harry's sole remaining brother, said, raising his glass. 'Truer words may not be spoken.'

Harry lifted his own glass. 'To them no longer with us, may thy spirits soar, and thy memory live long.'

The Sutcliffe-Earnshaw clan drank as one, and a rare silence descended over them, deep enough to include even the youngest members; then, as one, conversation broke out: compliments about the house and feast; enquiries over the various trades represented around the table; and news of a more homely nature.

Harry reclaimed his carving knife and meat fork, then dropped them once more as Martha screamed in agony.

'Reet then, lass, that's the last of 'em gone home. Gave 'em all a reet scare tha did.'

'I scared mesen, love. Thought me insides were ripping apart.'

'So where's pain?'

'Round me hips and in front.'

'But babby's not coming?'

'Nay, not yet. Pain's been coming on awhile, but nowt as bad as that afore.'

'Tha should've said summat, love. Tha's been overdoing it. Tha should've been resting.'

'Too much to do to rest.'

'How's tha really feeling though?' Harry did not want to start arguing, not now.

'I've been better, Harry, and that's the truth, but pain's lessening now.'

'Lizzie says it happens sometimes if babby's lying wrong.'

'Hmm. Lizzie's no midwife,' Martha pointed out.

'Nay, but she's had bairns of her own.'

'So have I.' Martha glanced at the ceiling where, in the room above, Edna had finally been put down to sleep after watching her mother's collapse and the near hysteria of her relatives.

'I'll be reet,' she said, her voice softer. 'Don't take on so, Harry.'

He perched on the side of her armchair and chucked her under her chin. 'Don't ask the impossible, love. I'll allus fret over thee.'

Martha leant her head against his strong shoulder. 'Lizzie does have a point though,' she allowed. 'Plenty of women have pains like this in run up to a birth. I'll just have to take it easy, that's all.'

'Well, tha can now that Mary's here. She's moving in tomorrow.'

'What? On Boxing Day? She'll have to sort all Christmas boxes out. Tha'll have to make sure she gives reet ones to butcher and baker, we can't have them getting mixed up.'

'Aye, we'll sort it, Martha. Tha needs looking after, lass, and she's family, she's happy to do it.'

There was silence for a moment, then Harry rose, crossed to the sideboard and awkwardly poured himself a brandy. After only three weeks in this house, it still did not feel like his, and nor did the style of life that went with his new position.

'One for thee an'all, Martha?'

'Aye, it'll dull pain a bit,' she said and held out her hand for the half-full glass.

5.

Harry dropped his chisel with a curse as another scream from Martha speared through the cottage wall and into his workshop. She'd been at this for hours already and the shrieks had only increased in their intensity.

He listened but heard no more, so picked up his chisel and examined the stone. It pained him that there was naught he could do for his wife at present, but that was the truth of it and he had to accept it as did every other father-to-be.

Uttering another oath, he ran his hand over the F in *WIFE*. Or what was supposed to read *WIFE*. It looked more like a P now. He offered the late Florence Butterworth a heartfelt apology, knowing it would be the living he would have to answer to for the grave error. Her son, Robert.

Poor woman; it was bad enough her name did not appear on her own memorial stone, now it read: *RICHARD BUTTERWORTH AND HIS WIPE* with only the husband's dates below.

He would do what he could to correct it, and he chiselled away the offending stone to inscribe the correct F, deeper than the other letters, but at least her station in life would be spelled correctly. He pondered whether Robert Butterworth's wife, Martha's friend Sarah, would suffer the same fate.

Martha would not, he knew that, and once more he stared at the wall in the direction of their bedchamber as the volume of her screams rose again. If, God forbid, she did not survive this birth, he would ensure she'd be named properly, her name on their family memorial clear for all to see.

More likely, 'twill read MARTHA SUTCLIFFE RELICT OF HENRY SUTCLIFFE, Harry thought with a stray smile. Despite her current distress, she was strong, much stronger than he, and apt to outlive him. *Would she be proud of me enough to be known as my relict, my widow? Or would even that be an indignity too far for her?*

More screams prevented him from answering his own question, and he threw down his chisel before he could make any more errors upon the Butterworths' gravestone.

'Harry.'

He looked up to see Emily at the door.

'It doesn't sound as if the child comes easy.'

'Nay, Emily, 'tis a hard birthing for sure. No surprise considering how hard she's been carrying this bairn these past months.'

'If anyone can do it, Martha Earnshaw can.'

'Sutcliffe.'

'Aye, of course. I meant nothing by it.' Emily stepped aside and returned the harsh glare of the new arrival.

'Sarah, what news?' Harry asked.

Sarah glanced at the gravestone Harry was carving for her in-laws, then stared back at Emily, although she elicited no further reaction.

'I think tha should come, Harry.'

'What?' Harry blanched and another scream answered him. His wife had not passed.

'Just to be close by, offer her comfort,' Sarah qualified. 'Old Peg is with her now, but this is an hard one. Martha needs to know tha's near. Though be warned, she'll not show thee much appreciation till the birthing is complete.'

And mayhap not even then, Harry thought as he nodded

his understanding and followed Sarah to the cottage. He did not pause as Emily placed a brief hand on his arm as he passed; nonetheless, he felt and appreciated the comfort she offered him.

Sarah slipped through the bedchamber door, careful to open it no wider than necessary; she did not want to give Harry any larger a view than necessary from his vantage point in the corridor.

'He's just outside the door, Martha.'

'Oh, sitting comfortably is he?' Martha yelled between grunts, each one crescendoing to a hoarse scream. Sarah forbore to point out the heavy tread of Harry's hobnailed books as he paced the boards outside.

'Well he might! He'll never get near me again. If he tries, I'll make sure I pass on every ounce of this agony.' The last word was barely recognisable from a shriek, but everyone within hearing understood. Including Harry. His pacing stopped and both Sarah and Peg heard the crunch of his chair back against the wall as he dropped into the seat. Martha was oblivious.

'Can tha not widen thy legs any further, lass?' Peg had been encouraging her to do this since she'd arrived an hour ago, but to no avail.

'I've already told thee, no I ruddy well can't!' Martha screamed. 'There's summat wrong, has been for months, tha knows that.'

'Her legs and hips just ain't working right,' Sarah interrupted before Martha could resume her earlier name calling. Peg had nearly left five minutes after her arrival due to the filth that had spewed from Martha's lips. 'Is there another way?'

Peg stared at the stricken woman on the bed for a moment, then accepted these were not the usual insults of a woman in the throes of childbirth. 'Aye, mebbe so. Help me roll her on to her side, Sarah, then we'll get her on to her knees, see if that'll help.'

'It'd better, tha awd carlin, else I'll have thee hanged for witchcraft.'

'Martha!' Sarah was horrified. That was not something to be joked about. A couple of hundred years before, near a dozen people, most of them women from just over the hill at Pendle, had been hanged for the same, possibly another in her own house on West Lane.

'What's tha dawdling at, lass?' Peg broke into Sarah's thoughts. ' 'Tis an idle threat, she knows I'd have her turned into a toad afore she could even blink at constable.'

Sarah laughed, even Martha made a strangled, gurgling sound that passed for a moment of mirth, then screamed anew as her two attendants manhandled Martha into a crouch.

The next pain elicited such a shriek, even Peg blanched, and Harry banged on the door, demanding to know what torture they were inflicting upon his wife. He obeyed Peg's sharp instruction to remain where he was.

Peg, who still had the strength of a farmer's wife despite being near seventy, grabbed hold of Martha's midsection, pulled, and dropped the mother's knees to the floor. Martha's head and shoulders collapsed on the bed in a temporary relief. Sarah leapt on to the soiled coverlet and grabbed her friend's hands, desperate to offer support; to do *anything* to help.

'Push reet hard now, lass,' Peg instructed, one hand buried in Martha's nether regions. 'I can feel the head. Tha's almost there.'

Harry winced at the curses emanating from his bedchamber, and uttered a quick prayer that the parson would not hear his wife's profanities, then hung his head in shame at his disloyalty.

247

He sprang to his feet and recommenced his pacing of the corridor. 'Twas not lengthy enough to ease his fears, and his hobnailed boots did the floorboards no good at all. *Martha'll have my guts for garters,* he thought when he spotted the scuffmarks occasioned by his turns at the window and stairtop. *I hope.*

He winced at another scream, even put his hands to his ears in an attempt to block out the sounds, then slumped back down on to his chair, head in hands. *How can anyone survive this? Mother or child?*

After a few moments of silence, he raised his head. *Why is she not screaming?* Then a new cry, a babe's. But relief did not come, Martha was too quiet.

Sarah emerged from the room, her eyes downcast.

'Look at me, woman! What is the news?'

She crouched beside his chair. 'Tha has a son, Harry Sutcliffe. A fine boy.'

'And Martha?'

'She'll recover.'

Harry eased his back with a sigh of relief. 'She lives?'

Sarah nodded. 'Aye, she does, but she's weak. She'll be abed for some time.'

'But she lives, she'll recover?'

Sarah said naught.

'Sarah Butterworth, tell me!'

'Walking will allus be difficult, and she'll bear thee no more children.'

'But she lives?'

'Aye, Harry, she does.'

'Can I see her? And the boy?'

Sarah glanced at the closed door. 'Not yet, it's been an ordeal, let her rest. I'll bring the bairn out when he's fed. Oh, and best Edna stays with Lizzie a while longer, till Martha gets some strength back.'

6.

Martha stared down the flight of stairs and gritted her teeth. A woman's laugh echoed up the dark stairwell and Martha turned sideways on to the steps, thumped her gnarled hawthorn walking stick on to the top tread and grasped the bannister with her free hand. Grunting, she forced her right foot down a step, then her left joined it.

A deep breath, then she jammed her stick on to the next step and she repeated the process.

She was greeted at the bottom by Emily Brontë. 'Good morn to you, Martha. I was just about to come up and help you.'

'Aye, so I heard,' Martha muttered as she brushed past the parson's daughter and thunked her way to the kitchen. She sank into her prized rattan chair by the fire with a sigh and eyed with distaste the basket on the table.

'Where's that been? I'd better not have to scrub the tabletop when she's gone.'

'Good morn, Martha,' Harry said, refusing to let his wife's sour temper spoil the day so soon. He was becoming well-practiced at this particular trick. 'How did tha sleep?'

'Like I were lying on a bed of thorns.'

'Better than nest of wasps the night afore.' Harry tried a smile to no avail.

'Hmph,' was Martha's only response.

'I've brought you fresh-baked baps.' Emily bustled into the kitchen and removed the cloth from atop her basket. 'And some new honey from the sexton's hives.' She placed the goods on the tabletop.

'Thank thee, Miss Emily, that's much appreciated. The sexton's honey is best int' village, ain't it, Martha?'

'Hmph.'

'My pleasure. But I must hurry, I'd like to get the rest of these to Weaver's Row while they're still warm.'

'Pass my regards to Lizzie and rest of 'em, will thee?' Harry said.

'They appreciate thy charity do they? Hardworking men and women the lot of 'em, earning their way, then you turn up to dole out the scraps from thy kitchen.'

'Martha!'

Emily held up a hand to forestall Harry's protest. 'You may call it charity, Martha Sutcliffe, but no one turns down Tabby's baking nor John Brown's honey.'

'Aye well, Tabitha Aykroyd must be into her seventies now, barely able to walk she is, and tha and thy family still have her keeping house as if she were a young lass.'

'Now look here, Martha Sutcliffe.' Emily planted both hands on the tabletop and leaned forward to glare at Martha. 'Tabby is as much a part of the family as I, Charlotte, Anne or Branwell. And you've never heard her complain, have you?'

Martha looked away and stared into the fire.

'Papa is the parson of this village, and we all know that however hard everyone works, there isn't enough food for all the hungry mouths. So Tabby and I turn what we can from the collection plate into flour, and we bake; all ruddy week we bake, so everyone in this godforsaken rookery of a village can eat!'

'Just making an observation. No need to get het up.' Martha glared at Emily. 'Bet the wives of this "godforsaken rookery of a village" love you calling on their husbands. Choosing which one to take for thyself is thee? Or has tha already chosen?' She looked at Harry, her accusation clear.

'You bitter old witch!'

'Now, now, that's no way for a parson's daughter to speak.'

Emily's colour rose further, her cheeks flaming red with her ire.

'That's enough, Martha!' Harry thundered. 'Emily has been nowt but friend to us. It ain't her fault tha's in pain.' He bent to pick up their son, Thomas, now a year old. 'Ain't his fault neither, and he needs his ma. Tha barely even looks at him.'

'Hmph.'

Harry sighed, walked over to his wife and placed their son in her lap. He glanced at Emily, whose temper, he saw, was not yet under her control. *If it ever were,* he thought ruefully. 'Come on, lass, there's no talking sense to her these days. Thank thee for bread and honey, and my regards to thy father. I'll see thee out.'

Emily re-covered her basket with the cloth, gave Martha a parting glare, which was returned in full, then turned and made her way to the front door, Harry close behind.

'I'm sorry, lass. Mornings ain't a good time for her. She's still in so much pain, has been since birth, but at least she's getting about easier now than she were.'

'But the birth was over a year ago, Harry.'

'Aye, and don't I ruddy know it.'

Emily touched his arm. 'Don't give up hope. I have some more of the preparation Mrs Hardaker makes.' She gave him a small bottle. 'She's still not happy about making it up without seeing Martha, you know what druggists are like, but she trusts me. And knows Martha of old.'

'Thank thee, Emily. It does help, even though she won't admit it and I have to sneak it into her food.'

'Just take care, Harry, she'll have you in the gaolhouse for trying to poison her.'

Harry grunted. 'Nay, she won't.' He cheered up as the thought struck him. 'Without it, she'd never get upstairs on her own. Happen laudanum's the only thing ever gives either of us a bit of peace.' He laughed. 'Anyroad, she needs me to earn our living. She wouldn't want to rely on alms or thee for her bread, even if I really were poisoning her.'

'That won't be an issue after next week.'

'What do you mean?'

'I'm departing with Charlotte for Brussels on Tuesday next.'

'What?' Harry's mouth dropped open in shock. 'You're leaving? *You*? But—'

'I know, I know, but we're serious about founding this school, and Charlotte is convinced a few months studying in Brussels at the Pensionnat Heger will give us vital experience and make it much more likely to succeed.'

'A few months?'

'Weeks if I can help it.' Emily smiled. 'You know how I get if I'm too long from the moors.'

'Aye, 'tis like a sickness in thee.'

'So you know I won't be away long.' She glanced at the house. 'Martha should be cheered, at least. She hates the very sight of me, it seems.'

'Don't tha mind her. She's a jealous woman, in all things. Allus has been. And pain's making her worse.'

'Mrs Hardaker has upped the amount of laudanum.' Emily indicated the bottle that Harry still held in his hand. 'That should ease the pain; the pain in her body anyway. Branwell swears it heals pain in the mind an'all. Maybe my absence will help to heal the pain in her heart.'

'I'll miss thee, Emily,' Harry whispered.

'Aye, I know. I'll miss you too. All of you.' She turned to encompass the dogs, duck and pheasant that patiently awaited her. 'Wish I could take all my friends with me.'

Harry knew he was excluded from that sentiment, it was only the company of animals and birds that Emily craved. Those and family.

7.

Edna grasped hold of her mother's skirts, trying to hide in the folds as a dray cart, laden with casks, thundered down West Lane, barely a foot away.

'Oh don't fret, lass,' Martha scolded as she knocked on the door. ''Tis only a drayman. Scared of owt, tha is.'

'How do, Martha, thank thee for coming,' Sarah Butterworth said as she opened the door.

Edna shrank even further into the protection of Martha's skirts. Sarah had only just survived the outbreak of smallpox a couple of years before. Glad of her life, she nonetheless rued the loss of her looks; her face now a patchwork of disfiguring scars left behind by the foul pustules.

'Aye, well, sorry for thy troubles,' Martha said. 'What else are friends for?' She followed Sarah into the house and deposited Edna and Thomas into the care of Sarah's eldest girl, Betty. Aged seven years, she'd be following her elder brother's footsteps on to the mill floor any day now.

'He's upstairs,' Sarah said. She lit a candle and led the way up, solicitously walking slowly to give Martha time to climb the stairs.

'In here.' She pushed open the door to a small, dim room and used her flame to light two more.

'Ain't this the haunted room?' Martha asked.

'Aye, none of kids'll sleep in it for fear of the Pendle witch. He has no choice now, though.' Sarah nodded to a trestle table under the shuttered window.

Martha walked over to the small, still figure of Edward, and crossed herself. 'Such a shame, and him only seven.'

'Eight,' Sarah corrected. 'He turned eight last month.'

'Of course he did, damn fine day it were too. Strapping lad he were, such a shame,' she repeated.

'Aye, he were a good worker. Old Man Rook thought highly of him up at mill. He had a good future ahead; family won't be same without him.'

They stood in silence a moment, regarding the child's body. Betty could only look forward to a spinner's wage, Edward could have had his own loom in a few years and earned a decent wage weaving pieces for the Rooks. *Ain't going to happen now.*

'Aye, a right shame,' Martha said again.

'Aye.'

'Reet, so what needs doing?' Martha had had enough of sentimentality and got down to the business at hand.

'The lot, I'm afraid. Wash him, dress him, then sew him into his shroud. Our Robert's gone to see Tobias Webster about coffin boards, then parson will bury him next week.'

'Next week? Why so long?'

'He has his own bereavement, ain't you heard? His sister passed last night. All funerals have to wait.'

'Miss Branwell's passed?'

'Aye. That's why we're doing this. Doris is up at parsonage, laying out Miss Branwell, and I'll not have my Edward lying here still with mill dust on him. Bad enough it killed him, he'll not suffer it in death an'all.'

'It were the mill lung?'

'Aye. Either that or the consumption. Result's the same, anyroad.'

Sarah bent her head to her son. 'He's loosening up now.' She eased his left arm out of his jacket and Martha limped round to take care of his right.

Sarah lifted him to remove the woollen garment, folded it neatly, and placed it on the seat of a wooden chair. 'It'll do for our lass's boy, Stephen. He's growing fast that one.'

'Aye, 'tis a good jacket,' Martha said.

'Sewed it mesen,' Sarah said unnecessarily. Almost everyone in the village made their own clothes.

She untied his shirt, then moved the body into a sitting position so she could lift it over his head.

Next were his breeks, then his long johns, and soon the eight-year-old boy lay pale and mottled with blue on the makeshift table.

Sarah fetched a bowl of water and placed it on the wooden boards by his feet. Both women wrung out rags and prepared to wipe away the dirt from Edward's skin.

'So if Miss Branwell's passed, the sisters will no doubt be returning home,' Martha said.

'Aye, more than likely. They'll want to be here for their aunt's funeral, no matter how far they have to travel. She more or less raised them after their ma died so young.'

'Hmm.'

'Tha still fretting about Emily and Harry?'

Martha shrugged.

'They're just pals, Martha, allus have been, ever since they were little. Tha knows that.'

'She allus hangs about him.'

Sarah tsked. 'No she don't. She stops by to say how do, the workshop and house is right by the parsonage. 'Twould be an insult if she didn't.'

'Far too ruddy often if tha asks me.'

'She ain't got no eyes for anyone, except them creatures that follow her around everywhere.'

'She's a rum 'un.'

'Aye, that she is. And so's thee, Martha Sutcliffe, if tha can't see that Harry only has eyes for thee.'

255

Martha screwed up her face in a scowl.

'He still ain't touched thee? Not since . . .' Sarah knew better than to mention Thomas's birth, even though she'd lived every agonising minute with Martha.

'Won't let him.' Martha shrugged. 'Last bairn all but crippled me. I ain't chancing another.'

Sarah said naught, but stroked the cheek of her son.

'I'd love more, but Robert won't come near me now.' She indicated her face. 'Hardly ever here, either. It's just me and the girls now.'

'Well, what a pair of misery guts we are!'

Sarah managed a slight smile, then looked up at her lifelong friend, expecting her to have more words of wisdom. She was unprepared for the look of horror on Martha's white face.

Sarah turned to see what had frightened Martha so.

A figure, a woman, hung from the rafters in the middle of the room, little more than a foot away. She slowly rotated on the rope that encircled her neck, creating deep purple welts, her tongue protruding from her swollen face, cocked to one side. Inch by inch, the head straightened, and Sarah later swore she saw that grotesque mouth stretch in a smile.

She would see no more though; with a piercing shriek, she bolted from the room.

Sarah's scream broke Martha's paralysis, and she limped around the room, as far away from the apparition as she could manage, and followed her friend.

As she approached the top of the stairs, Sarah had reached the bottom, flung the door open, and charged into the street.

Straight into the path of a heavily laden wool cart.

The horse's shriek matched Sarah's and the drayman's for intensity, and the animal reared up as Sarah floundered beneath its pawing hoofs.

Robert Butterworth, returning from his meeting with Tobias Webster, was quick enough in mind to grab hold of her, and he hauled her away from the descending horseflesh.

'What the Devil does tha think tha's doing, woman? Scaring the horse like that! Get back inside with thee. All this carry on and our son lying dead upstairs!' He shoved her back into the house.

'I'll take care of him, Robert, you look after Sarah,' Martha said with a gulp. 'It's too much for her.'

She glared at Sarah, warning her not to mention the phantom they had both seen. Robert would not appreciate such tales. She made her slow way back to the room, pushed open the door, and sighed in relief. The only occupant was Edward.

8.

'Good morn to you, Harry Sutcliffe.'

Emily received no response bar the rhythmic clanging of Harry's mallet upon his chisel.

'How do, Harry?' she shouted, then laughed as the master stonemason jumped and dropped his tools.

He glared at Emily then inspected the stone he was working on. 'Lucky for thee, there's no damage done,' he said. 'Good morning to thee.'

Emily grinned at him. 'You're in a world of your own when you're carving.'

'This is the last impact the dead have on this world,' Harry said, indicating the stones. 'Each name and date should be my best work. Though it were almost my own name that needed carving today. I wish tha'd take more care when tha discharges thy father's pistol of a morning, Emily.'

She shrugged. 'I can't point it at the moors, I might hit a hare or lapwing. Papa jests he'd almost be safer firing it himself, even with his sight failing the way it is.'

'At least he's never pointed the damned thing towards village, and I were never scared of morning's shot afore!'

Another of Emily's rare smiles graced him. 'I'd never hit you, Harry Sutcliffe.'

'I'm surprised he still keeps it by his bedside at night, it's been many years now. Branwell must take more care on his way home from Black Bull on his visits home too; any noisier and he'll have his father mistaking him for a rioter.'

'Aye, Charlotte's said the same thing. Papa will never lose his fear of the Luddites, though, and the riots he bore witness to in Hartshead.'

'But he's safe now surely? It's only mills and their owners that are being targeted.'

'True, but feeling still runs high. So many children are maimed or worse, and so many families starving now their work can be done faster by machine. 'Tis not only spinners now, there are new contraptions for carding, gilling and winding. If they devise a loom that runs on steam instead of manpower, many more will starve.'

'Folk have it tough round here, and no mistake,' Harry said. 'Thank the Lord for thy father, if he hadn't had old Mr Barraclough take me on as apprentice all them years back, Lord only knows where I'd be now; and me family an'all.' He shuddered at the thought of little Edna and Thomas going to the mill every day to slave under spinning mules from dawn until dusk and beyond.

'Aye, Haworth's naught but one large rookery as it is,' Emily said, staring downhill at the village spewing coal smoke from every chimney. 'Reduced to a slum, no more.'

'Surely 'tis not so bad as that,' Harry protested.

'Oh it is. I've seen more places than you, Harry Sutcliffe, and Haworth does not measure well. The water stinks, effluent soaks the streets, and sickness thrives. Papa conducts so many funerals, he's exhausted with it, they each take a toll. It's not right, Harry. People should live better.'

'Aye, that they should.' Harry struggled to order his thoughts. 'But who shall make it so? The men are so knackered by their work, they have neither time nor heart to fight for better, and 'tis not in the interests of those who are idle to fight.'

Emily dropped a copy of *The Fleet Papers* on to the

stone on which Harry had been working. She said naught, trusting Harry to know they were the work of the anti-Yorkshire-slavery activist, Richard Oastler, who continued to campaign, despite his ongoing incarceration in The Fleet prison for his debts.

It took Harry a moment, but then he understood. Emily had talked of him before. He picked up the publication.

The Fleet Papers; being Letters to Thomas Thornhill Esquire of Riddlesworth from Richard Oastler his prisoner in the Fleet With occasional Communications from Friends.

'Read it,' she said. 'Tell people about it. He speaks true.'

'Aye, I'll spread the word,' Harry said after scanning the article, his head spinning in dismay with details of corn laws, poor laws and diatribe against the long working days of the mills. 'I'll need time to take this in, but I'll help Oaster's cause if I can, small as my part may be, if it helps the poor sods who still have to send their nippers to mill instead of school.'

Emily nodded and opened her mouth to say something more, but the ringing of a bell forestalled her.

'It's mill bell,' Harry said. 'Summat's up, come on, lass!'

He took off running down Church Lane, then up West Lane and on to Lord Lane to Rook's Mill. Emily's mastiff, Keeper, kept pace with him, so he knew Emily was not far behind. And, apart from a few souls ahead, he knew the rest of the village not already working in the mills would be there too. All fretting over who was hurt, and praying it was no one of their kin.

The bell continued its toll.

9·

'What's gone on?' Harry asked Bartholomew Grange, who stood at the mill door, blocking the way.

Everyone stopped for a moment as the constant rumble of spinning jennies and mules faded into silence. Even Big Bart looked uneasy.

'One of little 'uns got trapped in mule,' he said, his voice like thunder in the unaccustomed silence.

'Who? Let us in, man! What's happening?' A chorus of voices at Harry's back echoed his own words.

'Let us in, man!' Harry shouted at Bart, and reached for his lapels. Bart was big, and he was hard, but Harry worked with rock every day, and was likely the only one in the village who could take him on, and Big Bart knew it.

He stared at him in silence a moment, then flicked his gaze to Harry's feet. 'No hobnails on mill floor, Harry.'

'What? Someone's hurt, and you want me to take me boots off afore I come in? This ain't the big house tha knows, Bart!'

'No hobnails on mill floor,' Bart repeated, no expression on his face. 'Place is full of wool fluff; any spark from nails could have whole place going up in flames.'

'Come off it, Bart,' Harry said and tried to push past him. 'They need our help. Someone could be dying in there.'

Bart lifted Dasher, his alley strap, and Harry stared at him in shock. Bart was a big man, yes, and a hard man, but he'd never been a cruel man.

He met Harry's stare. 'Only takes a second,' he said. 'Me

brother were killt that way over at Beckhead Mill. One pair of hobnailed boots, one spark, and whole mill floor were engulfed with flame afore any bugger could get out. Happened in a second and three hundred dead. No hobnails on mill floor.'

Harry nodded. Bart was right. He bent to free his feet of his boots while Bart repeated his words to the rest of the villagers. 'Boots off. No hobnails on mill floor.' He had no need to shout; he was used to making his words heard over machines, no one had any trouble hearing him when the machines were quiet.

Finally in stockinged feet, he let Harry pass, the others hurrying after him.

The stonemason ran down the main gangway, coughing on the wool fibres in the air, so thick it gave the impression of a snowstorm. He pushed his way through the gaggle of women and children, then stopped short at the sight of his sister, Lizzie. She had a little 'un in her arms.

Harry couldn't see who it was and part of him didn't want to know. By the amount of blood streaked over them both and the floor, there was no helping the child.

He looked the machine over. One of the new mules; the low horizontal carriage would normally be unrelenting, pulling and spinning the wool fibres through rollers until it reached the end of its traverse, clanging against the support stanchion before travelling back to the main body of the machine to wrap the yarn on to spindles.

He gulped as he saw white flecks of bone amidst the blood on the second stanchion.

Harry knelt by his sister. 'Give her to me, lass.'

Lizzie slowly turned her head to him and he gasped. Her normally rosy cheeks were stark white, her eyes dark and wide, looking like caves in her normally pretty face.

'Lizzie?'

'She's hurt too. Her hand. Getting Betty out. Ain't spoken since.' Harry didn't see who had spoken, his full attention was on the two before him.

'Betty?'

'Aye, Betty Butterworth.'

Harry recognised the dress then, the poor lass was Martha's friend, Sarah's girl. Eight years old.

'Lizzie,' Harry said again and this time thought he saw a glimmer of recognition in her eyes. 'Lizzie, it's me, Harry. Give Betty to me, I'll look after her.'

'It's all right, Lizzie,' Emily said from beside him, and Harry looked at her in relief. She'd know what to do.

He bent to take Betty from Lizzie, and gasped at the state of Lizzie's hand. The mule had crushed it as she'd tried to get Betty out. He couldn't look at Betty, or what was left of her. *Even her mother won't recognise her*, he thought with dismay. *Only the dress, the one she'd made herself and were so proud of, told of her identity now.*

'I'll take care of Lizzie, Harry,' Emily said.

Harry nodded, stood, and turned to see Martha and Sarah at the front of the crowd of bootless men and women. Sarah stared at Harry. She must have heard, but hadn't taken note yet.

'Sarah,' Harry said. 'Best tha don't look, love.'

'No.' The word was quiet, desperate, and she collapsed against Martha. Harry met Martha's eyes and knew she was thinking the exact same thing he was.

Thank God Edna don't have to do this work.

'Give her to me.' Robert Butterworth ignored his wife as he pushed past her, making both Sarah and Martha stumble in his wake.

He glared at Harry, who stared back. He saw no compassion in Butterworth's face and wondered how deep it was buried. Too many in this village had simply lost too much.

He took his daughter, and Harry noticed his hands shook. But he showed no other sign of his distress. The villagers parted to let him through, and Sarah and Martha followed, Martha's stick thumping a funereal tattoo as they went.

Harry turned back to Lizzie and Emily, and knelt back down beside them.

'How bad is it?'

Emily didn't look up at him, but carried on her work. She'd torn strips from her petticoat, but didn't even blush as she did so. 'Don't tell Papa, he can't afford another, and I don't need it, not really.'

Harry smiled at her, then flinched at a particularly loud thump from Martha's stick at the other end of the mill floor. 'How bad?' he asked again.

'It ain't going to be much use no more,' Lizzie said, staring at the misshapen clump on the end of her wrist. She screamed as Emily wrapped one of the lengths of cotton around it.

'Sorry Lizzie, we've got to stem the bleeding. Doctor Ingram's on his way, he'll set the bones and do what he can for you. He'll give you something for the pain too.'

'It'll have to be downstairs,' Bart said. 'Need to clear the floor; get machines up and running again.'

'You can't be serious!' Harry looked up at him, then noticed a child even younger than Betty scrubbing the blood away from the spinning mule.

'Make sure tha gets into all them cracks and crannies,' Bart directed the boy. 'We don't want no blood on new yarn.'

He looked back at Harry and shrugged. 'Mill got to run, Harry. Mill's got to run.'

Harry nodded. He had to look after Lizzie now, and Bart weren't the problem here, the Rooks were. If anyone were going to take *them* on, they'd need to think it through first.

Harry opened the door to the Black Bull and a riotous fug of shouts and odours assaulted him. He smiled ruefully; after tending to Lizzie all day, and quieting Martha's fears about Emily once more, he had hoped for a quiet drink. That was clearly not to be.

A slap on his shoulder sent him reeling towards the bar and he ordered ale, then tried to make sense of the arguments. Big Bart seemed to be taking the brunt of the men's tempers, and Harry made his way through the throng of his neighbours, all of whom seemed to hold the overlooker responsible for today's disaster.

'There were nowt I could do,' Big Bart said, his roar easily heard over the din. 'It all happened in a second. Everything were well, and then, then . . .'

Harry stood before him and placed his hand on Bart's shaking shoulder.

'And then what?' A new voice was raised. A strident voice, full of grief and anger, which silenced the pub. 'Then your mule crushed the head of my little girl. My little Betty. We've none left now. No more Butterworths. All gone. Taken. By your damnable machinery!'

Bart looked Robert Butterworth in the eye and calmed. 'Tha sent her to work there.'

'What did tha just say?'

'Tha heard. I do me best for them lasses, whatever age they are when they're sent out to work. She were too young to be on mill floor, and tha knew it, but tha'd had her working there ower a year already.'

Men stepped back, leaving the way clear for the two men squaring up to each other.

265

Harry moved between them. Robert Butterworth wasn't soft, but he was no match for Bart; and no amount of fury would give him enough strength to hurt the overlooker. If he tried, Bart would fight. He needed to hit out. And Bart would beat the living daylights out of the man, grieving father or no.

'Move aside, Harry.'

'No. This is not the answer. This does not honour any of the mill youngsters.'

'Too right,' Will Sugden, the innkeeper of the Black Bull, put in. 'Take it outside or drown it in ale, them's thy choices.'

'They'll drown it in ale, on my tab, Will.'

As one, the men of Haworth turned to the man who had walked into the middle of this. Zemeraim Rook, his father and brother at his shoulders.

'I mean it. Tonight's ale is on the Rooks. Tonight we commiserate, we remember, and we talk. Tomorrow we take steps to stop this happening again.'

'And how does tha mean to do that?' Butterworth sneered.

'We'll enforce the twelve-hour rule, there'll be no more exceptions, no matter how much you plead for more hours for pay. No woman or child will work more than that per day. And they'll take an hour and a half of rest during the day.'

'It's still twelve hours though! What about the ten-hour rule?

'Aye, it is, but only nine on Sundays. There's a new act going through Parliament as we speak, which means machinery will soon have to be fenced in, and we've already started on that. As for the ten-hour rule, we'll have to see what Parliament says about that in time.'

'Too late for my Betty,' Butterworth snarled as he

stepped up to Zem Rook. 'Eight year old and her life crushed out of her.'

To his credit, Zem did not flinch, even when the spittle from Butterworth's words hit his cheek. 'Eight, Mr Butterworth? You insisted she was nine when she started with us last year. You know full well children under nine should not be on our workforce.'

'Tha knew damn well she were seven when she started, just like most of t'others crawling under thy machines.'

'I distinctly remembering asking you to swear to her age of nine. I have your thumbprint on her record of work to prove it.'

Men shuffled away, eager to drown the truth in free ale. They all knew the law that forbade anyone eight or younger from working. But they also knew that births had only been registered since the queen came to the throne. No one over the age of six had a birth certificate, and when it came to feeding too many mouths on not enough coin, the Butterworths were not the only family in Haworth who had claimed their daughter to be 'small for her age'. Most of the men now guzzling their ale had done the same thing, and their shame was overcoming their sympathy.

Butterworth looked around at them, recognising he would get no further. He looked back at Bart who stepped up to him, placed his brawny hands on the smaller man's shoulders, and said, 'I did all I could. Tha did all tha could. We can do no more. Come, drink with me.'

Friends once more, the two men turned to the bar, where a space was cleared for them. They sat on a couple of upturned casks and were handed tankards of best porter. Those tankards would not be empty until both men were passed out on the filthy floor; sorrows well and truly drowned. At least for the night.

Harry turned to the Rooks, just as they were about to leave. 'There is more that can be done.'

Zem met his gaze and raised an eyebrow.

'Making life easier in mill is one thing, but what about at home?'

'What do you mean?'

'Thy weavers and woolcombers. Does tha know how many men, women and children are crammed into them cottages tha rents out? Most of space is given over to looms and the woolcombers' charcoal fires. As thy mill grows, so does thy workforce. They all need to live somewhere. I bet fewer would be taken by smallpox and t'other plagues if they weren't so crowded in. That's what Reverend says, anyroad.'

Zem regarded Harry for a moment, then looked around the room, sensing the charge in the atmosphere, before turning to his father and brother. Harry could not hear what was said, but could see they had a decision when Zem turned back to face the room, head high.

'What do you have in mind, Mr Sutcliffe?'

'The site of the old woolcomber's shed, the one that burned down a few years ago, next to Weaver's Row. I can build thee four cottages on that scrap of land. And me family needs the extra work now that Lizzie's hand were maimed in that machine of thine.'

Zem nodded. 'We'll give some thought as to where else to build.' As one, all three Rooks bowed their heads once, exited the Black Bull, then replaced their top hats for the short walk to their carriage.

10.

Martha dipped her rag into the water bowl beside her, wrung it out and put the cooled fabric to her daughter's brow. She stroked Edna's cheek, whispering encouragement to the eight-year-old. 'Come on, lass, look at thy ma, let me see them beautiful eyes of thine.'

She dripped water on to Edna's lips in the hope that some drops would find their way into the girl's mouth, but there was no response, and tears filled Martha's eyes as she looked down at her daughter. Wrinkled, blue-grey skin and dark circles around her eyes, hot to the touch, and heart beating double time, there was no mistaking the signs of the cholera. Half the village was down with it.

Edna groaned as cramps took hold of her again and expelled what little sustenance, and liquid, remained in the small body.

'Doctor Ingram's with the Rooks,' Harry said from the doorway, and Martha jumped. 'Whole village is suffering; there are so many shutters closed on Main Street, it's heartbreaking.'

Martha looked at him and said nothing, then turned back to her daughter. There was nothing to say.

'I'll go get Emily, mebbe she can help.'

'She's here again, that ruddy basket over her arm,' Sarah announced as she entered Lizzie's cottage on Weaver's Row.

'What, Emily? Where is she?' Martha paused, turning away from Lizzie and dropping her cloth into the bowl of cool, murky water.

'Where do you think? Talking to thy Harry.'

Martha's colour rose. Since Edna had died, she had spent most of her time with Lizzie, looking after her and her husband Thomas, and Sarah had taken to coming to help. It was no secret that since Betty's death, Robert had been finding comfort in arms other than his wife's and she could not bear to stay home in an empty house.

'I wish he'd never suggested building them cottages. She's there every ruddy day, and he laps it up!'

'Tha'll have to watch him better, Martha. Tha knows what men are like.'

'Not our Harry,' Lizzie croaked. 'Not him.'

Martha wrung out the cloth, and stroked her sister-in-law's burning face. 'Hush now, Lizzie, keep thy strength.'

'He's a good man is Harry,' Lizzie whispered before sinking back into sleep.

'Martha.'

She looked up at Sarah, who had gone to check on Thomas. Heart sinking, she struggled to her feet and crossed the small room to Thomas's bed as Sarah passed her hand over his face to shut his unseeing eyes.

Martha sighed. 'I'll go tell Harry. He can sort coffin boards out while we lay him out. Will tha watch Little Thomas while I'm gone?'

'Aye. They'll be running out of ground in that churchyard at this rate.'

Sarah got to her feet, and closed the shutters, then she checked on Lizzie again, before making her way to the kitchen to search out black ribbon; it would be needed for the family to wear, and to cover the doorknob to warn visitors. She'd make a wreath for the front door as well from laurel and yew, and wind the ribbon around that. She couldn't collect the greenery yet, though, first she needed to ensure there would only be the one wreath to make.

***

'It seems I only see thee when there's a funeral on these days, Martha,' Harry said as he watched his wife dress their remaining child, Little Thomas, in his Sunday best.

'Aye, well.'

'I thought I'd be seeing more of thee while I were working on them new cottages, what with tha spending so much time at Lizzie's.'

'Aye well, her brood keep us busy, especially with her only having one hand.'

'But Sarah seems to be there every day too, can she not do more?'

'Tha spends thy time talking with thy friends, I'll spend my time with me own.'

Harry stared at her, then understood. 'Not this again. Emily *is* a friend, no more. If tha don't believe it of me, tha should believe it of her.'

'Hmph.'

'Martha, please, not again, I don't know what else to tell thee. There's nowt going on, all she does is pass the time of day.'

'Several times a day from what I hear.'

'Martha!'

She stopped what she was doing as Harry raised his voice, and sent Little Thomas waddling out of the room, then stood to face her husband, her face set.

'Not today. Not when I'm burying me daughter and me brother. Just give it a rest, will thee?'

Martha said naught, but her eyes prickled as she watched her husband give up on her and go to find his son.

She followed them down the stairs to the front parlour where Thomas and Edna were laid out ready for the funeral.

'It's reet that he's here,' Harry said. 'I know it's more work for thee, Martha, but Lizzie couldn't have coped well on her own.'

'I'd have managed fine, Harry,' Lizzie said from the door.

He sighed and turned to deal with the living. 'It weren't a disservice, Lizzie, I know tha'd have managed, I just want to make it easier for thee, that's all. Tha's me brother's widow, he'd want me to look after thee.'

Lizzie softened as her gaze went to her husband's coffin, three times the size of Edna's. 'Aye, I know, Harry, and I thank thee for that. There ain't many folk who'd take on a crippled widow and her brood.' She raised her gloved stump of a hand.

'Stop talking of thysen like that,' Martha scolded. 'Tha's got another hand, and it ain't slowing thee down much.'

'That's true enough.' Lizzie crossed the room, and added more flowers to both coffins. 'They look peaceful don't they? As if they're sleeping.'

'Aye. Harry's had a photograph took of 'em. They won't be forgot.'

Lizzie nodded.

'Reet then, is there anything else that needs doing afore the parson gets here?' Harry asked.

Martha and Lizzie examined the room: the coffins were placed against the back wall, draped in black and white ribbon with a multitude of flowers; and as many chairs as could be crammed into the room were arranged in rows. 'No, we're ready,' Martha said, with a nod from Lizzie.

Harry grimaced, nodded and strode to the front door to prop it open for their guests and allow them to view Thomas and Edna before the service began.

Harry, Martha and Lizzie followed the parson and pallbearers past their friends and neighbours, and out into the sunshine. All three were numb, and barely aware of the service they had just sat through to commemorate their lost family.

The youngsters: Georgie, Little Thomas, and Stephen followed behind, pleased to be out in the fresh air again instead of the stuffy room, and leading the rest of the mourners out of the house and down Church Lane.

From the back of the procession, the large pine box and smaller white casket seemed to be moving on a sea of black crêpe and ribbon. At the gate, only those closest to Thomas and Edna entered the churchyard, everybody else continued to the King's Arms to make a start on the ale and food that Harry was laying on for them.

The family, plus Sarah and one or two other close friends, gathered around the Sutcliffe family grave as Reverend Brontë began the rite of committal.

Harry stared at the elaborate memorial stone he had carved after Baby John's death five years before. Elaborate scrolls and a frieze carved around the edge, he'd also carved a statue of a young child into one of the supports that would carry the altar stone. He had a second one to put into place when they replaced the stone. Harry stared at the names already on there, and gulped as he remembered carving Edna's name two days before in preparation.

He had thought himself hardened to it by now; he'd carved so many of his friends' names, and their children's as well as his own kin, but none had been as hard as carving his daughter's.

He caught the hand of Little Thomas, his sole surviving child, and was pleased to feel Martha's hand creep into his other, then realised Lizzie clasped Martha's free hand. Their numbers may be diminished, but they were family, and they would make the best of the days to come; together.

II.

'How's our Mary doing?' Lizzie asked.

'Tha could at least let me in and sit down afore tha grills me,' Martha grumbled.

Lizzie stepped back to allow her friend to clump past her into the kitchen and settle down in the most comfortable chair.

'She's ont' mend, stop fretting, Lizzie. The coughing's subsiding and doctor's happy that it ain't consumption after all. Probably her lungs are weak from mills and soot. She'll be on her feet again by end of week.'

'That's good news,' Lizzie said, and put some water on to boil. 'Will tha have some dandelion tea?'

'Aye, that'd do me reet,' Martha said. 'Has tha heard about Bart Grange?'

'Aye, dead of the consumption last week.'

'Aye, but that's not all. He were the last in line, and instead of burying him in family plot near church, Rooks have bought Granges' grave.'

'They never have! What about bones? And where'll they put Big Bart?'

'Up top of new bit – alongside parsonage by field wall.'

'That's terrible – they should be left to rest in peace.'

'Aye, Harry's livid. Reckons it's too disrespectful, even though there's no bugger left to mourn them. He's shocked at parson for allowing it.'

'Well, I hope he's making Rooks pay through nose for it. Oh that'll be Sarah.' Lizzie bustled to the door to let her in. 'I wonder if she's heard about it.'

'Were that Emily's voice I heard?' Martha queried when the two women joined her.'

'Aye,' Sarah said with a glance at Lizzie.

'She's been there every ruddy morning, and afternoon too. What the ruddy hell is she playing at?'

'Oh Martha, hush. There's nowt going on, tha can trust Harry, he ain't one to fool around on thee.'

'Tha can never tell,' Sarah disagreed. 'It were months afore I knew my Robert were playing away.'

'Well, I've had enough. I'm going to find out what's going on, and if I don't like it I'm putting a stop to it. I'll be up int' weaver's gallery, I'll be able to see what they're saying from top of steps.'

Lizzie and Sarah shared another glance as Martha heaved herself up from her chair and clumped towards the internal stairs to the gallery above.

Lizzie shouted after her, 'No good'll come of it, Martha. You'd do better staying down here with us.'

She received only a harrumph for answer, accompanied by the thumping of Martha's stick as she scaled the treads.

'How do, Ellis.'

'What did you call me?' Emily Brontë turned on Harry, her face twisted into her fiercest scowl.

Despite himself, Harry took a step backwards, nearly falling over the stone behind him waiting to be faced. He held his hands up, still clasping hammer and chisel, to ward her off. 'Steady on, Emily. I'm reet then, am I? It is thee that wrote that book, tha's Ellis Bell?'

'No! No, I am not!' Emily stamped her foot to further stress her denials.

Harry ignored her. 'Aye, tha is. It's thee that wrote it. "I wish I were a girl again, half savage and hardy, and free . . . Why am I so changed? I'm sure I should be myself were I

275

once among the heather on those hills." Them's thy words, Emily, no matter what's written ont' cover.'

Emily glared at him, her fists clenched, and Harry wondered if her basket would hold up to the force of her fingers, but he wasn't going to let his advantage go now.

'Anyroad, ain't Bell one of the curate's names? And if tha's Ellis, I'm guessing Currer is Charlotte, and Acton, Anne. I'm not daft, tha knows. Anyroad, no bugger else could write about moors like that – reading *Wuthering Heights* were like seeing the moors through thy eyes.'

'Does Martha know?'

'Ha! I knew it! And no she don't. I weren't sure mesen till just now. I've been teaching her letters, and she's reading it at moment, though I doubt she'll work it out. She don't know thee like I do.'

'You can't tell her, Harry Sutcliffe, you have to promise me. It'd be all round the village by noon.'

'I don't keep secrets from me wife, Emily.'

She scowled again, and Harry gave in. 'All right, I won't tell her, I'll keep thy secret.'

Emily relaxed and Harry grinned at her.

'So, who's Heathcliff based on, anyone we know?'

'No.'

'The only lad daft enough to scrabble around moors with thee were mesen.'

'Don't flatter yourself, Harry Sutcliffe.'

'I can't help but notice there's a similarity in the name an'all.'

'There's similarities to most names in village. It doesn't mean folk are in the book. It's just a story, with characters not neighbours.'

Harry raised his eyebrows, and Emily shrugged.

'Well, mayhap I did get some inspiration from the goings on in Haworth.'

'I knew it!' Harry grinned at her.

Emily shook her head at him, opened her mouth, then with a glance upward, shut it again and started up the stairs to the weaver's gallery, basket over her arm. Halfway up, she paused, made to turn, then changed her mind and continued upward.

Martha stepped forward into the doorway, blocking Emily's entry to the gallery. She smiled at the smaller woman, who was further disadvantaged by having to pause on a lower step as Martha loomed over her.

Emily glared at her, but Martha did not move aside.

The background noise of the looms working softened then tailed away as the weavers realised something was happening and they paused in their work to watch and listen.

'I can't get past.'

Martha made no reply, but crossed her arms, strengthening her position.

'Please stand aside.'

'It's time we had a little chat, Miss Brontë. Tha's spending far too much time with my husband and I would prefer it if you would desist.' Martha looked at her in triumph at her well-worded demand. No one would be able to say she wasn't polite.

Emily flushed a deep red, and moved forward until there was just one step between them. Martha did not move, but Emily was not one to be cowed.

'There's nowt improper happening, you know that well, just as everyone else does. If you don't like Harry talking to folk, maybe you should try talking to him yourself.'

It was Martha's turn to colour, but she was aware she had an audience and stood her ground.

'I can still read lips from me days int' mill, tha knows.

Comes in reet handy it does.' Martha grinned at Emily. 'I've read that book an'all. Some of it, anyroad, I'm not quick with me letters like thee and Harry.'

Emily gasped. 'Martha, no!'

'Harry's *my* husband; he ain't *thy* Heathcliff. Tha'll make me a laughing stock with that ruddy book!'

'Then stop talking and don't tell anyone,' Emily hissed. 'I don't want folk to know. As far as the world knows, Mr Ellis Bell wrote that book, and that's the way it can stay.'

'Well.' Martha uncrossed her arms and rested her hands on her hips. 'If it's privacy tha wants to keep, tha'll have to do summat for me to keep me mouth shut. Stay away from my Harry!'

'Martha!' Harry had noticed the quarrel and rushed up the steps.

Emily took advantage of Martha's momentary distraction, and pushed by the larger woman, then hurried through the gallery.

'What the ruddy hell's going on here?' Harry stared after his friend as she reached the far steps and scurried down them.

'Is Martha reet? Did Miss Emily write that book everyone's been on about?' Alf Thackray asked.

Harry turned to his wife. 'What's tha done? What was tha thinking? Tha's full of spite, Martha Sutcliffe, and there's nowt uglier than a spiteful woman!'

'She's writing ruddy love stories about thee!' Martha protested. 'And having whole world read 'em. The pair of thee have humiliated me! Even Robert Butterworth *tried* to keep his dalliances private – thine are ruddy *published*. Ruddy Heathcliff, my arse!'

Harry stared at his wife, barely recognising her as the woman he'd fallen in love with ten years ago. Now he felt only disgust at the woman she'd grown into, and grieved for the woman she could have been had life been kinder; or if she'd chosen different words and actions over the years.

'Well, if I started out as Heathcliff, I reckon tha's the inspiration for the monster he becomes at end. That there lass,' he indicated the direction in which Emily had rushed, 'has more kindness, more sense, and an hell of a lot more goddamned plain *decency* than thee ever had. And she sees people true; she sees me, and she ruddy well sees thee for who tha is!'

Martha gasped in shock as his words ignited lightning in her heart that tore her apart, setting fires of rage, jealousy and humiliation burning through her, consuming her. The emotion exploded from her and she screamed as the world spun; she couldn't make sense of what she saw: stone steps, the still looms, and Harry's face, spinning away from her.

Part Four

April 2017

"He's more myself than I am. Whatever our souls are
made of, his and mine are the same."

Wuthering Heights
Emily Brontë, 1847
Haworth, West Yorkshire

1.

The shrill staccato shriek spears through my skull, accompanied by a dull, throbbing roar. Over and over, piercing the darkness; the sound a lightning strike on my brain; the roar the thunder of my pulse. The storm isn't just overhead, it's *in* my head. Gratefully, I sink back down into dark, silent oblivion.

A piercing bolt of white shocks me back into awareness. I lie still, trying to make sense of the sounds. Regular, clipped, like the piping call of a lapwing, only much louder.

There are more, beyond the loud one – quieter birds calling their rhythm. *That's right,* I commend myself on the realisation. *It's a rhythm, yes. But this is no song. So why* is *it so drear? And where's Harry? And Little Thomas?* Harry's face flashes before me and I flinch back from the memory.

I rise from the darkness once more, awareness seeping into me like the dawning sun's rays – gentle at first, then more insistent. *It's quiet! No lapwings!* Instead, a new pain; my eyes now. In place of darkness, all is red; a bright, resolute red – not like the dawning sun at all but a setting one the night before a glorious summer day.

I squeeze my eyes tight against it. *That's better.*

'Verity? Verity are you awake?'

My breath freezes. *Who's here?*

'Lara, I think the light's too bright, will you close the curtains?'

Movement, the scrape of a chair, then the redness dims and I relax my eyelids.

That name again – *Verity*. It sounds familiar, but I can't place it. *Who is Verity?*

'Can you open your eyes?'

It is imperative that I do so. At least two people – strangers – are sitting over me as I lie here helpless. I need to see; to assess the danger.

I try to lift my lids, without success. *They're stuck! What's happening to me?* Again – some small success – a chink of light. *Too bright.* I squeeze my eyes shut.

'Come on, Verity, you can do it. Come back to us.'

A hand strokes my arm, another my face. *Don't touch me!*

I draw in a breath, gather my determination around me, and force open my lids. It's like prizing apart two woolcombs.

The lids on my right eye give way and I immediately shut them again. I can feel my breath coming faster, as if I'd walked up Main Street. *Just from opening an eye for a second?* I think with terror. *What's happened to me?*

As my breath calms, I try to make sense of the indistinct image my eye records before snapping shut. It's no use, everything's blurred.

I flinch when a cool cloth is placed over my eyes, then gently drawn away.

'There, that's better,' one of the voices says. 'Wiped the sleep away, it should be easier now. Try again, Verity.'

My fear eases. There is gentleness in that voice and action; concern.

I try again. Now they open, the cloth has done its work. Again I slam them shut, but this time in a blink; a series of blinks as I allow light into my world and thoughts, giving my eyes time to get used to it.

Two heads appear over me. Strange heads. Women, but not women. *Angels?* No, angels would not have such blood-red lips and blackened eyes. *Devils.*

A small cry escapes me and the darkness rushes back to claim me, then a child's voice, following me down: 'What's wrong with her, Mummy? Why isn't she Auntie Verity anymore?'

'Welcome back.'

It's one of the she-devils. I slowly turn my head to look at her.

'Sorry we crowded you yesterday. It was too much, overwhelming. We were just so pleased to see you awake.'

These are not the words of a devil. I blink, then blink again, trying to focus on her features.

'Jayne's taken Hannah to get a cup of hot chocolate,' the woman says. 'It's quiet now, they've muted the machines – finally, all that beeping was driving me mad!' I flinch as she laughs, showing teeth.

'It was worse on the ward, a dozen of the things, all going off – a right racket. But they moved you into a side room when you showed signs of waking. It's much better in here. Sorry, I'm babbling.'

The woman laughs again, this time without showing her teeth. I realise she's holding my hand. I stare into her face. She looks familiar somehow. *But who . . .*

'We've been so scared, Verity. When you and William collapsed like that, and then just lay here, day after day. Thank God you're awake. Oh Verity—' She breaks off, tears running down her face, leaving strange, dirty lines. *Coal dust?* But no, it don't look reet.

'Who . . .' I try to say, but my throat is so dry no words emerge.

'Here, have some water.' The other woman's back. And the child. 'Support her head for me, Lara, that's right. There, drink.'

She's pushing a cold tube between my lips.

'It's water, just suck.'

I do as I'm bid, and cold, fresh liquid floods my mouth. I close my eyes in pleasure as I swallow, then suck again. I've never tasted water like this before.

'That's enough,' the second woman says, pulling the strange tube from my mouth. 'The nurse said just a little bit, your body needs to get used to it again.'

I stare at her. 'Who . . .' An audible sound this time. I try again. 'Who's Verity?'

Silence. Before I receive an answer, I sink back into sleep – the effort of waking is too much.

My eyes open, gently this time. The light is dim and the room silent, and I relax back into the bedding in relief. I'm alone.

But where am I? I wrinkle my nose at the strange, harsh smell as I look around the room. The walls are smooth and plain; no stonework visible, no wallpaper either. The curtains at the window are so thin and flimsy, I struggle to think of them as curtains; they're far too short as well, finishing almost a leg's length above the floor.

And what kind of bed is this? I grasp the metal rails to each side. *'Tis half cage, and not big enough to share, even with a bairn!* Yet it's so soft and comfortable. I rub the blanket between thumb and forefinger. Thin again, but warm enough and with some kind of loose covering. Clean too – not a speck of coal dust or fluff.

The pillows, though! I move my head from side to side. I have never rested on anything so fine and soft.

I wrinkle my nose again. *What* is *that smell?* Sharp,

stringent. *Caustic soda? Lye?* No, not quite. I've never smelled anything like it.

Disinfectant.

Of course. But what's disinfectant?

Brow wrinkling as well as my nose, I jump as the door opens and a man walks in. Tall, clean-shaven and with no hat, he wears the plainest frockcoat I've ever seen. It's white! How can a gentleman walk the streets in a white frock coat? It will grey with soot and coal in seconds!

He wears numerous strange ornamentations in his top pocket. And the coat itself is too short for him. *Why on earth can he not fasten his buttons? Or wear a neck tie? He's walking into a woman's private room half undressed!*

'Ah, good, you're awake,' he says, with no greeting or manners at all.

The doctor, I think – though I know not why. This is not Doctor Ingram.

He says no more, but moves to the foot of my bed, takes the clipboard hanging there and flicks through the pages.

I furrow my brow further in consternation. *Clipboard?*

Still silent, the man – this *doctor* – moves to the side of my bed, takes one of his ornamentations from his pocket and points it at me.

I scream at the unexpected blinding light.

'Nothing to worry about, just look past my shoulder while I check your eyes.' He flicks the light left and right, further confusing me. I've never known a doctor, or even a druggist, do such a thing. *And how on earth is he fuelling the light? It cannot be candle nor gas.*

Batteries, I think, then frown again at the strange word.

'Watch my finger.'

I stare at the man. *Is he mad? Am I in Bedlam?*

'Just follow it with your eyes.'

I decide to humour him, and watch his finger move left, right, up, down.

'Hmm,' he says, making a note on his – *what is it? Ah yes, clipboard.* Then he takes a seat. *He is sitting on my bed!* I stare at him in outrage.

'Do you know where you are?'

I continue to stare at the strange man who finds it appropriate to sit on a woman's bed.

'You're in hospital,' he says.

Hospital? I look about me again. Bright, clean, too large, and this strange, rude doctor. *So it is the madhouse then.*

'You've been in a coma for three months.' He looks at me carefully and I stare back in shock.

Three months? I've been in the madhouse these past three months? How is Harry coping without me? Did he put me here? What of Little Thomas? Fear threatens to overwhelm me and for a moment I cannot catch my breath.

'We've run MRIs and CAT scans, but can find no reason why both you and your friend have been afflicted in this way.' He pauses. 'Can you tell me what you remember?'

I look at him blankly, then gasp as I remember Harry's face falling away, but I can't say owt to this stranger sat on me bed. *Harry! What have I done?*

He sighs, then smiles. 'I'm rushing you – I'm anxious to work out the puzzle and am getting carried away. Let's start at the beginning. Can you tell me your name?'

'Martha Sutcliffe.' I know that at least. Or do I? The name seems wrong now that I've uttered it, and the doctor has a strange look on his face. Worried.

'Martha Sutcliffe,' he repeats.

'Yes. No.' I realise I don't know. I'm certain now. That isn't my name. I stare at the man, feeling helpless. Tears prickle at my eyes and my breathing quickens. *Who am I?*

'Don't worry.' He pats my arm. 'You've only just woken, things are bound to be confusing at first. It's nothing to worry about, we'll just give it a bit of time. I'll come back and see you tomorrow.'

The door opens. 'Are you ready for us?' A woman's voice.

'Ah, I'm not sure. Are you up for a visitor? It might jog your memory.'

I say nothing. A woman dressed in a strange blue smock pushes someone into the room.

I stare at the man in the wheeled contraption.

'Harry!'

'Martha! God, please no, get me out of here! Get her away from me!'

Darkness rushes back to claim me and I spin away from the image of the husband I killed. I know now, this is the madhouse, and Harry the devil that will plague me for the rest of my days and beyond. But I'm not in Bedlam, no. I must have died too, I'm in Hell.

2.

'Here you go, Jayne, coffee,' one voice says.

'Double shot?' says the other.

'Of course. I don't know how you sleep at night, the amount of caffeine you drink.'

It's the she-devils with the red lips, I realise. I keep my eyes closed.

'Any sign of waking?'

'No. I wondered a minute or two ago, but nothing.'

'We should swap her water for your coffee, Jayne, that would keep her awake.'

The two women laugh. *Are they talking about poisoning me?* I focus on keeping my breathing steady so they won't realise I'm listening to their plans.

'Vikram says The Rookery is nearly ready,' one of them says – the one called Jayne, I think.

'Yes, it's looking great. Mo is just finishing off the tiling in the en-suites and he's decorating Verity's apartment too.'

'There's nothing in the budget for that.'

'He's doing it as a favour for me.'

'Ah, so that's going well, is it? Good, I'm glad. You deserve to be happy, Lara.'

'Happy? With Verity just lying here?'

'You know what I mean.'

A sigh. 'Yes, 'course I do. I'm just remembering how excited Verity was about The Rookery, and meeting William. Then that *stupid* séance! Oh why did I do it?'

'We were trying to help, Lara. Nobody could have predicted Verity and William reacting like this – and if we'd even thought it *could* happen . . . Well, to be honest, none of us would have believed it and we'd have carried on anyway.'

Silence. I imagine the one called Lara nodding and hear her sniff.

'Too much was happening in that building, it was freaking us all out.'

'Yes, and escalating too. Those birds, and then when I saw the Grey Lady.'

'I know, Lara. And I'm sorry I ridiculed you when you first talked about orbs and spirits.'

'It's fine. You need to see or experience something to believe, otherwise it's all claptrap. I understand.'

'Well, I know better now, and it was all centred round Verity and William.'

'I wonder who Martha and Harry are. Were.'

My ears prick up. *Were?*

'I've been doing some research,' Jayne says, her voice quiet and careful. 'They're both mentioned in the parish records – their marriage is recorded anyway: April 1837.

'So they definitely lived in Haworth.'

'Yes, and died there.'

Died? Both of us? What about Little Thomas? Don't tell me he's gone too.

'Maybe they're trying to talk through Verity and William, send a message. It's strange that they both woke at the same time, spouting the same names. It's got the nurses in a right state. Some won't even come into their rooms, and the doctors have no answers; nobody knows what to make of it all.'

'Has anything else happened at The Rookery while you've been staying there, Lara? Anything at all?'

'No, nothing. I've told you already. Even those awful birds have gone since Vikram put rubber spikes on the window ledges and guttering.'

'Good, he said they'd do the trick. If there's nowhere for them to perch, they'll move on.'

'You really like him, don't you, Jayne? How's it going?'

Silence. *What's she doing?*

A clap. 'That's wonderful! And about time, you've been on your own for far too long!'

'It doesn't seem right with Verity . . .'

'Verity won't mind a bit. She's only ever wanted you to be happy, you know that.'

'Yes.'

I open my eyes and stare at them both. 'Who's Mo?' I croak.

They stare at me, then slowly smile, and both lean forward. Jayne grabs my arm, Lara my hand, and I notice she's scraped most of the nail varnish off her finger nails.

'Verity?'

'Yes.' I nod. 'Yes, it's me.'

'Ah, Ms Earnshaw, back with us I see, good, good.'

I blink until the blob of pale colours coalesce into a man. The doctor. I say nothing. I don't quite know what to make of him.

He looks down at his clipboard, turns over a few pages, then puts it down and clears his throat.

'Your case is . . . most perplexing.'

I raise my eyebrows.

'We can find no sign of any kind of injury, nothing to explain why you've been unconscious for three months.'

I stare at him, it seems I can do no more.

'And . . . well . . . I'm afraid we have so far been unable to determine the cause.' He wrinkles his forehead, clearly expecting me to make a comment, then continues when I remain mute.

'What is even more perplexing is that your, er, friend, passed into unconsciousness at the same time, and, er, well, appears to have woken at exactly the same moment as yourself. As you know, he suffered matching delusions, although has not come out of it the way you have. He still thinks himself to be somebody called Harry.'

'What?' The news shakes me out of my stupor. *Is William still stuck in the past?*

'As I say, we can find no physical cause, so I have asked a colleague from Psychiatry to come and talk to you both. Although I will still want to see you regularly as well in case any symptoms re-emerge, or you experience any other, well, strange behaviours or beliefs.'

'Strange behaviours or beliefs?' I question.

He shrugs his shoulders. 'How else would you put it?'

The door bangs open, followed by an immediate apology as Lara spots the doctor. I realise I don't know his name, then another thought grips me.

'Lara – William still thinks he's Harry.'

'Yes, I know, Mo and Vikram are still trying to get through to him. His sister, Rebekah, will be back at the weekend, hopefully she'll be able to help.'

'I'll deal with Harry,' I say. I pull off the sensor clamped to my finger, and fling the blankets back.

'Ms Earnshaw, I really must caution you to stay in bed.'

I ignore him, swing my legs over the side of the hospital bed, and place my feet on the floor. I crumple after taking no more than three steps.

Lara helps me back up – neither she nor I would wait for a nurse – and I look at the doctor, my eyes wide with fright.

'As I was trying to explain,' he begins, then glances at Lara and softens under her furious glare. 'You have been in bed for three months. Muscles lose their condition very quickly, and I'm afraid it's going to take some work to build your strength back up.'

'What do you mean, some work?' Lara asks.

I lie in the bed, out of breath and terrified. *If I can't stand or walk, how on earth am I going to live in and run a three-storey guesthouse?*

'Physio,' the doctor says. 'Somebody will be along shortly to get you started, but if you're determined enough, you'll be back on your feet and running in a few weeks.'

I've had enough. I close my eyes and will oblivion to take me away. Just for a little while. Then I'll worry about learning to walk again.

3.

'I need to see William,' I say after the doctor has gone and I've gathered my strength.

'Verity, no, you heard what the doctor said. You need to concentrate on getting your strength back,' Jayne says.

I glare at her. 'I've been *asleep* for three months. During that time, I lived another person's life. It sounds like William still is. I've got to help him out of it.'

'I grant you it's strange you had the same dreams—'

'It was *not* a dream!' I stop, realising my voice has risen into a shout. 'It wasn't a dream,' I repeat. 'I *was* Martha, I wasn't dreaming about her, I was living her life, feeling her emotions, walking in her shoes.'

'And William still thinks he's Harry,' Lara says.

'Exactly – he's still trapped. I've got to help him. Maybe the sight of me will shock him out of it.'

'*Shock* him out of it?' Lara questions. 'Exactly how does this story end?'

I shake my head. I can't tell my two best friends that I killed Harry. No, that *Martha* killed Harry. I repeat the gesture, this time in confusion, trying to make sense of the last image of my dream. *Did Martha kill him, or have I just* assumed *she did?* I'm no longer sure what is real and what isn't.

'I'll go get you a wheelchair,' Lara says.

'But the nurses,' Jayne protests. 'They'll stop us – you heard the doctor.'

'The nurses are freaked out by the pair of them – haven't

you noticed they won't come in here or into William's room unless they have to?'

'I just thought they were busy,' Jayne says. 'They're run off their feet.'

'Well, that too.' Lara smiles at Jayne. 'Either way, they won't stop us. I won't be long.'

She slips out of the door and is gone before Jayne can say more.

'It'll be okay, Jayne. I have to do this. I have to help him get back to himself.'

Jayne sighs, then sits down by the bed and takes my hand. 'I know you do, Verity, and I'd do the same. We just don't know what we're dealing with and I'm scared that you confronting William, or Harry – or whatever's doing this to him – will only make things worse.'

I squeeze her hand with a small smile in reply.

Jayne approaches the door of my room, checks both ways, then beckons us forward.

Lara pushes with rather more enthusiasm than I expect, and I grip the armrests of the wheelchair as it careens through a ninety-degree angle between the doorway and corridor.

A stern-looking nurse in a dark-blue uniform looks at us in surprise, then frowns. 'And just what, exactly, is going on here?'

I feel like a schoolgirl again, caught running in the corridor by a teacher.

'She's feeling very cooped up,' Jayne says. 'We thought we'd take her out and about for a change of scenery.'

'I see.'

I regard the woman, doing my best to keep my face blank. I wonder if I imagine her shudder when she meets my eyes.

'Very well. But Don't be long. The physiotherapist is due in an hour to start—' she glances at me, then looks back at Jayne before continuing '—Ms Earnshaw's rehab.'

I narrow my eyes. *Why doesn't she speak directly to me?* She bustles past, still refusing to look at me.

'I think you're right, Lara. That woman looked terrified!'

Neither Jayne nor Lara say anything, and I don't blame them. What is there to say?

Lara starts pushing again, and my wheelchair trundles forwards. For the first time I wonder if Jayne's right, and I should let William find his own way out of the past.

I open my mouth to tell Lara to halt, but instead she tells me, 'Here we are. This is his room,' as Jayne pushes open the door.

I see Vikram and another man first – Mo, I guess from the way his eyes light up when he sees Lara. Vikram looks at Jayne in just the same way. They're both half-standing, half-sitting on the windowsill and I wonder why they aren't using the chairs by the bed.

I look at him then, William, and recoil at the look of horror on his face.

'It's okay, William,' I say, hoping at least a part of the real him is awake and can hear me. 'It's me, Verity, you're safe.'

The others in the room stare at me in confusion.

'Harridan!' William – no, Harry – shouts. 'Murderer! Get thee away from me! I have no wish to see thee!'

Lara gasps from behind me. I ignore her. I *have* to get through to William.

'That was Martha, William. And a long time ago. She didn't mean to do it.'

'Tha broke me neck!' William – no, Harry – screams. 'Killed me after I loved and cared for thee!'

'No. Martha killed Harry, William.' I struggle to keep my voice calm. 'You're alive, you're William Sutcliffe. Harry and Martha lived a long time ago – they're both long gone.'

'Get away, get away, get away from me, thee hear?'

'What on earth is going on in here?' The door bursts open and the nurse we'd spoken to in the corridor bustles into the room.

She looks at me – glares. 'I might have known.' Then she turns her gaze on Lara and Jayne. 'A change of scenery, you said. Get her back to her room, while we calm Mr Sutcliffe. He needs to rest.'

I realise another nurse has entered behind the bossy one, and she's already at William's bedside, syringe in hand.

'Sorry,' I whisper. 'I thought I could get through to him.'

'Just get her back to her room. Everybody out. Now.'

We obey, Vikram now pushing my chair as Lara – tears threatening – walks with Mo's comforting arm around her. No one speaks.

4.

The physio helps me stagger back to the bed and I fall on to it. I lie there for a few moments, out of breath, waiting for the hot trembling in my legs to calm down.

They begin to feel less like jelly and more like flesh-and-blood appendages of my body, and I heave myself fully on to the bed with a grunt.

Another rest, then I turn and manage to get myself under the blanket. I lie back on the pillows panting with effort. This is ridiculous, I've only walked a few yards to the bathroom and back! *How am I going to manage all the stairs at The Rookery?*

It'll be months at this rate, yet they're sending me home in a couple of days.

A knock at the door, and I force my features into a smile as Lara's head pops round it. 'Are you up for visitors?'

'Always,' I say, my smile turning genuine as Hannah bursts into the room, runs to the bed and jumps up to give me one of the most welcome hugs of my life.

I squeeze back, holding her tight, although even that hurts and tears are threatening. Not of sadness, but a jumble of emotions. Relief, joy at being loved, fear and love of my own for the little girl in my arms, her mother, and her other 'aunt'.

'It's good to see you,' I say.

'Let Auntie Verity breathe,' Lara says. 'You're suffocating her.'

I shuffle over a little to make some room. 'Here, you stay up here with me, Hans.'

'How are you feeling?' Jayne says as she takes one of the chairs and Lara the other.

I frown, then catch myself. I've come to hate that question in the last few days, but I know Jayne is asking out of genuine concern.

'I'm okay – getting there, anyway. Is there any news of William?'

Lara narrows her eyes at me, knowing I'm avoiding telling them how I really feel, but Jayne answers before she can say anything.

'He's coming out of it, but is still quite confused. Occasionally he talks as if he's still Harry, but Vikram says he can see more and more of William every day.'

'Do you think he'll see me?'

'Not yet, Verity, sorry.' Jayne leans over and grasps my hand. 'He's still very confused, and after last time . . . well, best to give him some space; he'll come to you when he's ready.'

I nod, unsure what to say. I was feeling so sorry for myself only minutes ago, yet William is still struggling to free himself from Harry and Martha.

'How about you?' Lara asks. 'Are you still aware of Martha?'

I consider her question. 'Not in the same way as when I woke up. I can still remember everything, even how she felt – I felt it all myself and it's like a memory. But I know I'm Verity, I *think* Martha's gone.'

'Think?' Jayne pounces on the word.

I shrug and give Hannah a squeeze. 'How can I know for sure? All I can tell you is that while I have her memories, I'm fully cognisant that she's a third party.'

'Fully cognisant,' Lara repeats. 'You've seen the psychiatrist then.'

I give a small laugh. 'Yes. Not that she was any help. She

300

has no real idea of what happened, and the best she can say is that it was some kind of mental break.'

'But William having the exact same one at the same time,' Jayne says. 'How does she explain that?'

I shrug again. 'Mass hysteria.'

'Mass? It only happened to the two of you,' she protests, 'and whilst I don't know William, judging by his friends he's not the hysterical type, and I know you're not.'

'As I said – no real idea.'

'Is she going to keep you in?' Lara asks.

'No.' I try to smile. 'No, she's happy that whatever the episode was, it's over and I can go home on Monday.'

'That's fantastic news!' Lara and Jayne say together, beaming as Hannah says, 'Yay!' and snuggles into me.

'Isn't it?' Lara asks, seeing right through my fake smile.

'Of course it is, I just—' I pause and take a deep breath to prevent new tears forming before admitting, 'I don't know how I'll manage. All those stairs and all that work. I can barely get myself to the bathroom and back.' I wave in the direction of the en-suite bathroom door and lose my battle with the tears.

'How am I going to get around The Rookery? It could take weeks, even months before I'm fit again – my muscle strength has just, just *gone*.'

'Don't worry, Auntie Verity, it's because you've been lying down so long. Your muscles will come back, you'll see.'

I smile at Hannah as she accompanies her assertion with a rather impressive bicep curl, then I glance at Lara – I know those are her words.

'You heard the physio,' she responds. 'Walk a little further every day. Keep pushing yourself, but rest when you need to. You're the only one who can rebuild your strength, and I know you can and will do it.'

'And you're not alone,' Jayne adds. 'Lara and I will be with you as much as possible, and the boys have been brilliant. I can't wait for you to see how The Rookery looks now, you'll be amazed.'

I stare at them. 'What do you mean? Have they carried on working? What have they done?' I start to panic, my breathing becoming faster as I think about all the decisions I should have been there to make. All the plans I'd made being taken over by others. *What have they done to my home?* I'm struggling to take in enough air, and Hannah looks alarmed.

'Calm down and stop worrying. Everything's okay,' Lara says.

'It looks really cool, Auntie Verity, I can't wait for you to see it!'

I look back at my friends and my breathing slows as trust reasserts itself at the smiles on their faces. 'Tell me.'

5.

I gape at my friends in amazed wonder. Lara has overseen the build every day in between taking Hannah to school and back, and all three of them have spent their weekends there to help get things ready.

Once my prepayment to Keighley Builders was used up, Jayne put up her own money to fund the rest, and has waited until now to ask me to sign the necessary paperwork for me to reimburse her.

On top of that, she's managed both builders and Lara to ensure the build will come in near or even on budget.

'Vikram has been an absolute star,' she says. 'You owe him big time. He's been joining us at the weekends – on his own time – to help with cleaning and buying furniture and stuff. All you have left to do is trial the toiletries to decide what to put in the guest bathrooms – and I'm afraid Lara's ordered you quite a few to test.'

Lara shrugs. 'Got to get it right – who doesn't love those little bottles of gorgeousness when they go away? It's such a disappointment if it's nasty, cheap stuff.'

I grin at Lara. 'Quite right – we can all test them, then compare results.' I turn my smile on Jayne. 'Vikram seems very keen,' I say with arched eyebrow.

'He's Aunt Jayne's boyfriend,' Hannah informs me. 'And Mo is Mum's.'

'Hans!'

'Well he is. You're not very good at keeping secrets, Mum. I have eyes and ears, you know.'

The three of us stare at Hannah, Lara's face turning a very unflattering shade of beetroot, then Jayne and I can no longer contain our laughter.

'Is William still your boyfriend, Auntie Verity?'

I sober and we all fall silent.

'No, Hannah. He's poorly at the moment, and I don't know what will happen, or if we'll still be friends.'

'You're sure to be when he's himself again,' the child asserts. 'Everyone says so.'

'Hannah, why don't you go and get a drink? You know where the machine is.'

'Coke?'

'Diet Coke. And one for me too. Would you like one, Verity?'

Suddenly I have a monumental craving for sweet fizz. 'Yes, please, full-strength for me though, Hannah, I haven't had any sugar for three months!'

She raises her eyebrows at Lara, waiting for her mother's permission. After receiving the required nod, she looks at Jayne, who holds up a travel mug. 'I'm okay, thanks Hans. I still have coffee.'

She collects some coins and skips out of the room, delighted at the prospect of pop.

'Now she's gone, you two – spill. I haven't had a chance to ask you properly. When did you and Vikram get together, Jayne? Exactly who is Mo, and how long have you been seeing him, Lara?'

'Short answer, a couple of months now,' Jayne says. 'We've all been spending a lot of time both here and at your place. We just clicked.' She waves a hand, embarrassed.

I smile, it's been too long since she's been interested in a man, and Vikram is a decent one. A bit abrupt at times if I remember correctly, but then so is Jayne. They're a good match.

I turn my attention to Lara, my smile widening at the grin on her face.

'Mo works with Vikram. He's a tiler, in fact he's there now, working on the en-suites.'

'Tiling?' I'm shocked. The last time I saw The Rookery, it was a building site, and I'm still struggling to comprehend the length of time I've been in hospital.

'It really is nearly ready, Verity,' Lara says, taking my hand. 'I know it must be hard, but you've been here a long time. You can still open for Easter if you want to.'

'Easter?'

'Yes, it's in a couple of weeks.'

'Two weeks?' I'm stunned. We only just celebrated Christmas.

Lara squeezes my hand, and Jayne moves to sit on the bed. 'It'll take a while to orient yourself,' she says, ever practical. 'We haven't done anything about guests yet. No advertising, and while we've registered you with the online booking sites, we've not made the listings live.'

'We wanted to wait until you were home and well again,' Lara puts in. 'You should be the one to click those buttons.'

'And we wanted to help but not take over,' Jayne finishes.

'Have we done right?' Lara asks.

Tears are pouring down my face, and I grasp both their hands in mine. 'I don't know how to thank you both,' I manage to say. 'I could have lost everything, have nowhere to go.'

'You'll always have somewhere to go,' Jayne says as they both embrace me.

'What's happened?'

Lara turns. 'Nothing, Hans. We've just been telling Auntie Verity about all the work that's been done at The Rookery. She's only crying because she's happy.'

305

'Oh.' Hannah thinks a moment. 'If Auntie Verity's going home, does that mean we won't live there anymore?'

A shaft of horror again spears my heart, and I glance at Lara, then Jayne, then back again.

'How am I going to manage all those stairs?'

'Don't worry, Verity, we've thought of that,' Jayne says. 'You mentioned to Vikram about having the downstairs doorways wide enough for wheelchairs and pushchairs, and we realised it would take you a while to get your strength back.'

'We've made it a fully disabled-accessible room,' Lara interrupts. 'Grab handles in the bathroom, walk-in shower with a drop-down seat, all the necessary rails everywhere.'

'We thought you could use it until you were strong enough to live upstairs again. You'd have everything you needed.'

'What about a kitchen?' I break in.

Jayne continues, 'The kitchen for guest breakfasts is all ready. You can use that for yourself too, and you can get around every area downstairs in a wheelchair if you need to.'

'At least at first,' Lara adds. 'And when you're ready for guests, you can send them up to their rooms and maybe hire one of the local girls as chambermaid, or . . .' She pauses to wave her open palms in a gesture similar to jazz hands. '*Or*, during the Easter holidays, Hannah and I can stay in your apartment, and I can take guests up and help with their rooms.'

Tears overwhelm me yet again. 'I don't know what to say,' I gasp. 'Thank you.'

'Stop doing that with your hands, Mum, it's weird.'

This time, Hannah is part of the group hug.

6.

'Ready?' Lara asks.

'Definitely,' I say and smile, although I'm far from sure about it. On the one hand I can't wait to get out of the hospital. But on the other, I'm nervous about returning to The Rookery. And my trepidation is not just about managing a three-storey guesthouse in hilly, cobblestoned Haworth while dependant on crutches and a wheelchair.

What will I find there? And, more importantly, what – or who – will find me?

'Can I push?' Hannah asks.

'Only if you're careful and don't go too fast.'

'Okay!' She gets behind my wheelchair, grabs the handles, and throws her weight behind her push, but I don't budge.

'You need to take the brake off, Hans. Here, now try.'

'Thanks, Mum.' She squeals as we career across the room.

'Yeah, thanks Lara,' I say, hanging on for dear life.

'Don't worry, Auntie Verity, I won't crash you, I'm getting the hang of it!'

'Oof,' I say as my knees bang into the door. 'Maybe let Mum get me out of the room, then you can do the straight bits.'

'Okay.'

'Sorry, Verity,' Lara whispers in my ear as she manoeuvres the chair on to a more productive course.

'It's fine,' I say, uncontrollable laughter spilling out of me. 'I haven't ridden the dodgems for years!'

'They're not that easy to control, you know.' Lara just manages to avoid another bump.

'Me now!' Hannah says.

'Verity?'

'Why not? This is the most fun I've had in months!'

'Don't encourage her, Verity. We've got a long walk to get out of here.'

I clutch the armrests again, as Lara grabs the handles to help Hannah retain control and avoid us crashing into the nurses' station.

'Whoa,' the man sitting there says. 'Looks like you've got an awkward one there.'

'She's doing her best,' Lara defends her daughter.

The nurse smiles. 'I meant the chair. Let's see if I can find you a better one.'

'Oh. Yes please. Thank you.'

I don't have to see Lara to know she's bright red and refusing to look at Hannah. She won't hear the end of that one for a very long time.

'Here, try this. Do you need a hand transferring?'

'No, I should be okay, thanks,' I say and use one of my crutches to lever myself up to my feet, then back down to sit in the new chair.

'This one's much better, thank you!' Hannah sings out as she pushes me – now in a straight line – down the corridor.

Lara is strangely quiet as I hang on, and I breathe a sigh of relief when we reach the lift doors with no further mishap.

'I said not so fast, Hans,' Lara pants as she catches us up.

'This isn't an awkward one, Mum. I didn't bump Auntie Verity into *anything* with this one,' Hannah replies as the lift pings and the doors open.

I'm face-to-face with William. His face drains of colour but he tries to smile.

'Hi,' I say.

He nods.

'Hello Verity,' Vikram says from his position at the controls of William's wheelchair. 'How are you feeling?'

They both glance at Lara and Hannah, then look back at me in my chair, trying to hold on to my crutches as well as the armrests.

I shrug. 'Getting there. Well, you know.'

William nods. 'Going home?' he asks.

'Yes, not quite sure how I'll get on though.' I smile and nudge the crutches. 'You?'

'Not yet.' He lapses back into silence and the lift doors start to close.

'Oops,' Lara says and William sticks out a leg to halt the doors.

'Come on, William, we're holding them up.'

William doesn't look at me again as Vikram pushes him past us and we take their place in the lift.

'Well, that was awkward,' Lara says once we start our descent.

'He's still not the proper William,' Hannah says.

'What do you mean, Hans?'

Hannah lifts up her shoulders to her ears then drops them again in response to her mother's question, but remains silent.

I remain quiet on the journey home. Lara does her best to distract me, but I can't forget the way William's face paled at the sight of me, nor the stilted words – I can't call it conversation. At least I saw William rather than Harry, but who did *he* see? Me or Martha?

'Verity.'

I startle out of my reveries and look at Lara, then out of the window – we're parked outside The Rookery.

'Sorry, lost in thought.'

For answer, she smiles, lays a gentle hand on my forearm, then gets out of the car and walks around to open my door and hand me my crutches.

'Thanks.' I haul myself out of the car and catch hold of Lara as one of my crutches slips on the wet cobbles.

'Welcome home. What do you think?'

I look up at the new voice. 'Jayne, what are you doing here?'

'I've taken a week off work so I can help you settle back in.'

I smile at her then look up at the façade of The Rookery and freeze.

'Don't you like it?'

'I told you we should have waited until she was home,' Lara says.

'It's supposed to be a surprise – a welcome home, but if you don't like it, we can get it redone,' Jayne says.

I stare at the signage, at the three rooks above the lettering. 'Three for a funeral,' I say.

'What?'

'One for sorrow, two for mirth, three for a funeral.'

'No Verity. It's one for sorrow, two for joy, three for a girl,' Lara says.

'I'll google it,' Jayne says, ever practical. 'Come inside and sit down. I know you have to keep walking, but you're also not supposed to overdo it.'

'I thought Vikram put those pigeon spikes on all the window ledges,' I say.

'Only upstairs and the roof edge,' Jayne says. 'He says no birds will roost on the ground-floor window ledges, there are too many people about. Now come on, stop worrying, and come inside before you fall.'

I force a smile on to my face.' I can't wait to see what

you've done inside,' I say as I negotiate my way up the steps and through the front door.

'There's wheelchair access at the side,' Lara says, 'but this is what most people will see when they come in for the first time. We wanted to give you the full effect.'

I stop as the feeling of foreboding that overtook me outside diminishes. To my relief, the reception area is laid out exactly as I'd envisaged and arranged with the build team, with desk before me, a lounge area to my left, and open-plan dining room to my right.

The wallpaper is a tasteful gold and pale blue pattern; classy without being chintzy, and I grin at Jayne, already looking quite at home behind the reception desk.

Before I can speak, Lara has bustled me to the new downstairs guest room, and I sit on the bed in relief.

'You look exhausted, Verity.'

I nod. 'That trip took a lot out of me.'

'Your strength will come back.' Lara rubs my arm in reassurance. 'Have a rest and come back out when you're ready. We've ordered you a wheelchair from Amazon, and it should arrive tomorrow, will you be all right on crutches for today?'

'I'll manage. Thanks, Lara,' I say as she leaves me in peace to recover, and I look around to take in the room.

They've done a fantastic job, and have stuck to my visions for the décor, but it doesn't feel quite right.

I haven't chosen the wallpaper or the furniture. I haven't placed it. Nor have I chosen the curtains, bedding, carpet – even though I may well have made the same choices as my friends.

I sigh. I'm being ungrateful and know it.

Jayne and Lara have done an amazing job and I'm extremely lucky to have them. If they hadn't taken it on, the build would have stopped, I'd have nowhere habitable to stay and would not be able to start renting rooms out to guests for months yet.

I give myself a mental shake, then clump to the bathroom on my crutches. I eye the grab handles and rails with a mixture of relief and distaste; hating that I need them, yet grateful that they're there.

It's only temporary.

I turn to exit, and see rows of small toiletry bottles arranged neatly on the windowsill and shelf above the sink. The samples to test. I peek into the shower cubicle. Yep, at least a dozen bottles of shower gel, shampoo and conditioner. I giggle to myself – Lara clearly enjoyed that job!

When I'm ready, I make my way back to Reception, where my friends are waiting for me. I give them a big grin. 'I don't know how to thank you both.'

'Do you like it?'

I nod. 'It's perfect. You even remembered what I said about wallpapers.'

'Of course we did.'

'It was ages ago.'

'You know our Jayne,' Lara says. 'Never forgets anything, just files it away in that head of hers.'

'And you've been grateful for it on more than one occasion,' Jayne retorts as she taps a computer keyboard. 'Ah, here we are.' She scans the screen. 'You might want to sit down.'

My heart sinks. *What now?* But a seat is a good idea at this moment and I limp to the nearest armchair as Lara dashes around the desk to check out the screen for herself.

I catch a look between the two women as I sit. 'Just tell me,' I say. 'Whatever it is, just say it.'

'Well, you're both right. About the rooks. The modern

version of the nursery rhyme is one for sorrow, two for joy, three for a girl, and four for a boy, and it counts the birds you see, whether magpies, rooks or crows.'

'But,' I prompt.

'But there's an earlier version. The one you quoted outside, Verity.'

'How much earlier?'

'Do you know any other lines?' Jayne asks in lieu of answering my question.

'Er, let me see. One for sorrow, two for mirth, three for a funeral, four for birth. Umm, five for Heaven, six for Hell, seven for the Devil, his own self.'

'If seven's for the Devil, what's a whole flock of them for?' Lara asks.

'Parliament,' I correct. They ignore me.

'Well,' Jayne says. 'There are a couple of older versions as well, but that one . . . That one, according to Wikipedia . . .' she tails off.

'Just say it, Jayne.' I think I know what she's going to say and feel almost resigned to it.

'The one you just recited was published in a book of proverbs and popular sayings—'

'When?'

'1846.'

'When Harry and Martha lived,' I say.

'Hmm.'

'It means nothing,' Lara says, hugging a tearful Hannah. 'It's coincidence, that's all. It's a common verse and there are all sorts of versions.'

'Yes, well said, Lara,' Jayne says. 'We're letting fear and imagination take over. Enough of that. Lara, will you get the champagne? It's time to celebrate Verity's homecoming, not worry about creepy old nursery rhymes.'

7.

'Off to bed now, Hans,' Lara says. 'They'll be here soon.'

'Aw, can't I stay up a bit longer, Mummy? Say goodnight to Mo and Vikram too?'

Lara rests her hands on her hips and regards her daughter with pursed lips. 'All right. But just half an hour.'

Jayne and I exchange a glance at the theatre of Hannah's bedtime routine.

'An hour.'

'Half.'

'Half an hour, then TV.' Hannah grins, knowing she's won when the knock at the door interrupts negotiations and her mother winks at her.

'I'll get it,' Jayne motions at me to stay on my chair. She's been warning me all day not to overdo it. And whilst frustrating, I'm beginning to appreciate her concern. We've been preparing for tonight all day, and every muscle in my body hurts. I'm looking forward to a fun, relaxing evening with my friends.

'Evening,' I say, greeting Vikram and Mo with a smile.

Mo crosses the room to Lara to give her a quick kiss, then crouches in front of Hannah.

I crane my neck to look behind Vikram, but no one else is with them. I'm not surprised at the absence, only at the sense of loss I feel.

I glance back at Mo as Hannah erupts into giggles, and my smile becomes genuine once again as I catch the glance that passes between Mo and Lara. I haven't seen Lara look so happy for a very long time.

I turn my attention back to Jayne as she asks Vikram, 'No William?'

He shrugs. 'We invited him, and he may turn up.'

'Or he may not,' Mo butts in.

Vikram pushes his lower lip up in a scowl. 'Aye. It's hard to know with him at the moment. But if he don't turn up, he'll be missing out by the smell of it.'

'A proper roast,' I say, trying to ignore the subject of William. 'Roast Yorkshire lamb, veg and potatoes, homemade mint sauce, the works. What would you like to drink?'

'Don't you dare wait on them, Verity. They know where the kitchen is, they can help themselves.'

'Should do, we built it,' Vikram jokes and points Mo toward the kitchen door.

'You're not the boss tonight, Vik, it's your turn to get the drinks in,' Mo retorts. The uneasy formality collapses and the atmosphere lightens.

Jayne goes with him to choose a bottle of wine for us and I wonder if they're trying to hide something from me. I give myself a mental shake – being stuck inside for so long is playing with my head, they probably just want a moment alone.

'I've basted the lamb,' Jayne says when they emerge laden with glasses and bottles. 'It's nearly there so I've taken it out to rest while the veg and spuds finish off.'

'Thanks, Jayne,' I say as I accept a glass of red.

'How are you feeling, Verity?' Vikram asks. 'I can't see any crutches, are you finding it easier to get about?'

'Yes, thank goodness! I still need crutches on the stairs, but I can walk on the flat now without too much pain. I just need a stick by afternoon, and I'm getting stronger every day.'

'You'll be back to normal in no time,' Lara says.

'Yes, it's scary, though, just how fast muscles deteriorate, and how hard it is to get back into condition.'

'You'll be fine once you're open,' Mo says. 'Running up and down all those stairs all day will get and keep you fit.'

I laugh. 'You can say that again!'

'Have you had any more thoughts about when to open?' Vikram asks. 'You were hoping to be up and running soon.' He flinches at Jayne's elbow jab then realises what he's said and gives me an embarrassed smile with gritted teeth. 'So to speak.'

I laugh again. 'Very true – in all sorts of ways! I'm taking up Lara's offer of help, and am planning on a soft opening just after Easter, no fuss. Hopefully if I start slowly and build, I'll be able to manage.'

'That sounds sensible. Shame though, I was looking forward to a big opening party.'

'We can always have one of those later in the year – midsummer or something,' Lara says.

'Has anything else . . . odd . . . happened?' Mo asks.

'No, thank goodness. All quiet.'

'That's good,' Vikram says. 'Maybe it's over.'

'Maybe,' I say. 'Hope so.'

'I'm going up to my room now, Mum. 'Night, everyone,' Hannah says.

'Of course, Hans. Just remember, half an hour of TV, then lights out.'

Hannah nods, wends her way around the room to bestow goodnight kisses, then disappears up the staircase.

'Is she all right?' Vikram asks.

Lara sighs. 'Not really. She was scared when Verity and William were in the hospital, but she's dealing with it. I'll go up and check on her in a few minutes.'

No one knows what to say, and we all jump at a knock on the door.

Vikram shoots to his feet. 'I'll get it.'

'Mate, you made it!' he exclaims, then stands aside to allow William access.

He moves a few steps forwards, then stops, looking unnerved at being the centre of attention. 'Hi,' he says. 'I-I thought it was time . . . and with the lads being here too . . .' he tails off after glancing at Vikram and Mo.

'Welcome, William,' I say and clamber to my feet. 'It's good to see you. What would you like to drink?'

'Black Sheep if you've got it.'

'I'll get it,' Jayne says. 'I need to check on the veg anyway.'

'Come and sit down, mate,' Vikram says. 'What's that?'

'Oh, I thought, well . . .' William stops, then looks at me. 'It's a housewarming present. I started working on it months ago, before . . . well, you know. Before you even bought this place. I-I'm sorry I didn't tell you about it, but, well, you know . . .'

He turns the large picture frame and I gasp, then stare at the painting. I'm standing at the top of a stone flight of steps. Steps I recognise. Steps that are no longer there, but once rose up the wall to my back to the weaver's gallery. The last image Harry would have seen.

8.

'That was delicious,' Vikram says as he pushes his chair away from the table to give his belly a bit more room. 'Can't beat a proper homemade apple pie.'

I catch the glance between Jayne and Lara and hide my smile. I wonder which shop on the high street it came from; whichever one it was would be seeing a sharp rise in sales.

'Would anyone like coffee or are you happy on wine?'

I catch another glance between my two best friends and my heart sinks. *Now what are they planning?*

'Let's stick to alcohol,' Lara says. 'At least till we show you this.'

'Show me what?'

'You remember the CCTV Sparkly had such fun and games installing?' Vikram asks.

I nod, although in truth had forgotten all about it until now.

'While you were in the hospital we—'

'We watched it,' Lara cuts Vikram off. 'We needed to find any clues at all about what happened, why both of you zonked out that night.'

'And you found something?'

'I'll say we did,' Mo butts in.

'It's all set up behind reception to play back,' Jayne adds. 'Do you want to see it?'

I glance at William as he flicks his gaze to me, and as one we push our chairs back and move towards Reception.

'I think that's a yes,' Vikram says, smiling at Jayne.

Our friends gather around us, and I take hold of the mouse.

'You just need to click there.' Vikram points to the arrow icon.

Lara leads the way out of my living area into camera shot, Jayne hot on her heels, Vikram doing his best to protect them with the chair.

'Where's Verity?'

'And William?'

The three look at each other in terror, then Vikram draws a deep breath, warns Lara and Jayne to stay back and opens the door a crack.

Squinting, peering into the dim room, he steps back in surprise and the door swings open, presenting a view of the living and dining area.

The birds have all found a perch, covering almost every surface – except for one area around the table, an area they all seem to be watching; maybe guarding.

William and I are in a heap on the floor, clutching each other, neither moving, with two orbs spinning and dancing above us.

'Will? Will, mate, can you hear me?' Vikram edges into the room, but the birds hold their perches.

Jayne and Lara follow, calling my name.

I don't answer, and the birds don't take flight.

'Rewind that, will you?' William says, leaning forward on his seat. 'What just happened there?'

'Did you see it too, Verity?' Lara asks.

Shocked into silence, I nod.

Jayne rewinds the footage, saying, 'Lara saw it straight away, I had to rewatch it a couple of times before I could see.'

She clicks on Play, and we lean forward to get the best view of the screen.

The orbs whirling and dancing above us part, then disappear. One zooms into William's chest, and the other into my forehead. They do not reappear.

Vikram reaches our prone bodies and shakes William's shoulder.

No reaction.

He places two fingers on William's neck.

'There's a pulse. Verity too, but they're not responding. I think you'd better call for an ambulance.'

9.

'Well that was less than subtle,' William says as the two couples make their excuses and go upstairs.

'Not really.' I laugh.

'No,' he agrees. 'Well, at least things are starting to make sense now, kind of.'

'Yes, that footage is pretty unequivocal. Those orbs were Harry and Martha.'

'Must have been. But why would they do this to us?'

I have no answer for that, and we sit in awkward silence while we both scrabble for something to say.

'She did finish *Wuthering Heights*, you know. Martha,' I say, at last.

'Did she?'

'She knew she got it wrong, jumped to false conclusions. That you . . . that Harry wasn't Heathcliff.'

'Hmm.'

'She never forgave herself.'

'Good.'

'She was terrified of losing Harry; of what might be. Life was so fragile back then.'

'Still is.'

I pause, wondering how to draw William out and get him talking. 'Who do you think it was?'

'What?'

'That Emily loved so fiercely.'

William smiled. 'Emily did everything fiercely, why not love too?'

'But who?' I persist.

'I reckon it wasn't a who at all, she certainly didn't love Harry like that. I reckon it was a what, a where.'

Confused, I pull a face. 'What are you talking about?'

'I mean, that's how she loved the moors: intensely, passionately, with deep abandon, even when the weather closed in, and when they turned on her and nearly killed her. Remember the bog burst?'

I nod.

'It never stopped her going back up there. The animals she helped – saved from the moors – they hurt her sometimes, bit or clawed her, but she never minded.'

'And when she was away from the moors, she fell ill,' I say, remembering.

'Aye, she used to say that if she was ever forced to live anywhere else, she would die.'

'No wonder she never married.'

'She was only thirty when she died, she had time yet.'

'Not in those days,' I remind him. 'People married young 'cause they died young too, especially in Haworth.'

'Aye, you've a point there.'

'Heath,' I say. 'It's another word for moor.'

'Aye, and there are a few cliffs up there too.' William grins. 'She did things her own way, did Emily. One of a kind, that girl, always was.'

We lapse into silence.

I regard him for a few moments, but he doesn't meet my gaze. I decide to tackle this head on.

'You're scared to be alone with me, aren't you?'

'No. Well, yes, a little bit. I look at you and can see Martha, standing at the top of those stairs, staring after me. It's . . . bewildering, and frightening. History has a habit of repeating itself.'

'It's already tried, and failed,' I admit. 'It's done, history is history.'

'What do you mean?'

'Antony.' I reply, then heave a breath to bolster my resolve. 'When I found out about what he was up to . . .' I falter, and William reaches out to take my hand. He meets my eyes, and I decide to believe in the encouragement and reassurance I see there. I will not make Martha's mistakes.

'When I found out about the other women, the catfishing.' I pause again, then sigh. I have to do this or it will never go away. 'I was so hurt, so angry. I felt so betrayed, so humiliated, I *wanted* to kill him. No!' I reach out to keep hold of William's suddenly withdrawn hand. 'Hear me out.'

I take another deep breath, then caress the back of William's hand with my thumb.

'I didn't. He was right there, at the top of the stairs, just like Harry and Martha.'

'But you didn't push?' William interrupts.

I meet his eyes again. 'Not only that, but I used every ounce of willpower I possessed to *not* push him.'

'Is that supposed to reassure me?'

'Yes. Don't you see? I'm not Martha. I haven't lived her life. I fought against the hurt and betrayal. I fought the instinct to push. I am not a killer.'

William gazes into my face, unnerving me with his close scrutiny. 'But you were scared you could be.'

My features crumple and tears spill. 'Terrified,' I confess. 'For an instant, for one terrible instant, I really considered doing it. I could have said he'd tripped and no one would have known I had it in me to kill. He's a clumsy bastard, I could have got away with it.' My voice had reduced to a whisper.

'But you didn't, did you?'

No. Not said, just a shape formed by my lips.

'Then you're *not* a killer.'

I can't speak or meet his eyes any longer.

He grasps my hand now. Hard.

'Don't you see, Verity?'

'What?'

'That's what this is all about. We know from your father's name that you're related to Martha somehow.'

'So I have a murder gene, is that what you're saying?'

'No, dammit!' William takes a calming breath, sits back down after his explosive words, and places his hands on his knees after I pull away from him.

'You were given the same test, don't you see? And you passed. Where Martha didn't. You've just not accepted that because the "could have" is so strong in your conscience; it stopped you accepting that the important thing is that you *didn't* push.'

'What?' I'm thoroughly confused now.

'You didn't kill Antony, despite what he did and how much you wanted to,' William explains. 'You didn't kill him, Verity, you are not Martha.'

'But I came so close!'

'And didn't do it. And Martha came back to make you understand that.'

I stare at him, a glimmer of acceptance of what he's saying shining in my heart.

'You're not a killer, Verity,' he repeats.

'No. No, I'm not, am I?' I laugh – a strange, strangled sound, but a laugh of relief all the same. 'I didn't kill him. I really, *really* wanted to, but – I didn't,' I add, seeing the alarm in William's eyes. 'I didn't push.'

William smiles at me, and I sit back, my body feeling weak, as if I would crumple.

The fear and self-loathing that has been keeping me upright since that morning suddenly drains away. 'I'm not a killer, I'm not that person.'

William moves closer, tentatively it has to be said, but

forward propulsion all the same. He pulls his chair along, until he's as close as he can be without sitting on my lap, and wraps his arms around me.

I pull back.

'I understand now why Martha came, why she's been here, but what about Harry? He's been with you – there were definitely two orbs – why? And why did they push Jayne and attack Antony?'

'My guess is it was Martha who did both of those – she was the one who let anger get the better of her, who lashed out.' William takes my hand as he speaks and rubs his thumb over my skin.

'That does actually make sense. She was frustrated, unable to communicate, and trying to do so in the only way she could.'

'Jayne, and especially Antony, were getting in the way of us meeting.'

'But why was Harry with her?'

'To keep her in check maybe?'

'Or to warn you to stay away from me?'

William laughs. 'Just the opposite. He's forgiven her, don't you see? He came here now to help Martha communicate her message. Whatever she did—'

'Whatever she did? She pushed him down the stairs and broke his neck!'

'But he's forgiven her – he understands, he still loves her and wants to be with her. The only one who can't forgive her is Martha herself, and Harry wants her to understand that. And he's letting us know too.'

I stare at him. *Does he really believe that?* I remember my dreams when I first

 arrived in Haworth, Harry had been with Emily, not Martha.

He recognises the scepticism in my eyes and sighs, grins,

then says, 'All right, fair enough, that's unlikely. He's probably punishing her still, won't ever forget it or stop hating her, but is making sure we get it right while he's at it.'

'Now *that* I can believe,' I say with a small smile.

'It's only been a hundred and eighty years or so,' William adds. 'She still has millennia to repent.'

I eye him cautiously. '*You're* not going to hold a grudge, are you?'

He smiles properly and shrugs. 'Well, it does kind of run in the family . . .'

The humour evaporates.

'In the family,' I repeat. 'You're a Sutcliffe, you're a direct descendant! That must be why it took you so much longer to shake off Harry in the hospital.'

'I guess so.'

We stare at each other, stricken as the implications sink in.

'But you must be descended from one of Martha's brothers at the closest, and that a few generations back, so we're only very, very, *very* distantly related,' he adds, then leans forward and kisses me. 'At least we know Little Thomas survived long enough to have children.'

I pull back. 'One more thing.'

'What?' He sounds exasperated.

'The Grey Lady. How does she fit in?'

He opens his mouth, then closes it again with a frown. 'I'm not sure. Emily was there, wasn't she? I mean here.' He points at the wall between The Rookery and Weaver's Row.

'Yes. And Lara said something—' I pause, trying to remember.

'What?'

'That the Grey Lady is an, an imprint, like a recording in time. Repeating the same action over and over again.'

'So what? She's repeating that final climb up the steps before Harry's death, and has done for all these years?'

'I guess so.' I shrug. 'Although the last time I saw her, she turned and looked at me.'

'Maybe she has resolution too, now, and can finally rest in peace.'

'I hope so.'

10.

Two Weeks Later

'Morning, Verity,' Lara says as she enters Reception. 'Are you ready for the big day?'

I pull my lips into a tortured smile and Lara laughs.

'Don't look so worried. The Rookery is ready, and Hannah and I will stay for the rest of the Easter holidays – by that time you'll be able to cope with the stairs much better and you can vacate the downstairs room and let that out too. You're not on your own, you know.'

I give her a proper smile and relax. 'Thank you so much for giving up your holidays to help me out.'

'Are you kidding? This is an adventure – we have our own apartment for three weeks, and in a guesthouse.' She pointed upwards to indicate my quarters. 'And we're spending the holidays with good friends. Hannah loves exploring the village and moors, and there's always something to do. She thinks she *is* on holiday, don't you, Hans?'

Hannah looks confused, then shrugs. 'I guess so. Can I take Grasper out later?'

'You'll have to ask Aunt Jayne when she gets here.'

'Okay.'

'Speak of the Devil,' I say at a knock at the door, and go to let Jayne in.

'Morning,' she sings out as she enters The Rookery.

Lara giggles. 'Looks like you had a good night.'

Jayne blushes, then shrugs. 'I'd forgotten what it was like to wake up next to someone in the morning.'

'You and Vikram getting on well then?' Lara asks.

Jayne nods, her face still red, and I give her a hug. 'It's great to see you so happy.'

'Yes, yes, okay,' Jayne says, embarrassed. 'Have you got the coffee on?'

Lara laughs, walks to the sideboard and gestures at the freshly made pot of coffee waiting for us.

'Well pour it then, don't just show it off, you're not hosting a game show.'

'I hope Vikram knows what he's getting into,' I say with a chuckle.

Jayne gives an embarrassed grimace. 'The first thing he does in the morning is get me a coffee,' she admits.

'Aunt Jayne, where's Grasper?'

'He's at Vikram's house, Hannah. With it being Auntie Verity's big opening, he's better off out of the way.'

'Oh.' Hannah's face falls in disappointment.

'Don't worry, we can go and get him later and you can take him out for a walk.'

'Okay.'

'Right, well, shall we have breakfast, then we can get on with the day?'

'Just what I was thinking,' I say. 'Come on through to the dining room.'

'Well, that went pretty smoothly,' I say, pleased with myself, 'despite all your different orders.'

'It was a test run, Verity. When guests are here, they'll all be ordering different things, and you need to serve everyone at the same table at the same time,' Jayne says. 'Whether you still need that walking stick or not.'

'I'm not talking to you for ordering poached eggs. That was just cruel.'

'But delicious and perfectly cooked.'

Lara smiles and tops up our coffees. 'What's up, Verity? You seem a bit out of sorts this morning.'

I sip my drink, then position my cup on its saucer. 'I think I understand the orbs and the Grey Lady.' I pause.

'Yes,' Lara encourages. 'For what it's worth, I think you and William are right about them, and I don't think any of them will be seen again. They've done what they needed to do, and are at peace now.'

'That's not it, though, is it, Verity?' Jayne presses.

'No. It's the birds. Why did they congregate here? Why were they tapping the windows and breaking them?'

'Yes, Mum, I've been thinking about that too,' Hannah says. 'What were the birds doing?'

Lara sips her coffee. 'To be honest, I don't think we'll ever know for sure. It could be that the old tale about graveyard rooks being the souls of the dead, or maybe the souls of children who died before being christened, are true, and Harry and Martha being here made it easier for them to interact with us.'

'Or?' I push.

'Or Martha and Harry were trying to use them to communicate.'

'But it was Emily Brontë who had the connection with animals and birds,' Jayne points out. 'Could she have been trying to warn Verity? Trying to prevent Martha taking her over?'

'That does make sense, Jayne, I'm impressed,' Lara says with a proud grin. 'Emily saw Martha at her worst, and was also invested in the village and doing what she could to ease suffering – whether animal or human. It makes sense she would or could use the birds to stop Martha causing more harm.'

I nod, the words whirling around my head.

'Have you been dreaming again?' Lara asks.

'No. Well, no dreams of Harry and Martha anyway, although I have been having nightmares. Probably just thinking about the opening.'

'It's no good just thinking about it, you've got to do it an'all, you know.'

'William!' I stand with a smile, unsure whether I should greet him with a kiss. Before I decide, the moment is over.

'What's that?' I ask instead, indicating the large, slim parcel he's carrying.

'Well, when we first met, I promised a certain somebody a painting.'

Hannah squeals. 'Is it my portrait? Have you painted me, Uncle William?'

I glance at William in consternation at the word uncle, but he's smiling broadly and offers the parcel to Hannah. As she takes it and all attention is on her, he leans over and kisses me.

I glance up, meet his eyes, and smile. My heart flips as he grins back down at me. At last, I only see William when I look at him and, as far as I can tell, he no longer sees Martha in me.

'William, that . . . that's amazing!' Lara says. 'I can't thank you enough. What do you think, Hans?'

Hannah is gobsmacked and stares at the painting. 'You've painted Grasper too.'

'Is that okay?'

'It-it's perfect! I love it! Thank you, Uncle William.' She leaves the painting on the tabletop and runs over to give him a hug. The smile on William's face expands further, and I step over to the painting to have a proper look.

He has really caught Hannah, not only superficially, but something in her expression that is simply . . . Hannah. She's cuddling Grasper, who is looking at her in adoration;

they're alone on the moors, with a reservoir in the background and a hovering kestrel above.

I glance up at Lara and see she is close to tears. Jayne gives her a squeeze and grins at her, but doesn't tease her. I can see Jayne is moved too.

'I'm going to hang it in my room, I can, can't I, Mum?'

'Yes, of course you can. Or we can hang it in the lounge if you want, so everyone can see it.'

'Umm, I'll think about it,' Hannah says, and I realise how much she's matured over the months I was absent. Physically she's still the same Hans, but she seems much older now somehow. *She's growing up*, I realise. *Fast.*

'Has everything gone live?'

I glance up at William, aghast. With the excitement of Opening Day, I'd completely forgotten to look.

'Let's check now then.'

I nod and cross to the reception desk to boot up the computer, while Jayne and Lara clear the breakfast things. Hannah is fixated, staring at her picture, exclaiming every time she notices a new detail.

I check my own website first, and make sure the booking page is now working as my web designer promised it would, then go to booking.com to check The Rookery's listing is live. William peers over my shoulder and rests his hands on my hips.

'Congratulations, Verity,' he whispers. 'You're officially open.'

I turn to check the others are still otherwise engaged, and wrap my arms around his neck. 'Thank you,' I whisper back.

'What for?'

'Well, you know. Sticking around and helping me after everything, well, after Martha—'

'Shh. That's all over, stop worrying. We're Verity and

William. Martha and Harry have gone. Or has something happened?'

'No.' I shake my head. 'These days I only dream about you.' I stretch towards him and he meets my lips in a lingering kiss.

'No time for that, you've got a business to run.' Jayne's voice breaks the spell, and I pull back from him with a rueful grin.

I turn to admonish her, but am surprised to see her proffering two champagne flutes.

'Bucks fizz,' she clarifies, as Lara appears behind her with two more glasses.

'To The Rookery,' Jayne toasts. 'May God bless her and all who stay in her.'

I grin at the parody of the queen's ship-launch blessing, and sip the orange juice and champagne.

'To good friends.' It is my turn to toast.

'And to success and happiness – in all things,' Lara adds.

'I'll drink to that,' William says. 'And I have another gift, I think now is the ideal moment.' He fishes out a brown-paper-wrapped package from his back pocket and hands it to me.

I glance up at him in question.

'Open it.'

I pull the paper away to reveal a flat board attached to a chain. *Vacancies* I read, then turn it over. *No Vacancies.* It's hand-painted, with a moor-landscape background, and the lettering is picked out in black. I look closer. Each stroke of each letter is styled as a feather.

'It's perfect, thank you, William.' I grin up at him and give him another kiss. A short one this time. 'I'd completely forgotten about a sign.'

He reaches into another pocket, pulls out a hook attached to a sucker, takes back the sign, and hangs it on the large window next to the front door.

'Now what?' Lara says. 'Is there anything that needs doing?'

I shake my head. 'Now we wait.'

'Well, I'll leave you to it,' William says. 'I need to open the gallery, but I'll pop back at lunchtime.' He gives me a peck on the cheek and waves to Lara, Jayne and Hannah. 'Have a good day – I'll put the word out on Main Street too, let people know you're open.'

'That would be great, thanks.'

II.

'Anything?' Jayne asks when she returns with Grasper, ready for his walk with Hannah.

I shake my head. 'Nothing. Five hours open and not a single enquiry.'

'Don't look so down, it's only the first day, it'll take time for word to get out, we just need to be patient.'

'Or maybe not,' Lara says, nodding at the window.

I glance out to see Vikram and Mo walking alongside a young couple and gesturing at The Rookery.

'Have you any rooms free?' Mo asks, throwing a wink to Lara. 'We met Carole and Bob here in the Bull. They've come out for the day and have decided to stay on, but haven't booked anywhere, can you help?'

'We certainly can,' I say. 'Welcome to The Rookery. How long would you like to stay?'

'A couple of nights,' Bob says. 'We didn't realise how much there is to do around here, and Carole really wants to go to an event at the museum tomorrow.'

'Oh, the Branwell Brontë talk?'

'Yes, and Bob wants to see the Flying Scotsman.'

'Oh yes, that's very popular – do you have tickets?'

'Yes, we bought them this morning.'

'Great – I hope you enjoy it. It's £100 per double room per night with full, home-cooked breakfast. Can I ask you to fill out a registration form, and also an authorisation for your credit card? You won't be charged until you check out.'

'That sounds fine,' Bob says, and Carole picks up the pen to fill in their details.

'We also include a complimentary bottle of wine – there's red in the room, or if you prefer we can change it for white.'

'Oh that's a nice touch. Red's fine, thank you.'

'You're in Emily's Room, which is at the back, so you have a view of the parsonage, and Lara will take you up. I hope you enjoy your stay.'

'Thank you.'

Lara ushers them to the stairs and upward, and I turn to thank Vikram and Mo, but realise Jayne has already taken care of them.

'You realise Will's been up and down Main Street telling everyone about this place,' Vikram says. 'Don't be surprised if you get busy.'

'Aye, but you'd better let him know when you're full, else you'll be turning people away.' Mo chuckles. 'The man's on a mission!'

I colour as they laugh, but can't help a big grin spread over my face at the thought of William herding tourists up the hill to The Rookery.

'Must want this place to be a success for some reason.' Vikram winks at me, then steps out of the way as another couple enter.

'Is this the place run by a real Earnshaw?' the man asks.

My colour deepens. 'It is, yes. I'm Verity Earnshaw, welcome to The Rookery.'

'The man in the art gallery said you could trace your family back to the Brontë era, his too.'

'That's right, yes.'

'And between them, they inspired at least one of Emily's characters,' Vikram put in.

I don't answer, but fill in the paperwork and send them upstairs with Lara as soon as she returns.

When we're alone again, I turn to Vikram. 'Don't do that, please.'

'What?'

'Use Harry and Martha like that, after what happened. Just let them rest in peace.'

'The best way you can ensure they rest is by getting things right. You *and* William,' Jayne says. 'And that includes filling this place. After what you went through, why wouldn't you take the advantage that comes from it too?'

'And anyway, it's not like it's a lie, is it?' Vikram says.

'See, it pays to get in with the locals,' Jayne says as Lara shepherds another couple up to their room. 'I don't think you're going to have any trouble filling the rooms, not with Vikram and William on the case. You'll need more rooms at this rate!'

'Calm down, Jayne, it's only the first day, and we're not booked up yet. I'm still taking up the downstairs guest room, and the single room is empty.'

'Perfect, just what I was going to ask you.'

I turn to see a woman of my own age standing in the foyer, William behind her. *I need to install a bell on that door.*

'Welcome to The Rookery,' I say, and flash a smile at William. 'I see you've met our local artist.'

The woman and William burst out laughing.

'You could say that,' he says eventually, oblivious to my discomfort. 'Let me introduce you. Verity, this is my sister, Rebekah. Rebekah, Verity.

'Oh!' I turn bright red with embarrassment. 'I'm so sorry. It's good to meet you.'

'And you, I've heard a lot about you. Hello, Jayne, nice to see you again,' she adds.

I'm confused for a moment but realise they must have met when I was in hospital.

'So how are you? I keep quizzing this one,' she links her

arm with William's, 'but getting information is like dragging blood out of a stone.'

'It's a bit difficult to explain over the phone,' William defends himself.

'Why don't you come for dinner tonight? We'll fill you in on all the details, and we can get to know each other too.'

'Sounds perfect.'

I check her in, just in time for Lara's reappearance.

I turn the sign over to read: *No Vacancies*.

'Full already? See, nowt to worry about,' William says and embraces me. Stick with me, lass, we'll be reet.'

I nod. 'Will you stay tonight?'

'Sure?'

'Aye.' I'm aware of the silly grin on my face but can't do anything about it.

'Then there'll be no keeping me away.'

I grab William's arm at a tapping sound, and we turn to see a familiar black shape perching on the stone ledge outside the window. The rook pecks the glass again and both of us freeze. It holds my gaze for a few frenzied heartbeats then flaps away.

The End

If you enjoyed *Parliament of Rooks*, please consider leaving a few words in review. Reviews are very important to an author and do help me understand what you enjoy, as well as guide other readers to books they would like to read.

Thank you – Karen Perkins

For more information on the full range of Karen Perkins' fiction, including links for the main retailer sites and details of her current writing projects, please go to Karen's website:
www.karenperkinsauthor.com/

Glossary of Yorkshire Terms

Allus – Always
An'all – As well
Anyroad – Anyway
Apeth – Idiot/fool
Aw reet – All right
Awd carlin – Old woman
Breeks – Breeches
Fret – Worry
Mesen – Myself
Neps – Clusters and knots of wool fibres
Noils – Short wool fibres
Nowt – Nothing
Ower 'ere – Over here
Owt – Anything
Reet – Right
Shoddy – Lowest quality wool, made from recycled
garments and/or the sweepings from the mill floor
Summat – Something

Acknowledgements

Parliament of Rooks is a work of fiction, and is inspired by the work and lives of Emily Brontë and her family, as well as life in Victorian Haworth. Whilst Harry and Martha are wholly fictional, all other mention of ghosts and hauntings are based on local tales, legends and reported sightings.

I have made the circumstances of the Brontës' lives as accurate as possible, although have fictionalised Emily's day-to-day life, words and actions. When the concept of this book took shape, I envisaged it as being more about the mills and living conditions than the Brontës, but as I wrote, Emily's character became stronger, and her part larger – and I am not willing to argue with Emily Brontë! I hope I have done her justice.

The Crow Hill bog burst did occur in 1824. The huge mudslide took place during a thunderstorm after days of rain, and it is believed that Anne, Emily and Branwell were playing on the moor at the time, although with their servant Sarah Garrs rather than a young friend, and took shelter at Ponden Hall. Patrick Brontë believed it to be an earthquake and wrote a sermon about the event.

A number of people and institutions helped me research this book, and my thanks to Mark Mosley at the Bradford Industrial Museum, the Brontë Parsonage Museum, and Haworth Ghost Walks.

The modern village of Haworth is reflected accurately, and I enjoyed the days I spent there researching. The Rookery is a fictional establishment, but is inspired by Wilsons of Haworth (now under new management and called Weavers), where I stayed during my visits. My thanks to Martin and Dale Wilson for their warm welcome, and for being so accommodating and patient with all my questions and odd requests (including a solitary ghost hunt in their dining room, just in case the Grey Lady did appear on December 19th. If she did visit, I missed her!). Returning to my room hobbling and exhausted from wandering around Haworth's hills and cobbles, the cake waiting for me in my room was always extremely welcome. They set the standard that Verity aspires to in her own venture, and if you are planning to visit Haworth, I highly recommend booking a room at Wilsons – you will be very well looked after.

Thank you to Tessa Price who braved Haworth's ghost walk with me on Halloween, and was happy to explore the graveyard with me later that night, on our own. A good friend indeed!

I'm deeply appreciative of Louise Burke for editing Parliament of Rooks, as well as all the other help she gives me, and also Cecelia Morgan for designing another stunning cover.

Thank you to Sandy Heydinger for videoing her dog Lola dancing with orbs of light, which inspired Grasper's part in this book.

I'm also very grateful to Christina Robinson, Louise Turner, Tessa Price, and fellow author JJ Toner for reading *Parliament of Rooks* in the month before publication. Their sharp eyes and the extremely helpful feedback they gave me before release has saved me more than a few blushes!

Finally, but by no means least, I would like to thank you for reading. The support and encouragement – whether through reviews, comments or more detailed feedback – I've received has been overwhelming, and deeply motivating.

While researching for and writing this novel, I have found a number of books and sites to be extremely useful, including, but not exclusive to:

Aspin, Chris (1982), *The Woollen Industry*, Shire Publications Ltd, Aylesbury, Bucks, UK

Atkinson E (1998), *Haworth in the Brontë Era, B.H. Babbage's Visit to Haworth*, Fretwell Print and Design, Keighley, W Yorks

Barker, Juliet R. V. (1994), *The Brontës*, The Orion Publishing Group, London

Hewitt, Peggy (1985, 2004), *Brontë Country, Lives & Landscapes*, Sutton Publishing, Gloucestershire

Lister, Philip (2006), *Ghosts & Gravestones of Haworth*, The History Press, Stroud, Gloucestershire

Mason, Kate M (1989), *Woolcombers Worsteds and Watermills, Addingham's Industrial Revolution*, Addingham Civic Society, Addingham, W Yorks.

White, Paul (2014), *The Brontës & Haworth*, Whinray Books, Ilkley, W Yorks

Wood, Stephen & Palmer, Ian (2009), *Haworth Through Time*, Amberley Publishing, Stroud, Gloucestershire

www.bronte.org.uk
churchofengland.org
www.haworthchurch.co.uk/history
www.haworth-village.org.uk/
kleurrijkbrontesisters.blogspot.co.uk
www.ponden-hall.co.uk
www.thecompassmagazine.co.uk/haworth-bog
www.thehaworthband.co.uk
www.victoriana.com
victorianmonsters.wordpress.com
www.weasteheritagetrail.co.uk

Fiction by Karen Perkins

The Yorkshire Ghost Stories

Ghosts of Thores-Cross
The Haunting of Thores-Cross: A Yorkshire Ghost Story
Cursed: A Yorkshire Ghost Short Story
JENNET: now she wants the children

Ghosts of Haworth
Parliament of Rooks: Haunting Brontë Country

Ghosts of Knaresborough
Knight of Betrayal: A Medieval Haunting

* * *

The Great Northern Witch Hunts
Murder by Witchcraft: A Pendle Witch Short Story
Divided by Witchcraft: Inspired by the true story of the
Samlesbury Witches

* * *

The Valkyrie Series
Before Anne Bonny and Mary Read, Gabriella Santiago
sailed the Carib Sea...

Look Sharpe! (Book #1)
Ill Wind (Book #2)
Dead Reckoning (Book #3)

The Valkyrie Series: The First Fleet (Look Sharpe!, Ill
Wind & Dead Reckoning)

About the Author - Karen Perkins

Karen Perkins is the author of the Yorkshire Ghost Stories, the Pendle Witch Short Stories and the Valkyrie Series of historical nautical fiction. All her fiction has appeared at the top of bestseller lists on both sides of the Atlantic, including the top 21 in the UK Kindle Store in 2018.

Her first Yorkshire Ghost Story – *The Haunting of Thores-Cross* – won the Silver Medal for European Fiction in the prestigious 2015 Independent Publisher Book Awards in New York, whilst her Valkyrie novel, *Dead Reckoning*, was long-listed in the 2011 *Mslexia* novel competition.

To find out more about Karen's current writing projects, as well as special offers and competitions, you are very welcome to join Karen in her Facebook group. This is an exclusive group where you can get the news first, as well as have access to early previews and chances to get your hands on new books before anyone else. Find us on Facebook at:
www.facebook.com/groups/karenperkinsbookgroup

See more about Karen Perkins, including contact details and sign up to her newsletter, on her website:
www.karenperkinsauthor.com

Karen is on Social Media:

Facebook:
www.facebook.com/karenperkinsauthor
www.facebook.com/Yorkshireghosts
www.facebook.com/groups/karenperkinsbookgroup

Twitter:
@LionheartG

Instagram:
@yorkshireghosts

Printed in Great Britain
by Amazon

16111336R00206